THE WRATH OF ARTEMIS

MATT LARKIN

INCANDESCENT PHOENIX BOOKS

TITAN ERA
OKEANUS
THULE
HYPERBOREA
ILLYRIS
SALON
KELTIA
RASSENIA
MNEMOSYNIA
OLMECATL
THRINAKIA
TARTESSOS
KARKHEDON
KARTH
KEMET
MEMPHIS
TIWANAKU
TIWANAKU
INUMIDEN
THE GREAT VELDT
OSIRION
KUSH
HY-BRASIL
KONGO JUNGLE
KGAUAGADI DESERT
AZANIA

KER-YS
XIRONG
ISSEDONIA
NYXLANDS
WAKOKU
YAN
ARIMASPIA
JINYANG
HYLEAN WOODS
YINDAI
FLAMING MOUNTAINS
JADE MOUNTAINS
KIMMERIA
XIANYANG
YING
YAMATO
PHLEGRA
THEMISKYRA
GEBI DESERT
XIAO
OLYMPIAN MOUNTAINS
KOLCHIS
XIANG
BO
WANGGEON
ELLADOS
IOLKOS
KOLCHIS
DANGUN
PHAEAKIA
ILIUM
PHRYGIA
KUNLUN MOUNTAINS
DELPHI
THEBES
ARAD MOUNTAINS
AXEINOS SEA
BYBLOS
ITHAKA
ARGOS
KORINTH
LESVOS
PHOEBA
PHOENIKIA
YUESHANG
KROKYLEA
KRONION
SKYROS
LYDIA
VYADHAPURA
NERITUM
NAXOS
ORKHIS
TYROS
AEOLIA
HELION
NUSANTARA ISLES
ATLANTIS
KNOSOS
HAWAIKI
THALASSA
AIAIA
ATLANTIS
UGART
NUSANTARA
NESHIA
MUGEDANG
BADIAN STEPPES
NINEVEH
ASUR
DREAMING DESERT
EMPTY DESERT
BABILIM
DREAMING LANDS
BULU
BABILIM
RAPAI
KISSATU
MU
DURANKI MOUNTAINS
SHALMALI
NYSA
SUMERU MOUNTAINS
HURSAG MOUNTAINS
TAKHKHASILA
BARBARIKON
PATALIPUTRA
HINDUSH
DHANYAKATAKA
KUMARI KANDAM

THE WHISPER

It starts with a whisper, a haunting intimation of a World askew. That we are, in the end, caught in a death spiral, time nearly played out, whilst entropy tugs ever harder upon the Wheel of Fate.

Looking now into the dying embers, we at last apprehend Truth, and in it the revelation that the vaunted tales of old were not what we thought ... And neither, in fact, were we.

For if we have lived before, might not all we've dreamt be but our souls' memories of Worlds become dust ...

A QUICK NOTE

For full colour, higher-res maps, character lists, location overviews, and glossaries, check out the bonus resources here: https://tinyurl.com/hw52dzss

And if you liked this book, be sure to check out my offer for a free novella at the end.

PROLOGUE

Asura Era, Silver Age

On the outskirts of Kosala rose a verdant mountain, from the peak of which Matarśivan could make out the spires of the great city. By now, Rama would have returned with his rescued bride and slain Ravana. That his people worshipped the Adityas as gods, that Rama himself bore their blood, seemed momentous, yes, but far less so than that for which he had summoned the Circle.

The others flew in, singly or in pairs, joining him upon the stone landing. When they had left their homeland, they had come here, chosen this place for such councils, and built an open-air platform ringed with benches. Here, they had debated the course of the World. Here, upon the seat where Matarśivan now sat, head in his hand, they argued over what action to take when the war between Adityas and Danavas had ravaged those left in their care.

That conflict had ended the first great Age of the World and it had seemed there was no going back. Now, the Danavas—Men called them Asuras, now—had retreated to the fringes, though their curse had transformed no few of the Adityas into monsters, as well.

And the Dodecadic Circle debated, wondered if they did enough. The Men and Adityas in this land called them Rishi—sages—and trusted them for guidance, even if they did not always listen. It was the nature of Man to heed only advice which affirmed their desires, he found.

Today he must give the Circle new cause for debate, and he could not gauge which way it would go. This day, beneath the merciless sun of Kosala, he must ask them to question the precepts that had guided them for nigh four millennia.

Matarśivan had seen Men break when forced to question ideals held long enough. He'd seen them lie to themselves rather than admit a belief they had clung to might have led them astray. He'd witnessed, time and again, how such things became a part of a Man's identity, such that one could not sever the Man from the belief without rending him in twain. And, in the end, even the Watchers were still Men.

But what alternative lay before him? Was he to allow them to continue their ignorance? Was he to let them mire in the misapprehensions—the *lies*—that had so long steered their courses? And what if he was wrong?

Oh, he was not so arrogant as to deny that possibility. Maybe it was he who had faltered, had been misled by the wild, dread apparitions that plagued his mind now most every day. A millennium and a half he'd searched, investigated, and sought proof ... But found naught conclusive. Just more doubts, more questions, more fear: what if all of it was lies, torments brought upon himself by his fears and failing sanity?

He dared not ask Agni, both for fear of revealing his doubts, and for fear of the Archon's reaction if the worst was true.

Aditi settled down beside him, her face a mask of concern. She alone among them would have any idea of the depth of his worries, though he had not shared the whole of them. Far from it. The others

... well, he had, in fact, curtailed some of his investigations rather than risk drawing their ire or attention before he was certain.

But these were his *brethren*, his allies from the dawn of history. If he could not count upon them, to whom should he turn? If they were deceived, he owed it to them to show them the Truth, no matter how it haunted. How it *cut*, even to their piths.

When the others had settled around him, Narada rose, arms folded across his chest. "Well, Matarśivan? Why are we here? Another Age is ending, we can see that, and a great many things require attending to."

Danu, behind him, glowered at each of them as if all that had befallen her descendants was their fault. As if the Rishi bore responsibility for the slaughter and defeat. As if the curse the Danavas had laid upon half the Adityas was not punishment enough.

Matarśivan, too, rose, taking in his fellow Watchers one by one. Introspective Mitra, face unreadable as he watched Matarśivan. Unflappable Atri, who would stay whatever course the others agreed upon but so rarely lent his voice to the debate. And, of course, Arundhati, wise and steady, and so obviously wracked by curiosity as to his purpose. Matarśivan loved them each, in his way, though none more than Aditi.

And he was about to shatter their World. To shake the foundations upon which they had stood and leave them unsteady and uncertain of everything, most of all themselves.

Twice, he opened his mouth, then shut it in aphonic stupor. If he demurred now, if he turned away, they might enjoy centuries more in blissful ignorance. But would they all later pay a price for his reticence? And did the Truth itself not demand revelation?

Forcing his hands to stillness at his side, he focused upon only one of them. Kratu, who, of any beyond Aditi, might prove most inclined to listen. "For some time, I have seen things before they happen. My mind reveals visions, sometimes far distant ones, sometimes events that will soon unfold. But thus far, naught I have beheld, not a single vision, can I say is patently false."

Latsatian, to Kratu's left, leant forward. "Do you intimate the Archons have given you a new gift?"

Oh, that seemed unlikely. "Perhaps. Perhaps it is some new manifestation of Prana you will all develop in time." Though, so long had passed, his hope of that had dwindled. Whatever had happened to him didn't seem about to spread to the others. "Either way, I am convinced I have gained some ability to apprehend greater Truth."

Vinata snorted. "Beyond what we all see in the Roil, you mean? We are to believe that the Archons—or whoever—chose you alone to reveal this aspect of Truth to, trusting we should take your word for it? Does that not bespeak hubris, Matarśivan? If our gods wished us to know something, they could simply reveal it to all of us."

Indeed, there was hubris in thinking he alone knew the Truth. Matarśivan found it hard to avoid fidgeting. He, a four-thousand-year-old immortal, wriggling before his peers at having to tell them that which they would not relish hearing. "What if they do *not* wish us to know?"

At that, the others exchanged looks, and Atri and Yami leant together, falling into whispers he could not make out.

"You tread upon the banks of blasphemy," Vinata spat at him, though Mitra laid a restraining hand upon her arm.

Oh, he would more than tread upon blasphemy. He would dance all over it and demand they do the same. Almost, he could feel the gods' wrathful gazes settling upon him to even think it. "I have foreseen a future bleak beyond imagining, but one that seems inevitable if what I have begun to fear should prove real. I have seen the end of the World." Or several endings, though he could make little sense of that. "There is ... *something* that I ... fear feasts upon the Wheel of Life itself."

Now, all of his fellow Watchers had risen to their feet. Some gaped at him, while Yami took a threatening step forward. "You imply the Archons remain oblivious to such an abomination."

"I doubt ... they could remain unaware." The word complicity stuck in his throat. It choked him. Their *gods* abetted whatever eldritch power seemed to lurk in the darkness beyond the cosmos.

They allowed its obscene gorging. That was the only explanation he could see. "I ... believe they have used us to foster great civilisations in order to pit them against one another. That they wished for war and death and chaos as a means of keeping spinning the Wheel of Life, to feed the Darkness upon a feast of souls."

"Blasphemy!" Yami roared at him.

Before he could prepare himself, a beat of her black wings hurled her at him. Her fingers grasped his throat and bore him down into a heap.

His head smacked hard against stone and white haze filled his vision. All sound and sight blurred.

He flailed, trying to dislodge the Watcher, but without breath could not begin to grasp his Prana to flood into his limbs.

Then she was gone and his senses came seeping back in.

Screaming, cries. The scent of blood.

Yami's head was broken open upon one of the stone benches. The grey of her brains had splattered the area, and Aditi stood over her corpse wailing.

Gasping, Matarśivan struggled to gain his feet but only managed his knees.

All of them, the whole of the Dodecadic Circle it seemed, was screaming. What had he done? What had he *done*?

As he worked to rise, Atri leapt over his head, his descending fist slamming into Aditi. And then they were caught in melee and chaos and raining blows.

"Flee!" Aditi shrieked at him. "Matarśivan, flee—"

Her last words before falling, broken as Atri's fist caved in her throat. Before Vinata rent her wings.

Before his beloved, precious, darling Aditi hit the ground, dead.

PART I

If we take it as true that the future is woven for us by the Moirai, that we cannot escape the grasp of Ananke, a question rises ever to our minds: Are we, in fact, culpable for our actions? For thoughts and deeds and feelings born not of ourselves, but predicated upon an endless chain of causes stretching back to the beginning of time? Am I then naught save the sum of infinite moments that compounded to create an illusion of me?

— Urania, Analects of the Muses

1

PANDORA

754 Bronze Age

The collapsing bubble of the Box deposited Pandora within the confines of an alley, her appearance sending a nearby colony of rats scrambling away from piled refuse with annoyed chitters. Blinking away the disorientation—and damn glad she'd not appeared in the midst of the rats—Pandora rose, steadying herself against the alley wall. In one hand she held the Box. Beautiful, hateful, tormenting, and oh so precious, this vessel into which she had poured all the hopes of changing Fate.

To hold it once more, years after having lost it, felt akin to regaining the use of a lost limb. An impossible boon, a surging relief that threatened to have her heart bursting in elation she could scarce believe, much less put into words. But beneath all that joy—tears welled from it—was fear, too, for she looked at this Box just as the Gnostic Cabal had looked upon their Time Chambers, infusing it with desperate hopes of escaping the ouroboros.

The Cabal had, so far as Pandora knew, failed. Vorsanos had

become Kronos, Kronos had fled through time, and, in the end, Kala had slain him in the distant, snow-blighted future Hekate would create. Neither seeing the future in the Oracle Mirrors nor time-walking using the Chambers had allowed the Cabalist to change aught. Fate had stalked him through the halls of time, cornered him, and claimed him.

That knowledge struck like a fist to her gut. It tried to blast the hope from her lungs and leave her resigned, giving in to the fatalistic ennui that always lurked in the shadows of her doubting soul. But Pandora had sworn to Nemesis—*Athene!*—that she would never stop fighting, and it was more than an oath; it was an assertion of the greater truth of her soul.

She stared at the Box, its metal cool in her hand. It dared her to use it, to strive once more, to fight against the constricting coils of that ouroboros. To try, always at least one more time, to find the way toward true freedom of will. With a sigh, she tucked the device into her satchel and strode forth, into whatever polis she now found herself in.

The place was foreign to her and, given that twilight had most shopkeepers already packed up for the eve, it took her longer than she might have liked to identify her surroundings. It was not as if she could walk up to a passerby and inquire as to what city she was in, though the mental image of their expressions at such a question did bring a smile to her lips. Mostlike, she'd find herself named a madwoman and locked up or thrown outside the city for fear her condition might prove catching.

Instead, she strolled the breezeways until she caught enough snippets of conversation to recognise the local tongue as Phrygian. The only city of this size in Phrygia was Ilium, the place Artemis had claimed to have last seen Pandora before their fateful encounter in Babilim. The thought of Artemis had Pandora's chest clenching in its familiar tightness. Even her eye was twitching. How had Pandora allowed their friendship to flounder thus? Why had she not been able to do more to avert the conflict she had foreseen coming betwixt them? Every step she had taken had seemed, at the time, so needful.

But then, that was what Ananke meant, after all: *necessity*. Things happened as they must, based upon causal chains. Even this moment, even her regrets and self-recriminations now, were predicated upon events in her past that led to the pattern of her thoughts, to the movements of her soul. How was Pandora to hope to overcome a fundamental law of the universe, to deny causality itself?

If she was to have a chance, any chance at all, it must lie in the absolute mastery of the Box. Every time she had used this thing, her control had improved. Maybe, given enough knowledge and pratice, given a clever enough means to outwit the Moirai, she could find a way to save the future without unmaking the past. Such were her musings as she came to stare up at the walls surrounding the royal citadel of Ilium.

Beneath the citadel lay the lower city, where she had appeared, a place thick with tenements and workshops, with markets where the real people of this land plied their trades and hoped to peddle enough goods to return home with food for their families. And above all of them rose this towering edifice of kings, almost a literal mountain looking down on them the way Olympus soared over Elládos. Pandora wondered if the king here, whoever it was in these days, was better than the rulers of other lands.

Either way, if she was to find Artemis, assuming she had reached the correct time, she would need to head within the palace. Perhaps the citadel guards would have taken in her Heliad eyes, assumed her a Nymph, and admitted her despite her dirty, battle-stained clothes and dishevelled appearance. Perhaps they would even believe if she named herself as Nike. Or she might admit *herself* to the palace and thus test how fine her control with this Box had become.

For a time, Pandora walked the wall's periphery, judging the distance to the terrace far above. A few citizens and at least one guard seemed to take note of the strange woman examining the wall, but she paid them little mind as she performed a few trigonometric calculations in her head. Thus far, the Box had never caused her to appear in immediate danger, so perhaps Prometheus had installed some sort of safety feature that ensured she could not transport herself inside a solid object, or appear in midair, or under the sea, or any such fatal situation. Still, she thought it best to remain as precise as possible; why even take the chance of missing the terrace?

When she had checked her calculations twice, she removed the Box and began twisting the gears and panels. In Vulgeth, Amirani had told her the Time Chambers moved one through both time and space, and that, in fact, they *had* to move one through space to function. But the Box was a more subtle tool, a masterpiece predicated upon its creation, as Prometheus had used his experience examining the Box to later create it in the first place. So perhaps, with care, Pandora could move herself through space without any meaningful shift in time. Or, if she did move through time, then let her move by but a few heartbeats, so as to make no difference to her ends.

"You there!" someone cried from behind her, and she turned to see a guardsman headed her way, a wary look on his face. "It's rather late for a woman to be out alone."

Pandora favoured the man with a smirk. "Oh, but alone I've braved the sea of time, and survived the thrashing of its wild waves. Alone, I have walked through dark spaces others fear to even name in whispers." When the guard faltered, gawping at her, Pandora winked, and activated the Box.

The bubble of light rose up, engulfing her, making her ears pop. Next she knew, the World had shifted, and she was kneeling upon the terrace, a magnificent view of the stars spread out before her. She tried to stand, but a second wave of vertigo drove her back to her knees and forced her to remain there until, at last, her vision ceased to swim. That was odd ...

As she rose once more, a servant sweeping the area around the balcony stumbled back, mumbling. "Forgive me, lady. I did not know anyone was up here." The man seemed afraid to even raise his head. Were most aristoi in this place such oafish brutes as to castigate a servant for doing his assigned tasks?

Pandora strode to the man's side and gently touched his elbow. "I am seeking for the Olympian, Artemis. Is she here?"

The man swallowed hard but nodded and scampered off, with mumbled obeisance Pandora had not sought.

With a sigh, she turned and made her way to the edge of a battlement. Leaning against it, she gazed up at the moon. Was that Thoth himself—itself?—the Elder God? Prometheus had told her the Elders Gods, once called Archons, had commanded the Watchers. Now, she could not shake the sense the moon itself watched *her*, and its regard, imagined or not, made her feel like a scrambling insect underfoot, allowed to exist only by the indifference of giants.

She and Prometheus had found precious little time to speak of such things on Mu, more was the pity, given he had at long last begun to offer real answers to her questions. Perhaps he had judged she had journeyed far enough, learnt enough, to handle the truths he must unveil to her. His awful Ontos; that knowledge that had shaken a Watcher, born at the dawn of time, to his core.

She heard someone running toward her, and when she turned, Artemis skidded to a stop several feet away. "Did Zeus send you here for me?"

Pandora could have sworn she'd had almost the same conversation with the woman in Babilim. And the thought of that, of how it had ended, it once more had that ache in her chest throbbing. Something between a cry and a chortle escaped her, for she could not say for certain whether elation or deepest of sorrows should have come from this moment. She was afraid, was terrified, this would prove the last time she would see Artemis on friendly terms. The thought of that sent a fire more intense than even the Phoenix burning through her core. Before she knew what she was doing, she'd strode forward and flung her arms around Artemis. Even as she did so, she recalled that was how Artemis had greeted *her* in Babilim, before Pandora had tried to kill her emperor.

"Gods, Artemis," she sobbed. "I'm so sorry for everything ... what happened or will ... f-for the mistakes I've made. I want us only to be friends, always ..."

Artemis pushed her back to look into her face, plainly bemused. "What are you on about?"

All Pandora could do then was laugh and wipe her eyes. "You know, I, uh, I missed you."

Artemis half smiled, seeming almost shy at the admission. "And I you." She hesitated. "So you no longer serve Zeus."

Pandora looked hard at the woman. "I never served Zeus. I fought alongside him during the Titanomachy because Ananke wove it so."

"And the Gigantomachy."

Pandora nodded. "A means to secure release for Prometheus, only. I had no desire to see Zeus's benighted order endure a day longer than it must. And you? By your question and presence outside the sphere of Olympus, I take it you have broken with the Olympian Order?"

Artemis chewed on her lip. "A great war impends between those who yet serve the corrupt kingdom of Olympus and those who would see Man freed of Zeus's yoke." Pandora almost sighed. Much though she loathed Zeus, Mithra would prove an even greater threat to Mankind. And Artemis was going to serve the god-king unless Pandora somehow changed the future. "Stand by me in this war, Nike, that we may rectify the mistakes of the past."

She shook her head. "Would that I could. Maybe, one day ..." She shut her eyes against the future she knew was coming, held them closed before fitting Artemis with her gaze once more. "I have other, more pressing ends I must attend to first, Artemis. Do you know aught of the Unseen Order?"

"No, I've never heard such a name."

Not yet, then. "Well, it was worth asking."

The Phoebid shrugged. "You spoke of Prometheus. He is here, in fact, and I think he will be glad to see you."

Pandora's heart leapt; Artemis's words almost too welcome to give credence to. Had the Moirai, at long last, deigned to offer her a helping hand? Artemis beckoned her to follow, and Pandora did so, almost giddy.

WHEN ARTEMIS ESCORTED Pandora to Prometheus she found him, not alone, but rather with a teenage girl, sitting in a garden, practicing meditation. The child, auburn haired and fierce aspected, reminded her enough of him she thought they might be kin. Prometheus's eyes opened as she drew nigh, though Pandora thought her sandals soundless upon the damp summer grasses, and a vibrant smile lit her lover's face, his gaze seeming almost lucent blue.

"Kassandra," he said, and the girl started, then turned to look at Pandora. "This is my beloved, Nike." Because, of course, Prometheus realised Artemis knew her by that name.

The Phoebid patted Pandora's shoulder and left her to her reunion, calling for the girl to follow and leave Pandora alone with Prometheus.

"She's not your daughter, is she?" Pandora knew jealousy was such a petty emotion, but the words burst from her before she could stifle them. While Pandora flitted about through the timeline, oft passing fortnights or longer without seeing her lover, for him it could be *centuries*. Would it not be unfair of her to expect him to touch no other woman in all the vast span of history?

Prometheus's wry smile told her he had well-judged Pandora's thoughts, his amusement at them all the more infuriating. "She is not my daughter," he said, rising, and coming to stand beside Pandora. He took her elbows in his hands and squeezed. "Kirke wrote to me and asked me to offer what guidance I could for a young Oracle who cannot control her abilities."

Pandora embraced her lover and held him close, wanting the reassurance he was really with her more than aught else at the moment. When at last they broke away, she looked at him. "Kirke remains exiled upon Aiaíā?" When he nodded, Pandora sighed. At some point, she ought to arrange to visit her granddaughter there. For now, she didn't even know if the current year was before or after she had encountered Kirke in Themiskyra, either in absolute time or in reference to Kirke's point of view. "When am I?" she asked after casting a look around to make certain no one was in earshot.

Prometheus frowned. "The late Bronze Age, during the rule of King Priam."

Pandora nodded, mind whirring. Marduk had spoken of a great war in Priam's lifetime, fought between Ilium and Elládos. For the nonce, the city she saw looked to be one at peace, so Pandora assumed that had not yet unfolded. "I think we must speak alone."

"The king has granted me private chambers."

Pandora nodded.

PANDORA HAD NOT, on asking for privacy, originally intended her first action to be yanking her clothes off with such fervour the seams tore. Yet the moment the door was shut and she and Prometheus were alone, her body took on a mind of its own, the fiery blaze of the Phoenix in her breast demanding she embrace life. Only when they lay twice sated, entangled in one another's arms before the hearth, could she summon the presence of mind to give voice to the myriad questions that haunted her.

One, the worst, she feared to ask and yet saw no choice, much though she dreaded the answer. "You ... you are a servant of the Moirai."

Prometheus pushed himself up on his elbows so he could look at her. The firelight cast a golden glow upon his skin even as it glinted off his sapphire eyes. Eyes almost identical to the ones Athene possessed when she revealed herself as Nemesis. Was that colour a sign of the pact made betwixt the Moirai and their avatars? "A long, long time ago, I had to make a choice. Even as you so desperately seek the answers, so too did I. In exchange for the Ontos, I made a pact to serve as a guardian of history."

"Like Nemesis."

He frowned, shaking his head. "The gifts they gave her are different, and I think, so far as chronology even applies to them, they chose her later. Perhaps they found me less pliant of a servant than they had wished, though I, in my way, do uphold their Tapestry."

She could not shake the sense something lay unspoken, upon the tip of his tongue, words he refused to give voice. "How is that different than the ideology of the Unseen Order? Are you one of them? Your former Watcher brother, Mithra, *leads* their Order, Prometheus. Mithra or Enki or whatever name he calls himself at present. It was he who brought me back to Ogygia, the day Zeus threw you into Tartarus, and now I am given to think he *knew* what I would find in your workshop, back then. So tell me now, are you working with them?"

"No."

Now she rose to sit before him, legs folded beneath herself, all the pent-up frustration rising to the surface until it felt apt to burst forth like the Phoenix's flames. "Yet you espouse the same goals as them!"

"Insofar as we both agree history must unfold, yes. I hold not entirely with them, nor with the Gnostic Cabal, and yet I am bound with some kinship to both. The Watchers, the Dodecadic Circle, we were torn apart, Pandora, but it did not sever bonds forged from millennia of common experience. Even if pain and recrimination transform such a bond from love into loathing, still it remains the strongest of emotions, and noways pure. It is possible, even and especially at such times, to hold the ashes of love and the fires of hatred in one's hands at the same time. Who but those closest to us could ever engender such passions?"

And he was left caught in a maelstrom of conflicting emotions. "In Mu, you called Nemesis as Vinata, but I saw her later, and she was ... our granddaughter, Athene. Conscripted to serve the Order."

Prometheus now rose, mirroring Pandora's position, pain creasing his face before he pushed it away. The Watchers, she knew, had a frightful ability to mask their emotions, to retain a preternatural calm that only rarely cracked to reveal humanity beneath. "Athene ..."

"Have we so failed as parents, as grandparents, that our daughter will become a plague upon Gaia, that our granddaughter should fall into the service of the Unseen Order? On Mu I heard some insanity about Hekate *binding* an Elder God? What utter *madness* has our family unleashed upon the Earth?"

Prometheus let his head fall into his palms, leaving her to wonder how many of these revelations were news to him. He was stricken with shock, that much was plain, a shuddering breath tore out from him, until she couldn't stop herself from reaching across the space between them and placing a comforting hand on his shoulder. Yes, because in times of greatest strain, even his mask would crack. Her lover looked up at her touch, blinking away tears. "I tried *everything* I could imagine to change Fate, even before I bound myself to it. And on learning of the awful end, I tried means further still to save her. But if there is any play that might shift the course of Fate, it must needs prove a subtle one."

Pandora swallowed, withdrawing her hand. So he had failed to save Pyrrha from herself, though he had tried. All of this unfolded in service to his greater goal, she had no doubt, but she could not see the end of the path they were on. Or rather, she could not see it end in aught save blood and pain, and oceans of regret vast as the span of history. "Your plan somehow involves the Destroyer, of that I am almost certain, though I lack too many details." He opened his mouth, but she raised a hand to forestall his objections. "No, I know you fear to speak some things aloud, lest other servants of your mistresses uncover the depths of your gambit. But tell me, how can you place hope in a source of *carnage*?" Pandora grimaced. "Herakles? Is that the sort of man you think can save us?"

He shook his head. "Herakles was not the Destroyer, but rather an incarnation of the Destroyer's soul. That soul might be born in the interim, prior to the need for an Eschaton."

Pandora huffed. "Either way, the man killed his own children. He brutally assaulted Priam's father, Laomedon. Inside his breast is a boiling cauldron ready to overflow at the slightest provocation. Truly, if he is not the Destroyer, still he earned the title." Her lover looked to the hearth, staring in the flames for so long Pandora began to suspect he looked there for pyromantic insights about what she had said. Then something else sparked in her mind. "Herakles *was* not the Destroyer?"

Prometheus looked back to her, not masking the sadness in him.

"He died, more than a decade ago, and his death set in motion events beyond control and, in some cases, even beyond my ability to predict in the deepest of probability trances. I can say he will be born again and, mostlike, die again well before his actual incarnation as the Destroyer becomes needful. As to the rest, his abilities, in large part, are psychic ones. He unconsciously calls upon the skills and memories of his past lives, warriors all. In times of great danger, such memories rush to the forefront and turn him—"

"Into a *weapon*," Pandora finished for him. "You made a weapon out of a *man*. And that weapon turned itself upon his children. The moral imprecations of using a person thus aside, what use is a tool without control?"

Again he shut his eyes. "Long did I muse over the question of why that happened, for never in all his prior incarnations did such a thing occur."

"You said that nature was only supposed to arise in him if his life was in danger." Pandora knew her tone was accusing, but the years of secrets and half-truths had left a bitterness in her she had not, until this moment, realised ran quite so deep. Or maybe that anguish in her breast was the ache left by the ruination of their daughter's life. "Are we to believe his wife and children threatened him with mortal peril?"

Prometheus raised a finger in acknowledgment. "If we discount such an absurd occurrence, we are left with two possibilities. One, the Destroyer's soul has endured so much over its numerous incarnations it has begun to arise when unneeded. Or ..."

Pandora huffed. "Or an external stimulus drove him to it." She folded her arms over her chest. "Fine. Fine. Suppose I take it as given the Destroyer is needful to keep the World balanced, or to fulfil your greater plan, whatever that might be. Still, I'm left to ask where that leaves *us*. I admit I'm not well disposed toward the Gnostic Cabal considering they held me in a dark cell for *years*, but I at least share their goal of breaking the Wheel of Fate. And you, my love, remain a sworn servant of the Fates. Your mission seems far more in line with the Unseen Order than the Cabal."

He looked again to the fire. "You do not understand. If, upon seeing both sides of a coin, you find neither side tolerable, you are left to strive after a third alternative, one which no one else could even conceive of."

"Refuse the coin entirely." Some middle ground by which he could both uphold and, at the same time, subvert Fate? Was that even possible? It would be the longest con in all history, then, for it must needs stretch from the dawn of time to the moment of its culmination. Pandora swallowed as some semblance of Prometheus's gambit began to take shape in her mind. He could not speak it aloud, no, but she saw it, nonetheless, an incipient apparition taunting her with its scope. He would follow through with Fate until such a nexus moment as he might change its course. All the air blew out of her, and Pandora settled back down, defeated. How was she to come up with a better plan than one which he had spent tens of thousands of years perfecting? His machinations reached across the entire ambit of time, all toward his most desperate of ends.

Part of her, a vast part, thought her role must then be to aid him in whatever way she might do so. He was, on a scale beyond aught she had ever imagined or attempted, trying to save the future, to save Mankind, to save everyone, no matter the cost to himself. He had endured millennia of pain and loneliness, on a chance, however slim, of averting whatever terrible future he had foreseen. She started to reach for his hand, to grasp it and show her support for the war he fought on behalf of them all.

But her fingers dropped and she could not close the distance. "I know you have your mission, my love. But I have mine, as well. At present, that comes to tearing down the Unseen Order and stopping the Deluge the Queens of Mu will unleash because of Mithra."

"If such is the Eschaton, you cannot stop it."

Heat rose in her breast at his dismissal of her deepest need. "Then I will use my last breath trying!"

Slowly, Prometheus nodded. "Of course you will, love. It's who you are, and I adore your tenacity." He paused, glancing once more to the fire. "Look to the Anunnaki." Pandora frowned. They were the greatest Titan bloodline of Kumari Kandam, she thought, though she'd read little more of them. "I've reason to believe the Order connected to their line. Beyond that, so far as I know, three of the Watchers joined the Unseen Order. Mitra—now Mithra—you know, who was Enki, one of the Anunnaki patriarchs, not unlike Kronos in that way. Vinata, once Mitra's lover, became Nemesis, perhaps at his behest. Atri, now called Sraosha, guards the bridges of the Underworld, and I should not expect contact between you." He grimaced. "I have seen a fell vision in which he and I fight, and I have little choice but to slay a brother ... I do not look forward to such a day." He patted her knee. "That is all the aid I can give at this point."

And more than she had expected. She closed her hand over his, still upon her knee. "I shan't give up on Pyrrha, either."

"Nor I, though I saw her die, long ago, and I never found a way to change it."

His words carved a fresh wound into Pandora's soul, and she grimaced. So many things wrong with time, and she without a clear path to fix any of them.

2

___

ARTEMIS

742 Bronze Age

*I*n the woods north of the polis of Athenai, beneath an almost full moon that no longer pulled at her soul, Artemis watched her apprentice turning a rabbit on a spit. The boy had shot, skinned, and now cooked their supper without her needing to offer the least guidance. That, of course, had left her with the strange admixture of pride and a sense of loss all parents must feel on seeing the children outgrow the need for them, even if the boy was not her blood.

Hippolytus would be sixteen soon, and already his face had come into its first beard, or at least hints thereof, that *he* would have called a beard. After Atalanta's death, Artemis had thought she would never attach herself to another child, but the way the boy had looked to her with that muddle of admiration and need, it had pierced her like the truest of arrows. He'd been so like Artemis's lost adoptive daughter. So *eager* to be all the things Artemis was, as if she were a paragon worth emulating.

And who was she, really? Convinced she could escape the fetters of patriarchal oppression, she'd fought and killed for Zeus. She'd murdered her grandfather to chase a dream of a better society, but like all dreams, in the end, it had become naught save grit stinging her eyes and a bitter memory of *almost*.

Now, if Zeus knew Artemis was in Elládos, he'd have come for her. The tyrant king tolerated no question to his authority and in walking away from the mountain, she had bucked his will. Athene had made plain, years back, he expected her return, and she had ignored the woman, though Athene had named her sister then. But Artemis could no longer, would no longer, be a party to the corruption of Olympus. Whether she liked it or not, that meant Athene had set herself up on the opposite side of a brewing conflict.

Still, for the nonce, Artemis had striven not to bring down Zeus but his wayward bastard, Dionysus. Perhaps that was why the Olympians yet tolerated her rather than hunting her down. Or perhaps her brother, Zeus's precious Oracle, had bought her time and grace.

"You've scarce said a word all night," Hippolytus commented, and she realised her apprentice stared not at the spit but at her.

"Hmm?" Artemis slapped her palms against her knees and huffed another sigh. "The wretch has grown into a new form, and I find him nigh impossible to track."

Her apprentice did not need to ask of whom she spoke, for she had told him rather a great deal of Dionysus. She had told him, even, how she had slain his prior incarnation and he had somehow used Ariadne's body to reincarnate himself as a babe, then risen and spoken to her. Taunted her. Artemis did not know for certain, but she suspected that, though only thirteen years had passed since then, still the new Dionysus had mostlike attained adulthood. With a new face and a new name, he worked in secret, and she could not find him.

The boy hefted the spit off the flames and set to carving off slices. "You said Athene once offered you alliance against that abomination. Perhaps the offer still stands?"

Artemis had no idea. Given she spent her time flitting back and forth between here, training Theseus's son, and scouring Elládos, Phlegra, and the lands beyond for Dionysus, Athene could have located her had the woman wished. Athene was an Oracle herself, if not nigh so strong as Apollon, and could have used her hydromancy to find Artemis, or so Artemis assumed. She had not done so, and Artemis had studiously avoided interaction with other Titans whenever possible. She had just returned from Salon, in far Illyris, and found no trace of her quarry there, either. Was it possible he had fled Kêr-Ys and crossed to Kumari Kandam or even Hy-Brasil? Gaia was vast, and she was, at this point, hunting at random, wandering in the dark and hoping her prey would stumble across her path.

She accepted a hunk of meat her apprentice offered. "It might." Or showing her face to the Olympians might earn her orichalcum fetters and Zeus making an example of her. A man who could throw his father into Tartarus had no scruples about casting his wrath in any direction that suited his whims. Like the simians of Hy-Brasil who flung their faeces at those who displeased them, Zeus would happily cake his hands in shit, if only to ensure it splattered on those who vexed him, as well.

"There's going to be a second Titanomachy, isn't there?" Hippolytus asked.

Artemis started. Were her thoughts so plain even the boy could suss out her fears? The last war had nigh destroyed the World of Man. Had Nike not slain that Tartarian abomination, Artemis could not imagine what carnage would have unfolded. And if pushed to extremes, Zeus was far worse than Kronos had ever been. He could not be allowed to live, and yet, the cost for his downfall could prove earthshaking.

Part of her had almost toyed with the thought of allowing Dionysus to continue to work toward his father's undoing. But the avatar of Pan had stripped Artemis of her free will. He had enslaved her, body and mind, for years. He was, in her eyes, as much worse than Zeus as Zeus was than Kronos. A sick chain of ever-increasing madness, where every link must be rent asunder. "Maybe you're right," she said at last. She needed aid against Dionysus, which meant she needed to call on another Olympian. The question, she supposed, was who.

IN THE END, the choice was taken from her because her brother arrived by pegasus outside Athenai polis, clearly having known where to find her. For a brief moment she stared at Apollon, a little at a loss after not having laid eyes upon him for years. Her twin spread wide his arms, flashed his irritating love-me-I-am-glorious grin, and waited for her to embrace him. Much though she wanted to cuff him upside the head—stupid, shining Heliad everyone elevated over her by virtue of naught save a cock—Artemis grudgingly stepped into his arms.

"It's been long," she said.

Apollon snorted. "Did you think I did not keep my eye upon you with every whorl of the clouds?"

Artemis pulled away and shook her head at the aeromancer. Had Apollon known half of what she had endured at Dionysus's hands, he'd have been there, arrows flying, she had no doubt. Still, she allowed him his pompous air of wisdom. Let him play the all-knowing Oracle if it suited him. "Then why come to me now, after so many years?"

"I have located Ares," he said. The words were drawn out slow, as if of some import. Or pretension.

Artemis shrugged. Ares was but another sadistic wretch sprouted from Zeus's loins, true, but in keeping his father busy with his rebellions, he proved a boon to her rather than a hinderance. "I've no care for solving this squabble betwixt father and son."

"Perhaps not, but Ares has captured Athene. He plans to use her hydromancy to counter the fact Zeus has gained some semblance of the Sight."

Artemis's stomach dropped out from under her. Zeus with the Sight? How in Nyx's vast darkness had that happened? "Athene won't help Ares against her father."

"No, and when he cannot convince her, I imagine the torture will begin. It is best we do this together, Sister."

The import of her brother's words settled upon her like a comforting hand squeezing her shoulder. Because Apollon was on Artemis's side—and clearly had been for some time. She did not need to speak it aloud; she was certain the gratitude in her eyes was readily apparent.

Her brother offered her a small nod. "Ares has a camp in the hills of Phlegra, a half day southwest of Iolkos. If you are swift, you may find Athene there, though the God of War does not tarry overlong in any one place. Perhaps he fears the Oracles serving Zeus would locate him."

"As you have."

He flashed his idiot grin. He truly thought the sun shone from betwixt his teeth, didn't he? "Sadly, no, despite our king's commands, I have not been able to locate his son so far, though my efforts never cease."

Artemis glanced past him, to the pegasus. "Give me a moment to see my apprentice off."

"Be quick," Apollon warned. "Best I am not gone long enough for Zeus to suspect you and I have contact."

Artemis sat behind Apollon on his pegasus as they soared across the innumerable Aegean islands and made for Phlegra. No matter how she twisted, he managed to sporadically jam his elbow into her ribs in the name of controlling the mount. His antics made for a long flight, giving her enough time to muse on whether she'd been remiss in not coming to her brother herself for all these years. Had he taken this much time to come around to seeing things her way, or could she have had an ally all along, had she but asked? Apollon forever thought himself better than her, true, but other than that, her twin had never betrayed her in all their millennia-long lives.

Carrying two across such distances drained even a pegasus, and the moment they spotted the continent, Apollon allowed the animal to land and graze. They both knew it would fly back to Olympus when it was rested. By unspoken accord, they broke into a swift pace, hurrying over the coastal plains and toward the distant hill lands that blanketed so much of Phlegra. This place remained wilder than Elládos, giving it an appeal Artemis could not deny. There were dangers, of course, Gigantes and centaurs prime amongst them, but for someone like Artemis, she felt right at home.

Soon the land began to slant upward, but Titan stamina kept their progress steady. "Any idea what we'll find in Ares's camp?" Artemis asked as she scrambled over a rocky slope, careful of her footing. From the top of a hill she could make out a pass, winding through the valleys, that might mean faster progress. Ever since Apollon had mentioned that Ares might begin torturing Athene, mental images of it kept flashing in her mind. Would he beat her? Cut her? Something more permanent like severing digits? Each such thought brought a fresh wince from her. She'd known Athene as a child, had helped train her. Had loved her as a friend when she was grown. Much though she loathed the woman's father, the thought of harm befalling Athene felt like razors churning in her gut.

"Gigantes," he said. "Like Demeter before him, Ares gathers to him those rejected and cast to the fringes by Zeus's order. Hungry mouths eager for their share of the land's bounty, I suppose you could say."

"Hungry mouths eager for something worse, if they're Gigantes," Artemis retorted. She skidded down the slope, her sandals dislodging a tiny avalanche of scree in the process. At the bottom, in the valley, she glanced back to him and saw him sliding down after her. "Or do you imply you sympathise with their monstrous desires?" Driving Man-eating monsters out of civilised lands was one of the only things Zeus had done Artemis did not despise the king for.

"No ... Filthy, dirty creatures. I only mean to say, Zeus has fomented a fair crop of enemies, so it is not impossible for them to unite against him."

The thought of that left a sour taste on her tongue. What bitter desperation it would take to turn to monsters just so one could fight a greater monster? Could she ever take that step? Could she tolerate fighting alongside those Man-eating beasts against which she had fought most of her life?

"I know what you are thinking," Apollon chimed when Artemis resumed her trot. Soon, she would need to start hunting for sign of a camp. They must rely on stealth, for if Ares had a small army of Gigantes, a frontal assault would end with her and Apollon in the bellies of those monsters. "But perhaps some crimes are worse even than cannibalism and the insatiable need it engenders in Titans."

That brought Artemis up short, and she looked back to him once more. "Some are worse, indeed." Dionysus was far worse. As was his father. So maybe Apollon had a point after all. Given a long enough life, it was bound to happen eventually.

ONCE APOLLON HAD PROVIDED a rough area with aeromantic insight, it had not proved difficult for Artemis to scout out Ares's camp. The God of War had chosen a ravine where a granite outcropping provided shelter from the elements, creating an almost cave-like recess. The lay of the land meant the camp could not be easily attacked or even detected from above, and to approach from below would mean taking a narrow pass easily held by a pair of Gigantes.

"We could shoot them," Apollon offered. "Hit them in the throat or face and they'll go down without having time to alert other forces."

In truth, it was the first plan she'd considered, and had Apollon not reminded her the ruler of Olympus was, in fact, more despicable than a Gígas, she might have gone through with it. But if they came in and started slaughtering Zeus's enemies, they harmed their cause. Much though she loathed the Gigantes and their disgusting addiction, Artemis had not come here to kill them. Besides, even with the element of surprise, the two of them would struggle against a Gígas war band.

"We have to try to convince Ares to release her."

"You want to negotiate, then." Apollon puffed out his chest. "Well, Ares may yet prove a useful ally against his father."

Artemis grimaced at that. What times had they come to, that she would countenance such an idea. "Follow my lead and cover me. If they refuse to talk, I may need to make a hasty withdrawal."

After nodding, Apollon hopped down to a lower rock, upon which he could crouch and take aim at the camp's entrance. Once he was in position and signalled her, Artemis too scrambled down. She passed her brother and dropped all the way to the base of the ravine. Hands empty and raised in peace, she stepped into the line of sight of the guards.

The both of them were swollen to heights of over nine feet, their forms looking bloated and bestial. Maybe consumption of Man-flesh served but to reveal the true natures of their savage souls. One snarled and hefted a club at her approach. Artemis kept her shoulders loose, ready to draw the knife at her back in an instant should either of these creatures make to attack. "I've come to parley with Ares."

The left guard relayed her message over his shoulder and Artemis let her hands drop. One she kept on her hip, closer to the dagger's hilt. A moment later, Ares strolled into view. A mat of ashen hairs covered the Titan's exposed arms. His visage had taken on a wolf-like aspect, his vicious grin hinting at fangs in a too-long maw. So the son of Zeus had himself become a Gígas.

Artemis struggled to keep rank disdain from her face. Like his father—like most Titans, and all Olympians, she supposed—Ares suffered from an overabundance of pride. Wounding it would turn him into a beast in truth, she had little doubt. "I've come for Athene."

"Who?"

Artemis stared at him. "That's what you're going with?" She had expected him to deny holding his sister prisoner. Not to pretend he didn't know who his sister *was*.

Perhaps the idiocy of his response dawned on him because he waved away his comment. "Well, but we're in the midst of a family discussion and you're no blood of ours."

Praise Thoth for that. "I know that you hold her against her will, Ares. So what do you want? You cannot believe she will ever aid you against your father. Not Athene. Not her." She was mired so deep in the need for Zeus's approval she could never dig herself free of such a prison.

"She will!" the man snapped. At once, he began pacing in a half circle, as if preparing to pounce. "She has to. She has to open her fucking eyes and see the man is tinged with madness."

Artemis laughed at that. "Tinged with madness? Your father has *marinated* in madness for thousands of years. Insanity weeps from his pores in place of sweat."

"Aww. I see you have met Papa, haven't you?" The God of War giggled. Ares, now, *he* was tinged with madness.

Artemis wondered if the entire Kroniad genos was polluted with some sickness of the blood. She had never seen mental aberration in Kronos, but so many who hailed from his line seemed touched by it. Or maybe, Olympus itself corrupted the mind, in which case, she too might well have derangements of which she remained unaware. A disquieting thought. "Athene will not aid you, and I don't think you truly wish to harm your sister." At least, she had banked on there being *some* semblance of familial loyalty between them. Artemis could never, under any circumstances, imagine hurting Apollon. And her brother had now all but walked away from his position as one of the rulers of the World for her sake.

"Maybe I'd rather harm you." Whilst they may have shared in loathing his father, she could not forget Ares was petty and keen to lash out at someone if he didn't get his way. Rather like his father, really.

"If you insist, I can challenge you to single combat. We can see if you deserve the title Men give you." Among the Olympians, it was hard to say for certain who would come out ahead in a fair fight between Artemis, Athene, or Ares. It had come as a shock to learn Ares had defeated his sister, but that didn't mean Artemis could not overcome him. She was, so far as she knew, the fastest of any of them.

The only Olympian she was certain she could not take in a struggle was Zeus himself, because of his accursed command of lightning.

Ares continued pacing, seeming to weigh her indirect challenge. Perhaps he too thought he might fail, or maybe he realised he had precious little to gain and much to lose. Because he whirled on her and pointed a finger that, she saw now, ended in a claw-like nail. "Give her back to Father and you aid his cause."

"Maybe. But at the moment, it is Athene's cause I am concerned with. Release her, and I'll take her from here with me. It will give you time to move your camp." Ares snarled, licking his lips with a too-long tongue. "She will force you to kill her," Artemis pressed, hoping he could not, *would* not do so.

Ares threw up his hands. "You hate him too."

"Yes."

"Then fight with me. Help me bring him down."

Maybe Apollon was right. Maybe sometimes one had to choose the least vile option. "The day may come for it, when I have attended to more pressing matters first. But that day can only arrive if, on this day, you release your sister into my custody."

"Bah! So be it. Take her and be gone, then." Once more he pointed that claw-finger at her. "But see to it that one day arrives sooner rather than later."

Artemis nodded. She hoped it would.

3

ATHENE

742 Bronze Age

Fettered in orichalcum, Athene sat against the cool wall of a cave. She did not know quite where her brother had brought her, though somewhere in Phlegra she assumed. His war camp was well concealed, bustling though it was with warriors and Gigantes. Ares had kept her in the recesses of his subterranean hideout, away from the greater portion of his forces, such that she could only guess at his true numbers. He had chosen this spot for her, she supposed, because of the tiny pond beside her, into which he hoped she would focus her hydromantic abilities. The reflection of stalactites on the surface created the illusion of a deep lake brimming with underwater stalagmites, but Athene knew better. The waters here had no more depth than Ares himself. Her brother flailed in the dark, nursing wrath he scarce knew what to do with.

Though the lay of the cavern prevented her from seeing much, Ares had to keep the torches burning here if he wanted Athene to gaze into the pool. Through the flicker of their dancing lights, she had caught sight of one of her brother's guests. That had been the sage, Tiresias, long advisor to the kings of Thebes. From Herakles—even the thought of her fallen son tore through Athene, a searing knife eviscerating her soul—she had heard the immortal sage had once fallen afoul of King Aeëtes of Kolchis, though never the details. How came such an Oracle to consult with a rebel Olympian?

For these questions, she did indeed look into the waters, watching the blurred sparkle of torchlight over its still surface and letting her mind slip into trance. But the answers came not when she willed, but when *they* willed.

Now, Athene must drive the other champions of her people into the fray—no doubt the choice Father would have directed, though she'd send men like Odysseus and Nestor and Ajax to their deaths—or she must join it herself. Athene could not bear to watch those she had befriended here mount their pyres one by one. The thought evoked the wound that had become Herakles. It was an injury she knew now, after decades of watching it weep inside her heart, would forever remain raw and bleeding, incapable of receiving the healing boons time was meant to bestow upon it. Some blades bit too deep. Some wounds turned not to scars but to pains that became one with the person bearing them, defining a new reality with them.

In thinking to save Mankind through its heroes, she had let one after another into her soul, and one by one, she watched them fall to the final fate that lay ahead of all Men. Perseus and Bellerophon and Theseus and Jason and so many others all dead now. All turned to ashes and blown away on uncaring winds. Herakles.

Herakles.

So, Athene had strapped on her panoply, trod among the Elládosi, and stemmed the Ilian advance. Her people would not break this day. This day, she would not watch the burning of Odysseus or Nestor or Ajax or his half-brother Teukros or any of the others.

She had not, on donning armour and taking up arms, expected to find herself come face-to-face with her brother. Had he already begun wading among the melee, or had he joined it on learning of her taking an active role? Either way, a feral, lupine grin spread across his features as he trod toward her.

&

"WHAT DID YOU SEE?" her brother demanded, and Athene started, the images flitting across her mind turned to haze.

So deep in her trance, she had not noticed his approach. She licked her parched lips before turning to stare daggers at Ares. "Naught that will ever aid you against Father."

Ares bent close to her, frowning, his jaw trembling as though he might break into weeping, though she had never once seen tears in his eyes in all their centuries of shared life. His backhand cracked against her jaw, sending her head smacking into the cavern wall. Spots bloomed across her vision.

"Why, why, *why* make me do such a thing?" Ares giggled, prancing around as Athene blinked away the spots. Of course, even as they began to clear, pain blossomed in her skull. Without Pneuma to toughen her flesh and bones, his blows fell like hammer strikes against her. "Ah! Should I pull your hip bones out of socket? Would that entice you to cooperation, little sister?"

Athene didn't bother hiding her groan. "You think ... an Oracle can concentrate whilst in the throes of agony? The Sight requires a meditative state, Ares." Had the man ever achieved aught like the calming of his mind in his entire life? She doubted it.

He looked at someone behind him and barked a command. Then her brother huffed, pointed a finger at her in some vague threat, and stormed off. Moaning, Athene shifted, trying to find some way to rest her head against the wall without touching the swollen spot.

Bound in orichalcum, prey to the fickle whims of her captor, it carried a dreamlike taste of foreknown memory. Not this moment, though, but a dream yet to come, worse still.

For a time, Ares was gone, and Athene dozed, somewhere in the space betwixt pained delirium and deeper release of sleep. Her brother had allowed her precious little rest in the days he'd held her prisoner ... had wanted her pliant ... kept her deprived of all necessities ...

His rough hand seized her chin and hefted her upward, forcing Athene to scramble to her feet lest he wrench her neck. It was not the awakening she'd have preferred. "Your pet she-bear has come to ransom you."

Half-conscious, starving, and battered, she struggled to understand what in Tartarus he was on about. Next she knew, he'd unlocked the chains. The moment her wrists were free of the manacles, Pneuma began to flow once more, biting like the sudden return of blood to a limb fallen asleep. Once she could catch hold of the channels rushing through her, she directed some of the flow into Tolerance, pushing down pain, allowing her to ignore physical deprivations.

His words began to take shape in her mind as he escorted her to the cavern entrance, and even before she saw Artemis, she knew it must be her. Indeed, the Phoebid and her twin were both here, apparently having come to save her. Athene doubted Ares's claim about a ransom—would he trade her for mere drachmae or even Ambrosia?—but they must have offered her brother something of value.

Not knowing what to say, she cast a look of profound gratitude toward Artemis, and the other woman nodded in answer, obviating the need to put into words all Athene felt in that moment.

4

KIRKE

728 Bronze Age

"It doesn't work." Zeus's words, more growl than statement, sat heavy in the air within Kirke's manse, like a toxic cloud. Yeah, Kirke had known there would be trouble the moment he'd come plodding along the path to her prison once more. Zeus carried trouble in his wake anywhere he went, a veritable lodestone for anarchy and suffering.

Two years since she'd seen the gods-be-damned King of Olympus, but she could have happily gone two centuries. Or longer. He represented the sole interruption of her solitude she did not, would *never* welcome.

"Eh, you mean to say you did not gain the Sight."

The pale-eyed king glared at her as though she were some maggot that had dared crawl its way out of his meat and he considered whether to throw her out or eat her regardless. "It has not revealed the Unseen," he snarled.

Unseen? Had not Pandora asked about something along those

lines, back when she and Artemis had first helped Zeus win his throne? "I-I don't understand. That's all the Sight does, show you things others cannot perceive, and yeah, sometimes—oft enough—we might wish we didn't see it, either. The past and future are this mesh of knots and we think seeing them can ... can ..." *Can allow us the freedom to change them, but as Pandora had said, time is an ouroboros.* She wanted to tell him the Sight would never reveal aught he could change. She wanted to explain—and maybe to *taunt*—that he would sooner induce fish to soar among the clouds than achieve any expediency from his Sight.

Since provoking him would have been about as wise as pissing over a pit of vipers, Kirke kept her mouth shut. One of life's great challenges.

Just when she was about to explore for need to, in some way, point out his ignorance, his fist collided with her temple and all thought spilled out of her head. Next Kirke knew, she was on the ground, Zeus's sandal upon her sternum.

"Open those golden eyes and look at me, bitch." He pressed down with his foot until she felt her ribs creaking. Air was forced from her lungs. Her heart felt apt to burst within her chest. "I did not fly across half the Thalassa to have you explain what the Sight does. I have come here because you are going to make it *better*."

Kirke wheezed, unable to make the least answer. Stark terror crawled along her spine and wrapt around her guts.

Zeus flexed his fingers and crackles of lightning leapt between the digits. He extended his index finger and began to reach it toward her face.

Tears almost blinding her, Kirke managed a weak nod, and Zeus stood, easing the pressure off her chest. At last she drew in a painful breath, gasping, clutching her bruised ribs. "I'll ... keep ..." She couldn't form words. Couldn't work her tongue. "... Working."

"See that you do, you useless whore. I will have progress when next I come here." He left the rest of his threat unspoken, and Kirke was not certain whether to call it a blessing. "Now," he said, "why did your mother never answer my summons?"

Kirke wished she knew. Or rather, she could guess. After having given Hekate the Box, Kirke had tried to visit her mother's dreams to no avail. Because Hekate had no doubt used the blighted device, and the Moirai alone knew when or if she would return from it. "I've not ... seen her ... in two years. I am imprisoned ... here."

Zeus growled again, hardly pleased, but seeming to accept the answer. For now.

So Kirke worked, day and night, striving to create a more perfect Nectar. Throwing oneself even into an impossible task seemed somewhat better than dwelling upon the price of her inevitable failure. So what if she considered fleeing Aiaíā most every day? If she imagined a thousand ways to escape, whether it be pleading with Eos for a boat, or stealing one, or even trying to swim for the Phoenikian coast, though the attempt would mostlike end in her death. Yeah, oft she considered such plans and discarded them, unwilling to die, and certain that, even if she lived, Zeus would find her and make it all so much worse.

He had the Sight now, thanks to her. If he wasn't certain to find her before, he surely would do so now. Kirke was forever trapped in this manse, the final victim of her alchemical pursuits. Had Zeus never taken Io—had Kirke not forced it to happen!—she would never have begun brewing Nectar in her futile attempt to free Mankind from beneath Titan heels. What horrors she had wrought with the Art, and how little it had all availed her, or anyone, in the end.

Maybe that was all the Art could do: make things worse. Seeking magical remedies always ended in disaster.

In the times when she could bear staring at phials and beakers and alembics no longer, or when she needed to let her tinctures stew and settle, she took to weaving. The Moirai had woven their frightful, infinite Tapestry across the ambit of history, and Kirke had seen more of its shape than anyone, Man or Titan, ought to ever witness. Trying to capture even a piece of that awful creation within her weft served to ward off the madness that ever tried to creep upon her like a thief in the night. No one, she supposed, could bear witness to pieces of the Ontos and retain the precarious balance of humility and self-importance Men called sanity.

Other times, she walked in the woods, talking to squirrels and wolves and birds. "So, yeah," she told a chukar who wandered across her portico, "I'm basically employed by the king of the whole fucking World. Yeah. Makes me a big deal, you know? I mean, it's not technically employment because he doesn't pay me. And he beats me and threatens to rape or torture me. So, really, you might say I'm more like a slave than a hireling. I mean, if you did say that, I'd call you an arse-hole. Maybe tell some village hunter where to find you so he could plant an arrow in a place you wouldn't want it to bloom. Hmm." She threw up her hands. "Oh, don't look at me like that. Fine, I'm sorry, all right. Can I … can I call you Chicken? It's important to name things. Yeah. So, the king, right? He's got an ego big enough to flatten a mountain range and keep on rolling. Really, he's only the king of Elládos and maybe Phlegra or something." Though the little gossip she heard from the village claimed Ares now stood in rebellion out of Phlegra, so there was that. "Yeah, but he thinks he rules the whole earth and the heavens and probably the moon, or whatever. So, Chicken, what I mean to say is I get to spend the rest of eternity as a semi-slave to a megalomaniac. But sure, I guess you've got problems too. Tell you what, share them, and we'll see who has it worse." She stared at the chukar and the bird stared back with black eyes laced with epic stupidity. "No?"

She shrugged. Chicken, it turned out, was a terrible conversationalist.

She awakened in twilight, a city of jagged spires rising just beyond where she knelt, the sight like some many-spined behemoth. Then it did move, for the ground bucked beneath her, cutting short her attempt to rise. A cacophony erupted, Gaia groaning in her violent heaves, spires shattering

and raining stones like hail across the darkened city. The tumult sent her tumbling as the land broke apart, and Kirke slammed hard into a rising shelf of earth.

The impact dazed her, left her moaning, not quite certain how much time had passed. She pushed herself up on hands and knees and gaped in absolute terror at what unfolded before her. The sky had splintered, pieces of it plunging earthward like a cracking dam about to burst. Through the rifts rent in reality writhed intimations squirming tendrils, like some thousand-armed cephalopodic nightmare, worming their way into the Mortal Realm.

Kirke slapped a hand to her mouth, too stricken to scream. A thought came to her, appalling in its clarity, and more so because she could not imagine whence came such an idea. But the dread apprehension remained: what if she beheld not the breaking of reality, but the falling away of a facade, like plaster flaking off a crumbling wall?

Those profane tendrils stretched down, toward the blighted, falling city, giving her a better—more terrible—look at the abomination seeping into her world. The arms seemed to glint with endogenous motes of light beneath the surface, as if composed of both stars and the infinite darkness between.

KIRKE MOANED ON HER DIVAN, drenched in sweat and clutching her blanket. There was an unspoken rule among sleepers that no horrors of the night could get a sleeper still wrapt in her blanket, she was fair certain. Oneiromancers who lost control of their Art tended to have the most vivid, most gut-wrenching nightmares. It was not the first time she'd awoken with tears in her eyes, afraid to ever close them again.

Nor would it be the first time she would swear off drinking herself to sleep every night. The lies one told oneself were sometimes all that kept one sane.

5

___

HERAKLES

731 Bronze Age

A torrent of spring floodwaters had transformed the lowland valleys into a churning soup of mud and debris, with nests of unseen roots making any fording treacherous at best. Hand to his brow to keep the drizzle from his eyes, Herakles scanned the horizon for a means to continue their southern trek. Grey smothered the sky, left it hazy as a night drowning sorrows in bottomless amphorae of wine.

"Can't you just kill someone to right this?" Deianeira whined.

Herakles whirled on his new wife, wondering once more—as he had so many times since they had wintered in her homeland of Kalydon—how he'd allowed Meleager's ghost to convince him to marry the prince's sister. Oh, he knew, of course. Faced with his friend's unhappy shade, a shade damned in the Underworld no less, how could Herakles deny the man's one request? Even if it was still Iole's face he pictured at night, when Deianeira's inanities at last gave way to her fitful sleep and her incessant somnambulant mutterings.

"Kill whom, exactly?" he asked when he had forced down his spark of irritation.

"You fought that river god for my hand. Kill the river now!"

Herakles frowned, not bothering to point out he'd defeated a siren who tried to abduct her and would have done the same for anyone he'd found in danger from the Otherworld. Deianeira didn't seem to fathom that slaying a river god did not equate to him being able to thrash a flood itself into obedience, and he'd grown weary of explaining that sort of thing.

The woman huffed, placed a hand on her belly in an obvious attempt to remind him she bore his babe, and then slumped upon a mossy log. She had misjudged how slick it would prove, though, and immediately slipped off to spill on her arse. His wife wriggled around and stared at the offending chunk of wood. "Did you see what it did to me?"

In times such as these, Herakles found it difficult to decide whether the woman acted in earnest or merely leant into such displays in the hopes of earning some attention from him. Either way, he seized the log with his right hand—his left had never quite healed —and hurled it off into the floodwaters. "It shan't harm anyone ever again." It took an effort to keep his face straight saying such, and he turned from her. "Stay here, if you will, and I'll try to find us a safe place for crossing."

"I *told* you we left too soon," Deianeira moaned.

Rather, they had tarried overlong in Kalydon. He needed to return to his new farm and see about the planting if he was to have a crop worth the harvesting come autumn. Besides which, he imagined had they dawdled much longer in his wife's homeland, she would have claimed herself too heavy with child for overland travel. Not deigning to answer her complaints, he plodded in search of any route that would not take them days in the wrong direction.

MUD SQUELCHED between Herakles's toes, slicking the inside of his sandals and turning his every step into a challenge. Still, he did not mind overmuch. Stalking the woods, even in the spring rains, it offered a kind of peace he'd found wanting these past months. He always felt himself strongest, freshest, during storms, as if the rains cleansed his soul and washed away his cares. He'd not seen the shades of his boys since he'd completed his labours, oft though he'd looked, so he had assumed them released at last from the torment that had imprisoned them. Their freedom meant his own, and he took every chance to breathe in full, savouring the petrichor.

The denizens of the forest had slunk away to their burrows and holes, waiting out the weather, and leaving him to the solitude of his thoughts. Here, alone, he need not struggle forever to keep from snapping at his new wife and her maundering stream of fatuousness.

He clucked his tongue at the thought and shook his head. Such thoughts were unbecoming, though. It was not Deianeira's fault she was not Iole, and he had promised himself never to punish her on that account. Mayhap he ought to have refused Meleager's desperate plea—yet how could he?—but he had not done so and now must live by his word.

The road one might have taken always carried melancholies, as if, but for a snag in the weft of Fate, life could have held greater happiness. If Eurytos had not broken his oath, if he had allowed Herakles to marry Iole back then, Herakles would have had ample grounds to deny Meleager. By now, he and the woman with whom he ought to have spent his life would have built a home together. They would have laughed over bowls of spiced wine and handfuls of roasted walnuts, their joy filling the space of that farmhouse until it seemed warmer and more festive than the great megaron of Mykenai.

In the quiet, he could hear her voice. In the beats betwixt the *shlump* of his sandals, he could almost catch the bits of her keen wit, sharp with merciless teasing. No puerile whinging from her, no, for she would be there beside him, a partner.

Oh.

Herakles paused mid-stride as the thought struck him like a gut punch. That was it, was it not? In the months since he'd last seen Iole he'd thought of her ever and anon—her laugh, her smile, her voice—and his heart had settled upon her more than it had upon anyone before. But it was more than that, for in Iole he might have had a *partner* with which to *share* a life. In Deianeira, rather, he had undertaken to care for a woman incapable of standing on her own and thus unsuited to ever exist in mutual support. Meleager had asked Herakles to take care of his sister, and that's all it could ever be.

Or perhaps he judged her too harshly. Perhaps, in time, she too could find her way and mature into someone he could depend upon. She would never be Iole, true, but ...

Herakles thumbed his brow. It was cruel to fault his wife for not being another person. No, he would do better by Deianeira than these sullen musings. He'd find a ford, get her home, and together they would find a way to the happy life he'd so long sought.

AFTER FINDING A CROSSING—MORE treacherous than he'd have liked, with rocks rising high enough above the floodwaters to create rapids —Herakles made his way back to where he'd left Deianeira. Before she came into sight, her wild shriek reached him.

Has that woman managed to fall into the water? The thought popped into his head an instant before he broke into a mad run, sandals slipping upon the mud, nigh sending him careening into an oak. The rain had picked up, further obscuring his view. "Deianeira!" he bellowed. He didn't know if she could swim, gods damn it all! "Deianeira!"

Another scream, this one more frantic and farther off. But if she could scream, she was not drowning yet, praise Zeus. Herakles dashed out of the trees and swept his gaze across the churning waters. She had to be somewhere nearby. Just there, fresh loam glistened where he'd yanked up that log, so this was the place. She could not have gone far from here, he was certain ...

There!

Halfway across the valley, a man had her over his shoulders, fording the waters. No, not a man, Herakles realised with a sudden pit in his belly. That was a damn centaur, dragging his wife to the far shore, intent to do who-knew-what with her. Herakles rushed to the water's edge. But he'd never chase down a centaur, even if he did not first need to swim across this turbulent expanse.

"Deianeira!" he roared again.

His wife cast a frantic glance in his direction, but naught more. Oh, by Tartarus's black walls! Herakles unshouldered his bow. He'd get only one shot, and if he failed to fell the centaur, the beast would vanish into the forest with Deianeira.

A black-fletched arrow. The hydra's toxic blood had proved potent enough to lay low even a head of Ladon, the Old One drakon who had guarded the golden apples. Such arrows had wrought woe enough, Herakles knew, but too they had brought down most any monster he'd ever struck with one.

Only one shot.

He nocked the poisoned arrow and drew back until that ebony fletching tickled his cheek. Because of this toxin, Artemis had lost a lover. His left arm, once mangled by Kerberos, screamed in protest, and Herakles gritted his teeth against the pain. His arms shook, though not only from the strain of holding drawn the bow, but from the rising sense of dread. Should the tip so much as scratch Deianeira, agonised death would lie ahead of her, and there would be naught Herakles could do to spare her from it. But if the centaur managed to escape with her, it would no doubt subject her to worse torments.

"Apollon guide this shaft," he whispered. As the centaur's hooves touched upon the far shore, Herakles loosed.

The creature's squeal carried over the distance as it fell, pitching over sideways and sending Deianeira spilling back into the floodwaters. He could ill afford to delay, so he tossed aside the bow and dove into the churning muck. Icy mountain meltwater sent a shock to his core, forcing him to call upon Pneumatikoi to keep his focus. To give him the strength to surge forward, blinded by the mud and desperate and knowing he would prove far too late to save her.

But when at last he crawled upon the opposite bank, Deianeira was there, beside the corpse of the fallen centaur. His wife shivered, glaring at him as though all of this was somehow his fault. "What took you so damn long?" she moaned, teeth chattering in the process.

His gaze passed over the monster that had abducted his wife, noting that the beast had torn the arrow from its flank, for he saw the gaping wound, streaked by blackened veins. When at last his regard settled on the human visage of the centaur, Herakles's breath caught —he knew this one, had seen it look upon him with murderous wrath glinting in its eyes. Guilt smacked him like a blow to the temple and Herakles dropped to one knee. For this *was* his fault. He had slain Nessus's father Diomedes—Ixion—in front of Nessus as one of his labours, and Nessus had sworn vengeance.

A trembling hand went to Herakles's mouth. The centaur had taken Deianeira only as a means of revenging himself upon Herakles, and his wife had nigh paid a horrible price for Herakles's deeds. "A-are you harmed?"

"Of course I'm harmed! Can't you see I'm cold as a Hyperborean's crotch? And I'm all *wet*! I thought I told you to smash the damn river."

Numbness seized his heart. "I'll build a fire to get you warm." He had killed Ixion both because Eurystheus had demanded it and to free prisoners from the centaurs. Iole's brother Iphitos had been among those captives, in fact. Even his attempt at doing the right thing, his effort to prevent further carnage by destroying a monster, had led to yet more violence. There seemed no way free of this sick cycle.

Or dare he imagine it would end now, with Nessus dead?

Dare he believe he might yet make a life of peace?

While the dream had seemed close enough to grasp moments ago, now, he felt it begin to flit through his fingers.

6

ENODIA

216 Golden Age

From the lakeside, Enodia watched as Poseidon, spurned by young Pyrrha, shoved the girl into the waters. As her younger self swam to shore, Enodia advanced, embroidered cloak wrapt around herself, pausing at the spot where Pyrrha would make land.

Even now, beset by the torments of death, she had entertained the thought of breaking the cycle. But she had seen the folly in that line of reasoning. Her path lay in her future, and she could not walk that road until she had ensured her past led her here.

So she offered a hand and, when Pyrrha accepted, pulled the girl to her feet. "I saw that."

Stubborn and proud, the girl wrung out her hair before discomfort outweighed dignity. Then, shivering, she stared at Enodia with a hint of defiance. "He mistakes his simply being present for wooing and a lack of revulsion for interest."

Enodia wanted to laugh at that, but she wasn't sure she could do so and still conceal the hollow ruin of her voice as a revenant. Instead, she shrugged. "The powerful cannot conceive of their so-called lessers not worshipping them."

The girl offered her an approving look. "I'm Pyrrha."

Enodia nodded. As if they needed introductions. But then, she knew what to say, the words coming to her with ease as though she had practiced them, despite this moment being so long back in her memory she could recall only blurred images. "And I am Enodia, a sorceress formerly of the Circle of Goetic Mysteries. I have felt you, Pyrrha, and sensed your potential from long ago. I can help you open your mind and reach that potential if you so desire."

The girl gaped at her, fair teetering with nervous excitement.

"You're offering to teach me sorcery? It's real?"

That drew a snort from her. She clucked her tongue. "Mmm. It is real, but your bumbling around in the Penumbra will not give you such power. If you ever managed to confront a spirit thus, it would mostlike slip inside your body and ride you like a horse, sating its perverse desires using your flesh. It would feast upon your soul and leave you an empty husk, perhaps after enduring centuries of slavery."

Pyrrha shivered again. "Why?"

"Why then would people like me dare hold concert with the denizens of the Ether? Why would any save madmen touch the Otherworld?" Enodia took a step forward to grab the impetuous girl by the arms. What a naïve fool she'd been back then. That innocence now tasted loathsome, hateful, and she could scarce restrain the urge to throttle the whelp. "I offer you more power and knowledge than you could ever have imagined. Is that not what you have sought after, combing through the dark? Did you imagine such would come with neither risk nor price?"

But Pyrrha fixed her with a level gaze and offered the only answer she ever could have. "Teach me."

For two years, she instructed Pyrrha, teasing her with secrets of the Realms beyond, hints of the power she might one day wield. In the ambit of the World, Enodia knew of no other sorceress to rival the breadth of her knowledge or control of the arcane.

And now she no longer needed sleep or mortal sustenance. She had no use for Ambrosia, for her ruined corpse would sustain itself so long as she feasted upon the flesh of Man. Where once the thought of such, of what Dionysus had made her taste, had churned her gut and left her with bouts of self-loathing, now her existence depended on it. There were always deaths, fresh graves aplenty to dig up and sate her hungers upon. Murder remained as popular as ever, and on those rare occasions when Men did not deign to die oft enough, she would hasten along the process.

She was not, however, without limitations.

The sunlight stripped her of her Otherworldly strength and stamina, leaving her lethargic and exacerbating the pains that forever wracked her. And the Box ... Again and again, she had sought to speed along her journey using it, but it would not open. However it had been designed, it seemed only to respond to the living. It had brought her here, millennia in the past, and left her stranded, uncertain how to reach the future she had left behind save to live through it *again*. In constant torment.

A thousand times a day, Enodia considered ways to end her wretched existence. Her mind sought to escape her agonies by lurching in wild gyrations until she wondered if, one day, it might not return from the dark recesses into which it delved.

Still, Pyrrha made the progress she must. She learnt the things she had always learnt. She said the words as if reciting lines from a play, and Enodia found herself both playwright and audience.

A sense of the surreal lulled Enodia into nigh total silence as she led Poseidon down toward the beach, having implied Pyrrha awaited him there for a liaison. The boy heard what he wished, and Enodia had not the least scrap of pity for what would soon befall him. Indeed, she found herself scarce able to dwell upon Tethys's son or his fate at all.

Everything played out so perfectly it felt as though she could see the threads of the Tapestry, tugging upon all their limbs like puppets. Even her. Especially her. And though she wished to see herself as free of such fetters now, still they bound her, compelled her steps, her words, her thoughts.

But she would spite both the Moirai and the ravenous Elder Gods. Through her Art, she would free herself and, perhaps, even the souls of all Mankind.

Thus did she escort Poseidon to where Pyrrha had formed a summoning circle, setting him on a path where he could walk to the girl without glimpsing or disrupting the glyphs. The boy pranced down, clearly ill at ease, yet drawn onward by the pull of his cock. Enodia could go no further though. Pyrrha may not realise it, but that circle would bar her mentor as well. One more weakness of her state as a ghost.

Pyrrha's voice—how timid it sounded to Hekate now—thrummed through the Ether, reverberating in the Penumbra, as a host of spirits drew nigh. Perhaps to entice the boy and make him cast aside any lingering doubts, the girl shrugged off one side of her peplos, exposing a breast. Strange, Enodia had forgotten doing that, and seeing it now, it seemed so crass.

"What are you saying?" Poseidon demanded of her.

"Nereus," Pyrrha answered, flicking blood from her fingers into the prince's face.

That sent him stumbling away. "What the fuck?"

"Nereus, Prince of Pontus!" Pyrrha shouted.

And the Deep One spirit—a Telkhine of Pontus—waiting inside the Penumbra, flung itself at its newly designated host. It dove into him, sending him spasming as it yanked his mouth open and began to wriggle its way inside him. The process of possession failed to disturb Enodia any longer.

Moaning from outside the circle drew her attention. A tall shade, his throat badly wounded, hurled himself against the barrier, slamming Pyrrha's wards. Enodia frowned at what she beheld. Okeanus ... Poseidon's father, drawn from his misery by the plight of his son.

Okeanus looked to Pyrrha, eyes gleaming with that fell rage Enodia knew too well. Utter wrath born from years of suffering, the pain of fatal wounds never quite fading away. And as Pyrrha's fear led to the faltering of her will, Okeanus might manage to break through her circle.

That Enodia could not allow.

Enodia's cants thrummed through the Ether, intertwining with her necromantic abilities to wrap invisible chains around Okeanus's soul. The dead were her domain, and she would dominate any who dared interfere with her ends. The ghost fell to his knees as she approached, looking to her with sudden dread—a terror beyond the understanding of the living, though Enodia knew it all too well.

She pressed her palm against his brow, and Okeanus flailed, his spectral body dissolving into liquid shadow, cast down into the Roil. The shade's own laments had left it trapped in the Penumbra, reliving its final agonised moments. Here, Tethys's husband died afresh with each passing moment, locked in eternal torment. Still, Enodia would not delude herself into believing a brighter end awaited Okeanus in the Underworld. If the shade avoided getting consumed by one predator or another, it would find itself drawn into the ranks of one of the numerous necropoleis. There was no respite for the dead.

When she looked back, Poseidon, claimed by Nereus, stared at Pyrrha whilst Styx screamed about what had befallen her brother.

Enodia allowed herself a grim smile. All as it had ever been.

As of course she must, Tethys banished Pyrrha from Thebes. Enodia had no idea how much her father could sense of her or how easily he might detect her if she remained in the Penumbra. Just how far did his own psychic abilities reach? Could he see into the Spectral Realm? Could he sense, as she had, when some eidolon drew close on the far side of the Veil? Enodia was never certain. Not wanting to take the chance, she avoided eavesdropping on his futile attempts to dissuade Pyrrha from pursuing the Art.

It was too late for that now, and Papa no doubt knew such all too well.

In the two years since her death, he had not looked for Enodia, so far as she could tell. Perhaps, with her dead, he no longer considered her his child. Or perhaps he believed her now beyond all hope of redemption. As if she had ever any chance of that.

One day, thousands of years hence, he would meet her in the wake of Europa's kidnapping. He would look upon her, ravaged by fire and the machinations of Fate, and know that he had sent her to that death. The thought tasted of vengeance yet offered no hint of sweet satisfaction. Merely a bitterness and the vague sense she had failed him as much as he had her.

When Pyrrha left Thebes, Enodia followed her to Korinth, watching from across the Veil to ensure all unfolded as it must. On occasion, she would show herself to the girl, impart further guidance —nudge the girl another step down the paths of damnation that lay before her.

The sense of surreal fulfilment would crop up from time to time, immersing Enodia, dragging her under the flow of its currents and carrying her through rapids and wild turns until, at last, she would burst through the surface, gasping for breath.

And find there was none to be had. For she would never breathe again.

WHEN PYRRHA WENT TO DELPHI, Enodia watched Themis—after meeting the girl—make a hurried flight toward Kronion to confront Hekate about what she'd learnt. From the shadows of the Spectral Realm, she witnessed the slow unfurling of the Tapestry in all its awful splendour. The Gnostic Cabal would see the presence of a timewalker and think to use Hekate to their own ends, but Hekate would turn from them, as ever she had. All of the Cabal's schemes amounted to little more than a pitiful threnody for the death of their illusions of free will, even if they refused to open their eyes to that truth.

In Delphi, foolish, young, fated Pyrrha drank Python's tonic, and when the Gloomwood and Pan rose to claim her soul, a fierce desire to bind the dryads came over Enodia. But such would prove unnecessary she knew. Instead, from across the Veil, she trailed Artemis, pricking at the Titan's nerves until the Phoebid realised something was amiss. Until she followed the churning of her gut to the Otherworldly orgy unfolding within the glade and, struck by its perversity, killed a dryad host and saved Pyrrha.

Damn, but Enodia had missed Artemis and the way they used to be. She missed all the innocent friendships Hekate had sacrificed along the way in her drive for power. Such musings were pointless, of course. There was no going back.

When at last Pyrrha snuck away from Artemis's cottage, Enodia found the girl in the woods and knew where she would head. Thus, Enodia placed herself in Pyrrha's path, crouching beneath a tree in the fragile hope that sitting would alleviate the eternal pains shooting through her core. It didn't.

"You had a brush with a tendril of an Elder God," she told the girl, not lifting her gaze.

Pyrrha balked. "Artemis calls them Primordials."

"Yes, they have many titles and many names." They, she thought, may well have come from somewhere outside the World, somewhere older. Formless, lurking predators from beyond the cosmos, waiting to devour it all, when at last Papa's cycle of Eschatons collapsed in upon itself and he could no longer forestall their hunger. Unless Enodia stopped them. "Names, you see, hold a power of their own. They are how we see ourselves, yes, and a mask we wear to shape the perceptions of others." She turned to look up at Pyrrha. "Just as you, perhaps, should have a new name."

"What?"

"Pyrrha was a scared girl banished from the court of Thebes. You must reinvent yourself as a proud, irrepressible sorceress. A mistress of the night. You have become both necromancer and now oneiromancer. Surely you have shed your childhood guise."

The child folded her arms, lost in thought. "Um ... Soteria? Oh! Maybe, Propulaia?"

"Choose whatever you wish, child."

Her apprentice scowled. "Oneiromancy is ... understanding my dreams."

"Yours and those of others. The greatest oneiromancer of our age is called Morpheus, and he too is a member of the Circle of Goetic Mysteries. Perhaps you can learn from him if you can convince your friend to take you."

The girl's gaze turned off looking after her friend. "She is afraid of something."

Of course she was, for Artemis, older and more attuned to the pulse of the wild, sensed the unspeakable threat the Primordials represented, even if she could not quite form that knowledge into coherent thought. Her worship, even of Thoth, was tinged by flecks of unacknowledged fears, creeping around her mind like skittering spiders in the dark. The Elder Gods, the greatest of the Primordials, they drew adulation toward them by their unknowable natures. But though cults and tribes across the Earth worshipped them, the awe remained forever coloured by the knowledge that the primal forces were not benevolent. That, for the most part, these beings were so far beyond the ken of Man that an individual life was beneath their notice.

And if the greater part of humanity knew what Enodia knew about the predators upon the Wheel of Fate, terror would paralyse the whole of Man, or else transform the race into a wreck of gibbering madness. Few could face their own utter insignificance and come away unscathed.

"Everyone is afraid of something," Enodia said, a groan of fresh pains escaping her as she rose. "If you want to further your studies, you will need more mentorship than I alone can provide." A truth, only because it had *already* proved the truth. Pyrrha must go to the Circle because she always had.

"I'll speak to Artemis about going to Phoenikia."

And when Artemis and Pyrrha had gone, the young girl primed to don the mantle of Hekate and begin her long road to here, Enodia climbed the rugged slope beyond Delphi. Beneath the gibbous moon, she spoke an invocation to the quiescent spirit of the mountain, beseeching it to open its yawning maw. Tremors sent scree tumbling into gulleys. The roots of stubborn trees broke free of the shifting ground, dangling over a new pit like so many arthritic fingers.

"Hold this wretched thing," Enodia commanded in Supernal, the Box in her hand. "In the deep places, keep it wrapt in a cloak of earth until one should come to ask for it."

The Box would not avail the dead, and, with what little hope Enodia could still muster, she dared to believe no one else would need use the thing again, nor further the hateful whorls the Fates had woven into their Tapestry. As she tilted her palm down, the device that had wrought so much chaos—that had, indeed, given rise to her life—spilled into the void, tumbling end over end, swallowed by the mountain, granite jaws closing around it.

INTERLUDE: ACHILLES

800 Bronze Age

Blood trickled down Achilles's arm, slicking his fingers where they gripped the hilt of his xiphos. The wound meant naught. He had carved his way through a hundred men to reach Hektor, reaping their lives with all the indifference of a farmer threshing wheat. Some having borne witness to his speed, his prowess, had fled, and those fortunate few had lived, for Achilles had little mind to chase rabbits when his true prey stood now before him.

Curly-haired, lisping, handsome, vaunted Prince Hektor whom the Ilians called their greatest champion. He and Achilles paced a circuit around the undefined periphery of their battleground, eyes never leaving one another. Though Achilles spared them no glance, he knew both armies had paused in their slaughter, watching the impending duel. Did they know the Ilian hero would choke upon his own blood and feast on dirt this day? Did they see his death in the eyes of their souls?

Oh, but Hektor knew it, that much was plain writ across his

bearded visage, struggle though he might to hide it. He twirled his sword in affected bravado, yes, but his eyes made plain he knew Achilles had come to send him to Hades.

Their javelins were spent, shattered upon their shields. Their spears were broken, cast aside. Now, it came to blades, and Achilles's was, according to Athene, the blade once borne by Herakles and forged by famed Hephaistos. No finer weapon had spilt blood in this war, of that he had no doubt.

Achilles pointed his xiphos at Hektor, still circling. "You brought this upon yourself! You, who thought to have slain immortal Achilles!"

And in so doing, Hektor had broken the dam of Achilles's rage and unleashed a flood that must soon drown all of Ilium. The prince, despite himself, cast a glance over his shoulder as though he might think to flee. Should he venture it, Achilles would chase him down like a fox before a hound and gut him like the craven he was.

That, too, Hektor could see plain enough, for at last, his circling ceased, and shield before him, he advanced to meet his doom.

ACHILLES WAS a boy of seven when Patroklus came to foster at his home in Phthia. Though rumour claimed thirteen-year-old Patroklus had come to them in exile after the killing of another boy in his home, Achilles at once thought him the embodiment of the heroes of old. Here, he thought, stood before him the model of famed Bellerophon or valiant Perseus. While Patroklus might have shunned the company of a younger boy, even the son of his host Peleus, he instead threw himself in Achilles's games. Together they chased down the Nemean lion once slain by Herakles, though the sheep acting in stead of the lion little loved being chased across the fields with a stick. They slew the sea serpent Ketus—a grass snake—to rescue fair Andromeda from the rocks. They joined the Seven Against Thebes, eager to restore the son of Oedipus to his birthright in a war waged over a pile of standing rocks.

As they grew, Achilles looked to Patroklus and saw in him, perhaps more even than in his own father, the model of what a man of Elládos ought to be. Patroklus would tell him all the truths of the world his parents had concealed from him, and for that he earned Achilles's undying respect. He told him how Peleus and his brother Telamon had sailed with the Argo, in days now long gone. He told him how, at Zeus's behest, Thetis's father Poseidon had forced his daughter to wed Peleus, though none quite knew why. Patroklus had explained how Thetis, a Nymph who thought herself above demigods like Peleus, had raged yet found herself powerless to deny the will of Zeus.

Their wedding had been a grand affair, the likes of which of had rarely been seen in the days since the close of the Silver Age. Many of the Olympians themselves had attended, Patroklus said, and Achilles could scarce imagine it.

It was Achilles's mother who first warned of a future of bitter war that must haunt her son's steps, some two years after Patroklus had come to them. Mother had little love for Father, even Achilles could tell this much. She spent her days in solitude, wandering the seashore or haunting caves where the tide would come to lap at the rocks, as if she imagined joining her father in the depths. But Thetis had a touch of the Sight, or so she claimed, and saw things others did not in the shifting of the tides. Thus she came one day, when the two boys sat playing at draughts—Patroklus had taught him the game and always won—to see King Peleus.

"His shall be a short life of immortal glory or a long one of obscurity," Mother said, and Father had paused mid-sip.

Father heaved an affected sigh before setting his goblet upon the table and fitting Achilles with his weighty gaze, almost as though he had known such a time might come. "The centaur, Kheiron, trained my brother and myself in the arts of war in our youth. If Achilles is to have his glory, perhaps that grizzled stallion has yet a few things to teach."

Father, of course, had no intention of asking whether Achilles

would have chosen the option for a long, uneventful life. No such
future could lay before the son of Peleus.

"I'll not go unless Patroklus comes as well," Achilles blurted.

So, to Mount Pelion and the centaur they had gone.

ACHILLES'S adamant xiphos sheared through the rim of Hektor's
aspis, a second piece of his paltry shield carved away. The Ilian
dropped his shield arm, thrusting above the ruined protection with
his own blade, but Achilles danced aside with ease and kicked
Hektor in the shin. His sandal struck the man's greaves, the armour
preventing a fracture, though the impact sent Hektor stumbling backward, toppling onto his arse.

Shame had to precede death for him, for the swift end Achilles
had delivered to his comrades was too merciful for the warrior who
had stolen Patroklus from him. Blood cried for blood, pain for pain.
And when anguish rose up in towering waves fit to inundate a man's
World, then the one who had summoned that wave must needs
drown beneath it as well. Without Patroklus, life had lost its lustre,
and Achilles longed for the honest, hopeless grey that would await
him before Hades's gates. But for that final trek, he would have
company aplenty.

So he waited, allowed Hektor to gain his feet. "Behold the great
champion of so-called Troy," Achilles taunted and banged his sword
upon his shield. "A boy fallen in the dust."

With a wheeze, Hektor hefted his sword and shield once more,
perhaps too breathless to manage any barbs of his own. The Elládosi
feared this man, though not nigh so much as the Ilians—and, yes,
indeed, his fellow Elládosi too—feared Achilles. They dreaded his
coming, and with due cause. When battle was joined, a primal
instinct seized him, like the chorus of some distant song, as avuncular
as once Patroklus had been. It guided his movements, honed his own
instincts—ingrained by Kheiron—to a razor edge that allowed him to
counter any number of foes. Combined with his demigod speed and

vitality, entire phalanxes fell before him. He had vaulted over shield walls, carved through spears, and single-handedly toppled war bands that could scarce land a blow upon him.

Oh, but then, Hektor had already wounded him. The Ilian had cut the beating heart from Achilles and cast it amid the charnel, though he'd known it not at the time.

"We are, both of us, walking corpses now," Achilles spat at his foe.

UPON HIS SHIP, moored far from the fighting, Achilles sat, cool beneath the shade of sails and yet ill at ease. Patroklus had accused him of sulking, the words of his idol ringing truer than Achilles would have liked. How did the man always manage to make Achilles feel himself once more a boy in need of lessons? How, after ten bitter years of this ceaseless, pointless war—years in which Achilles had won more glory than any ten men combined, when he'd slain the indomitable Amazonian queen, even—could he be brought to shame thus?

Oh, but Agamemnon had wronged him, and Achilles had sworn not to rejoin the battle until the proud king came begging for his sword. Until the lord of Mykenai bent his knee and lowered his face in shame, until he forfeited his honour and admitted he could not do this without Achilles—until *then*, Achilles would abide here, drink his wine, and while away his days.

Aged Akamas had visited him, hoped to induce him back to the battles with promises of glory or bounties. "There are girls aplenty for the taking beyond those walls," the son of poor Theseus had said, though he, of course, had never come nigh to touch his father's glory. But Achilles had waved the man away, for he had won honour enough already and now had it stolen from him.

Odysseus had come imploring, as if Achilles might forget it had been the king of Ithaka who'd compelled him and Patroklus to join Agamemnon in the first damn place. "Our countrymen die in droves," Odysseus had chided, "and yet you idle in the sun."

Achilles had scoffed. "Unlike some, I never swore an oath to aid the husband of Helen. If the situation is so dire, then force your so-called leader to choke on his pride and beg my forgiveness for his affront."

"I can bring back Briseis, if it is but the girl you want."

It had given him pause, though only for a moment. "I do. But it is Agamemnon who must return her, not wily Odysseus on his behalf."

Still, Patroklus had taken the Ithakan's word to heart. He had insisted upon wearing Achilles's famed helm and armour, claimed the panoply would inspire the Elládosi to rally and hold the beach they had nigh lost. And Achilles had been unable to deny his friend, much though he wished to force Agamemnon's hand. He had never been able to deny Patroklus aught, even when he had known better.

Oh, the rivalry between the Mykenian king and Achilles was an old one, from the first days of the war. The king had it from an Oracle that to win he must sacrifice his beloved daughter Iphigenia. And the bastard had lured her to her death by promising her she would wed Achilles. Though Achilles had not known the girl, when he had learnt of Agamemnon's misuse of his good name, he had raged and seethed and damn nigh left the war before it began. Odysseus had soothed him then, with crafty words and meaningless platitudes about the needs for Elládos to unite against foreign foes. But Achilles was no longer a seventeen-year-old boy, and Odysseus's machinations would no longer avail him.

And still, Patroklus had gone.

So Achilles sat and teased the sunlight along the length of his xiphos, casting plays of light and shadow and trying to block out the rising chorus of voices in the depths of his soul. Those voices bade him join the battle once more. To kill. To destroy. And he was left asking himself if the violent depths of his soul sought to aid his fellows or rather exulted in carnage. He was uncertain he wished for an answer.

Thus did his friend Antilokhos find him, desultory and bored. Nestor's son had become fast friends with both Achilles and Patroklus when the war had begun. Like Achilles's own father, Nestor had sailed with Jason—his cousin—aboard the Argo and swapping those tales of old had proved common ground for the pair. Even if ancient Nestor himself rarely wished to speak of the voyage and had implied, on occasion, it had little in common with the valiant heroic tales bards spun from it.

Still, despite it, Achilles could not quite shake his youthful reverence for the quest, for he and Patroklus had oft mimed stealing the Golden Fleece from cruel Aeëtes or facing monsters upon the sea to escape with the prize.

"What stops the Elládosi from sailing away from here?" Achilles called as his friend boarded his ship, his dour look making plain the battles continued to go against them in the days since Achilles had withdrawn. "I plan to ready the Myrmidons and quit these shores next wind and tide allow it. Come with me, and we can stop by Pylos. Hunting and feasting appeal more than fighting over a woman most of our people care not a whit for."

Antilokhos swallowed, shifting uncomfortably from foot to foot. Blood spattered his cuirass and had seeped into the grooves of his helm. "Would that we had heeded such advice sooner."

Achilles rose, a sudden apprehension seizing him. Dread wrapt its icy fingers about his throat, and almost, he forbade Antilokhos from speaking, as if he could block out the truth of horror by refusing to acknowledge it.

"Sad news, and I am the wretched, unwilling messenger. Patroklus has fallen."

No. Impossible. Like Achilles, Patroklus was a fine warrior, trained by Kheiron, and few could stand against him for long. He shook his head, trying to form some coherent denial, but words slipped away. The pit that had opened in his stomach gawped wide enough to swallow him whole.

"He was slain by Hektor," Antilokhos continued, "in single combat, who mistook the man for you. I ... I am sorry, my friend."

That name. Yes, one of the few on the battlefield who might have threatened Patroklus. In that one moment, that one day in which his friend had fought without Achilles by his side, he'd been snatched away forever.

A wail erupted from him, animal in its unvarnished intensity. Such was the purest of all grief.

ॐ

LIKE A STRIKING SERPENT, Achilles's sword danced, darting in and out, carving pieces from Hektor. The Ilian warrior fell back, powerless against the torrent of Achilles's assault. The adamant blade flensed slivers off aspis and panoply, gouged biceps and sliced through greaves to notch bone. Hektor toppled back to the dirt, his wobbling blade raised in warding.

But Achilles had enough of toying with the man.

A swipe of his xiphos lopped the Ilian prince's hand off at the wrist. Achilles twisted round with his swing and drove his blade through the prince's chest. That adamant sword parted the bronze cuirass as easily as flesh and punched hilt-deep into Hektor.

He leant close to the dying man's ear. "There's no honour left for you. And for what you've taken, your kin shall share in my anguish."

Already, he could feel the inferno of his rage threatening to cool, and Achilles knew, once it fled, there would be naught save the cold of death left inside his breast. So he stoked his wrath before it could dwindle. He lashed Hektor's ankles with a leather band and, ignoring the gasps of onlookers, bound the prince's corpse to his chariot.

Let them all see what had become of their champion. Desperate to hold onto his fury, Achilles whipped his horses into motion, dragging Hektor behind, pulverising the body as he circumnavigated the insurmountable walls of Ilium.

He did not know when he'd begun screaming in wordless rage, but he could not stop.

Maybe he would never stop.

PART II

At their height, Men called the Phoenikians the Sea People, for they controlled the whole of the eastern Thalassa, dominating all trade from Neshia and Nusantara, and serving as intermediary between those lands and Atlantis as well as Lydia. To those who challenged their trade dominance, they were the most fearsome pirates the world had ever known. Yet even they crumbled before the expanding might of the Babilimian Empire.

— Kleio, Analects of the Muses

7

PANDORA

754 Bronze Age

"Of the Anunnaki," Artemis said with obvious reticence, "I can tell you precious little. I've had to meet but a few of them ..."

They walked in Ilian gardens, the memory of the beautiful verdancy of Babilim's own splendour, and her time with Artemis there, raw and throbbing in her mind. A part of Pandora's soul longed to say something here that would reinforce their bond, that would avert the future that must befall them. Except, it was not Pandora's future; it was already her past, and she could not shake the look of betrayal in Artemis's eyes that day from her mind. It was, she suspected, a look that would haunt her for the rest of her life.

Ever she tried not to dwell upon it, but the fragrant scents of jasmine insisted on reminding her, moment by moment, of the last such conversation she'd shared with this woman. "You hold back," Pandora said, steering their course away from the jasmine blooms and toward a fresco painted along one wall. "Though I hate to pull forth unpleasant memories, any knowledge you have might prove a boon."

Artemis gnawed on her lip, looking at the artwork. It depicted a great herd of horses running free across wild steppes. The animals were considered sacred to the people of Ilium, Pandora knew, though she'd never read much of how that had come about. When the silence had stretched long enough to become awkward, Artemis sighed and turned to Pandora. "If one lives long enough, one accumulates a great many shames and regrets, some bright enough to burn through the haze of compounded millennia of memories."

"Oh," Pandora said, shaking her head, "believe me, even those who live but a few decades acquire regrets, and those too seem oft the most pellucid of memories."

"Heh." Artemis folded her arms across her chest and began to stroll onward, forcing Pandora to follow. "A long—" She paused. "A long time ago, when I was yet young, by Titan standards, I let Hekate —Thoth, it wasn't even her name then!—I let her convince me to follow my father and maternal grandmother in pursuit of the Art." She unfolded her arms and shook her head. "Not the last time I made a poor choice out of my desperate love and friendship for Hekate ... I ..." She seemed to choke upon the words.

Pandora laid a hand upon her bicep, hoping to reassure her. All it served to do, however, was remind of the pummelling Pandora had levied against Artemis in the last gardens. The fury of the Phoenix had risen in her, and, slamming Artemis against tree trunks as she had, Pandora might well have broken the woman's spine. And now, here she was, forcing her to relive buried pains in the name of friendship. "If this is too much ..."

"Why should it be too much, Nike? I bear the responsibility for my actions and whatever woe resulted from them." She blew out a steadying breath and turned back down amid greenery. Whilst the gardens represented pain for Pandora—the guilt of *her* actions—the plants seemed to calm Artemis, so she could not well begrudge the woman such small comforts. "For a brief time, I studied with the Circle of Goetic Mysteries. The Outer Circle, they called us novices.

Some of the Anunnaki were among the Inner Circle, or at least one that I recall." Another pause, and the Phoebid swallowed. "I remember her—her name was Inanna and she was vibrant and beautiful. Her I shan't ever forget, because I killed her."

Pandora winced at the self-recrimination in Artemis's voice, but scarce knew what to say to such an admission. "Why?"

"Because, like a fool, I touched upon powers which I could little fathom, much less control, and something slipped inside my soul. A bear spirit, from the Moon. It became part of me and it took me years to learn any measure of control over its savagery. In those first moments, not even knowing I was aught other than an animal, I mauled Inanna; I sent her no doubt abraded soul screaming down into the Underworld, speeding her toward damnation.

"Aghast at what I had done and what I had become, I gave up the Art. Only once, in more than four thousand years hence, have I have touched the greater arcana again. At my weakest moment ... I made another mistake. One more regret upon the ever-growing pile."

Pandora paused, snatched the Phoebid's wrist, and pulled her into an embrace. "We cannot change the past." Though Pandora remained persistent in trying. "We can only do as best we may to make right our mistakes." She held Artemis close, wanting, despite her words, to change *her* past and spare Artemis her future. "I'm sorry; I'm sorry about all of it."

"Ha." Artemis snorted into her shoulder. "What have you to apologise for?"

Pandora pulled away to look into the Phoebid's argent eyes. "More than you can know." Part of her wanted to tell the woman of her time-walking and thus unburden her soul of its myriad weights. But doing so would only compound Artemis's burdens, and so felt selfish. Instead, Pandora found herself with an almost overpowering urge to provide Artemis with some fuel for hatred against her, as if doing so might somehow justify the horrible ending of their friendship which impended. "For a start ... I am Pyrrha's mother."

Artemis snickered, then, upon realising Pandora was in earnest, began to chew on her lip like she thought to gnaw clean through it.

"You speak of regrets," Pandora said. "Perhaps my greatest regret was that I could not be there to raise my child; I was, by conspiracy of Ananke, separated from her when she was a babe and saw no hair of her for thousands of years."

"Her mother ... died in the Ambrosial War."

There was relief in confessing her failings, though it left Pandora flushed and breathless. Prometheus had allowed Pyrrha to believe her mother dead, at the time, because the girl could never have understood the awful truth of the situation. Pandora had never once seen her lover lie, but he had mastered the art of allowing others to draw faulty inferences through his careful omissions of certain details. "I didn't die; I just couldn't find a way back from where I was trapped."

And here she was, following the well-beaten path of lies of omissions, the road Prometheus had laid out before her. And she could, bitterly, understand the necessity for it. How did one avoid lying when the truth would prove so damning to another person?

Artemis rubbed her arms, looking glum, almost morose. "You know ... she died. Centuries back, she died."

Pandora knew it, even if she had no details. Still, hearing the words from Artemis made them seem too real. All she could manage was a nod.

The Phoebid cupped her cheek and drew her into one more embrace. She planted a kiss on the top of Pandora's head. "I'm sorry." The words, mumbled into her hair, were clear. Powerless to change aught, and yet, a balm upon Pandora's wounded soul.

"So am I. About everything."

IN THE MORN, Artemis took her to see Kassandra, the Oracle princess of Ilium. Though the people believed the girl the firstborn of Priam and Hekuba, Artemis told her that Kassandra was, in fact, Priam's bastard from a liaison before his marriage. From the look of her, perhaps her mother had some Heliad blood, for she had fiery hair common among that genos, albeit without the golden eyes. Of course, Pandora had also heard of Hyperboreans and others with auburn hair, as well.

Kassandra was nineteen, Artemis had explained, and had spent some time training with both Apollon and Prometheus to learn mastery of her oneiromantic gift. Nevertheless, the girl remained touched by the things she heard, driven to bouts of eccentricity and perhaps even madness. At least, madness was what most of the populace of Ilium thought the girl afflicted by.

Still, Artemis claimed it was the girl's cryptic words that had allowed her—with aid from Hekate out of the Underworld, a thought that had Pandora's heart leaping with renewed hope for her daughter!—to overcome a foul abomination called Dionysus. Thus had Artemis suggested perhaps Kassandra could help Pandora learn more about the Anunnaki before she headed for Kumari Kandam. If there was a chance for knowledge here, Pandora could not afford to pass it by.

The princess stood upon the terrace, not far from where Pandora had first appeared here. In fact, she seemed to be staring at the spot, as though the tiles vexed her. Or as though she *knew* something had gone amiss here, some disruption of space and time that her mind, different from other people's, could perceive.

Artemis drifted away, affording Pandora privacy with the touched princess, but when Pandora came nigh to the girl, Kassandra did not look her way. Rather, the girl stood there, rubbing her arms despite the day's scathing heat, mumbling something under her breath.

"Kassandra?" Pandora ventured.

Dancer-like, the princess whirled upon Pandora, though her gaze flitted side to side as if expecting something step out of the empty air. "There comes a time, amid ancient peaks, where Fate circles back in wicked volutions, smouldering in the eyes of four desperate women. Four and one, all come round, to burn forever in the space 'twixt long-stretched moments."

Pandora frowned, shaking her head. "I don't fathom your meaning." She spread her hands in what she hoped would prove a placating gesture, trying to soothe the girl's obviously frayed nerves. "My name is Nike, Kassandra, and I've come to ask you for your aid."

Kassandra's eyes widened as though she looked upon something beyond Pandora, the girl turning pale. "It starts with a whisper, a haunting intimation of a World askew."

Whether her words or her tone, something about it sent a shudder wracking through Pandora, and she fell back a step. "I need to know about the Anunnaki. I need to know where to find them and if they can be reasoned with."

"That we are, in the end, caught in a death spiral, time nearly played out ..." She spoke as though in recital of some litany she had heard, like the words of an eerie song stuck in her head.

Hearing her speak thus had the hair on the back of Pandora's neck rising, the more so because, though she had never heard such words before, still they held a frightful familiarity for her as well. As if her soul apprehended a piece of something her mind had forgotten. For a time, she stood there, her jaw flapping in silence. "The ... Anunnaki ..." she managed at last.

For the first time, Kassandra's gaze met her own, something akin to panic in the girl's wide eyes. "Out of the darkness they came ... Remnants of memories, tattered but not quite broken. In the peaks past all known ... did there raise sanctum. It fell amiss, a daughter's betrayal."

Pandora's mind reeled, struggling to parse the incoherent snatches of Kassandra's words. Without some context, it was like trying to solve a puzzle in the dark whilst uncertain she even had all the pieces. There was no help for Pandora here, and she could not shake the sense that, in even asking Kassandra these questions, she only served to burden the poor girl. "I am sorry to have disturbed you, Princess. Artemis said she would take you out riding this afternoon. Would that suit you?"

Kassandra's only answer was a wan smile.

WHEN PANDORA RESOLVED to leave Ilium, Prometheus accompanied her. Together, they took a ship bound for Helion. On the forecastle, watching the waves lap against the hull and the leagues vanish behind them, they stood, their fingers intertwined upon the gunwale. They had not spoken overmuch, at least not of weighty things. Oh, they passed conversation on the trivialities that comprised the greater portion of life, and thus, perhaps, a piece of its meaning.

"Given the choice," Pandora said, "I'd live somewhere warm, I think, resplendent with sunshine."

"You mean like Atlantis."

Though the island had been her home since childhood, Pandora shook her head. Atlantis was doomed, unless she saved it, and she didn't think she could quite forget that. Rather, she had recalled her years in the dark beneath Vulgeth, in the Time of Nyx. And before that, the nigh sunless, merciless cold of the mist-choked world Hekate made of the future. Pandora had endured enough of darkness and cold, for such lurked ever behind and before, and she wanted most of all to dwell in the now. Whenever now ended up being, assuming her quest to save the future did not end in her own destruction.

She knew it might well cost her life, of course, but neither of them spoke of such things, least of all now. By tacit accord they drifted toward pleasant thoughts, even banalities, because they could no longer bear the burden of wounding each other with harsher realities.

"I think not only warm but removed from the press of people and their ceaseless demands. I imagine ... something akin to the home we strove for in Ogygia, the home where we had dreamt of raising Pyrrha. But not there, nor any place where the World would find us and draw us back into its swirling currents."

"Mmm," he said, squeezing her fingers. "A tropical island, then? Far from the Thalassa. There are countless tiny isles in the sea betwixt Dangun and Mu, many with scant inhabitants."

"Where we could ..." She did not dare to give voice to such a fancy. She could not say, *where we could live out our lives and raise another child*. Maybe Ananke would never prove so kind as to permit such a life to them. Certainly not to him, bound to the Moirai from the dawn of time to until its last, gasping moments. But still, maybe they could, at some point, steal a portion of *now* and call it their own.

"Yes," he said, in answer to her unspoken questions. Yes, to everything, for he wished for it too, and too, he knew that naught could last forever. Prometheus must know that better than most any other person on Gaia, and Pandora could only pity him for the loneliness such knowledge must engender. He was doomed to spend eternity watching all he knew crumble to dust and slip through his fingers, and from that doom, she could offer only respite, but never reprieve. The thought of it brought back that familiar pain in her chest, and she fought it by squeezing his hand back. Such was the only weapon at her disposal.

IN HELION, they took a room in a guesthouse, neither having an inclination to call upon Helios in his gleaming, golden palace. The Sun Titan's ego remained massive enough it seemed to press against anyone in the same room as him, leaving them breathless and ravaged, or so Pandora imagined. Instead, they sat in a modest common room, sipping imported Phoenikian wines. They watched sailors and merchants come and go, beset by simple, earthly concerns that, nevertheless, must have felt momentous to them. The price of salt in the market, the exchange rate between currencies, the overcharging harlot with those smoky eyes. Pandora heard every meaningless complaint these men uttered and was tempted, at first, to disdain them as petty.

But such men were the people she was trying to save from the deluge that Tiamat would unleash. If their worries were petty in comparison to the weight she carried, still such woes were the stuff of life to them. Perhaps the man bemoaning salt prices would, if he paid the higher rates, find he could afford less food to preserve with that salt. Perhaps the man longing for the harlot had suffered some personal loss or desperate loneliness that left him seeking a human connection he had failed to make any other way. It was arrogant of her to think it her right to judge lives she had not herself lived.

Without drinking, Pandora swirled the crimson wine about in her wooden goblet, aware Prometheus watched her more than the people around them. Of course, knowing him, he had mostlike observed all of them as well. "You recall the first day we met?" She snorted at the thought. "When first I met you, I mean, not when you saw me in that vile cell." What a strange relationship they shared, that she should need to specify *which* first meeting. The thought brought the hint of a wry grin to her face, though a hint was all she could manage.

Prometheus nodded, once. "Kelaino's symposium. You were eavesdropping upon my private conversation with my niece."

Pandora blushed at the reminder. Even back then, she'd had a knack for ramming her nose deep into unwanted crevices in search of answers to every question. She'd felt she needed to solve every puzzle Gaia could offer up, never once imagining the scope of the mysteries she would soon find herself swept up into.

"Why such reminiscences now?" he asked, though Pandora assumed he must know well enough. Because, looking to the less burdensome past, before she'd seen the scope of the ouroboros, was like looking toward the fanciful distant future that would, mostlike, never materialise. It served as a distraction from the weight bowing each of their shoulders and the knowledge that Ananke would tear them apart once more. How could it not, when they must pursue separate ends?

"You're never going to tell me everything," Pandora said, not bothering to answer his question.

"I hardly know *everything*, Pandora." There was a hint of a smile in his sapphire eyes. "Some things I know because I have experienced them in a different order from you. Some things I glean from the fragmentary, oft inscrutable images I behold in the flames. Others, I calculate based on probabilities and insight into human nature, which, taken in conjunction, allow me to predict many outcomes. But everything? No, not even close. We are, all of us, wandering in the darkness."

Pandora frowned. "Yes, but you have a candle."

That drew a faint chuckle from him. "A dim fire that, oft, serves more to reveal the depth of the shadows than drive them off."

Now Pandora threw back her wine, wincing at its welcome burn before letting her goblet clatter on the table in a signal for a refill. "In Mu, before the end, you said I had told you I would need aid escaping from the Time Chamber, and thus you were there, waiting for me."

His mirth slipped away at once. "When?"

"Just before the Queens of Mu sought to summon Tiamat."

He nodded, taking that in. Prometheus oft stilled his face into a mask, and yet, Pandora had begun to see beneath it. Enough to guess that he had not, in fact, known about Tiamat afore now. "I think, perhaps, I must go to Mu then. If the world shall turn about the actions of these queens, I will need to understand them."

"And be there to ensure they follow the course Ananke demands of them." Wine had loosened her tongue. Or perhaps it had laced it with barbs. Even knowing it, Pandora could not stop herself from glowering.

"From time to time, the Moirai do insist upon one action or another of mine," he admitted.

When a serving girl had poured her a fresh cup of wine, Pandora sipped at it as well. "Beloved ..." she mumbled, wiping her mouth with her hand. "How can we not find ourselves at cross-purposes, when your gambit depends upon the Eschatons unfolding, and I strive to stop the rise of Tiamat?"

Prometheus did not answer for a time, tracing his index finger along the wooden rim of his goblet. At last, he looked up at her. "It is not cross-purposes when we aim for similar ends, even if we must take different means. Both of us seek to save Mankind from the predations of horrors which lurk beyond their ken. Both of us, having seen the Ontos, or pieces thereof, have chosen, rather than to quiver at the Darkness, to become guardians against its incursion. If we are not always aligned at every moment, trust, at least, that we shan't ever be enemies." He hesitated. "That I could not bear."

Nor could she, and the fear of it had turned her gut sour. "So you will make for Mu, and I for Kumari Kandam." If the Unseen Order was caught up with the Anunnaki, she needed to move among them to learn all she could of them. It might prove her only chance to stop Mithra.

"Yes. And I suppose I shall see you, in years to come, in Mu."

Their time together there had proved painfully brief, but he didn't need to know that now. Let him, in the time between, cling to hope that it would provide another stolen moment for them.

Sometimes hope was all one had.

8

THESEUS

742 Bronze Age

Bedraggled and harried, the kin of Herakles had come to Athenai and, pursued by the war band of Eurystheus, cast themselves upon the mercy of Theseus. Upon the steps of his megaron, Herakles's nephew Iolaos had rounded on the herald, or so Akamas had told it, for the twelve-year-old boy had borne witness before summoning his father. Akamas had told Theseus that the herald claimed to have been waiting outside the city, primed to come in and seize those Iolaos had in his charge. Which had been enough to send Theseus storming to his gates, blade in hand, and thrust himself between Iolaos and the one sent to claim him.

"Your king may be mighty but he holds no sway here," Theseus declared loudly enough the gathering throng would mark his words. "And if you intend to come into my city and seize those seeking refuge within by force, you shall swiftly find yourself disabused of such notions."

The herald sneered, though his eyes betrayed a dawning realisation that he had overstepped.

"Leave now," Theseus commanded him, "before my patience and my hospitality grows threadbare."

And so the Mykenians had gone, and Theseus had seen Iolaos and his people brought within the megaron and housed among his own kin. There, in chambers fit for visiting royals, bedecked with rich curtains and plush carpets, were the guests housed.

Antigone, now eighteen, the height of her Nymph ancestry plain —little though Theseus could believe it—tended to aged Alkmena, who was given the finest of those quarters. When the old woman was well settled, Antigone had gone to attend the other women. There was Megara, Iolaos's wife, as well as two younger girls Theseus assumed to be Mekaria, Herakles's daughter, and Leipephile, Iolaos and Megara's girl. What words of comfort Antigone offered them, Theseus had no idea.

Iolaos and young Hyllus joined Theseus and Phaidra in private council, held in Theseus's own chambers. Had Hippolytus, now almost a man grown, not been off with Artemis once more, Theseus would have taken his elder son into council as well. The youth seemed forever on some hunt or other, though, and so it was only Theseus and his wife who met with Herakles's unhappy kin.

A part of him knew it, before Hyllus spoke—impossible though it seemed. Still, when the boy confirmed his invincible father had fallen, it knocked the wind from Theseus and he found himself staggering, kept standing only by the supporting arms of Phaidra behind him. Tears welled in his eyes, fractalising the light from the brazier and all but blinding him. Numb, he listened to Hyllus relate the tale of his mother murdering his father, the boy fighting against weeping himself.

All his life, Herakles had seemed a bastion of strength. He was a fixture of the land, like the Olympian Mountains, and as inviolable as those peaks. And he was *gone*. The thought left an ache, awful in its own right. And somehow, at the same time, summoning up the shades of Pirithous and of Theseus's parents and of everyone he'd ever lost. Once, years back, he'd striven to conquer death and learnt the vanity of his course. Now, all he could do was draw Hyllus into a sheltering embrace. "You are safe within these walls, son."

❧

THESEUS HAD SET AKAMAS, who had two years on Herakles's son, to watch over Hyllus. Theseus's son had failed to draw the boy out of himself, though he'd at least gotten him to sit in the sunlight and take a repast. From the balcony above, Theseus and Phaidra watched the pair.

Phaidra sighed and leant on the balustrade. "This is not over, you know. Eurystheus, craven though he is, will come for Hyllus. He loathed your friend and will not sit restfully on his throne until every threat to his rule is extinguished."

Theseus could only groan. "Herakles ought to have slain him the moment he was free of the chains of those labours."

Phaidra *tsked*. "You know better than that. All your friend wanted was a life on his farm. You think he'd have had peace if he began murdering kings? Did he not tell you with pride, how he'd strung his sword above his hearth and thought never to draw it again? He strove to escape the violence that had permeated his life."

"He failed."

"Oh, and you make it sound so easy, King."

He soaked up her unspoken rebuke. Years ago, with aid from some of the Argonauts, he'd slain many of the Pallantides when they had plotted against him. Some vestiges of that bloodline had survived, though, and in the intervening years made no end of trouble for Theseus. They stirred up the aristoi, always questioning his rule, implying him less wise than his father had been. Yet they never made the mistake of breaking any law, never sparked violence, never gave him due cause to arrest the troublemakers.

"The latest rumour claims you take the princess of Thebes as your pallake ..."

Theseus almost choked on his rage, his stomach dropping at such a thought. "Antigone is a *daughter* to me!"

Phaidra nodded. "It's not me that needs convincing. But Kreon has agreed to cede the throne of Thebes to her brothers and they petition for her return. How does it look if you refuse her kin?"

"Oedipus entrusted her to *my* care." In truth, the dying king of Thebes had claimed Theseus's oath to look after all his children, but Eteokles, Polynikes, and Ismene were in the care of Kreon. Athenai could little afford to antagonise Thebes by demanding the king turn over the heirs to the throne, whatever Oedipus might have wished. So he'd contented to let Kreon raise the other three of the dead king's blood—Kreon's grandchildren, after all—and leave them be.

"Hmm." She extended an open hand toward Hyllus where he sat, ignoring Akamas's attempts to draw him from his dolours. "And now you collect more children for our little house."

"We live in a palace." Because *that* spoke to her point. But sometimes petulance was called for. Especially when dealing with a wife smarter than oneself.

"Husband. Even more so than Antigone, Hyllus and Mekaria have enemies. If you keep them here, you make their enemies the enemies of Athenai. No one wants a war with Thebes, and the Pallantides will say you provoke one. They will use this to turn the people against us."

He whirled on her, dropping his voice to a whisper. "So I ought to let Eurystheus murder children? The children of a man I loved like an older brother?"

"No." Phaidra sighed. "There is no right choice here. But know that this may come back upon us, upon *our* children."

"Artemis would never let aught befall Hippolytus." A lame protestation, if ever there was one. Indeed, Phaidra had been kind to refer to Theseus's bastard son as *theirs* at all. He knew his wife struggled with resenting the young man. Perhaps sensing that unvoiced bitterness was what had driven Hippolytus to his apprenticeship with Artemis in the first place.

"And Akamas, then?" The ice in her voice made plain he'd misstepped.

Theseus heaved a sigh. "The aristoi can little object to a war against Mykenai if we *win*."

"Oh what precarious ground you tread upon, husband." She clucked her tongue.

"Antigone will be safe with her brothers," he admitted, though it felt as a knife in his guts. All these years raising her, and she had become his daughter in his heart. The thought of sending her to foreign lands, of perhaps not ever looking upon her smiling face again ... it carved out a piece of his insides. "When they take the throne, she shall return to Thebes."

Let the aristoi be sated with that much. He would *not* turn Hyllus and Mekaria over to their deaths. Not even if it meant war.

&

As usual, Phaidra had the right of things. Eurystheus came with his army, marching through Athenian hinterlands. Displacing farmers. Stealing cattle. Doing worse to the people, Theseus had little doubt.

Perhaps Eurystheus thought himself invincible, given his superior numbers or the vaunted prowess of his house's blood, Tethids and descendants of Perseus that they were. Either way, shock was painted plain upon his face when Theseus and the Athenians cut down his phalanxes and left his war bands strewn over gore-drenched fields.

Rivulets of blood streaked Theseus's face, more drenching his tunic. He'd lost his helm in the melee and now tugged at bits of viscera tangled in his hair. A squelching mess of gristle had wedged between his toes. All of this, it had been men. Some friends, some foes. Some who had sworn to the service of Athenai, though Theseus had never known their names.

And there Eurystheus knelt in the filth, hand over a wound in his neck, dark blood seeping betwixt his fingers.

Panting, morose, and disgusted, Theseus stalked over to the fallen king of Mykenai. "This is what you sought, Eurystheus?" he asked, gesturing at the charnel house war had made of land meant to give food and life. "Does this slaughter sate your bloodlust?"

Eurystheus chortled, the sound wet and sickening. "You could have simply given me his brats."

Theseus had no need to ask who *he* was. "So you'd have murdered children?"

The king sneered, defiant, perhaps, knowing death already circled him like a murder of hungry crows. "Instead you sent a great many young men to die in their place."

Theseus pointed his bloody xiphos at Eurystheus, his arm trembling as much with rage as battle fatigue. "Don't you dare seek to turn this around upon me with your false equivalencies! As if victims are to blame for carnage wrought by monsters not given their way. Herakles never sought your throne. His ambition never reached beyond planting barley and growing vineyards. All the vitriol you spewed over him was for naught! You brought your kingdom to ruin over fears of shadows in the corner of your mind."

Another snorting wheeze, and this time, blood sputtered from the king's mouth. "Oh ... your own kingdom will surely thank you ... for the deaths of their young ... on behalf of a couple of foreign whelps."

Theseus plodded forward until he stood but a hair from the other king and stared down at him. "Your body will lie in an unmarked grave here, alongside the men you led to their deaths. Your sons will arrange no kingly funeral procession, Eurystheus. And your shade shall wander the banks of Styx, unable to pay the ferryman for passage to Hades's gates, whilst your memories slowly wither and turn to dust in your mind. I have seen what becomes of the unsent dead, Eurystheus. Eternity is *darkness*."

At last, true fear arose in Eurystheus's malicious eyes.

It was the last Theseus saw of him.

❧

When Theseus returned to his megaron in Athenai, he found—as though Eurystheus had been blessed with the Sight—the Pallantides gathered in his hall, accosting his son. Akamas had his hands raised in an attempt to placate the throng, but the elder men paid little heed to a twelve-year-old boy. At a glance, it seemed to Theseus that Peteus was the voice here. At least, the Pallantide had his finger in Akamas's face, his own son Menestheus lapping at his heels like a faithful hound.

Blood splattered and bone weary, Theseus stormed toward Peteus. So intent was the man in castigating Theseus's poor son over his father leading Athenai to war, he did not seem to hear the warnings of his supporters. Or at least, he did not react until Theseus's hand seized the back of his neck. With a heave, Theseus flung the bastard to the megaron floor. The buffoon skidded along the marble for several feet. When he came to a stop, he sat there gawping, as if in disbelief Theseus had manhandled him so.

Rather than bother addressing Peteus, Theseus looked to his dog of a son. "What laudable valour I find here, a fair phalanx of courtiers having cornered a *boy*. Have you the least inkling of the carnage I waded through to return here?" Theseus waved a hand to indicate browning stains bespattered his panoply, pointedly lingering above the hilt of his xiphos, where blood had crusted into the grooves.

"Carnage you invited to our door," Menestheus spat at him. Another day, Theseus might have named his defiance vigour. Might have appreciated it in the young man. As it was, it took an effort of will not to slap Peteus's son, damn the consequences.

"Be gone from my home," he grated instead. "I've no hospitality to share this day."

When the Pallantides and their flock had passed beyond his gates, Theseus whirled upon his seneschal. "Why in the dark of Poseidon's watery abyss did you permit them in whilst I was at war?"

The man dropped his eyes to his sandals, abashed. "Forgive me, my king. Queen Phaidra warned against sending our guards against them, and they were most resolute upon entering. It was ... I believed she intended to address them herself, but then your son returned and insisted upon consulting with her."

Theseus looked to Akamas, brow quirked.

"Hippolytus returned," the boy filled in. "Artemis had to trek off somewhere with her brother, in great urgency, so Hippolytus is home for now."

Which was well; Theseus had missed his other son, true enough. The young man was still going to catch an epic tongue-lashing for dragging his stepmother away from a situation like what Theseus had just witnessed. Already unstrapping his panoply—his people would gather and clean it, he knew—he made for the rooms he shared with Phaidra.

Should I embrace the boy before I lay into him for his brainlessness? Probably. Theseus *was* happy to have his other son back under his roof, even for a little while. He didn't much care for the boy vanishing for months at a time with Artemis, though an apprenticeship with an Olympian was too keen an opportunity to pass.

It was a shame Antigone had gone. She would have loved to have seen Hippolytus herself. The two of them had always been such a pair, and Theseus had half feared she would one day ask to join Hippolytus on his sylvan jaunts. Zeus, but Theseus missed her like he'd lost his own daughter. Mayhap, when all this Pallantide affair had been laid to rest, they could all make sail for Thebes for a fort-night or so. Phaidra missed Antigone even more than Theseus did, he knew, though she tried to hide it.

"Phaidra?" Theseus asked at the threshold of their rooms. He eased the door open. "Phaidra? Hippolytus?"

The sight that greeted him drove him to his knees. It punched his gut with the force of an arrow cleaving his core in twain. Suspended from the rafters by a cord of torn silk, Phaidra hung, limp feet dangling out of reach of the divan she must have leapt off. Her face had purpled, her tongue lolling from one side. A bruise and a split lip marred her visage. Her dress was torn, never properly redonned after

...

A wail, primal and resounding, filled the palace.

Theseus did not, at first, realise it was his own.

SHE HAD BEGUN SCRIBING on papyrus but managed little of it, her tears splotching the ink. Still, he could make out the name. *Hippolytus.*

It was plain enough what the boy had done to his stepmother, inconceivable though the thought would have been this morn. *Why?* That question sounded like a gong in Theseus's head, ringing again and again as he hunted for his treacherous offspring.

Servants had seen him flee the polis in a great hurry, taking his chariot and riding forth. His deed was done, his aim accomplished. He thought he could escape the consequence of so vile a crime?

Why? The sound of it was splitting Theseus's skull in twain. It filled the sum of his World. It drowned his thoughts, inundated his will, and ruined his soul.

"WHY?" Theseus shrieked at his son. Through the paroxysm of rage that had seized him, part of him knew the boy would not answer. Could not. Theseus had his hands around Hippolytus's throat. Had driven him down, choking, pushing his son's head beneath the lapping waves at the seashore. Still the question bubbled up like a torrent of bile held down too long. "Why! Why! Why!"

Theseus had raced his horse in front of Hippolytus's chariot as his son skirted the shoreline, perhaps seeking a way off the island. Theseus's passage had frightened the other steeds. They had toppled over, sending the boy spilling onto the wet sand.

Theseus didn't remember dismounting. Couldn't put the pieces together. But here he was, strangling. Slamming his son against the ground over and over, as if Gaia herself might crack and offer up a reason for this.

"Why! She was a *mother* to you! Why!"

Already, Hippolytus's thrashing had abated. His body's jerking came only from Theseus himself.

A dawning awareness of his crime crept through the haze of fury that had tinged his vision, and Theseus faltered. A wave—higher, wilder than the others—slapped him in the face. It left him sputtering, now himself choking, as much on tears as the brine that had washed up his nose.

His boy ...

He'd slain his own son.

Because of Hippolytus, Theseus had lost his beloved Phaidra. Because of his unspeakable, unforgivable act, a woman's life was ruined beyond repair. And still ... Theseus clapt a hand over his mouth to stifle his sobbing screams. Still, Theseus had become the vilest of kinslayers now.

In a day, he had lost wife and child both.

The wretched threads of Ananke had wrapt around his throat and strangled him as surely as he had choked the life from his boy. Now ... now Fate had left behind naught but a walking corpse.

Hollow.

9

ARTEMIS

742 Bronze Age

Together, Artemis and her brother returned Athene to her city. It had proved a long trek back from Phlegra, the first time the three of them had all been together in Artemis didn't know how long. Not since the Gigantomachy, she supposed, for by the time Athene had returned to Olympus seven centuries later, Artemis had all but walked away from the mountain.

Once, at camp along the way, Athene had scooted closer to Artemis, seeming at a loss for what to say and yet compelled to speak regardless. Most people were like that, Artemis knew. Silence unnerved them, so they sought to fill it, even if it meant giving voice to sentiments that would only grow weaker upon being spoken aloud. "I ... I didn't expect you to come for me."

Artemis had reclined against a knotted root and had almost dozed off when Athene had spoken, so she took a moment to mull over the words. Athene, perhaps, meant she had expected her beloved Father to come for her. Maybe she still, despite it all, imagined he cared for her so much as she did for him and thought the self-proclaimed king of the Earth would have upended mountains to find his missing daughter. Or perhaps she meant, after her last meeting with Artemis had ended on a note of mistrust, she never imagined Artemis would lift a finger for her.

"My sister is not the type to forsake friendships," Apollon answered, and Artemis started, looking to her brother. Was that what he truly thought of her? Her, the woman who had murdered their own grandfather? Or maybe he would have said she had done that, in part, because of her friendship with Hekate. But Pyrrha was gone now, probably long dead. Drowning in grief over Orion, Artemis had given herself to Dionysus, and because of that, she had failed Atalanta and Ariadne, as well. She was left wondering if any choice she had ever made had brought more weal than woe.

With a drawn sigh, Artemis turned back to Athene. "I could not bear the thought of you suffering at his hands."

Athene nodded. "Then will you ..."

"*No.*" Artemis infused the word with pure adamant, for she needed to be certain Athene was left with no doubts. "I shan't ever return to Olympus. My loyalty was to *you*, not to your father, and so long as yours holds to his corrupted empire, you and I can never be what we were, Athene."

Her harsh words had cleft the night, and from then, Athene had spoken little, retreating into the moil of her own, no doubt turbulent thoughts. On the ship from Korinth to the island of Athenai, the hydromancer spent nigh every moment staring into the waves, perhaps seeking answers in their undulant patterns. The thought of it, of Oracles finding their way through insights others could not access, sparked a brief bout of cantankerousness in Artemis, travelling as she did with two of them. Why should they have such recourse rather than need to muddle through their lives as others did?

But, oh so many times Artemis had wanted to go to Athene, to clasp her hand. To find some way to ease the wound she must have inflicted. But how could she do so when she had spoken the truth? It was Athene who needed to bend, to acknowledge her father as a monster.

Apollon, by her side on the ship, laid a hand upon her shoulder. "I am not so certain I would take it well, either, if someone insisted we must overthrow Father for his crimes." Her twin seemed to share her thoughts. She knew he had a point, too. Helios was not half—not a tenth—so bad as Zeus, but still, if he were, would she have the strength to rise against him? But then, for a time, she had sided with Zeus against the Ouranid League, of which Helios was a member.

"We did turn upon him, and for lesser crimes than those of the Olympian Order."

"We did ..." Apollon released her shoulder. "And then we came crawling back and implored him to join us and avoid losing too much in the coup. So you might say our rebellion was half-hearted at best."

Was it?

When the ship arrived in Athenai, she still had no answer, but together, the three of them headed for Theseus's megaron. The populace stopped and stared to see a trio of Titans—Olympians, no less—striding down their streets. Such a sight might have been noteworthy in the Golden Age. Now, in this day, it was all but unheard of, and Artemis fought the urge to squirm under the regard of so many eyes.

So she strove not to meet the gazes of those who gawked at her. Still, she heard the rumour, whispered amid the alleys. *Did Artemis come here to avenge her?* The words made no sense and she stiffened. Though she flowed Pneuma into Perspicacity, still she did not hear anyone speak such again, and neither of the other two reacted as though they had heard aught amiss. Her fingers twitched and she chewed on her lip, wanting to break into a mad sprint out of here but unsure where she needed to go.

Something was wrong here, in Athenai; of that, she was dead certain.

THE ANSWER HIT with the force of a mountain goat ramming straight into her chest. Phaidra was dead, had killed herself. The palace buzzed with gossip and panic, women claiming young Hippolytus had forced himself on his stepmother, and Theseus had raced off to confront the boy. Artemis staggered, struck by the sheer madness of the claim, and for a drawn-out instant, could do naught save stare at her brother. That sense of frenzied dread that had seized the megaron rose in her, redoubled. Once she tore free of it, Artemis flooded Pneuma into Alacrity and Lightness. She bounded out of the palace, through the city, flying from rooftop to rooftop, absolutely riven by the thought she would be too late.

Then she was out of the city and racing toward the shoreline. There, washed up by the incoming tide, lay the overturned, shattered chariot. And there Theseus, dragging the body of his son out of the waves. The king collapsed on his arse, hand over his mouth, aghast at having slain the boy.

The scene became a twisting blade, worming its way through her gut, shredding her insides with each slow turn. Artemis stumbled, one knee scraping across sand though she did not feel the abrasions. This could not be happening. She had been gone not a single month, and her boy ...

She was not conscious of having crawled to Hippolytus's still form. Next she realised, she had a hand upon Theseus's arm and was hurling him aside, sending him stumbling ten feet away to crash down into the sea. As if the teenage boy were still the toddler she had first met in Themiskyra, she cradled him in her lap. "Hippolytus ..." She was rocking him back and forth, moaning, only half certain what was going on.

"He suffocated just now?" Apollon was asking.

Artemis wasn't certain she had answered.

"Asklepoius!" Her brother said. "He was in the city, he might ..." Without another word, her brother took off running, a curtain of sand thrown up in his wake.

Athene had fished Theseus from the sea and tugged her descendant, one of her precious champions, to his feet. "What happened?"

"I ... I ..."

"Speak!"

Theseus swallowed. "He forced himself upon Phaidra and fury clouded my mind, a rage unlike aught I've ever felt before, tinging all my thoughts. I wanted him dead but I did not ... did not ..."

Athene dropped the king of Athenai, allowing the broken man to land with a thump on his arse. She turned to Artemis then, a wary look on her face, as though she feared Artemis might avenge her apprentice on Theseus. Part of her imagined it, her hands wrapt around his throat, squeezing the life from him as he had done to her boy. But if Hippolytus had truly committed such a vile act against Phaidra, how could she expect a husband to react differently?

So instead, she laid her cheek upon the still chest of the child she had helped to raise. *Not again, not again*, the thought parading through her mind in ceaseless procession, clouding out all other concerns. In his lifeless body, she held Atalanta and Hippolytus all at once, both stolen from her by cruelties of Ananke. So all she could do was lie there, part of her longing to join her boy in the gloom into which he had descended.

THEN ASKLEPOIUS ARRIVED, clinging to his father's back as Apollon bounded from the city and down to the shore. Artemis had not watched their progress, though she knew her brother could not manage so far or so swift leaps as she herself could. When she saw his demigod son hop down and rush over, she glared at him.

"What is a chirurgeon to do with the dead?" she snapped, holding the boy jealously to her chest.

Asklepoius dropped down to his knees in the moist sand beside her and pulled a phial from his belt, breaking the stopper. "Hold him up. Quickly! The longer his brain is starved of blood, the less chance I can revive him."

Revive? Was such possible? Had Apollon's son lost his mind, or had he learnt to defy death? She eased Hippolytus's body up so that Asklepoius could pour whatever draught he'd concocted down the boy's throat. Once it was done, the healer laid her boy back onto the sand and began to push rhythmically upon his chest. "How long since his final breath?" The demigod grunted in the midst of his efforts.

"I don't know. I don't ..." Tears had begun to stream down her face. What was this, now? This insane, unbelievable hope carved as deep into her soul as the wound of loss itself.

"Several moments, at the least," her brother answered. "It appeared the ... event ... happened before we arrived, but I had to fetch you."

Asklepoius slammed a fist down onto Hippolytus's chest with a force that must have cracked ribs. And then the boy sat up, gurgling golden ichor. He flung back his arms, veins straining upon his neck from whatever agony had seized him.

"Was that Ambrosia you just gave him?" Artemis asked, somewhat aghast the demigod would even have such, much less defy Titan law by bestowing it on a Man. Aghast, and still swelling with gratitude.

Hippolytus convulsed, doubled over, and curled onto his side.

"No," Asklepoius answered. "I had no Ambrosia to give."

Athene, however, had picked up the discarded phial and sniffed it. "This is *Nectar*."

Apollon's son looked back to her and shook his head. "A modification I made, not the pure stuff the Pleiades created."

"It is still—" Athene began to protest.

"He has saved my son!" Artemis shrieked, silencing the other woman. It took Artemis a moment to realise what she'd even said. Never before had she named Hippolytus *hers*. Never before having lost him. She stroked his brow.

"Mistress ..." Hippolytus moaned, turning over to look at her. Golden drool remained plastered to his lips, along with a mixture of phlegm and water and who-knew-what-else. "Something ... got into my head."

In the anguish of his death, she had not even had time to consider the depth of his deed. "You did it? Your stepmother?"

"I ... Oh, gods! There was something abhorrent in my head." She scowled at that, and he moaned. "Not lust, Mistress. Something ... *alien* and vast, deep as the ocean or ... or a trackless sylvan expanse in the darkest of nights. It took my will and twisted it, pushed me into the recesses of my own mind and held me there, forced me to watch as ... as ..."

Realisation hit her like a slap. Because she knew all too well that theft of self, that perversion of will. "*Dionysus.*" The word was a growl, a curse. He must have somehow given Hippolytus some of the Bacchic wine and used it to control the boy.

"You're saying—" Apollon began.

A sudden peal of thunder, deafeningly close, cut off her brother's words. "Blasphemy!" Zeus's roar managed to sound even above the ringing in Artemis's ears. "Not even gods shall have the power to raise the dead!"

"My king," Asklepoius protested, throwing himself prone. "Forgive me, it is not what—"

"Theft of Ambrosia!" The air took on a tangy, too-clean taste. Zeus's pale blue eyes turned luminous, flashing with lightning. Sparks coruscated between his fingers.

It all happened so fast that by the time Artemis understood, already the blinding bolt lanced down from rumbling clouds overhead. It was as if a mastodon had kicked her square in the chest. Artemis was hurtled from the shore, flung into the sea. For an instant, her body felt energised as though flooded with Pneuma, and yet convulsing, unresponsive.

Then the drowning deep smacked the back of her head.

SHE AWAKENED to currents of pain racing through her. Each breath felt as though it were drawn across a field of razors. She blinked, a skittering of light slowly resolving into stars overhead, their dappled light peeking through a canopy of leaves and branches. She tried to sit but managed only a moan. Her flesh had cracked and felt at once aflame and wet.

"Shh," Apollon said, scooting closer. Her brother held a torch and brought it nigh, inspecting makeshift bandages he had wrapt around her torso. He clucked his tongue and shook his head. "We need Ambrosia for you."

"How ... bad ..."

"Ichor oozes through from the wounds, and I think they'll be a long time healing."

"Hippolytus?"

Apollon turned to her and, even by the flickering firelight, she could see his eyes were red, his face almost broken. "Dead. Blown to pieces, along with Asklepoius."

No.

No, no, no, no.

"I, uh ... I dove into the sea to save you, though I assumed Zeus would have killed us as well. Perhaps Athene intervened on our behalf. I know ... only ..." His voice broke and he fell silent. "When I got to shore—elsewhere, of course—when I looked for her later, she and Zeus were gone. Of our children ... scarce enough pieces were left to bury."

Artemis had not the strength to weep or scream. She wasn't certain she even wanted to. It felt as though someone had carved out every last organ inside her and left her hollow. Or rather filled her with pain, but a pain of the body that paled compared to the empty despair of her soul. The one would heal. The other never would.

Dionysus had, it would seem, brought about his slow vengeance upon her, come round at last. This was the second time that abomination had stolen a child from Artemis, and he had known where to strike. "I'm ... I'm going to kill them."

Apollon nodded, face grim.

"Dionysus, Zeus. I'm going to kill them and anyone who stands with them."

Apollon grasped her hand, and even that touch hurt. "Then let us learn one lesson from Dionysus. Let us bide our time and strike when our foes are least prepared."

So, then, let the second Titanomachy begin.

IF ARTEMIS and Apollon were to bring down Olympus, they had always known they would need aid, and who better to start with than their own blood? The Heliads were proud, respected across the Thalassa, yes, but many remained wistful of the days when their genos had stood in eminence on the Ouranid League. So they had drifted among the Heliads, Apollon swaying those he could with promises of a return to the grandeur that had once rested upon their bloodline. Artemis was not certain she much cared for the prestige any longer, nor did she think her father deserved a throne, but anyone was better than Zeus.

For her part, she relied on more subtle strokes, for there were many who chafed under their present circumstances and many who had reason to loathe Zeus. Among them, of course, was her sister Phaethusa. Once, in a mercurial fit, Zeus had blasted Phaethusa with lightning—and Artemis now knew how badly that hurt—sending the woman and the pegasus she had ridden hurtling down in a ball of pain and death. It had been, Artemis had heard, the beginning of Phaethusa's banishment on Thrinakia.

Choosing to leave with Artemis meant defying their father, but for Phaethusa, maybe it was worth it. "If we succeed, Father will forgive all of his children any transgress," the Heliad said. "If we fail, Father's ire would be moot compared to Zeus's wrath."

"I have spent enough years in dread of Zeus's wrath," Artemis had retorted. "It is time he learnt to fear *mine*."

Hippolytus would be avenged. She would bring down both of the wretched men responsible for his undoing. Dionysus had brought about his first death and Zeus the second, and Artemis would attend to them in the same order.

"There is another who has endured exile for nigh five decades at this point," Phaethusa ventured. "Her aid might prove valuable."

At first, Artemis had not even known of whom her sister spoke. When her meaning dawned on Artemis, she frowned. "I have naught against Kirke, and you're right about seeing her exile ended. But how could she help us? Naught good will come from potions and poisons and such." The Art always wrought more woe than weal, and Artemis knew it better than most.

Phaethusa looked far away. "She has more talents than alchemy, even if that has earned her the infamy she wears like a robe of office."

So they had sailed for Aiaíā, and Phaethusa had led the way up to the manse in which Kirke had dwelt these past decades. Artemis was not certain solitude in a small palace in the woods sounded so awful. Then again, the idea of being bound to one place rankled and Kirke's imprisonment was even more stifling than the years Artemis had spent confined to Olympus.

They found the door open, but the place dark, and paused on the threshold. Kirke was inside, fiddling with some creation or other, seemingly not noticing them. Phaethusa glanced at Artemis, then rapped upon the doorframe, then stepped inside.

Kirke rose, turned to them, and seemed to choke on her words. Phaethusa had hinted that some ill will had passed betwixt them at the time of Kirke's exile but had declined to elaborate, and now Artemis was left wondering how bad it had been.

And if neither of the other women were going to cut through the fog of tension rising around them, Artemis would. She leant against the doorframe, folded her arms, and looked to Kirke. "You were right."

"Yeah ... well, I suppose that's usually a good way to start a conversation." Artemis's half-sister shrugged. "And it's bound to happen, time to time. I mean, I aim for more oft than not, but no one is perfect." Kirke indicated Phaethusa with a bob of her head. "Save for that woman, I suppose. You know with Father's light shining straight out of her arse and her farts smelling like summer dew and all."

At that, Phaethusa glanced back at Artemis, looking pained and perhaps wanting support. Artemis offered her a slight nod, then Phaethusa moved to stand before their sister. "Forgive me, Kirke."

Kirke teetered back and forth. "Yeah. All right. So Artemis turns up saying I'm right ... about something or other. Then Phaethusa apologises to my face. I take it I've stumbled into a dream, and not the prophetic kind. Is this about to turn nightmarish, then? One of you will sprout a second head and start singing off-key whilst the other tries to gnaw upon my knees?"

"You dream such things?" Phaethusa asked, voice laced with almost as much incredulousness as Artemis felt.

Kirke shrugged at that, then motioned to a divan carved in Phoenikian style. "If you've come here to be civil rather than to castigate wretched Kirke for some failing or other, then I suppose I can offer you up some wine. Phoenikian vintages, you know."

Artemis followed behind to help, and when Kirke showed her which amphora, she hefted it. Kirke chose some bowls and as they returned to the hearth, they found Phaethusa sitting on a rug before it. Kirke and Artemis joined their sister.

Since the rug had not enough space for all of them, Artemis sat on the marmoreal floor, easing a little Pneuma into Tolerance to keep from freezing her arse in the process. "You were right about Zeus," Artemis said. "You were right all along, and I ought never have convinced Father to back him in the Titanomachy. I ought to have slain him, despite Hekate's alliance with him. Maybe I could have managed leniency for her once that cur was dead. Maybe ..." Thoth! What terrible mistakes she had made in her desperation to escape from the oppression of her gender. She rubbed her brow, uncertain how to explain all of this.

"And I ought never to have turned you in to Father," Phaethusa said. Oh? Was that how this exile began? "How did he have us so desperate to win his approval?"

Kirke huffed. "He only ever cared for his sons. The rest of us were tools to use or barter as befitted his needs. Pasiphaë is dead, traded to Minos to win the favour of Zeus." She waved a hand at Phaethusa. "You and Lampetia are all but exiles on Thrinakia. I am banished here. And you," she turned to Artemis, who looked up at her address, "escaped such fates only because Zeus named you an Olympian and thus outside Father's authority. So, yes, Zeus is the greatest blight on the pox-riven face of Elládosi society, but he's hardly the only pustule."

Phaethusa frowned. "Such bitterness ill suits you."

Snorting, Kirke poured the wine. "Did the pair of you truly come here to the fringes of Father's domain to apologise to me?"

Artemis nodded. "That's the main of it. That, and to join you."

Once more, Kirke snorted at their fumbling attempts to make amends. "Yeah, sure I've got rooms aplenty if you want somewhere to live a while in peace. I promise, few people come to bother us." She seemed to smile at some private jest. "You can join me in my weaving," she indicated the looms in the back of the room, "or we can braid each other's hair or whatever insipid activities normal sisters do when not at one another's throats." Kirke paused only to sip her wine. "Perhaps gossip about men or other women or such."

"Not to join you on this island, Kirke," Phaethusa said. "We want to join you in the endeavour you began long back, to bring down Olympus."

Kirke looked to each of them in turn, before snickering. "Yeah, sure. Never minding that was a thousand years ago. Why not?" She set her wine bowl down and stared hard at Phaethusa. "Why not start again the vain pursuits that got me exiled in the first place? But before that, excuse me whilst I go bang my head upon the wall for the next fortnight or so."

Well, Artemis could understand her frustration and resentment. "You're not alone this time."

Kirke hesitated. "You two may be among the finest warriors in the Thalassa world. Rumour claims it, anyway. But still, the three of us cannot overcome the Olympian Order. You heard of those blighted witches, the Graeae, right? Sharing one eye betwixt the three of them? Hmm, yeah, that's us trying to live with one *brain* between us, and I can't imagine it enough."

Phaethusa bristled. "I did not come here for you to insult me."

"Eh. How do you know I wasn't insulting you before you got here?"

Artemis laid a hand upon Kirke's knee. "Kirke. Please. We are offering you the chance to change this world for the better. I'm sorry we were not there for you long back, but we cannot change the past. We—"

"No one can change the past," Kirke snapped.

And it sounded like Kirke wished they could as desperately as Artemis had. "The Olympians are not what they were. Ares has left the Order. My brother is with us, and I think I may yet win over Hestia, or at least ensure her neutrality. Poseidon finds himself embroiled with problems of his own, with his son Triton and granddaughter Triteia eroding his authority. A Telkhine civil war may well impend. Athene slew Demeter and Hephaistos long back."

Kirke silenced her with a raised hand. "And besides Zeus himself, Athene remains your greatest threat. If you move against her father, she will defend him." As if Artemis did not know that only too well. "Of course, Hermes, too is a danger. You never know when that arrogant cock is around." Her sister sighed. "Can you recruit Ares?"

It had crossed her mind, but the thought still left her bilious. "He's a psychopath and a Gígas who feasts upon Man-flesh."

Kirke winced. "Hebe? Hera?"

"I don't know."

Kirke glanced between her and Phaethusa. "Why come to me, then? Why not one of them? They are Titans, and more powerful by far than me. Nyx, why not try to convince our father?"

"You're smarter than any of them," Phaethusa said. She knew Kirke better than Artemis did, so Artemis could only assume it truth, but still, it shocked her to hear it spoken so frankly. Tales she heard of Kirke always spoke of her wickedness, her vengeful nature. Or perhaps it took a certain cleverness to have perpetrated the spread of Nectar for centuries undetected.

Kirke flushed. "Um ... thank you?"

Either way, Phaethusa was right, and they needed Kirke. More than that, they owed it to her. For so long, the woman had been pushed aside, named Nymph and considered naught save a commodity to be traded at her father's whim. So if Kirke was vengeful, Artemis understood why. If she was desperate for a little respect, Artemis too had felt that ache, down into the pith of her soul. "If the children of Helios all work together, we can rectify the mistake we made in the Titanomachy."

"All? Aeëtes?"

Phaethusa frowned at that. They had only briefly discussed him. Rumours of his cruelty far outstripped even the most outlandish tales about Kirke.

But offering Kirke support was not the only reason Phaethusa had suggested they come here. Her sister had believed Kirke might have the knowledge needful to deal with the first of those Artemis had sworn to kill. "There's something else."

Kirke nodded. "You are hunted by the reincarnated Dionysus."

Artemis stifled her shock at her sister's perceptiveness and returned the nod. "Before we can devote our full attention to Olympus, we must find the means to make a final end of that abomination."

Kirke kept glancing between Artemis and Phaethusa. "You will ... not betray me again?"

"No, *never*," Phaethusa swore.

Artemis couldn't believe she needed to ask. Or maybe she could believe it. She clasped Kirke's arm.

Kirke swallowed. "Then I will dream for you an answer to this Dionysus. And once one monster is slain, we can attend to the next."

"THERE IS this girl in Ilium, a princess, loved or hated by the Moirai," Kirke said.

Phaethusa folded her arms over her chest. "You mean she has the Sight."

The three of them sat on the portico, taking a repast of olives and a game bird Artemis had shot and cooked. Kirke had a store of apple juice gifted to her by Aunt Eos, and Artemis savoured the sweet tang of it on her tongue. She'd had few dealings with Father's sister since she was a child, but the woman seemed to approve of her and Phaethusa coming here to see Kirke. Approve, even though surely she knew it meant Phaethusa had violated her own banishment.

Kirke mumbled something over a mouthful of olives. "She's an oneiromancer, and an unusual one. She hears voices in her dreams."

"You're already an oneiromancer," Phaethusa objected. "What need have we for a Phrygian child when we have a Titan-blooded sister with the same gift?"

"Yeah, true. And have I ever mentioned how endearing I find it when people without the Sight advise me on how it works, though they couldn't tell the difference between psychic perceptions and an angry gut from sour wine? I haven't? Huh. I could have sworn I had. Perhaps I ought to have it carved above my door for future reference."

Artemis tore a piece of her game hen and let the steam seep out. "I'm sure there must be a point buried in that mess of words, but I fail to see it."

Kirke snorted. "And they call you the greatest hunter on Gaia. Hmm." She sipped her juice and cleared her throat. "All right, fine, have a listen. The Sight is a term we use for psychic sensitivity and it can manifest all kinds of ways, yeah? So if someone is an oneiro-mancer, they use it through dreams, whilst pyromancers divine through fire, mediums see through the Veil, and necromancers hear the voices of the dead." She waved it all away. "Examples, only. The point is, even if you have two psychics cut from the same cloth, so to speak, they shan't be the same any more than the three of us are iden-tical, though we share a common father. One psychic isn't inter-changeable for another. I can dream whatever it is my mind can dream, and what I can't, I can't, so I won't, follow?"

"Yes," Artemis said, "despite your attempts at verbal acrobatics."

Kirke shrugged. "The tongue's a muscle, too, and needs exercise lest it atrophy." The woman let that sit between them until Artemis rolled her eyes. "So. I tried to learn of Dionysus and instead I dreamt of this girl, Kassandra, the princess of Ilium, hearing too much. Of course, there's always a chance she has as much to do with this as that hairy mole on Phaethusa's arse."

"I don't have a—" Phaethusa said.

"Anyway," Kirke interrupted. "There's also a chance Kassandra can dream up your answer, though I garner she can little control her talents."

"Sounds like *you* can scarce control yours," Phaethusa grumbled.

Kirke shrugged once more. "Search out your answer in Ilium and we can plan from there. If I can learn something else, I can have Eos send a message to you."

Yes. If there was even a chance this Kassandra could help her slay Dionysus, Artemis would take it.

10

ATHENE

742 Bronze Age

Athene and her rescuers were forced to make their way back overland, at least until they could take a ship from Thebes to Korinth, and thence on to Athenai. Athene had dared to hope Artemis coming for her meant the rift betwixt the woman and Olympus was healed, but Artemis made plain naught had changed.

"I shan't return to Olympus," the Phoebid had spat. "My loyalty was to *you*, not to your father. So long as yours holds to his corrupted empire, you and I can never be what we were, Athene."

And really, what more had there been to say after that? Athene would remain forever grateful for what Artemis had done, would love her for all they had shared over the years. Artemis had been mentor and companion through the Ages. But could they ever be true friends again, when their allegiances tore them apart?

They came to Athenai and headed for Theseus's megaron. But Athene could never have prepared herself for the tragedy that had transpired here in her absence. As she had hoped, Theseus had defended Hyllus from Eurystheus. But whilst that unfolded, young Hippolytus had raped his stepmother, and Phaidra had taken her own life in despair. Theseus had slain his own son in his fury, and Athene had been struck dumbfounded and almost senseless with the sheer madness and suffering wrought here. Apollon had gone to find his son Asklepoius.

It had grown worse from there. Even with Nectar, Athene would not have believed a chirurgeon could return life to the dead. She did not know how her father had caught wind of such—perhaps his own Sight had revealed this moment to him. But when she looked up, she saw the crackle of lightning fulminate across the darkening sky. Thunder bellowed in anticipation of Zeus's arrival.

"Blasphemy!" Her father roared. "Not even gods shall have the power to raise the dead!"

"My king," Asklepoius protested, throwing himself prone. "Forgive me, it is not what—"

"Theft of Ambrosia!" A blast of lightning erupted from above, blinding, leaving skittering afterimages dancing before Athene's eyes. The bolt slammed into both Hippolytus and Artemis, hurling the latter out to sea, while the former exploded in a torrent of gore.

The chirurgeon wailed, pleading for mercy. Before Athene could react, a second bolt split the heavens and crashed down upon Apollon's son. His flesh blackened an instant before it burst apart in steaming gobbets. Pieces of the demigod splattered over Athene in a macabre rain that had her shrieking in horror.

Next she knew, Apollon dove into the sea after his sister. Maybe Zeus would pursue them. Maybe slay them as well, given the apoplexy that had seized Athene's father at the moment. The thought so galled it yanked her from her stupor, and she flung herself at her father's knees. "Papa, stop! It is enough! The twins knew naught of Asklepoius's ... crimes." She almost choked on the last word, so bitter was it upon her tongue.

When he turned his gaze on her, eyes still luminous with crackling lightning, dread welled in her gut. Surely he could never turn his awful power upon *her*? The next instant, the light dwindled. With a hand on the back of her neck, Zeus yanked her to her feet. "Where in Hyperion's arse have you been?"

Athene was left gasping, breathless. The suddenness of the violence—the sundering of Olympus—defied reason. Or perhaps this moment had proved but the final snap that rent in twain a fixture long riven with cracks they had all ignored. Either way, Athene had no illusions about what it meant from here.

Her father had slain Apollon's son and the boy Artemis had raised as her own. If Artemis lived at all, Athene knew how she must needs react. She knew, because she would have done the same to whoever took Herakles from her.

There could be no patching the rift now.

§

WITHIN HER TEMPLE ON OLYMPUS, in her private chambers beyond the eyes of curious servants, Athene collapsed onto her divan with a huff of exhaustion and frustration. Part of her longed for sleep, yet she too found herself loathing the idea of slipping into dreams. Her mind lurched in wild gyrations, leaping from the way Ares had betrayed and wounded her to the moment, seared across mind and eyes, when the lightning struck Artemis. Did the Phoebid live?

Though it took momentous effort to push through the despair that gripped her, Athene at last climbed to her feet and stumbled over to her small table. There, the servants had already set out a clean basin of water for her to wash with. Rather than splash it over her weary eyes, Athene peered into the bowl. With one finger, she stirred the water, creating a faint swirl of ripples. Then she let the patterns tug at her consciousness. Where was Artemis? Did she still draw breath? Had she survived the strike of lightning that had obliterated her apprentice?

Athene's eyes glazed until, like the water itself, she too was rippling, swirling. The stuff of her flowed, untethered in time and space, and her mind fell away, into some space beyond either sleep or wakefulness. Shadowed flickers of Artemis came to her, phantasms of times they had shared, or places the woman had been. No sign of her in the now, however. Rather, the whole of the woman's existence lay tessellated before Athene, beautiful and incomprehensible in its scope, one moment almost indecipherable from the next.

Athene knelt heavily upon the table, the wood groaning in protest from the pressure she placed upon it, but her knowledge of such present circumstances remained tucked away in a far-off part of her mind. *Artemis …*

ATHENE GLOWERED. *She had known peace would prove impossible here. "You speak as though a self-proclaimed god-king who would rule all the Earth, by the sword if need be, is somehow more worthy. Somehow less a tyrant than the kings of your own homeland."*

"I am Lydian," Artemis fair spat. "And I do not come to treat with you, but rather with the Senate."

But even had Themistokles agreed to come himself, the answer would have remained the same. The general was right, Athene needed to do this, though not for the sake of the Babilimians but rather for the Athenians themselves. They needed to know they faced these foes with Titans at their backs. "They appointed me to speak on their behalf and deliver the simplest of messages, Artemis. Athenians will never bow before the Babilimian Empire. Elládos will not cave. If you would have peace, turn your ships back to Kumari Kandam. Flee across the Thalassa Sea and never think to encroach a single pace further than you have in claiming Kolchis. Fail to heed this warning, and you will face foes more dire than all of those you have fought thus far on behalf of Mithra, combined."

THE STARK CLARITY of the vision, as if her sight had settled upon a single tile of a mosaic, struck her for its strangeness. Athene recoiled, her motion disrupting the waters and sending her lurching out of the hydromantic trance she'd sought. She spilled onto her arse and sat there, mind reeling at the change in circumstance. Thanks to Kirke's Nectar, Athene's hydromantic abilities were stronger than they had once been, stronger than the average Oracle, who oft had little control of their gifts. Still, it was a rare thing if she could pull the answers she sought when she sought them. The flickers of foreknown memory that would arise in her mind were much like ordinary memory—oft sparked by a will of their own, to play out in vibrant, unreal panoply and quickly fade.

Her antechamber door swung open, yanking Athene from her musings, and she turned with rising indignity. Who would have dared intrude upon her inner sanctum unannounced and uninvited? Her father, perhaps, but she would have words with anyone else who so violated her privacy. As she rose, the figure who made her way in from the antechamber was not her father but her stepmother.

"You ought to have hunted down Helios's twins and seen them dead!" Hera blurted without preamble.

"They had just saved me from Ares days before," Athene protested.

"Bah! That traitor, too, you ought to have slain when you had the chance. They are all of them a threat to our order."

Athene balked. "Slain ... your son? My *brother*?"

Hera drew up short, frowning, then nodded. "Well, what is done is done, I suppose, and we must count it the will of Ananke, mislike it though we may."

Ananke ... The idea held a certain bitterness, especially as much as it had come to haunt Father. "I have seen something ... a struggle I cannot explain. It seemed as if, in days to come, Artemis works with Babilim against us." Athene had almost forgotten her visions of long ago, herself brought in chains before the god-king of Babilim. The flicker of Artemis speaking thus brought the dread of that future rising to the surface once more.

"Babilim?" Hera asked, her brow creasing. "Kandamians ..."

Athene frowned. "Stepmother? Is there aught you know of what such a vision portends?"

Her words drew Hera from her thoughts. "If you have seen woe, then I would advise you think on how to change it. Do not become a willing slave to Ananke. In the acceptance of the inevitable lies half the power the Moirai hold over us." She shook her head. "Besides, Babilim is but a minor polis, subject to the great Nineveh Empire. What fear should it hold for an Olympian?"

BUT LATE THE NEXT YEAR, sailors out of Neshia brought stories of changes sweeping over Kumari Kandam. Long it took for such tales to reach far Olympus. And yet, when at last Athene heard that news, it stole her breath and left her gasping as a chill sweat dribbled between her shoulder blades.

For tale said that a minor prince of Babilimian descent, one born in Kissatu, had overthrown the Ninevehan dynasty. This man, Kurus II, established a new empire, one with a capital in Babilim.

MANY YEARS LATER, word came, borne with the swiftness that only ill news could manage, that Zeus's bastard daughter Helen had been abducted by a prince of Ilium. Tale told it that the foreign prince, Paris by name, stalked into her chambers in the palace of her husband, Menelaus of Sparta, and carried her brazenly forth to his waiting ships. Athene found it hard to credit the man could have strolled through the palace and then the city streets with an unwilling woman across his shoulders, without a single witness taking note. Nevertheless, the insult remained, and Father took it as he needs must.

Hera's lip curled in sneering disdain—no doubt pleased at the affront to the get of one of her husband's infidelities—as Athene raced past her, toward the summit of the Throne of Zeus. Already, the soaring rumour had reached the king, she knew, for the perennial storms above Olympus churned as if stirred within a giant cauldron. Lightning flashed across the darkened heavens, accompanied rumbles of thunder that sounded issued more from the belly of some Old One abomination than any force of nature.

"I see the hand of the Unseen in this," Zeus snapped, though since he didn't look at Athene as she approached, she was uncertain he spoke to her. Sometimes, his thoughts burbled aloud these days, as if his mind could not contain their moil.

"You see the *unseen*, Father?" The winds had torn strands of her hair from her braid and they lashed her face.

Zeus whirled on her, face limned with wrath and creased with the strain that ever accompanied his visits to the Oracle Mirrors. The Seeing Pools took a toll upon all of them. Oh, she knew it only too well, for Athene, too, felt wrung out each time she looked into their fathomless, quicksilver depths in the hopes of gleaning some secret of days yet to come. No matter what she beheld, it seemed little to avail her or Olympus or anyone. Flickers of death and chaos—and her rising dread of Babilim—lurked ever at the fringes of her Sight, inchoate warnings of dooms that lurched closer with each passing year. As if the World had become drawn out and, no matter which path they took, it would collapse in on itself, the edifices of Man and Titan turning to dust beneath the rising tides of Khaos.

How it sapped the will, how it drained the soul to look into the future and see, ever and anon, the World drowned in torrents of ichor and oceans of blood. Such sometimes made it difficult to doubt Artemis's claims of how corruption had riven Olympus down to its core. If there was hope, it lay not in shadowy visions but in her own striving against decay.

"They think themselves clever beyond the ken of gods," Zeus spat into the wind. "They think all their subtle schemes and machinations worked in the shadows behind the gears of history go unnoticed ... but I *bear ... witness!* My father knew them of old! Bah!" He flung his hands up into the air, and the storm responded as though his hands created ripples in the clouds, bucking from impact. "Would that I had his wisdom now, Daughter. Damn the Unseen! Damn them all for their treachery in depriving me of Kronos."

Athene found herself unable to swallow, much less give voice to the protest logic would have had her speak. Father himself had bound Kronos in Tartarus at the dawn of the Silver Age. "Do we war against Ilium?" she finally managed to ask.

Something akin to confusion washed over his visage. His jaw worked furiously, as though he gnawed at some stubborn gristle that refused to be ground down. "Mwha. Bah. Let the mortals fight their wars. No, no, no. Ilium must be destroyed! Yes, its walls torn stone from stone in eternal warning to any who dare challenge the might of Zeus and Elládos!"

"Uh ..." Athene caught her windswept hair to hold it still. "So destroy the city, or leave it to the mortals?"

"Yes, godsdamn it! Must I explain all the vagaries of politics to you now?" Zeus stomped closer, his arms waving in spastic gyrations. "Yes, let the mortals destroy the city. Aid them, but it must be the Elládosi who conquer Ilium, Athene." He jammed a finger against her brow. "Think, girl! Think! We cannot expose ourselves to other Titans, much less the Unseen. No, no. Let Man, driven to patriotic frenzy by his misplaced pride, fight this war."

Was Father afraid of Ares striking at him now? She had heard Artemis had slain Dionysus, removing one threat. But still, Ares remained at large, no doubt seeking his chance to slay—and *eat* their father.

"Bleed them dry, Daughter, and perhaps we shall draw out our true foes."

At last, she managed to swallow the lump in her throat. Whether she aided them or not, the Men of Elládos *would* join together to avenge the insult, that much was true. Better, then, that she sided with her countrymen than let them sail alone. "It shall be done, Father."

11

ENODIA

271 Golden Age

*M*emory warned Enodia she must check in upon Hekate once a decade or so, ensuring the woman's course remained true, that her studies brought her greater and greater knowledge of the Art and all its forbidden secrets. But such intercessions took little of her time, leaving her free, oft enough, to wander the face of Gaia, scribbling further notes into her grimoire.

Hekate earned the wrath of the Circle of Goetic Mysteries by stealing that same *Sefer Raziel*, and Enodia, on occasion, found they came too close to finding her past self and dear Keuthonymos by her side. In those instances, she found it needful to divert pursuit. Sometimes she relied on oneiromancy to haunt, mislead, or terrorise, stalking the dreams of would-be hunters. Other times, stubborn pursuers, who refused dissuading with lesser arcana, needed fell curses to give over their search. Few men would bother hunting a thief while afflicted with the pox, she found.

But though her tactics oft distracted those who pursued Hekate, they failed to break the Circle. The sorcerers forever sought their precious, lost tome, as if they had known what to do with it in the first place.

Then, at last, Hekate cursed herself for a fool. For she had given herself the answer, as Enodia, though admittedly she had not revealed it for millennia.

Who was it, do you think, who broke the Circle of Goetic Mysteries and freed you from their hounding pursuit of their stolen prize?

Yes, Morpheus, Helios, and some others, they would live through whatever she did to the Circle. Others would prove less fortunate.

ON A MOONLESS NIGHT, walking within the Spectral Realm, Enodia trod through the twisted, shadow-wreathed streets of Byblos. Hekate had riven the Circle of Goetic Mysteries well enough, Enodia had found. Between stealing the grimoire, inflicting mind-rending night-mares on her pursuers, and the death of Hypnos, the sorcerers had fallen into chaos.

Damkina and Enki had abandoned the order they had created, perhaps in fear for themselves, or perhaps in simple indifference to the fates of those too foolish to ward against what had befallen them. Isis, perhaps the greatest of them, had walked away, returning to Kemet after some row with her sister Nephthys.

The void left the in wake of the departure of so many of the Inner Circle had given the Graeae sisters the chance to rise, even poor blinded Deino. But the Circle no longer felt secure within the city and had cloistered themselves within the Lodge of Whispers. There, within the darkened halls of their sanctum, they worked the Art, calling forth ancient spirits whose nature they did not begin to fathom. The Circle strove ever to bridge the gaps in their knowledge, to enhance their own power. In pursuit of those ends, no atrocity, no profane ritual could ever prove too dire.

Once, Enodia had believed they had destroyed themselves. After all, the dark ceremonies that had taken place here had so bruised the

Penumbra that it bled into the Mortal Realm in numerous convergences around the Lodge and, before they abandoned it, their sanctum on Sarpedon as well. The deepening, writhing shadows pooled about the Lodge, leaving the place accursed. Their actions would prove their undoing, but not without Enodia nudging things forward.

From across the Veil, she stalked behind Nephthys, careful to stay out of view, lest the sorceress decide to embrace the Sight. The Kemetian woman had always been obsessed with Sutekh, some god of Khaos she believed could be harnessed if she could but find the right ritual. Pursuing such a course had shattered minds and led to the eternal damnation of souls. Even now, Nephthys set to preparing a circle out amid the cairns rather than within the Lodge. Perhaps she sought a place to incant free from distraction, or perhaps she knew not even the power-mad Circle would countenance demonomancy on such a scale.

From a cask, the Kemetian drew forth macabre components still wet with the lifeblood of their former occupants. A liver set upon a flat grave. A heart that, based on its size, must have come from a child. A man's severed phallus. Nephthys's trophies oozed suffering into the Spectral Realm, the psychic echoes offering hints of the savagery with which the sorceress had obtained them.

Mostlike, Nephthys would succeed in drawing the attention of her loathsome deity, and perhaps it would have done Enodia's work in destroying the Circle for her. What was it? An Old One? Or, perhaps, as she suspected, if the Khaos god was one more aspect of a Primordial, once it had finished with them, the rest of the Mortal Realm would be left to wither beneath the creature's onslaught.

Enodia drifted closer until she stood before Nephthys. The other sorceress was so deep in her preparations she did not seem to feel Enodia's presence across the Veil.

As Nephthys began her cants, Supernal reverberations thrummed through the Ether, ripples that would spread out through eternity and call forth something that ought never so much as look upon the Earth. Even as Enodia prepared to step across the Veil, Nephthys's form took on substance, the sorceress now using the Sight to look through into the Penumbra and see the spirits that would answer her calls.

Bewilderment flashed over her face at finding Enodia standing arms' distance away. Given that Enodia had not bothered with either her hood or a glamour, she must have been quite the sight, one eye missing, the whole of her left side exposed bone. Before Nephthys could recover from her stupor, Enodia's hand shot out, wrapt around the woman's throat, and squeezed, bringing an abrupt end to the echoing chant.

"You had the right idea," Enodia said, ignoring the Kemetian's flailing attempts to dislodge her grip. Her struggles had a hint of Potency, but not nigh enough to compete with revenant strength. "Still, I think Gaia better off without you unleashing the horrors of Tartarus upon her face. It seems to me, fitting enough, that the countless spirits upon which your Circle has called ought to have the chance to express their displeasure. Have you ever seen the malicious fervour with which keres can pursue their ends?"

Somehow, the sorceress's eyes now betrayed even greater terror than they had at the thought of being asphyxiated. Nephthys swung an ineffective blow at Enodia. Before it could land, Enodia caught the Kemetian's wrist and snapped it with a simple twist of her own. Nephthys tried to scream, but Enodia's grip on her throat prevented any air from escaping.

Then, Enodia set to work, needing only small modifications to the circle the sorceress had so helpfully provided.

Nephthys's rasping shrieks as Enodia yanked off her fingers one by one served as a prime catalyst to summon forth a legion of keres affronted by the Circle in their rituals. Keres—darklings—were, of all spirits, perhaps the closest outside of demons to true Khaos. Darkness flowed through their veins like ichor. Their tainted minds and tattered souls thrived upon suffering, relishing even *their own.*

"Come forth Dainn, come Orcus, come Mantus," she called.

And from the deepest shadows of the Spectral Realm, they came.

Ashen skinned and onyx maned, they crawled from caliginous

wells, spindly limbs yanking their torsos forth with exquisite languor as if savouring their ingress into the Mortal Realm. Answering Enodia's cants, too eager to be revenged upon the sorcerers who had so oft tried to enslave them, they lurched, first into the Penumbra, then onward, wriggling out through the convergences the Circle had created. Through the echoes of suffering the sorcerers had wrought, the keres seeped into the world of Man.

A blight, yes, for certain, and yet one worth the price, if it meant the end of the threat to Hekate.

They would not long be able to remain in the Mortal Realm without hosts and, if they escaped this necropolis, a small price to pay.

Streams of ichor—stripped of its golden colour here in the Penumbra and reduced to no more than blood—wept from Nephthys's ruined hands as the sorceress dragged herself along the ground, making her vain but understandable attempt to flee from the darkness closing in around her.

"Destroy the Circle," Enodia commanded the keres, "and claim your overdue justice. This one, I will keep."

The darklings did not so much run through Byblos's necropolis as they did burst outward, scrambling along cairns and mausoleums like lizards or leaping into the air almost as if they could fly. They flowed in a tenebrous wave, surging in toward the sanctum. The wards upon those walls might hold them, for a time, but not for long.

"You would not know this," Enodia said, kneeling beside Nephthys and yanking the woman around to look at her, "but in millennia to follow, a king of the dead will rise to claim a throne of the Underworld. He will bind wraith after wraith to his soul and will, creating the most feared army in the Roil." She grabbed Nephthys's chin and pushed downward until bone crunched beneath her palm. Until a Titan skull collapsed into pulp, the Kemetian's wild flails of agony giving way to convulsive death throes.

Then, as Enodia stood, Nephthys's abraded soul wafted from her corpse. Her core ruptured, giving way to a seething mass of darkness even as her ruined aura transformed into a shroud to conceal the dead sorceress. Her abraded soul damned her to become a wraith, assuming no demon reached up from the darkness to claim her.

"I know how he does it," Enodia said. Before Nephthys could recover any semblance of control and strike out or flee, Enodia reached up under the nascent wraith's hood and pressed a palm against its brow. "I gave him the power, you see, though I could not exert so much of it myself whilst living. The dead, however, have some advantages when dealing with the dead."

The force of her will poured through Nephthys like floodwaters from a bursting dam. It wrapt around the ghost's desecrated core, around its tattered soul, stamping it with a simple mark.

A bond of eternal servitude.

SCREAMS ECHOED from inside the broken sanctum. The keres' maddening whispers had, in the end, driven fool Phobetor to sabotage the wards, allowing both the darklings and Enodia ingress into her former home. Then she had but to watch, as darkness took shape, lashing out with caliginous tendrils that ensnared limbs and held sorcerers fast.

She did not, however, feel inclined to observe the tortures the keres inflicted, not as hours stretched long through the night. In the darkened halls of this profane shrine, perhaps not even the rise of the sun would drive out these spirits. Bit by bit, they flayed skin, gnawed off fingernails, and lashed their victims with whips of shadow.

With caressing fingers and voices tinged with cloying sweetness, they reached into minds and bestirred nightmares not even Enodia, in her millennia as an oneiromancer, could have dreamt up.

They flensed flesh and soul until weeping shells begged for death, then dragged Phobetor into the dark, no doubt to feast upon his essence.

The Graeae sisters, though, the keres held in special regard. For those three had oft tried to call up the keres in Deino's futile attempts to restore her eyes. The keres thus tore all the eyes from the sisters, leaving them a single one with which they might share sight and cursing them to remain forever imprisoned within the confines of the Lodge of Whispers.

As Hekate watched, their flesh desiccated, muscles atrophying until gobs of skin hung from bone in mockery of human form. Their skin turned grey, ashen as the keres who worked their hex upon the Graeae.

Pity stirred within Enodia's breast. Perhaps no one deserved deathless agonies without reprieve. But given that Enodia herself must endure such a fate, her pity at those hunting her past self withered as quickly as their sinews, leaving in its wake naught save loathing and disgust.

Not every member of the Circle of Goetic Mysteries was here this night, but those who remained, on learning of this, would know their time had passed. She imagined them, huddled in the dark of their chambers, terrified of closing their eyes, forever wondering if the horror that had come for their brethren would climb from the shadows to claim them, as well.

The pursuit of Hekate was now the least of their worries.

FOR TWO THOUSAND years Enodia pursued the perfection of her craft. Before her death, she could not say for certain if any other sorcerer could have matched the breadth of her power or knowledge. After it, she felt fair certain, none living or dead could compare.

To her will, she bound shades and wraiths, and too, revenants across the Earth who would feed her information in her dreams.

There were few places upon the Earth or the Penumbra where she did not walk, scouring every tradition in the world for tales of old or forgotten secrets of the greater arcana. The Thalassa world into which she'd been born had always thought the Time of Nyx a time before time, an eternity of darkness without beginning. Enodia knew better. In that prior Era, so far as she could tell now, half the Earth lay in perennial shadow, half in scorching heat of a merciless sun. And

Vulgeth, upon the ruins of Falias, a jewel of Dark Faerie from an even earlier Era, had lain within a band of eternal twilight that must have looked somewhat like her experiences with Dionysus, in the Gloomwood.

From the forgotten ages of Eras swallowed by the mists of history she sought after every scrap of arcane knowledge that had ever come to Man or Titan. She found scattered references, even, of another race, one of two Elder Races, who had lived before but were gone now. Perhaps, she mused, over the passing of centuries whilst seeking these truths, this lost race had been the one to raise up the once magnificent cities of Dark Faerie.

If she could have still used the Box, perhaps she could have gone back, delved the truths of a younger Earth, and learnt all the secrets yet beyond her grasp. But such could not be, and she must content herself with the passing of Ages in one direction only. And when she had exhausted all she could learn across Gaia and the Spectral Realm, still deeper did she delve, peering into the swirling Khaos of the Roil.

And there, within the ravenous Dark, lay obvious confirmation of the consumptive nature of the cosmos, for those willing to apprehend it.

Beneath a crackling, bleeding sky, she stood upon bands of sinew spanning yawning abysses of seething mist. In the limitless expanses unfolding around her, half-concealed in fog and darkness, she beheld the shadows of monstrosities vast as living islands. Abominations writhed out of sight, as if unable to settle upon a single form, instead becoming masses of slithering blasphemy. The World—that blighted cosmos into which Man was born—unfolded around her in its awful, empty horror.

As if she needed assurance of her course. As if the whole of time had not conspired to demand she follow this path. "I will tame you," she swore into the void.

HISTORY, as ever, flowed onward in merciless procession. Time unfolded around Enodia as it always had until, at last, she recalled the day had come to act once more and ensure Hekate followed the course she must. Ananke was not done with her, not by a long way yet. If she was ever to escape its grasp, she must first play along with it, like a captive war slave lulling her master into complacency before striking when least expected.

Thus she came to Kronion, wracking her memory until she found a manor that tickled her mind, recalling days long past. By way of the Penumbra she passed through the walls, then stepped from the shadows into the hateful light of the setting sun and found a tree beneath which to rest her aching form.

Hekate was not long in coming. The Titan spied Enodia through the gate and, after a brief exchange with the doorman, strode over to meet her.

Standing above her, hands on her hips, Hekate glared down at Enodia, already no doubt thinking herself the ancient sorceress. "Are you here seeking me? I hardly have further need of a mentor."

A justifiable pride, perhaps, and yet Hekate could not imagine how much more she had yet to learn. Not just of the Art, though that would come, but of the World. Of Ananke's callous tendrils wrapt around them all, choking life away whilst no one noticed. Rising drew a grunt of pain from her. It almost always did. Given time, one learnt to live with pain—even the oceans of agony that accompanied unending death. But that pain was always there, always ready to step in and remind one of its presence. Unabating pain had a habit of sapping the will, if one let it. Perhaps that was why so many shades faded in time.

Wracked by fresh spasms in her gut, Enodia had little patience for her past self's arrogance. "Who was it, do you think, who broke the Circle of Goetic Mysteries and freed you from their hounding pursuit of their stolen prize?"

"Either way, I doubt they would have dared challenge me much longer, witch. I despoiled the minds of three of their number, slew dozens of hunters, and killed several of the Circle with my own hand."

Beneath her hood, Enodia smiled. She had forgotten trying to claim that. "Mithra slew Hypnos."

Hekate's shock silenced her for a breath. "He told you thus."

"Did he also tell me you plan to make for fabled Thule?"

The sorceress folded her arms. "You're an Oracle."

An Oracle? Well, an oneiromancer, she supposed. But then, Enodia had beheld more than Hekate could image, and firsthand. "I have seen things. Some of them involve you, as well I think you now guess."

Something between grimace and grin warred over Hekate's face before she motioned for Enodia to lead her deeper into the shadowed gardens of the manse. "What would you have of me?" the sorceress asked when they had trod far from any potential eavesdroppers.

"You did not seek me out here for pleasantries."

Enodia stifled a chuckle. "Hmm. We were never the sort to be pleasant, were we?" She leant against a tree in an attempt to at least shift her pains, if not abate them. "I will tell you what course you should take, Hekate, but you must do as you see fit." Because, of course, Hekate would do as she always had, though the illusion of free will yet remained to her. It was a hope that died the slowest of deaths, more painful even than the desecration of flesh.

Hekate spread her hands, bidding her continue.

"You are familiar with Kronos's youngest son, Zeus."

"A petulant brat with a violent temper and delusions of grandeur, yes. I've met him."

That, she supposed, summed Zeus up well enough. And yet, history revolved around him in violent eddies, *almost* justifying his monstrous ego. "You should seduce him."

Now the sorceress snickered, shaking her head. "Yes, that's usually my response on meeting someone with their head stuck so far up their own arse they can see their liver. Naught gets a woman in the mood like a toddler in a man's body."

Indeed. And yet ... "He is flush with more Pneuma than most

Titans could dream of, and you can siphon bits of it away from him in your bed, even while winning his trust."

"I could," Hekate admitted. "But I can think of about a thousand men in this city I'd rather take to my bed."

A flash of impatience shot through Enodia. Why must she follow the path so precisely? Why must she coddle and prod Hekate when she knew damn well how all this ended? It would save so much effort if she could but command her past self to follow the road ahead of her. Oh, but even this tedious conversation formed steps along that road, didn't it? "Zeus will be the future. He will rule this world one day soon. Would you rather not be by his side than risk becoming the target of his wrath?"

Enodia could not remember what she had thought this day, but the look on Hekate's face made it plain she recalled something. Athene? Well, best not to get too specific, lest she misjudge those thoughts. "You have also seen visions." That much must be true.

"Where is Zeus now?" Hekate said, a bitter, resigned look upon her face.

"At his father's palace here in Kronion, as luck would have it."

The sorceress grunted. "What do you get out of this?"

"Oh ... A child useful to the future."

SOME DAYS LATER, she walked the long wall of Kronion beside Hekate, the amber gleam of the setting sun searing her eyes and draining her strength. When its last light winked out, only then would she begin to feel herself. But this was when they had spoken—when Hekate had sought her ought—and so this was when they *would* speak.

"Zeus has been imbibing excess Ambrosia," Enodia told her younger self.

"What?" Hekate cast a shocked glance her way, though Enodia kept her gaze low. Her glamour disguised her, but she could not afford to risk Hekate recognising herself even through the illusion.

"How would he even get excess? The Ouranid League regulates what's available to all Titans. Is his father permitting this?"

"No, of course not. Why do you think he has gathered his little band of followers?"

"He's siphoning off the supplies," Hekate stated. "He's using his influence and whatever authority his father gave him to steal little bits at a time."

Always, a fleeting temptation to simply tell herself *everything*. To reveal her identity, to lay bare the necessity of Ananke. But that had not happened before, and she could not predict how Hekate would react. Or maybe she could. Come face to face with inevitability, with her future self, Hekate thought to spite Ananke by destroying that future. The time-shifted suicide that had birthed Enodia.

"More, perhaps, than you think," Enodia said. "Kronos is distracted with his fearful studies of the murky future and his dread apprehensions of what is to come." The Gnostic had apprehended both the damned state of Man and that his own end would be one of awful violence, though even Enodia did not know how he died, save that he feared a green-eyed timewalker.

"What fears should one of the rulers of the world have?"

Enodia chortled, forgetting how hollow and raspy it would sound. Hekate did not seem to notice, but she ought not let the woman dwell on it, either. "Ask your father."

"What?"

Enodia turned, looking out over the waters of the Strait of Korinth, squinting against the glare of the last, dying sunlight. How she had hated Papa for failing to tell her more of the future. And yet, here she was, doing the same thing to her own past self. Because her father had been as powerless as she now was. Like her, he must have sought that one, perfect moment, a nexus upon which he might change the designs of Ananke and reweave the Tapestry without unravelling the whole of it. But Papa could not do what Enodia would do. He had neither the strength nor will to follow the course she had laid before her.

What need to fear the Tapestry if she could destroy the Elder Gods that lay at its terminus?

"Zeus's followers are rewarded with more Ambrosia themselves," she said, still watching the flowing water, "but still less than Zeus, who consumes many times his allotment."

"That way lies madness." As if it ought to surprise Hekate. "If I turned him in to Kronos, it would be the end of him."

A pleasant dream, much like the illusion of free will. "But we don't want to be the end of him. A war is coming and Zeus will win. You need to help him, ensure he's had enough Ambrosia. We need a Destroyer fit to end an age and usher in a new one."

Though Hekate doubted Zeus would be the Destroyer. It was not his name upon the Tablet of Destiny Kronos had showed her.

Hekate fell silent, reeling at Enodia's words. "You want me to join his inner circle, to become a party to his conspiracy."

"You want power? This is how you take it. This how the world changes forever."

This was how the World was *made*.

❦

FOUR YEARS LATER, Athene was born. Much though Enodia longed to look in upon the babe, Hekate might sense her presence should she draw nigh in the Penumbra, and she could not make a convincing excuse to visit in the Mortal Realm. How long it had been since Enodia had last laid eyes upon her precious daughter? An *Age* had passed.

The aching hollow in her chest had naught to do with her missing organs.

Instead, she had to content herself with drawing Hekate to her with a dream. She met the sorceress beneath the shadow of Thebes's acropolis, past midnight, when the hateful sun would not enervate her. She leant against the cliff, no doubt almost invisible to any others who might have ventured out so late.

"There is a path before you," Enodia said when Hekate reached her, "winding through the dark of a moonless night. You cannot see the trail well, but you might trust that, if you keep your course true, greater strength may come to you."

"I've already borne a child to that narcissistic brute. What more would you have me do?"

Enodia smirked beneath her hood. "You are not overfond of his brother."

Hekate folded her arms across her chest. "If you tell me to lie with Hades, you and I are done."

"There is a ritual you might create, piecing together the secrets in your precious grimoire. An operation that, though most would balk, could lead to the creation of a most useful piece upon the game board."

Though her expression did not change, a glint rose in Hekate's golden eyes. "Tell me more."

12

KIRKE

739 Bronze Age

It was during one of Kirke's rare visits to the tiny village of her Aunt Eos that she learnt of the pirates. In times past, the Phoenikian civilisation had stood poised to become the dominant power across the Thalassa. Men called them the Sea People, and their combination of merchant fleets and piracy had ranged to far Karkhedon, one of their colonies in the west, and to trade with Nusantara in the east. But slowly, Poseidon had usurped the power of their god Dagon, and the seas fell more and more within the Telkhine, and thus the Olympian, sphere of influence.

Now, scattered ships sailed the seas without a tie to a homeland and preyed upon towns and merchants too weak to defend themselves. It was, perhaps, only a matter of time before a bunch of the ruffians decided to set themselves up in the local tavern, their captain acting like a king. They'd put some of Eos's few guards to the sword, and Kirke's aunt had not deigned to engage them herself in combat. Perhaps, after Ages of immortality, she feared death more than the shame of having her lands stolen. Or perhaps she knew, sooner or later, her brother—Kirke's father—would send someone to deal with the issue. Once he heard about it.

Maybe Kirke would have thought that sufficient too. Except she'd come to town to buy more wine, and that tavern—ironically named *Dagon's Gullet*—was the only real source of it. Which, of course, meant the pirates would have to go.

It didn't take much effort to slip into the *Gullet's* kitchens. Given her height and golden eyes, if the Phoenikians had looked at her, they'd have known her for a Nymph and never believed her a scullion. But the kitchen mistress, Khloe, she already knew Kirke and welcomed her with honey cakes. "Meant for them out there," the old woman said with a grin that would have sent the most vicious of badgers crying for its mother. "Now am I above a bit of petty revenge in making 'em wait a bit longer for me to bake a new batch?" A shrug. "I think I'm not, at that."

"How bad are they?" Kirke asked, leaning against the counter while taking a bite of the achingly sweet pastry. It stuck to her gums. In truth, she needed a drink, but that would come later.

Khloe scoffed. "Not bad if you don't mind men forcing the scullions to their beds at knifepoint, eating all the food, drinking all the wine, and killing anyone who says *what* to 'em, I suppose. Me, I minded all of it, more than a bit."

Kirke frowned and set aside the honey cake. After the mental image of savagery Khloe had conjured, she found she had little taste for saccharine treats. No, she thought perhaps something more bitter suited her current mood, and Khloe's words only served to reinforce the legitimacy of her plan. She had intended to have Khloe tell them that Aiaíā was under the protection of a witch and Men ought not tread here, lest they incur her wrath. It had all sounded grand in her head, deliciously pompous even.

Scaring off rapists and murderers didn't seem sufficient, though. Their victims, those alive, would bear the scars of such trauma their whole lives. Parents who had buried children would grieve until the day they too crossed the River Styx.

And the kitchen mistress was right. Such crimes called for vengeance.

"At dusk, I shall return with a tonic for you to pour in the wine," Kirke said. "Make certain none save the invaders taste even a drop." An afterthought occurred to her. "And make certain one of them receives but normal wine. We'll want a witness."

"For poison?"

Kirke imagined her wicked smile would have put even Khloe's to shame.

WHEN HYPERION HAD FLOWN his way across the sky and Thoth announced the arrival of night, when the pirates were drunk and raucous with laughter, then Kirke had returned to *Dagon's Gullet* with her potion and given it to Khloe. The kitchen mistress had ruined an entire amphora of Argothian red, a crime Kirke might, had she not herself insisted upon it, have considered unforgivable. It was not a pleasant sacrifice, but what was one to do?

She passed back out of the kitchen's rear entrance and waited, giving the whole crew time to imbibe their tainted draughts. Of course, such time meant Kirke had ample chance to dwell on what might happen to *her* if this particular brew didn't work as planned. Nectar was oft unpredictable, and this had been a batch she'd tinkered with more as a distraction from her work for Zeus than with any real intent to use it. Even if she had imagined somehow trying to get the king to imbibe it. Even if she had been working on the courage to act against her master.

But then, she was the alchemist who'd created Skylla, the centaurs, and Medusa. She had wrought transformations aplenty. So, yeah, this was going to work.

And for maximum effect, she should be there before the screaming started.

Of course, the moment the thought crossed her mind, the first scream rang out.

Kirke clucked her tongue. She had not quite timed that right, had she? With swift strides she closed the distance and flung open the tavern door. Even as she entered, most of the pirates were wracked with convulsions. Faces contorted, noses elongating into snouts. Backs arched and popped in twisting agonies, even as hands and feet fused into hooves.

Kirke stuttered, stumbling over her tongue, all her grand speeches forgotten. "B-behold," she managed at last, spreading wide her arms. "Behold the fate of those who dare cross the Witch of Aiaíā!"

As she spoke, another pirate came stumbling out of a back room, linens clutched over his nethers, eyes wide as an owl's. Behind him, a topless girl smirked in vindication, apparently pleased with the end visited upon his companions. Was that how Khloe ensured a witness? By sending one of her girls to seduce him?

Well, best make the most of it then. Kirke whirled on the last pirate who was not yet a pig. At least not on the outside. "The true natures that lurked within your brethren are revealed," Kirke proclaimed in her best imitation of her father's imperiousness. "Should you or your ilk ever dare to tread foot upon this island again, you will *envy* your unhappy comrades." She paused. "Before you leave, you will fall upon your knees and beg the forgiveness of those you have wronged." She pointed at the girl behind him. "Starting with *her*."

If it was possible, the pirate grew even paler. He dropped to his knees, his linen and modesty forgotten, and trembling, turned to the girl, hands raised in supplication.

She sneered at him. "Next time stick your shrivelled worm in one of 'em pigs." She snatched his linen, wiped between her legs, and shoved it in the man's face.

Naked, the pirate crawled his way out of the tavern, pausing before each person he met to whimper incomprehensible apologies. Tears and snot dribbled down his face, and, Kirke noted, his seed was smeared in his beard from where the girl had pushed it on him. Kirke stood with her arms folded over her chest, her face creased in the most baleful glare she could manage.

And when the intruder had left, every eye in the tavern was on Kirke. There was fear there, for certain, but mingled within the horror was something else. Something she had rarely seen in the whole of her long life. Respect. Gratitude.

INTERLUDE: PROMETHEUS

Asura Era, Silver Age

*A*diti's broken corpse lay upon the flagstones, her blood seeping out from the ruination of her wings and the shattered wreckage of her face. In stupefaction, Matarśivan stood there, screaming, thrashing against whoever held him back. He had to get to her. He had to change this, fix it. He had to … had to …

Kratu heaved him away. "Make her sacrifice mean something! Go, and I will try to soothe this."

"No …"

Aditi, too, had told him to flee. Her last request of him, and maybe she'd known they'd kill her for what she had done to Yami. Maybe … maybe … His brain had ceased to function.

More of the others had begun to turn their gazes upon him, though most remained preoccupied with the two dead women.

Make it mean something …?

Only half aware of what he was doing, Matarśivan took off running. He leapt from the plateau, manifesting his wings in the air.

A few beats hurled him skyward, the wind streaking his tears along his cheeks.

This could not have happened. This violation of all they had held sacred. The Dodecadic Circle ... was broken.

Aditi and Yami were dead, and the others would come for him, as well. He cast a glance over his shoulder, but none had fallen into pursuit as yet. Perhaps they had not the heart for it so soon. Perhaps they, too, stood mired in disbelief that their fellowship which had endured for four thousand years could break so suddenly. With such riotous permanence.

What a fool he'd been to think he could convince them to doubt their gods. The beings who had given his kindred purpose all their lives. Oh, he'd known how hard it was for anyone to doubt fundamental aspects of their identity, true, but he had underestimated how violently they would strike out against any who might cause them to question.

Yes, the questioning itself became a threat to them, the source of such rage as he had never before witnessed in his fellow Watchers.

And Aditi was *dead*.

Aditi. Aditi. Aditi. Aditi. Aditi.

The turn of events refused to settle in his mind. This truth violated *his* identity. She was dead ... But she could not be dead. She was his ... his ... purpose.

He did not know how long he flew, though the sun had set and a full moon had risen high above him. He landed amid the Sumeru Mountains, on a rock outcropping he fancied—though perhaps it was mere fancy—he and Aditi had once sat upon together, looking down over the expanse of Kumari Kandam that spread out below them, hills rolling like emerald waves.

She ...

She ...

An inchoate fear had begun to coalesce, a thought he had tried to push away but which now seeped into his consciousness. If all souls were drawn back to the Wheel of Life in death only to be reborn ... He might see her again, yes ... but not before ... before ...

If something was *feeding* upon the Wheel of Life, then she too must suffer the predations of that fate. Aditi would suffer torment he could only imagine must be like being eaten alive, and Matarśivan could not begin to guess how long such would last for her. Would her soul writhe in agony for moments as the maws in the darkness devoured her essence, or would her agony stretch over the course of centuries?

Certainly, if souls were reborn, they were not easy to recognise. Only in a few instances in all his long life could he even harbour a guess at someone he had met in their past life come again, and there was always doubt.

Or did whatever preyed upon the Wheel sometimes devour the whole of a being, leaving naught behind at all? Were those given another chance the fortunate few—though themselves still damned for having to find the same end once dead again—or were all souls spun out again, as the Archons claimed?

He simply had no answers. Moreover, even having an answer, he would remain utterly impotent to do aught about it.

Aditi was gone.

And so was he.

SOMETIMES, he mused as he tromped amid the ochre sands of the Dreaming Lands, one knew when madness had claimed oneself. Those fleeting moments of lucidity that punctuated the madness only served to deepen it, to season its pain like spice in wine.

In a drug-induced haze, he lay on his back, staring at the criss-cross of light that broke through the sandstone domes above. The roil of memory and dream bent back upon itself until one became the other.

Matarśivan ... The Elder God's voice in his mind was a distant thing, and he could not say whether he heard because of the drugs he smoked or whether they blurred Agni's words. Either way, he could not listen.

Dared not listen.

He wore a ring that weighted his hand down, but somehow, he dared not remove it, onerous though it had become.

Oh. Yes, one of those moments where his mind tried to peek through the brume that normally enshrouded it. Well, these people had the most excellent herbs to treat an overactive mind. Some believed they could enter dreams thus and reach a timeless reality. It had brought him here, and kept him here, he did not know how long.

He PASSED *a troop of kangaroos that offered quizzical looks to see a Man so far out from the coastal villages. They watched him before hopping away. Perhaps it was the cured pelts of their kindred he dragged behind him.*

On and on he plodded until he came to the sandstone domes of another village. The men met him upon the outskirts and guided him in once more.

He didn't think much about his words, though he must have spoken them, because they brought him berries and roots and tubers. Then they guided him inside and washed his feet. The blisters stung, though less so than when he'd first had to toss his worn-out sandals and tread barefoot across the desert.

When he had eaten and rested, a girl, probably no more than six years old, took him by the hand and led him deeper into the sandstone domes. This was when they gave him the herbs.

He WALKED IN SANDS, yes, but they held neither heat nor cold. They sky above was a kaleidoscope of colours all bled together. Or a smear of paint, cast lazily across the firmament, any sign of clouds as forgotten as was the sun, though glinting sparkles of light resembled stars.

This surreality had become his refuge, and here, he could walk for unbounded eternities without need for such indulgences as past or future or even a name.

Matarśivan ... The unwelcome voice had become more distant. The sounds it made associated with naught and were thus reduced to noise.

The sands were pink and packed tight beneath his bare feet. He plodded upon them until they carried him to the banks of a virescent sea. Cerulean bolts of lightning coruscated over the surface as if the whole of the waters were charged with energy, and beneath, he saw the shadows of gargantuan serpents slithering about. As he watched, one of the serpents breached the surface, revealing prismatic scales, before vanishing into the depths once more.

Idly, he wondered how many years he had lain in these drug-addled wanderings. Did they bring him into some unknown depths of the Roil? Some other space? Or was all this merely a figment of his broken mind?

He blinked, and the landscape rushed by him, as if a colossal wave had heaved him forward. Indeed, it had hurled him over the sea and he stood, once more, before the Tree of Life. Now, the Tree had become something that folded in upon itself in unfathomable angles. Bursts of light rippled along the bark in intersecting geometries that so boggled his mind he found himself slipping to his knees.

A susurration played in the leaves, running down the boughs until it came to settle upon the base as if the wind had gathered in one single spot to take his measure. Within the depths of the mountainous trunk, a motherly face creaked open, amber sap leaking from the cavernous eyes. The mouth broke into an indulgent smile.

"You no longer seek the answers. You embrace the ignorance."

"The answers brought no comfort." He heard himself speaking the words, and they said too much, like the one he'd been before the dreaming. "They cost more than could be borne and avail naught."

"That is a choice you can make," the Tree Mother admitted. "Dream and dream, and wander without name or purpose."

"Is there another choice?" he heard himself ask. No ... no, he could not ask such questions. No, not this again. Had he not learnt better than this?

The Tree was not indulgent, he realised, but demanding. It had, against all logic, seemed to lean inward toward him, almost bent double over his upturned face. "Perhaps, in the throes of deepest dream, you heard the whispers passed betwixt the living and the dead."

No. That was not why he'd taken to these lands. Was it?

"Maybe you heard them lament and demand answers from sisters who weave together threads of Fate. As in all dreams, it faded ... you forgot the way, the path you might have taken to find them."

"Find whom?" he rasped.

"The ones who hold the answers that haunt your periphery. The course you might take, if you are willing to lose what little of yourself yet remains. Do you even know the *why*?"

No, no, no. He didn't want whys or answers or aught more of life. He had lost ... lost ...

Aditi. That was her name.

He had lost her and lost himself.

"Who are you?"

Oh, deep down, he still knew. He was, had been Matarśivan. And perhaps he owed it to her to be so again. So the words ripped themselves out of his heart. "Tell me, then, how to find these Sisters of Fate."

Let him finally find the Truth.

The Tree creaked as the face receded. "If you would seek the Fates, go back to the beginning."

PART III

When we write of Titans, the mind drifts, as a matter of course, to those of Elládos, Lydia, and the other central lands of Kêr-Ys. Indeed, the immortal Titans of those lands are wont to think themselves alone kings of Gaia, striding through the Ages, peerless and unrivalled. Yet in such thinking lies hubris, for Titan blood has spread across the breadth of our broad world. From the Ennead of Hy-Brasil to the Anunnaki of Kumari Kandam, they too stand tall above Man. Denied Ambrosia, many of the other bloodlines remain, though long-lived, mortal. It is our natural state, much like Man. We have the aspect of Man; we can love and breed with Men until, our blood diluted by theirs, our descendants become indistinguishable from Men. Thus, one is forced to ponder how wide the gulf betwixt Man and Titan truly is.

    — Kleio, Analects of the Muses

13

PANDORA

754 Bronze Age

Founded in the Time of Nyx, Nineveh was, Pandora imagined, one of the most ancient cities on the whole of Gaia and thus a prime location for her to begin her search. Until recently, it had been the capital of a vast empire. But King Kurus II had conquered all of Neshia and moved his capital to Babilim. Pandora recalled Marduk expounding on the history of the city. According to him, Kurus had an Oracle son who succeeded him, but went mad. This would eventually craft the winding path that led to Mithra—Enki—taking over the throne of the greatest empire across the Mortal Realm.

Pandora strolled the breezeways of Nineveh, taking in the city. Beyond the river lay the expansive Badian Steppes, and she'd seen men training horses out there, preparing them for war. Here, though, the crowded markets overflowed with goods from across the continent, from Phoenikia, even some few she judged to be of Nusantaran or Kemetian origin. Fragrant incense created swirls of cloying smoke rising from one stall, while beside it, the next reeked of overripe mangoes and melons. The people here scrambled to make a living, haggling in almost frantic tones, seized by the frisson that infused a land whose people remained mired in ceaseless wars.

The city sat alongside the Tigara River, thus connecting it by waterways to the major polities across Kumari Kandam. It was strange, but in Pandora's time, she had considered the continent of academic interest but little political import. The Kandamians were forever at war with one another, with the enormous wall around Nineveh standing testament to that reality. Fractious city-states, prone to squabbling, and Titans without enough Ambrosia to challenge the Elládosi had made the Kandamians fascinating but hardly important on the political stage during the Silver Age. Gaia always changed, though, and stagnation became akin to decay. Neshia changed with it, and soon this continent would replace Kêr-Ys as the heart of the Thalassa world.

She did not pity Zeus's corrupt empire its inevitable slide into irrelevance. Her studies of history had made plain that patterns of oligarchy could not endure forever, even with immortal god-kings at their head. She would have assumed that, whether in one century or twenty, Mithra's empire would have shared the same fate, save the Watcher never intended his hold to last forever. It was, she suspected, all a means toward the end of prompting an Eschaton.

Her goal, then, became to avert the Eschaton, by whatever means proved needful. The thought that doing so might mean, even inadvertently, helping Olympus maintain its stranglehold across central Kêr-Ys had occurred to her, time and again, on the voyage across the Thalassa. It was bitter realisation, turning her stomach sour. Ananke seemed forever to conspire to force her to aid the man she hated most in all the breadth of Gaia. There was a sick part of her, one she did not like to look upon, that sometimes fancied she would welcome the coming Deluge if only it meant she got to see the look upon Zeus's face when he saw his doom washing down upon him at long last.

Pandora moved beyond the market, getting her bearings and judging the layout of the polis as a whole.

Though so much of Nineveh remained dedicated to defence or trade, a few years ago this had served as the centre of an empire, and civic buildings abounded in the wealthier districts. After a few days of exploration, she came upon a library down the road from the former royal palace. The palace itself had been relegated to offices for the military and the satrap the god-king had installed to rule this province. The library, though, was maintained by priests. Their religion seemed based around deities called Anu and Ki, which, Pandora gathered, represented the heavens and the Earth, respectively.

Though the library was not open to the public, the priests took her stature and aspect to mean she was Titan-blooded and, for a few drachmae, permitted her ingress. She had taken a room at a boarding house nearby, one favoured by wealthy merchants and minor political officials who could not claim hospitality from the satrap. Each day, she would walk to the library and—whilst a priest pretended not to watch her every move—peruse the papyrus scrolls recording the rise of the Ninevehan Empire. Each scroll was tucked into its own cubby in a vast honeycomb shelf, with dozens of such shelves arranged in a haphazard maze through the library. There was an order to the chaotic distribution of scrolls, though it took her two days to decipher that order.

Once she did, the pace of her progress increased, and Pandora would spend hour after hour squinting by lamplight, translating ancient Neshian texts.

"Perhaps something to write with?" a priest once asked, giving her a start and making her realise she had a crick in her neck. The man offered her a quill, ink pot, and several sheets of parchment.

Pandora accepted them graciously but did not deign to use them. Her eidetic memory made it unnecessary, though she might have turned to the parchment to help organise her thoughts, save for one fact: she suspected the only reason the priest offered her such aid was because he might glean from her notes what she was after. Those were not truths she was much inclined to share with anyone, much less men in service to her foe.

She needed to go back in her readings, farther back than the rise of the Ninevehan Empire, until she found reference to Anunnaki and their complex relations to the Neshian religion. According to the tales of priests, the Anunnaki were the descendants of Anu and Ki, much as some claimed Heliads held the blood of Hyperion himself in their veins. Of any such claim, Pandora remained dubious. Nevertheless, it gave her more of an idea what she was looking for.

"Enki and Enlil ..." she mumbled under her breath. The older the texts she had to deal with, the more archaic the tongue. Combined with scrolls so ancient she feared to touch them, her progress was slower than she might have liked. But the most prominent of the Anunnaki seemed to trace their descent from Enki and his consort Ningikugo, or from Enlil and his consort Mullilu, who some sources seemed to refer to as Ninlil, which she took as some sort of diminutive.

She shifted to another, older scroll. "The joining of the bloodlines ..." The passage seemed, as best she could judge, to reference the Time of Nyx. "The daughter of Enki wed the son of Nunamnir ... From their union came ..." The next part was faded.

The shuffle of feet had her looking up. Already, the sun had set, and the old priest—who had grown increasingly dismayed at not being able to determine what Pandora wanted here—had begun dousing some of the lamps. She suspected he misliked that she, both a woman and foreigner, could read ancient Kandamian scripts that many scholars here no doubt struggled with. Pandora, though, was in no mood to apologise for her gender or her gift for languages. So each day, the priest would offer her subtle or not-so-subtle indications it was time for her to be on her way for the eve.

This day, though, Pandora found herself little inclined to break off her search when she seemed so close to learning more about Enki. "Ereshkigal ..." The name felt odd on her tongue.

The priest, who had stalked within earshot, hissed as though he'd found a serpent nesting in his bed. "Speak not that name!"

Refusing to give in to the man's sudden panic, she raised a brow. "Who, or what is—"

"The fallen one! The dweller in the darkness, who rules Irkalla. We do *not* invoke her name."

So, what, this Ereshkigal was the Kandamian version of Hades? "But who was she? Clearly one of the Anunnaki."

"Dead," the priest snarled, "and best left that way." He pointed to the dark outside the window, and while he looked away, Pandora tucked the scroll into her peplos. "For the life of me, I cannot think what cause a foreign Titan *woman* has to browse our shelves, but regardless, you've no business here after dark."

As if his words didn't hold enough belligerence, the priest swept up the whole pile of her scrolls—making her wince as some crunched, bits of a papyrus flaking off—into his arms and toddled away with them. How a man with so little reverence for ancient texts attained such a position, Pandora could not even begin to imagine. Had he worked under her, she'd have thrown him on the street for handling a single manuscript with such insouciance.

She scrambled from the library, letting him think he'd managed to shoo her off—and hopefully, in his victory, he wouldn't notice the missing scroll.

⁊

"*The Descent of Inanna* ..." Pandora read in the scroll, huddled on the floor of her room in the boarding house. The oil lamp spewed reeking smoke around the room, and her eyes stung from the strain of peering at the fading script. The ancient language was more pictograms than letters, but crude ones, in strange triangular shapes or parallel and perpendicular lines.

Pandora had neither eaten nor slept, though her body craved both, and, in truth, a bath would not have gone amiss, either. Yet how could she tear herself away from her stolen knowledge when the connection between the Unseen Order and the Anunnaki seemed primed to rise up from the text and take form any moment? Always, always the next passage taunted her, even as the subtle shifts and revelations forced her to double back, re-examine her translations or assumptions. And yes, now she had begun to take notes.

"*Ereshkigal, firstborn of Ningal, firstborn of Enki, perished in shadow ...*" After stretching, she tapped a finger upon her lip, wrung out her shoulders, and sighed. But it called her, and next she knew, she was bent over once more, scribbling potential meanings for obscure metaphors. Shadow, here, she took to mean the Time of Nyx. During that Era, the people of Vulgeth lived in the Gloaming, a land of perpetual twilight. She had gathered, from her sporadic and one-sided conversations with the Gnostic Cabal, that half the world had lain in eternal, freezing night and the other half in scorching daylight. That Mankind survived only in the Gloaming betwixt the extremes, and barely that.

While the manuscript made no reference to Vulgeth itself, Pandora thought, mostlike, the demise of Ereshkigal must have fallen either in the Gloaming or perhaps in the lands of eternal night. "*While glories of heaven remained as yet unnamed, and the Dark lay as a burial shroud upon the land, it was then the golden child fell. And though all words, fair and foul, would have named it her place to wallow in the gloom, instead did the sorceress make herself its mistress. Like a smith of old might forge wonders out of ore did she cast herself a throne of shadow, in the empty places where the dead forever dwell. Thus did rise the dark gates of Irkalla.*"

All of that seemed, so far as Pandora could tell, but preface to a tale of the Descent of Inanna. The author rambled on, but so much of it seemed speculation that Pandora judged the manuscript was written centuries after the death of Ereshkigal, probably after the Time of Nyx had ended, even, and into the current Era. According to Elládosi folklore, Ouranos had cast out Nyx and brought Hyperion to the sky, ending the ceaseless night. The truth, so far as Pandora had uncovered, seemed far more complex. Vorsanos had been there, and she had no doubt he remained involved, but she suspected the shift in the basic nature of the Earth had as much to do with Amirani's Destroyer as it did with Vorsanos or his Cabal.

After a great deal of posturing about the glories of Enki and Enlil, the author went on to claim that Ningal and her consort Suen had more children, twins Inanna and Shamash. "Inanna?" Pandora mused aloud. That was the member of the Circle of Goetic Mysteries whom Artemis had slain as a bear.

"*Thus did Inanna follow in the footsteps of her sister and steep herself in the forbidden arcana preserved out of the Dark. Such were her voracious appetites that men would cast aside their lives in vain tumults as they strove for her favours.*" Somehow, Pandora didn't think the author meant Inanna's appetites for food. "*Yet for all her graces, Inanna walked the dark path, and in it, met her demise. But little did it suit the pride of Inanna to dwindle nor surrender the glories she had claimed before the eyes of Man. Thus did she come to the gates of Irkalla, come to call upon the sister whose face she had never once laid eyes upon. Some say she sought to claim the throne of Irkalla for herself; some claim, rather, Inanna believed Ereshkigal had the power to restore her to the world of the living.*

"*It was not with bowed head or reverence that she approached the black gates, nor with humility she presented herself before the gatekeeper Bidu. Rather, airs thick with pride fit to deny the tattered wretch death had made of her, she demanded audience with her sister. But great Ereshkigal had little love for the haughty insolence of her kin and forced Inanna to surrender a piece of herself at each of the seven gates of Irkalla. Thus, naked and bared down to her soul, upon soiled knees and with waning ego, did she at last come before the dark throne.*

"*And from there, with sneering glare, did Ereshkigal judge Inanna and find her guilty. Thus was Inanna bound within the wall of Irkalla, tied to the whims of her sister. Her fate serves as eternal warning of the cost of towering pride and how far it might lead one to fall.*"

A shudder wracked Pandora as she rose, rubbing the back of her neck. If this, if any of it was true, the Anunnaki were just as twisted as the genē of Elládos.

There was a final passage, the end broken off. "*Thus did the descent of Inanna sow the seeds of discontent within the breast of her mother, led her to question the purposes of...*"

The last bits might have crumbled with age, but Pandora half suspected someone had made a rather deliberate redaction. Inanna's mother would have been Ningal, but Pandora had no idea which purposes she had begun to question. Perhaps those of the Unseen Order, if she somehow believed them responsible for the deaths of two of her daughters.

Pandora frowned. Gaia, but she needed some sleep. Just a few hours, at least, and by then mayhap the proprietor of this place would have something cooked up on which she might break her fast. Would the priest even allow her back in the library after that? Well, time would tell.

IN THE TWILIT streets of Vulgeth, Pandora crouched in shadows, watching as spider-like vampires crawled along the walls. The land bucked and heaved in waves, buildings swaying until the peaks of cathedrals cracked and twisted, the city groaning in pain at its abuse. Vulgeth was dying, but a sickening surety rose in her that the place would still outlive her.

When a chittering abomination had passed overhead, Pandora broke into a scrambling, crouching run, a mad dash in hopes for shelter she knew could not exist.

A woman stood in the streets, wreathed in a tenebrous shawl that flowed and slithered about her form as if a living thing. Her black hair billowed in myriad directions, paying no heed to the northerly breeze nor even the tumult around her. A fell, incarnadine gleam arose in her eyes, her gaze boring through Pandora's soul and driving her to her knees.

Crevasses ripped apart the cobbles, the sound more akin to tearing fabric than crunching stones. From the rents sprang tendrils of liquid shadow, seeping around the woman, coiling up her legs, melding with her form, until Pandora could not say what of the darkness spawned from the ground and what from the figure. Slowly, slowly, she descended into the widening abyss beneath her, dark tendrils lashing her, dragging her into the depths. With claw-like fingers, she reached for Pandora, and against her judgment, Pandora found herself surging forward to catch the woman's arm, to save her from the burgeoning Khaos that sought to claim her.

But another figure, a man strode through the flood of shadows drowning Vulgeth, his gaze too locked upon Pandora. Darkness parted about his legs like waves breaking upon rocks and tumbling back upon themselves. Pandora had seen his face before on few occasions and was not like to forget it: Morpheus. The oneiromancer's face creased in a malevolent grin, as though he drank in her terror as vampires supped upon blood. The man stroked his dark beard once, no doubt aware of the horrifying figure he presented.

But his presence, though it induced fresh fears, served to remind Pandora: she had escaped Vulgeth already, and without encountering whatever woman was now being dragged down into the Underworld.

"Fascinating, is it not, the way the mind amalgamates the many terrors of our lives into visions that feel cohesive enough? How could you not find terror, here, looking into stark, abominable truths of such tragedies? But as you dig for knowledge never meant for your eyes, you must know, you risk exhuming the plot of your grave, timewalker."

Wake up! Pandora *raged at herself. Yet she was unable to will herself out of the dream.*

Morpheus's smirk only widened as if he knew well what she had attempted. The oneiromancer continued to sashay his way toward her, licking his lips in vicious delight over her frustration.

Pandora clambered to her feet and began to back away, though the heaving alleys made her steps uncertain. Stones had begun to tumble down from cracking edifices all around her, smashing into the cobbles and tearing loose fresh rents. Morpheus never stalled in his advance. A stone statue—carved in the likeness of some monster—broke loose from the rooftop and plummeted toward him. Rather than dive to the side, the oneiromancer waved a hand. The stone wings spread and the creature took flight soaring over Pandora's head instead of flattening Morpheus.

"Wake up, now, Pandora!" she wailed, pinching her arm in the vain hope of escaping him. What could he do to her here? Could he, in fact, kill her? If so, did that mean he too risked his life in such a confrontation?

Pandora willed the Phoenix to ignite upon her palm. She felt the heat rise beneath her skin but it failed to spark. She snapped her fingers, and still, no flame flared to life.

Morpheus chuckled. "In this space, you are like a child standing before a god."

Bands of liquid shadow lashed about her ankles, locking her in place. Pandora sent Pneuma surging into Potency, or tried, but her limbs refused to obey. The tenebrous strands held firm as steel; all her struggles failed to move her more than a single step. The coiling end of one band of shadow rose up before her, serpent-like, though it ended in a single point that seemed to gleam with razor sharpness.

"Desist," Morpheus commanded. "Abandon your wilful disregard of Ananke and submit to the Wheel of Fate."

"There is no torture on the face of Gaia nor even within your twisted mind that would drive me to accept that which cannot be borne." Pandora yanked at her prison once more, but it availed her no more than the first time. "Wake up, dammit!" She screamed within her mind.

The spike lowered until it came level with her shin. Then, with agonising slowness, it wedged into her flesh and began to worm its way upward like a splinter. Pandora gritted her teeth to stifle the scream that built in her gut at the torment. Her Pneuma failed to suppress pain in her dream, and tears dribbled from her eyes. She could see the awful shard of the thing working its way out beneath her skin. Like a bursting dam, she could take no more, and a wail of agony tore from her.

"Submit," Morpheus commanded.

"No!" Pandora gasped around her shrieks.

The black serpentine spike burrowed through her joint and slowly emerged from her kneecap. Pandora screamed until she ought to have torn her vocal cords. But of course, in her dream, she had no such reprieve. Nor could pain allow her the escape of unconsciousness.

"I'll ... kill ..." she tried to threaten, though the words failed to manifest around her endless screams.

Abruptly, the shadow was gone, as were the bands holding her feet. Pandora toppled over, landing face-first upon the cobbles and cracking her head. With a breathless groan, she managed to roll over before Morpheus knelt above her. The oneiromancer tangled his fingers in her hair and yanked her up. Her legs could not support her, and Pandora dangled, held up by her hair alone, though it felt as though it would rip out of her skull.

"You, I know well, would go to nigh limitless lengths in defence of your loved ones, timewalker. It is, perhaps, a family trait among your kin, yes? Do not think I would do less to protect me and mine. Continue down this path, and I shall visit you again and again, each time you sleep, until you fight against slumber's grip and life becomes a blurred, flavourless muddle. And when even your Pneuma-rich body can endure no more, and sleep claims you, there shall I be, ready to crack your mind, one endless night-mare after another."

Pandora moaned, imagining him well capable of carrying out his threat.

He dropped her and the ground rose up to slap her once more.

Pandora awoke having fallen out of her bed. She was face-down on the floor, face a mess with mucus and tears, lips caked in dried blood where she had bit down. Unable to muster the strength to rise, she lay there and wept. Agony throbbed in her leg, but she was terrified of looking to see what Morpheus had done to her. What if she could never walk again? What if even the Phoenix could not heal the catastrophic damage to her knee?

Oh, gods ... Oh, Gaia, it was all too much!

How was she to contend with the sorcerer's power to reach into her mind and claw it to pieces? She was as defenceless against his intrusions as she'd been against Tantalus's assaults on her body when she'd been a teenager. Pandora slapped an impotent palm on the floor, moaning. She had sworn never—*never*—to be that powerless again. But what could she, or another oneiromancer, do against his Art?

At last, she rolled over onto her back, wiping the awful mess of her face on her palm. A moment later, she managed to sit and forced herself to look at her leg. It bore no visible sign of injury, and, seeing it free of blood, already the pain seemed to ease in it. Gingerly, she rose, testing her weight on her knee. It bore it fine, and she was able to gain her feet.

"A nightmare, only ..." She'd known that, of course, but had been unable to shake the fear her torments must follow her into the waking world.

Still shaky and breathless, Pandora leant against the wall beside her tiny window. The guest house seemed dark, and so she batted at the shutters until they flew open, letting in beams of welcome sunlight. After the night she'd had, she did not think she would welcome the darkness again any time soon.

Unable to move, she stood there, ever so oft putting pressure on her knee, always half-convinced the next time would be the time it gave out. Hades, but that had all felt so real. Morpheus had been correct in his threat, too, for she knew she would fight sleep night after night until it rose up to claim her of its own accord. Then he would be there, waiting to prey upon her, unless she caved to his demands and abandoned her pursuit of the Anunnaki and the Unseen Order.

Do not think I would do less to protect me and mine.

Did he mean he was of the Anunnaki? He had the swarthy aspect of a Kandamian, but he'd always spoken Elládosi without accent and she'd thought him local there, or perhaps Phoenikian. And here she was, even now, moments after his torture, defying him in her mind. The thought brought a grim smile to her face. No, Pandora would not bow before the demands of either Mithra or his oneiromancer pet.

Neither, though, could she allow him to assault her mind night after night. She had not the stomach for such masochism, and besides, she would not risk that he might succeed in one day breaking her spirit. But Morpheus could not touch her dreams if he did not know where, or rather *when*, to find her. If she vanished into the timeline, how long would he search? A fortnight? A month? A year? Not for centuries, the idea seemed preposterous. Which meant, if she moved far enough forward or backward, and avoided drawing his direct attention, she should be safe to continue her struggles elsewhere.

Where, then? And when?

Prometheus had gone to Mugedang, and Pandora, having been

there, felt fair certain she could program the Box to reach the distant continent. If she visited the Queens of Mu after their ascension to power, but long before their desperation turned them toward summoning Tiamat, maybe she could sway their course. Maybe, with the right words, she could create a past that shaped their future, ensuring they would not countenance such a dangerous plan. It was a long shot, she knew, for Ananke mostlike accounted for it. But the only alternative she saw for the nonce was surrender, and that she would not do.

Better to strive for the impossible than submit to the inevitable. Ananke be damned. Pandora was going back to Mu.

14

ENODIA

1550 Silver Age

The Titanomachy came and went, years and centuries rolling by in languid waves whilst Enodia strove ever to expand her knowledge and gather to her will more bound ghosts. Hekate needed no further prompting to follow the course of her history to its natural conclusion. Not, at least, until that fateful night in Tyros.

Long had Enodia pondered the coming of that time. Long, too, did she muse on the necessity of pain as part of the birthing process. For Hekate's agonies would serve as the genesis of Enodia, and in the thousands of years since becoming the revenant sorceress, Enodia had toughened her resolve to adamant.

Through the undulant shadows of the Spectral Realm, Enodia plodded across King Agenor's palace. The sun had set and the guests already thronged the courtyards. Some of them, the more astute, shivered, suppressing chills at her invisible passing. Soon, her past self would come here, seeking to disrupt her even younger self's kidnapping of Pandora and Europa.

Like a bull seized in paroxysms of animal rage, Hekate charged ahead, willing to condemn herself and her bloodline to a void of non-existence if it but assured her of changing Fate. She was a child throwing a tantrum to prove rules did not apply to her. But history was merciless. It had always accounted for stubborn pride and self-delusion.

So Enodia stalked down to the wine magazine and crossed back into the Mortal Realm, stepping from the flowing shadows of the Penumbra into the natural, dancing gloom of a cellar lit only by a single oil lamp. How much suffering that tiny flame had once inflicted upon Enodia—when she'd been alive. Pains that, even now, never quite left the back of her mind. It was an unpluckable thorn that could, at the best times, be forgotten on a conscious level, if only for a little while.

With a careful hand, she bored holes into several of the amphorae bearing lamp oil, just enough to allow a slow leak of the stuff that would pool upon the floor. Then, in the back, she pushed over a large amphora of oil. Its crash sent shudders rushing up her spine. A pain so bright it managed to blaze through four thousand years of history.

She allowed herself a moment to regain her composure before stepping back through the Veil, into the colourless murk of the Spectral Realm. The way it warped and twisted its echo of the Earth had become so familiar it now seemed almost a comfort, natural in its unnaturalness.

After making her way to the palace vestibule, Enodia found a dark corner and, from the shadows, pushed back through the membrane and into the Mortal Realm. The harsh light of braziers assailed her eyes, but no one noticed her appearance.

Everything must play out as it always had. Here she was, coming to the final decades of her circular destiny, and finding an end that always seemed so distant now swept in with the swiftness of a mountain gale. Soon, she would step beyond the point where she might know her future.

She was not left waiting long.

Subtle as ever, Zeus ploughed into the vestibule, lusts inflamed by Hekate's oneiromancy, intent to claim his prize. Enodia's prize, however, trailed behind the King of Olympus, face stricken even back then by the demands Ananke saddled her with.

Her gaze brushed over Enodia, eyes widening.

Before that youngest Hekate could come for Enodia, though, a second Hekate rushed forward and shoved her younger self in convenient distraction. Not wanting to waste the chance provided, Enodia spun, hurrying back into the courtyard. Once free, she broke into a run, dashing into the chamber leading to the cellar. Down the stairwell, within the shadows, she stepped across the Veil, then stalked into a corner to await her pursuer.

A moment later, Hekate landed at the base of the stairs, having leapt them in her desperate chase. Now cautious, just beginning to apprehend the danger into which she had thrown herself, the sorceress advanced slowly, looking this way or that.

With her pulse up so high, her gaze searching mortal shadows, she did not sense Enodia's presence across the Veil. Because, of course, Enodia had known she would not. As Hekate passed, Enodia stepped through the membrane, moving to stand before the oil lamp.

"This mad circle of our history must end," Hekate declared. Ice crystallised around the woman's fingers as she pushed forward. There was no room for pity. "You cannot believe the course of our past and future behooves us." A pause, the woman sloshing around in the spilled oil. "Enodia, answer me!"

And so they came to it. One more crux of history. A moment of magnificent agony.

"How many men and women have deluded themselves in the throes of desperation?"

The sorceress spun, eye widening upon seeing Enodia blocking the stairway. "Still you believe you could find some way free of Fate, forgetting your opponent is *yourself*. Your every thought has already flitted through my mind. Your every scheme, every machination is doomed to fail against me, for I have already lived them all."

"Listen to me—" Hekate began.

"But I never do ..." Enodia slapped the oil lamp free from its shelf.

The lamp tumbled free, falling even as Enodia took a step back, up the stairs, watching dawning horror write its bitter tale across Hekate's visage. The instant it hit, that moment of shrieking, burning, of terror, Enodia turned her back.

She had not the stomach to watch it unfold a second time.

❧

WHEN, almost a century later, Keuthonymos found her lurking outside Thebes, for an agonising instant she both longed and dreaded that the wraith-revenant might recognise her, even beneath her cloak. But no, he could see her as a fellow ghost, that she remembered. Naught more had occurred to Keuthos, at least not that she recalled him revealing.

She lingered by the falls where once, eons ago, she had first met Enodia. There was a perverse comfort in places of familiar torment, not unlike prodding at a wound to see how much it might hurt. All the interminable years of her waiting were almost spent. At last she had come full circle, to the final moments when Hekate would need her nudging hand.

So she had waited, knowing that, sooner or later, the wraith would seek her out if she but made herself available. Ever loyal, Keuthos, even wracked by the ceaseless anguish of his frayed soul, could not turn his back upon Hekate.

"Your protégé flounders in dire straits," the wraith said when he drew nigh, little bothering with pleasantries. Perhaps his shock at realising the mentor who had so long guided his precious Hekate was, in fact, a creature not unlike himself stripped him of any desire to make introduction. He too remained hooded and cloaked, the rubescent gleam of his eyes concealed from any not peering deep beneath his cowl. The hunch of his shoulders betrayed the combination of apprehension and pain that must saturate his every moment.

"And you have trailed her since she fell under Dionysus's sway.

For some three years you've sought after any chance to break that hold but found none."

"No," Keuthos admitted. "There is something eldritch within that creature. It runs deep as the mountains, deeper even than this world."

The living thought they knew fear, yet none could imagine the unabating dread that comprised existence for the dead, forever beset by the nameless apprehension of ineffable predators lurking out of sight. Even a glimpse of such enormities would have struck the living mad. Perhaps the dead had no such escape, or perhaps, the both of them had already fallen into madness and found even its refuge an illusion.

"An aspect of a Primordial lurks within the soul of that abomination," Enodia admitted.

"Can you excise it?"

In her memory, Enodia had not even attempted to do so. Was that because, even with her army of ghosts, she could not yet hope to match the unbridled puissance that thrummed through such a being? Her aim, her final mission, it was to destroy all of the Primordials, most especially the Elder Gods. But if she revealed herself too soon, Ananke would conspire against her.

In answer, she offered a slow shake of her head, the denial a bitter one. How she longed to strike down Dionysus. Even in all the passing millennia, she had not forgotten the unbearable indignity of having her will stripped from her. It was a small wonder that sorcery abraded the soul, for there could be no greater affront than to steal choice itself from another being.

"I can, however, break its hold upon Hekate."

The growl that issued from beneath his cloak served as response enough.

PASSING THROUGH THE SPECTRAL REALM—THERE seemed little reason to conceal her nature from him when she knew he must have realised

—she and Keuthos made their way into what had once been Pentheus's great palace, ever careful to avoid drawing nigh to Dionysus himself. Doing so was not difficult, for the god's raw power bled into the Ether, staining it with palpable, corrupted vitality. He was like a cancer that grew, not only within a host, but out of him, polluting everything within hundreds of feet of himself.

Lurking in silence, within the shifting Penumbral shadows outside of Dionysus's sphere, they waited. In her palm, Enodia held the so-called oneiroi dust, an alchemical powder that would drive any who inhaled it into wild, even portentous, dreams. Oneiromancers sometimes used the drug to induct new students they thought had potential for the gift into the arcana. It would *also* serve to render Hekate unconscious.

Enodia had a vague recollection of being grabbed in the garden, but she could see no good way to share such with Keuthos and thus did not explain why she selected their particular refuge beneath a twisted mirror of a cypress grove. Spectral branches swept around them like skeletal fingers of a colossal wraith, their shifting so slow one might not notice it unless watchful for such. She wondered if the Echo had always warped these trees quite so viciously, or if Dionysus's extended presence in Thebes was dragging the polis ever closer to the Otherworld.

The latter, Enodia suspected.

Drunk and naked, Hekate stumbled along through the gardens.

In silent accord, Enodia and Keuthos stepped back across the Veil, and, when Hekate passed close enough, Keuthos stepped out before her. Inebriation slowed the sorceress's reflexes, and Keuthos caught her arms whilst she stared blankly up into the depths of his hood.

"Keuthos ..."

Before the sorceress could scream, Enodia stepped in behind her and slapped the oneiroi dust over her mouth and nose. Hekate's struggles lasted but a moment, before she collapsed limp in Keuthos's arms.

THEY BROUGHT HER OUTSIDE THEBES, to a glade beyond the lake's edge. Though they might have warmed the woman with fire, neither revenant would have much enjoyed being close to flame, and thus they left her, Enodia preparing a ritual to break the god's hold, Keuthos brooding in the shadows.

Her incantations lasting long into the night, Enodia casting the sum of her will against the tether with which the god had ensnared her past self. Bit by fraying bit, she sawed through the cords wrapt around Hekate's soul, ignoring the convulsions that wracked the woman as a result.

Hekate would survive, and the transitory discomfort of body or mind mattered little in the scope of eternity.

At last, ravaged by the effort of contending against even a shard of an Elder God, Enodia collapsed onto the ground. Even in the Mortal Realm, she felt it as the Roil sent invisible feelers in hopes of claiming her in her moment of weakness. Sickening, oily feathers caressed her insides, hoping to draw her down in the Dark with a thousand nudges.

If she allowed it, even for a moment, Aeshma would find her and come for its due.

Enodia would not surrender.

"Give her the Ambrosia," she rasped.

Rising, Keuthos took the flask she had given him, broke the stopper, and poured the brew down Hekate's throat. A small dose, but it would fortify her Pneuma and help her pull through the wracking of her body and soul. They could ill afford delay, for Dionysus would know his prize slave had been stolen from him now and would come looking for her.

Hekate coughed and sputtered, groaned, and turned to her side, still mired in the haze of lurid dreams, probably uncertain what was real.

"She's free of it now," Enodia said.

Keuthos moved to hover over Enodia, his loathing pouring down on her like rain. Even if he had recognised her as his beloved Hekate, still, hatred would have mingled with adoration in the wretched remnants of his soul. Such was the nature of the damned. Their acrimony polluted every other emotion, oil spreading over the surface of even the purest of water. How well Enodia had learnt that, in ages since her death.

"Can he claim her again?" Keuthos demanded.

Enodia wanted to groan. She wanted to curse at the revenant-wraith. The conversation held the flavour of half-remembered dream. Yes, Dionysus could reclaim Hekate. So why had he not? The answer seemed painfully apparent. Because no matter how enervated her efforts had left Enodia already, still she must once more strive against the god. "I can weaken him with a spell, though the process is long and will cost me."

She could see herself, expending so much Pneuma she would struggle to even hold possession of her corpse. That she would risk the dissolution of her soul, the chance that the Roil truly would swallow it, drag it down to the tortures the demon had so long waited to visit upon her. A dread rose then, a sudden, crushing realisation. She had not seen Enodia again after this moment. What if, in challenging Dionysus once more, she truly did destroy herself?

But she had to do it. Something had bought Hekate and Keuthos the time to reach the ruins of Vulgeth, and there was no one else save Enodia to achieve that. "He will not stop hunting for her, though. Zagreus's rage pierces even through the aspect of the Elder God. He will come for her."

Keuthos breathed out a raspy sigh. "How can we escape him?"

Enodia crawled over to Hekate, staring down at the semi-conscious woman. She did remember this moment, hazy and faded as it was. How much more suffering lay ahead for Hekate. How much pain and loss before she reached this moment the second time around. Sometimes, she thought death and transmogrification into a wraith had stripped her of all empathy, but ... She laid a hand on Hekate's shoulder. "She needs the power to confront him. Tell her to finish that grimoire."

Keuthos scoffed at that. "There are no masters left from which she could still learn. Even, I wonder, how much *you* might have to offer, sorceress."

Enodia rolled her remaining eye. The revenant could not begin to fathom the things she had learnt in the intervening millennia. Time, that most implacable of masters, had lashed her again and again, forging a sorceress without rival. "A great deal had I the time. But I must attend to Dionysus if you are to escape his sight." She withdrew her hand from Hekate's shoulder. "There is truth in your words, Keuthos. Few remain who could teach Hekate at this stage. But there were others, in Ages past, their wisdom forgotten in the buried halls of ancient wonders."

"Dark Faerie?" Keuthos groaned. "We have been to Gorias."

"The ruins of Falias lie in the Nyxlands. Guide her there, keep her alive, and she will find what she needs."

"So be it ... I will take her north, through the wild hills of Phlegra. Beyond, though I have not ventured there before."

I hope I see you again, Enodia wanted to say. Instead, she nodded, a silent, bitter farewell to her most precious friend. What wretches Ananke had made of them, dead and damned, and still refusing to surrender.

She *would* see him again, she resolved. A silent oath to herself.

15

ARTEMIS

750 Bronze Age

King Priam of Ilium received the Titans warmly, affording them the finest chambers in his palace, feasting them on fruit and fowl and shellfish. Apollon had implied, though not stated, they had come here as emissaries of their father, and of course, Priam sought to remain in the graces of the great Titan lord of Helion. The talk of the court, however, tended more toward the rumours of changes that swept across Kumari Kandam. It seemed, in recent years, a coup had turned the once mighty Nineveh Empire into the Babilimian Empire. Artemis had little reason to care about the goings-on of foreign continents, so instead she found herself watching Kassandra.

The Ilian princess could not have been more than fifteen. She had auburn hair and, save for her dark eyes, an almost Heliad-like aspect. She had wondered if they shared some distant kinship through one of the girl's ancestors. With subtle inquiries, she learnt

Kassandra was not the daughter of Priam's wife, Hekuba, but rather of some mistress Priam had taken to briefly, years back. A whisper of the name Damkina was the only answer she received, and she could not recall anyone by that name. Only that, on wedding Priam, Hekuba had agreed to raise the girl as her own, and did so, at least publicly, with open magnanimity.

Perhaps the queen loved the child; perhaps she pitied her. The princess tended to drift through the feast as though not entirely present in the courtyard, always staring off into empty spaces as though attending to conversations to which only she was privy. Kirke had called her an oneiromancer, but if so, it was not only her dreams that were haunted.

"In truth," Apollon was saying to Priam, "word reached me even in Delphi of your daughter's gifts." Well, not exactly in Delphi, but Artemis supposed a half-truth served well enough in this case.

"Gifts?" Priam glanced at his daughter and sighed. "Poor dear mumbles nonsense half the time and is lost in lachrymal dolours the rest. Only child I ever saw break into bouts of weeping on seeing a cloud drift across the sky or a drop of rain splattered upon her windowsill."

Apollon shook his head. "It's not nonsense she speaks of. She sees —or hears—things which she has no training to interpret." And Apollon had long established a reputation for training Oracles at Delphi. Of course, rumour also claimed he mostly only trained girls, and only beautiful ones. Artemis had never cared to ask her brother whether he bedded those under his tutelage; she rather did not wish to know the answer. "I can teach her to harness those visions."

"Would that abate her suffering?" Priam asked, and Artemis was touched by the sincerity of his question. He cared for his daughter, didn't he?

Artemis wondered if such training would, rather than abate suffering, serve only to give meaning to it. But her brother nodded, a grave look upon his face. "She can improve."

ARTEMIS STOOD upon the soaring ramparts of Ilium, admiring the sheer scale of the fortress. She had seen few works of Man ever raised stronger or higher than these walls. During the Titanomachy, Zeus had destroyed Menoetius and his army and razed the city of Ilium. The survivors of that massacre built back yet stronger fortifications in the wake of their tragedy. In the days since, she had never heard of anyone breaching these walls, though tale claimed Priam's father had fallen at the hands of Herakles after an altercation between the Elládosi and the Phrygian king. Thought of Herakles always tended to darken Artemis's mood, though less so since his death. Orion was long gone, and with his killer too having crossed the Styx, any ire against Herakles availed Artemis little.

Though the Argonauts may have slain Laomedon, still Ilium flourished under Priam. As the nominal ruler of Phoeba, the closest major polis to Ilium, Artemis had dealt with numerous Ilian kings over the years. They were proud, haughty even, and eager to tighten their hold across all Phrygia. And yet, she had found most to be fair and just, not eager for war across the borders of their homeland. Most of the time. She'd heard of a few ill-fated skirmishes made against the Amazons of Kimmeria, a mistake usually made only when enough generations had passed for memory of its cost to be lost to the Ilians.

Eventide had begun to bruise the sky when Apollon came sauntering over, stupid grin upon his face and eyes gleaming in the fading sunlight.

"Isn't she too young for you?" Artemis snapped, though she had resolved earlier to hold her peace on the matter.

He shrugged. "Old enough to marry, had her father ordered it." He winked. "Besides, kind of hard to find a mortal one's own age once one begins passing a few centuries."

Sometimes, Artemis thought the term "mortal" to describe Mankind a rather odd choice, as if Titans, though longer lived, were not mortal themselves without regular draughts of Ambrosia. "Have you garnered aught useful from all these months of ..." Artemis bit her tongue before saying something vulgar. "Of helping her hone her gift?" He did, after all, look rather pleased with himself.

"I think so, yes. Dionysus seeks to raise more Maenads out of Themiskyra." Themis must be livid over it, then. "He does so in a secret camp in the Katpatuka highlands. They dwell within hollow rock chimneys there, hidden from prying eyes. It sounded ... the things Kassandra heard ..."

"Sounded monstrous," Artemis finished. She could only imagine.

"She said ... I think we have to do it during the next full moon."

"Why?"

Apollon shrugged. "That I know not. Kassandra hears more than she sees, and it is difficult to make sense of it all. Only that, in the full moon, something Dionysus does not expect will happen. Something that will catch him off guard."

For all they knew, that could well be the attack they had planned against the bastard. Still, it was all they had to go on. "So we strike. And soon."

"We strike," Apollon agreed.

IT WAS impossible to gauge how many Maenads might lurk within the network of stone chimneys. Crouching on a plateau above, after nightfall, Artemis spied perhaps two dozen coming and going, bringing in water or game. She had to assume many times that number lurked underground, out of the heat of the day. In her mind's eye, she could see rivers of Bacchic wine flowing through the caverns. She could imagine the sensual moans reverberating off the walls as mounds of flesh writhed in prurient frenzies. Despite her fathomless loathing for the abomination, part of her body wanted to respond. It was an itch that begged for the reprieve of even a momentary scratch, even when one knew the scratching would only make one crave more.

Apollon nocked an arrow to his bow. He had dipped the tips in poisons provided by Kirke, venom she claimed came from some primeval stingray. Their sister had promised paralysis and death to any mortal and all but the strongest of Titans, should their aim hold true.

"Most, if not all of the Maenads are innocent women pulled under his thrall," Artemis said.

Apollon and Phaethusa exchanged looks with one another, no doubt imagining the difficulty in besieging this hold without relying on lethal force.

"They are stripped of will," Artemis reminded them, "their bodies turned into shells. This jealous, petulant god permits no doubts even within the recesses of one's mind. Can you imagine a worse indignity than denied autonomy over your thoughts?"

Apollon glanced at his arrow, his mislike of the situation plain. "Then perhaps death would prove a respite."

Like Aura? Like Ariadne? The woman had hanged herself in two different lifetimes to escape this monster ... "No. I want to save these women, not—"

"We didn't come here to save anyone," Phaethusa cut in. "We came for vengeance and to put an end to this accursed son of Zeus. Though by slaying him now, we *do* save all of his future victims."

She sighed. They were right, of course, but it left her wanting to retch, nonetheless. "I—"

The hair on her arms and the back of her neck stood on end, and Artemis spun, her dagger freed of its sheath in a single motion. Behind her, the gloom had somehow deepened, as if the moonlight could not even touch a welling pool of shadows. From it emerged fingertips, one after another, then a hand. Then Hermes was stepping through.

The instant he passed into the Mortal Realm, Artemis seized his tunic and flung him to the ground, dropping atop him, knees pinning his arms. The blade of her knife bit his throat, freeing a trickle of golden ichor.

"Another son of Zeus," Artemis growled, her face less than a foot from Zeus's messenger son. "Perhaps I can slay two of you bastards in a single night, eh?"

"Peace," Hermes wheezed. "I ... am ... *commanded* to aid you in ... your battle." At first, she thought him breathless with terror. But no, he struggled to keep quiet and lost, as if something compelled his will, too.

"Another trick of Dionysus?"

Phaethusa eased free her xiphos. "Kill him and have done."

"Sent by Hekate ..." Hermes grated.

"Hekate is dead," Artemis retorted. She had no time for this cur and had little cared for him even when they had been allies.

Hermes blinked, his misery writ plain upon his visage. "And yet, it seems, even so she maintains somewhat of the hold she had upon my will."

Artemis stared at the prone and helpless little shit. It was true, Hekate had given him his powers and, in so doing, had bound him to her will. She had, so far as Artemis had known, given Hermes and Iris few commands since, save not to spy on herself or her daughters. Was it possible he spoke truth now, and even from the Underworld Hekate sought to aid them against Dionysus? Did Hekate too have reason to hate Dionysus? Had he caused her death?

"So then," Phaethusa asked. "Can we trust him?"

"No," Apollon answered for Artemis. "But we can use any ally available to us."

With a glower, Artemis rose and allowed Hermes to gain his feet. Her brother was right. If Hekate had provided them with a tool, she would use it. "Go then. Slip inside and create a distraction for us on the opposite side of the cavern. When their attention is diverted, then we strike."

Hermes stared daggers at Artemis. Either Hekate did not permit him to speak, or he himself thought better of further provoking her, for he stepped back into the shadows and vanished from the Mortal Realm.

"So," Phaethusa said. "Are we simply going to gloss over the fact that we now, apparently, have a dead sorceress aiding us from the Underworld?"

Artemis allowed herself a grim smile at that. "Dionysus may have made an enemy more powerful than he expected."

†

ARTEMIS HAD CREPT toward the edge of the plateau, ready to spring. Uncertain whether they could trust Hermes, she thought it best to approach from a new angle no one would expect. Legend claimed that the Kabeiri had carved these strange structures back in the Time of Nyx, before abandoning them when Ouranos loosed Hyperion to soar across the sky. Artemis didn't know if she believed all that, but either way, the famed structures would have their uses.

Her brother's hand fell on her shoulder. "If you go in there, seeing those women as people you're here to save, it may get you killed. Even if it does not, it may cost us this chance to put an end to this god, and we do not know that another will present itself."

"I know." Artemis hated that he was right. More, she hated herself for knowing she would follow his advice.

"If any of them carry his child—"

"I *know*."

Apollon sighed. "Right. Phaethusa and I will take the front, as planned. Wait until the screaming starts."

"I know the damn plan, Apollon. I don't need my brother to lay things out for me as though I were a child."

He shrugged and slipped away, hopping down to the lower ledges where he could snipe anyone outside the caves.

Artemis blew out a steadying breath, then opened the sluice gates of her Pneuma, allowing it to flood into her limbs, making them stronger, faster. Making her body lighter. She sprung, hurtling fifty feet through the air to land against the edge of one of the chimney-like structures. With her lightened mass, she was able to skid down the edge until she caught hold of an opening. There she hung by one hand, forcing her tremulous breath back into rhythm. Waiting, counting ...

A shriek echoed from somewhere deep within the cavern, reverberating off the walls and carried up the chute to which she clung. She craned her neck around to the side, waiting until she saw some of the Maenads outside scramble into action. One of them dropped in a heap, no doubt brought down by Apollon.

Artemis heaved herself up to the gap, then wriggled into the chimney. The chute was scarce big enough to accommodate her Titan form. Using hands and feet, she slowed herself enough to keep from a free fall. At the end, she released herself and plummeted down amid a mob of crazed, naked women running hither and thither. Some cast about themselves after weapons, others ran like rabid beasts to bring down Hermes, who had begun an indiscriminate slaughter in the chamber beyond.

On the opposite side, Dionysus rose, his rubescent gaze locked upon her, piercing her breast like an arrow. For an instant, his momentous regard froze her in place. Primeval dread crept over her. A fear: what if he could overmaster her will once more? Artemis jerked the knife free from behind her back, and the spell over her was broken.

"You were a fool to come here, little champion." Like the Maenads, the god too stood naked, save for his antlered bone mask. By now, the creature ahead looked indistinguishable from the one she'd slain years back. Corruption born anew. "Just as your dead witch was a fool to send her minion. I shall tear the soul from your body and bring it with me when I descend into the Underworld. Your wretched Hekate may have built a kingdom for herself in the darkness, but I shall rive it in twain and, in so doing, free the soul of my mother from her grasp."

"You want to get to the Underworld?" Artemis snarled. "I can help with that."

She flung herself toward him, her blade cutting whirling arcs of death as she surged forward. Alacrity heightened her reflexes until the Maenads seemed to move as if half asleep. Arterial jets drenched

Artemis as she carved her way toward the abominable god. A Maenad ran shrieking at her, even as her knife hamstrung another of her kind. Artemis's Potency-infused palm collided with the woman's sternum, caving in her chest and sending her hurtling backward. She ducked and dodged blows, her knife opening throats, eviscerating bowels, severing limbs.

"You turn death into the finest work of art," Dionysus said, waving a hand as if to encompass the charnel house she knew she had left behind herself.

Artemis had no more words to spare for him. She seized a Maenad who charged her, spun the woman around, and kicked off her, sending herself shooting at Dionysus like a missile. The god snarled and caught her wrist, twisting it until the knife fell from her grasp. With Alacrity still drawn, Artemis watched it seem to drift to the floor like a feather. Using her other hand, she snatched the falling dagger and swiped. Her blade bit into flesh but held fast, as though she'd cut into the hide of a Hy-Brasilian rhinoceros. His fist descended on her like a meteor and Artemis scarce had time to flood Pneuma into Steadfastness.

Even with her Pneumatikoi, the blow sent her sprawling, held up only by his other hand gripping her wrist. The instant she could see again, Artemis kicked both of Dionysus's knees. It felt like striking solid rock, though he toppled, releasing her. She rolled backward, then did a handspring to leap to her feet, away from the feral god. The brief pause allowed her to see that Hermes and Phaethusa slaughtered Maenads on either side of her. Neither seemed able to reach her, but they denied Dionysus any reinforcements.

Could she defeat him without aid? There were more of his followers than any of them had expected, seeming to flood into the tunnel in an unabating river of madness, frothing at the mouth and moaning in the name of their god. Dionysus must have been gathering these wretches in secret all the years in between when she'd slain his last incarnation and now.

She'd lost her knife in the brawl, so she stooped to snatch up a club dropped by a dead Maenad.

Then an arrow ricochetted off the bone mask and Dionysus staggered. *Apollon, thank you!* Artemis leapt forward, pouncing upon the distracted god like a panther. Her club cracked upon his skull. The second blow snapped off an antler. Dionysus howled. His bone mask unhinged at the jaw, revealing triple rows of canine teeth surging up at her face.

Another arrow burst into that gaping maw. Black blood geysered over Artemis's face, blinding her for an instant. With a shriek, she kicked the god's ankle, caught his shoulder, and flipped him over her. Dionysus slammed face-first into the ground. Screaming, Artemis brought her club down onto his back again and again.

A Maenad seized her shoulder. Artemis slammed an elbow into her face. The woman's skull imploded in a mess of gore. She couldn't afford to think on it. Another strike against the back of Dionysus's head. The god bellowed, flinging back his arms and sending Artemis stumbling aside. He whirled on her. His fall had driven Apollon's arrow deeper into his mouth. It had to be wedged clean into his spine! Now those rows of masticating fangs chewed it up and spit it out, along with wads of blood.

"Die already," Artemis growled.

Another arrow caught him in the shoulder, but he barely jerked. If aught, he seemed to have grown in size. The brute was easily eight feet now, and growing with each fuming, furious breath. A massive, clawed hand descend toward her.

Its attack was interrupted as Hermes stepped out of the shadows and rammed a xiphos up into Dionysus's bowels. The god shrieked. Instead of seizing Artemis, he wrapt a hand around Hermes's skull.

Shit.

Artemis cast about for something more useful than a club, spied her dagger, and dove for it, coming up in a roll. As she rose, Dionysus snared Hermes's lower jaw with his other hand. With a single deft jerk—and a gut-wrenching tearing sound—he ripped his brother in half. The brain-splattered top half of Hermes's head was shoved into Dionysus's maw and vanished into crunching oblivion.

Bile scorched Artemis's throat. She could not afford to retch.

Out of nowhere, Phaethusa's sword appeared wedged in between Dionysus's ribs. The god swung at Artemis's sister, but the woman dodged, a blur of motion. Twice more Dionysus tried to snatch her—the thought of him doing to her what he'd done to Hermes!—but Phaethusa was a whirlwind of speed, reflexes even Artemis would be hard-pressed to match. While the god remained occupied, Artemis lunged herself. Her blade bit into his throat, and that had the god careening. Again, twice more, until blood burst from his throat in geysers.

An arrow bloomed in his left eye. His arms flailed wildly. A second arrow appeared in his other eye.

Artemis glanced back at her brother and offered an impressed nod. Dionysus collapsed to his knees.

"... the living and dying ... god ..." the abomination before her wheezed.

"Just dying this time ..." someone behind her rasped.

Artemis turned to see one of the dead Maenads had risen and now had a red gleam in her eyes. The skin from her left cheek began to droop, then pieces of it sloughed off.

"He won't be coming back this time ..."

"H-hekate?" Artemis gaped at the dead woman apparently possessed by the sorceress.

The possessed corpse looked to her. "Farewell ... old friend ..." The light in its eyes went out all at once, and the corpse collapsed back into a heap.

With two hacks, Phaethusa cleft Dionysus's head from his shoulders.

What remained of the Maenads fell to shrieking, wailing in the fresh madness that ensued following the return of their wills. For now, they were faced with the memory of what had been done to them. Of what they had been forced to become.

Artemis let the bloody, befouled knife drop from her limp fingers. "We live."

Had they truly succeeded? Had they ... won?

BENEATH THE WARM sun on a cloudless afternoon, Kassandra sat in
the garden, rocking back and forth, her gaze darting here and there
as if attending to gossip among the birds or whispers in the grasses.

"You've done it," Artemis said to the girl, ruffling her auburn
locks. "I almost doubted success would prove possible, and yet you've
given it to us."

Apollon had come to sit beside his protégé, grinning as if the
whole damn achievement fell at his feet rather than hers.

The teenage girl twisted her head around to stare at Artemis.
"Know you what dreams whisper to those cursed with waking?"

Artemis's brother had mentioned that, on their return, the girl's
babble had become more incoherent than before, but this was the
first Artemis had seen of Kassandra. "I don't know."

Kassandra wrapt her arms about her knees, her expression wan.
"Whispers like the hisses of nesting serpents, all a jumble. *Wriggling*
in the earth. Crawling, forever and ever. Hiss. Hiss."

Artemis glared at her brother. "How hard did you push her for the
answers we sought?"

His idiot smile had already washed from his face and now a scowl
replaced it. "The girl always teetered upon the precipice. You cannot
hold me accountable if she at last has plummeted to one side or the
other."

"I can if you *pushed* her." Artemis looked back to Kassandra and
stroked her cheek. "Shh, now. You can rest awhile."

"Rest?" Kassandra moaned. "To hear the uneven threnody come
humming up from the depths and worm its way through the untethered pieces of wavering souls." Tears welled in her eyes, but the girl
blinked them away.

Again, Artemis looked to her brother, her eyes imploring him to
fix whatever had happened to the princess.

"I did not do this to her," Apollon protested. "I helped her learn to
harness her gift."

Artemis pointed at the poor, moaning child. "This looks more akin to a curse than gift to my eyes, Brother." As Priam had told them, when first they asked of his unhappy daughter. With the gentlest of touches, Artemis eased Kassandra to her feet. "Come. Walk in the sunlight with me and let us talk of happier things." And maybe, just maybe, find a way back out of whatever dark place into which she had fallen.

16

KIRKE

739 Bronze Age

There was, Kirke thought, a certain appeal to using power to aid those unable to aid themselves. It offered more satisfaction than petty vengeance against those who had spurned her and far more than using her alchemy to make Aeëtes a king ever had. Thus, more than a bit self-satisfied, she sat in Aunt Eos's bower, sipping some Argothian red. Because of course her aunt had her private stock she'd never before deigned to share.

"That you will have my eternal gratitude goes without saying," Eos commented.

"Which is your way of not actually saying it," Kirke mumbled under her breath.

Eos clucked her tongue, though whether she had caught Kirke's snide remark or at some private thought, Kirke was not certain. "Were it up to me, I'd call these past decades penance enough for your crimes, Niece. Lesson learnt, I would say. Yes, I'd send you on your way, perhaps with a husband to watch over you and keep you out of trouble."

"Well, without one, I can only strive to do as well as you have." Eos's husband had abandoned her after the death of Aura. The moment the words left her mouth, she knew it was one more thing she should have probably kept to herself.

"Mmm. Indeed, let us hope." Her aunt raised her goblet, either too dense to note the barb or too polite to point it out. Since Eos usually had the grace and restraint of a hemorrhoidal bear with a wasp up its nose, Kirke imagined the former a smidge more likely. "Either way, I shall put in a word with your father about easing your exile, my dear."

She almost told the woman not to bother. Even if Helios decided his daughter had endured enough and lifted her exile, Zeus would never give her peace. Nyx, the Olympian King would probably see it as an excuse to have her dragged up his awful mountain and placed directly beneath his thumb. Helios was one of the few other kings in the world Zeus had a mite of respect for. Kirke had suspected the king not wanting to alienate her father was probably the only reason he had not yet forced himself on her or abducted her. He restricted his tortures to beatings and verbal abuse, which, for Zeus, was a song-worthy level of restraint.

She counted it a profound blessing he'd not deigned to return in some years, though Kirke did not know why. Tale of Elládos was sparse here. And since her aunt seemed in so magnanimous a mood … "Tell me, what news of the mainland?"

"What, Phoenikia?" Eos smirked over her wine. "No, you mean Elládos. Hmm, well … You know, I assume, about that war of the centaurs some years back."

Kirke fought to keep from wincing. She had heard, yes, that her monstrous creations had unleashed vicious savagery against the people of Phlegra and eastern Elládos. The horror of it had cut through even wine-haze to keep her sleepless on many nights.

"Well, according to Phoebe, this was all spurred by Dionysus.

Phoebe, of course, was involved with some kind of sorcerous cult in the early days, along with your father. Nasty stuff—"

"*Dionysus*? As in Semele's son, Dionysus?" Kirke had thought she'd seen him sent off to live in Nysa. She had not imagined him showing up centuries later to incite the centaurs into slaughter and rapine.

Eos shrugged. "Well, yes, I believe so. At least stories claim he was the one who slew Pentheus, that grandson of Kadmus, his cousin. So. Well." Her aunt cleared her throat. "Artemis slew Dionysus for his crimes, or so Phoebe told it."

"What in Hades's dark crotch is that supposed to mean, 'so she told it'?"

"Because she also claims he managed to get himself reborn and grow to adulthood in the space of months rather than years." Another cluck of that tongue of hers. "Well, I always told my brother messing with the Art would bring about naught save woe."

"It was the Art that broke those pirates," Kirke pointed out. Because it seemed a good idea to lose whatever favour she had won with her aunt.

Eos huffed. "And now we've, perhaps, got a grown-baby-man thing out there haunting Phoebe's granddaughter." She pointed a finger. "Tell me this isn't related to Phoebe being in that cult back then."

"The Circle of Goetic Mysteries," Kirke filled in.

"Yes, that one."

"The one I was conceived in."

"Yes, yes, well, I'm quite certain I want no details about how my brother managed that with that damn witch, Hekate, rest her poor accursed soul." Everyone assumed Mother was dead now, and who was Kirke to gainsay that?

"So you're telling me you think the fact that Artemis's grand-mother toyed with sorcery more than four *thousand* years ago somehow relates to Artemis's foe being reborn in some unnatural way?"

Eos sipped at her wine. "Would it not prove too much coincidence, elsewise?"

Kirke didn't know whether to laugh or weep. Or request a whole other amphora of imported wine. "Y-you do know the word coincidence implies the events coincide, yeah? You're talking about two events separated by vast gulfs of time and space. The only tether connecting those events in the least is that a drunk woman managed to work the name Phoebe into both sentences."

"See!" Eos pointed. "I told you, you drink too much. But, no, I don't think it your fault any of that happened. I mean, lots of other things are your fault. Oh, Hyperion's grimace, are they your fault, Kirke." And yet *another* cluck of that tongue. The damn thing should be locked away as a lethal weapon. "Who would have thought one girl could make so many mistakes? Well, but I'm sure you'll learn one of these days, especially now that you're out from under the influence of that dreadful mother of yours."

Kirke set her goblet on the floor beside her divan and rose, clearing her throat. "Well, lovely as this has been—and words escape me to even describe such astringent delights—I really ought to be going. Chicken will be wondering where I've gotten off to for so long." And Kirke was beginning to think the chukar would be better conversation than her aunt.

Eos smiled, too deep in her cups to have any idea what Kirke thought of her at the moment. "Do visit again, Niece. You spend too much time alone, really."

Yeah. Even Eos managed to utter truth once every so oft.

IT WAS a few years before Zeus came again. After the beatings, after he'd thrown Chicken alive and shrieking into her hearth and hurled her divan against the wall to smash it into kindling, he'd whirled on her. Kirke lay on the floor, one hand around her pummelled gut, the other staunching the blood oozing out of her probably broken nose.

"We cannot find Dionysus! We cannot find that accursed Unseen

Order! So what good is the Sight you have bestowed if it will not reveal the secrets we need to overcome our foes?"

Kirke wondered, distantly, what "we" he referred to. Did he work with her half-brother Apollon? So far as Kirke knew, Apollon was the greatest Oracle available to Zeus. Athene had her gifts, of course, and then there was Hestia. But Apollon was famed as the God of Prophecy, among other pomposity. Of course, Kirke dare not question Zeus on a good day, much less in one of his tirades. Huh. Well, she didn't think Zeus had good days. Maybe days with marginally less volatility than others?

"I ... uh ... I've prepared stronger brews," she said, struggling to her knees and crawling over to a footlocker where she'd stashed it. Were she to try to drug him with the tincture that might transform him into a pig, would the limited prescience she'd instilled in him warn him of the danger? Oracles were notoriously difficult to catch off guard, as their visions oft seemed to warn them of plots against their person. All save the one that would finally succeed, she supposed. Besides, Zeus held more Pneuma inside his body than any Titan she'd ever heard of. What if he resisted the transformation?

Oft though she'd imagined feeding him the pig-drug, she instead handed him the Sight-inducing Nectar. A craven, she always backed away from the chance to save herself. Gaia, she wished she had the strength to stand up to him. She wished she had a way to ... see a way forward ...

Zeus snatched the phial from her hand and stormed out of her manse without another word.

And Kirke scarce paid him any mind. Her home was filled with the wretched stench of burnt feathers and charred flesh of her avian companion. Her furniture was smashed to bits. Her face and gut ached like a horse had trampled her.

She pushed all of that out of her mind.

Kirke was an oneiromancer. Since childhood she had, on occasion, dreamt the future. Oneiromancy was, in the end, but an application of the same psychic phenomenon in which Oracles perceived the future through divination. It was a kind of Sight. So, what if she took the brew *herself*? Could she dream her way out of this situation?

Kirke stared down at the other phial of Sight-enhancing Nectar still in her locker. Zeus had been in such a hurry he had not bothered to ask if she had more. Slowly, Kirke reached for the phial.

She climbed along the rocky edges of Aiaíā's shore, letting the waves lap her heels and soak her sandals. The wind whipped her hair, threatening to tug strands loose of her braid, mocking her with its freedom. She imagined, as she had considered in days past, swimming the wide channel between the island and the Phoenikian coast. It was an impossible swim, though, and she could no more bring herself to attempt so suicidal an endeavour than she could slit her wrists. Thus, wandering, did she spy the ship drawing nigh, battered and worn, with kohl-lined eyes painted along the bow.

No pirates had dared defile her shores in decades. So who would come here, and not even toward the small town, by off the rocks, as if they did not know where to moor? Whoever it was, they had lowered a small boat and begun to row toward her, perhaps having spotted her watching them from the rocks.

Well, then. Perhaps she needed to stop by her manse and dig up a transformation potion, just in case.

One dose was not enough, of course. If Kirke was to dream her way free of Zeus, she would need commit herself to the path with all her heart. Oh, she had seen the dark depths into which Nectar addiction had led Athene. She had seen it all and knew the price. But sometimes, the price was worth it, if it meant escape from the unendurable now.

"MY FRIEND *and his crew seek refuge and a place to repair their ship,"*
Pandora said, still holding Kirke's arm.

"My aunt has a village, nestled between the northern and southern
mountain ranges. It's the only place for a large ship to moor safely, and I
imagine, if they can pay, they can find food and supplies." Kirke gave
Pandora a firm squeeze, as much to reassure herself the woman was really
here as for Pandora's sake, before releasing her arm. "As for you, you must
come with me to my manse. Yeah, I imagine we've got at least a thousand
things to talk on. More, maybe, if we've had enough wine."

"The right vintage does tend to render even the most prosaic of topics
compelling," her companion said.

Pandora looked to him. "This is Odysseus, king of Ithaka, come of late
from the siege of Ilium."

A RUMBLE SHOT through the ground, and Kirke's footing slipped. She spilled
onto her arse, scraping it and no doubt tearing her peplos as she slid several
feet downhill. Her foot caught on a ledge, arresting her momentum and
keeping her from taking a tumble that looked several dozen feet down. Even
Ambrosia-strengthened bones might break from such a fall, and Kirke had
no desire to put them to the test.

Before she could rise, the mountain hiccuped. Pieces broke away,
collapsing inward. An entire pine tree tore loose, its trunk crashing down
mere feet away from Kirke with a deafening crash. She was shrieking, arms
over her face, as a rain of pine needles drenched her.

17

ATHENE

800 Bronze Age

*S*at before a fire, amid the gathered elite of Elládos, Athene watched as Achilles and his Myrmidons marched by, having sacked another town loyal to Ilium. Something in this man, the fiercest of the Elládosi, it sparked an unidentifiable memory within the depths of her. She found herself at once fascinated by the man's audacity—and as captivated by his prowess as those around her were—and repulsed by his capacity for brutality. The man was a tempest given form, the storm within him barely contained by his flesh, ever threatening to erupt into indescribable violence. Athene pitied the man's foes and counted her side lucky he fought for them rather than against, but she did not think she could ever find herself much in camaraderie with him.

Or maybe—a thought had surfaced too oft to be ignored—she saw in Achilles too much of the person she had once been, long ago, consumed with rage and given over to acts of terrifying vengeance and nigh inhuman malice.

Nevertheless, she had granted him Herakles's adamant sword and shield, for in Achilles, she had seen the one who might end this war. In him, she too had placed a great many hopes.

"Sometimes," Odysseus said, the Ithakan following her gaze, "I think I made a mistake to recruit the man." Odysseus was the son of Laertes, an Argonaut Athene had once provided with minor aid, as well, so she considered patronage of his family a bit of a tradition. "Agamemnon all but demanded Achilles, you know. He said, 'if his is the greatest sword in Elládos, then it is only meet it must serve the greatest general in our lands.' He said that. Called himself a great general." The Ithakan tore off a hunk of venison and gnawed it. "Me, I'm all for boasting as the need arises, of course. Well placed embell-ishment on a tale of one's deeds flavours the dish like a sprinkle of salt." Odysseus swallowed, obviously drawing out his words to play up to his audience. "Aye, but someone ought to have told our great king not to dunk the whole damn leg of mutton in the salt barrel."

Ajax chortled, then coughed, choking on his bite of venison and shaking his head. As the son of Telamon, he was, in fact, cousin to Achilles, though Athene had witnessed little familial bond betwixt them. Achilles, had, perhaps, grown up too far removed from his cousin for them to know one another well. Athene leant over and slapped a hand on Ajax's back, allowing him to dislodge the offending bit, which he hacked into the fire. The effort earned him a display of sparks as the grease from his mouth splattered in the flames.

Beside the man, ancient Nestor snickered, probably more amused by Ajax's suffering than Odysseus's wit. "Agamemnon gets wind of this kind of talk," he said to Odysseus, "you may find yourself charging those cyclopean walls, naked, with naught save your waggling arse for support." Nestor had sailed with the Argo himself and was far too old for this war, yet love of his fellows had brought him here. That and, Athene suspected, perhaps the preference to find death swift and glorious in one last battle rather than allow it creep upon him by slow degrees. The passing of years stole the dignity of

Men, a thief that returned to prey upon one with increasing frequency, and Athene could not spare them such indignities.

Odysseus shrugged. "Heretofore, I've found my arse supports me well enough. If yours is somewhat wanting, perhaps you ought not let the young boys abuse it so."

Athene cast Odysseus a weak glare for his vulgar humour and the man decided, abruptly, his meal required his undivided attention. "I know the months wear on here, and time has a way of abrading caution." No one could remain forever in a state of constant readiness, forever on alert for dangers. Neither body nor heart could endure unabating strain. And, too, Athene knew well enough the coarse joking was how men at war held to their sanity, though she preferred they keep it under control whilst she sat among them. "But do recall, we have reason to believe Apollon and Artemis themselves are within those walls. Just because they have not deigned to strike against us so far does not mean we can forget a real danger lies not so far away."

"Yes, Goddess," Nestor said, solemn, bowing his head.

Though her father demanded mortals refer to Olympians thus, ever since her exile, Athene had found worship disquieting. Once, when she had protested to Bellerophon she was no goddess, it had sparked in him such fierce indignation he'd rebelled against Olympus and thus gone to his death. It was a lesson she would never forget.

"Well," Odysseus said, "I think we can call the evening's mood slain, skewered, and well basted at this point. Perhaps best we were off to our beds."

ATHENE DID NOT KNOW what madness prompted Agamemnon to snub Achilles's pride, ten years into the war. Perhaps the king, the leader of this vast alliance, had grown so thick with hubris his ego could not abide that his men worshipped his champion more than himself. Perhaps the man simply needed others around him to suffer as a means of ensuring his dominance in every situation.

Either way, Agamemnon affronted the Phthian, Achilles retired from the field of battle, and the tide turned against the Elládosi. They might have broken, then, when the champions of Ilium rode against them, chariot wheels churning the dust into clouds of choking doom. As their spirits waned, perhaps they would have fled toward their ships and sailed for home, and part of Athene wanted to watch it happen. A decade of blood had spilled across these sands, and it had availed no one and naught. Helen had not been returned. Of course, Athene was never certain whether Menelaus missed his wife or merely resented the insult. Of Athene's father, she tended to think the latter emotion won out. Either way, Zeus had commanded the fall of Ilium, and Agamemnon's vain mistake in distancing himself from Achilles had left her with only two choices.

Now, Athene must drive the other champions of her people into the fray—no doubt the choice Father would have directed, though it would mean sending men like Odysseus and Nestor and Ajax to their deaths—or she must join it herself. Athene could not bear to watch those she had befriended here mount their pyres one by one. The thought evoked the wound that had become Herakles. It was an injury she knew now, after decades of watching it weep inside her heart, would forever remain raw and bleeding, incapable of receiving the healing boons time was meant to bestow upon it. Some blades bit too deep. Some wounds turned not to scars but to pains that became one with the person bearing them, defining a new reality with them.

In thinking to save Mankind through its heroes, she had let one after another of them into her soul, and one by one, she watched them fall to the final fate that lay ahead of all Men. Perseus and Bellerophon and Theseus and Jason and so many others, all dead now. All turned to ashes and blown away on uncaring winds. Herakles.

Herakles.

So, Athene had strapped on her panoply, trod among the Ellá-dosi, and stemmed the Ilian advance. Her people would not break this day. This day, she would not watch the burning of Odysseus or Nestor. Not of Ajax or his half-brother Teukros, nor Theseus's son Akamas, nor any of the others.

She had not, on donning armour and taking up arms, expected to find herself come face-to-face with her brother. Had he already begun wading among the melee, or had he joined it on learning of her taking an active role? Either way, a feral, lupine grin spread across his features as he trod toward her.

Bright blood and golden ichor were splattered so thick upon Ares's panoply Athene could scarce make out the bronze of it. His crimson cloak billowed behind him. Here stood one well aware of the striking figure he cast amid the carnage of a field strewn with uncounted dead and dying. But carnage was Ares's great love in life. No pleasure of the flesh or mind could compare, for Athene's brother, with his exultation at violence.

Perhaps that was how they had come to this.

Her brother traced lazy circles in the air with his burnished spear, scattering blood drops from the tip of it. He beckoned, taunted. He dared her to face him. Even with her fierce ally, Ares thought her but a stumbling block in his path. One he, clearly, delighted at the thought of removing.

Athene approached, cautious, her shield up, her xiphos at the ready.

Or perhaps Ares already knew Achilles had removed himself from this war. Perhaps that was why he'd deigned to show himself. Could it be that even the God of War feared the demigod son of Thetis?

In mirror of Ares's twirling of his spearpoint, Athene flicked the end of her sword, circling ever closer to her brother.

"Last we clashed," he drawled, "I seem to recall wedging a blade 'twixt the bones of your forearm, Sister." He giggled, obviously amused at the memory. "I assume it hurt, yes? Sharp, piercing, delicious *pain*." Ares managed to turn that last word into an almost ritualistic chant, an idol upon which even the God of War might lavish his worship.

Athene's gut clenched at the memory of such agony. "Perhaps I can offer you a demonstration if you find the idea so fascinating." She lunged, but he was fast, whipping that spearpoint up and driving her back.

His reach gave him an advantage, forced her to keep dancing away, blocking his probing strikes on her shield without ever drawing close enough to counter. But then, Ares had never been one for patience or the long game. When his repeated attacks failed to find her flesh, his strikes grew more frenzied, a reflection of his growing fury. Bestial wrath glinted in his lupine eyes. Her brother snarled, his overlong tongue lolling outside his mouth as he lunged in. With her aspis Athene beat his spear skyward and drove into the opening. Her blade racked across his cuirass, shearing bronze but failing to pierce the skin beneath.

Not slowing, Athene kicked out at his ankle in a move Artemis had taught her long, long back, when she'd been scarce a teenager. Her sandal collided with her brother's greave, driving his foot backward but failing to send him tumbling.

Athene pushed inward, thrusting with her xiphos. Ares leapt backward, his bound carrying him some thirty feet away, out of her reach. A chariot careened past her, obscuring the battlefield with its rising cloud of dust, and Athene cursed under her breath. "Leave this place!" she shrieked at Ares, not knowing if he even remained in earshot but pointing her blade in his last known direction, nonetheless. "Leave the Trojan shore before one of us must end the other!"

No answer came to her.

Still, things had changed. Now, Titans had crossed blades on this battlefield, and there was no going back.

18

____

HERAKLES

742 Bronze Age

Mopping sweat from his brow, Herakles leant against the plough, admiring the rivets he'd dug. Come the morrow he'd start the planting, a crop of barley. In truth, he wished he could begin today, but the day had begun to fail, and already twilight bruised the horizon. Still, he did not much fancy returning to the farmhouse to listen to Hyllus and his mother bickering once more.

That the grown woman so oft sunk to the petty level of the ten-year-old boy only made the situation all the more intolerable. In idle musings, Herakles imagined walking away from the home he'd built here, starting down the road, and wandering to wherever his feet should happen to take him.

No, but he'd sworn to Meleager's shade to care for Deianeira, and moreover, he would never abandon his son.

The soft squelch of sandals in mud had him turning to see

Athene approaching. His mother, on arriving to find him prepping for planting, had insisted on lending her hand in the fields and must now have finished work on her chosen plot as well. Tracks of sweat cut through the layers of grime matted upon her face and neck, her khiton stained beyond repair, though she paid little apparent heed to her state, her mouth quirked in hint of a smile.

"You've yet to tell me the reason for your visit," he said, pushing off the plough to meet her halfway.

His foster mother's face fell at once and Herakles felt a twinge of regret at having yanked her from the simple pleasures of life in the idylls. That she had not mentioned her purpose in coming here no doubt meant she avoided it with a will, and he, wanting some distraction from the woes of his house, had forced the issue on her.

Now Athene rubbed a rag over her face, though the effort more smeared the dirt than cleaned it. She stared at the cloth before tucking it inside the fold of her equally filthy khiton. The woman shook her head and stared off toward the fading sunlight.

"What is it?" Herakles asked, concerned now. Her reticence bespoke a real fear, and if she was worried, then he was worried. He strode toward her until he stood but a few feet away. "Mama?"

"Kyknus was not the only one of Ares's brood he's tempted with the flesh of Man." She failed to meet his gaze, and he knew why. Athene of all people knew Herakles had hung up his sword and shield and had not the least desire to embroil himself in conflict once more. Battle had a way of bringing out something dark as pitch that lurked in the hidden corners of his soul. There was a presence there, a chorus of voices urging him to surging heights of greater and greater carnage, and he dreaded the thought of wakening that presence once more. Idle fancies of wandering the roads aside, only the simple life of a farmer kept in check the baser movements of his soul, and he feared what he might become should he allow those movements to rise.

Already, he had begun shaking his head, denying her words. For more than a decade, he'd not needed to take up arms, and he'd no desire to do so now.

"I did not want to trouble you with this," Athene said. "I've long sought for my brother, but he hides himself from my efforts and my Sight alike."

Herakles shut his eyes. "You fear another Gigantomachy."

"Or worse."

Another Titanomachy? A battle that had nigh consumed the whole of Gaia, and Ares risked it by fomenting rebellion against his father. *What has this to do with me?* he wanted to protest, though he knew the answer. A second Titanomachy would unleash chaos not seen in Ages upon Elládos, and no one, man, woman, or child, could avoid the suffering that would follow. "You wish me to aid in the hunt for your brother." *Our brother*, he supposed, for Zeus was father to all three of them. "And should I find him?"

"In truth, I don't wish harm upon him ..."

"But if you bring him before Zeus, he will face an end worse than death," Herakles finished for her. He'd seen what his father had done to Kronos, to Tantalus. To Arke, who cast herself to her destruction because her mind could never recover from the horror of her imprisonment in Tartarus. He scrubbed a hand through his beard. "And yet if either of us strikes him down, we become kinslayers."

"I find myself at a loss," she admitted. "That, and somewhat short of allies at the moment. There are no other Olympians to whom I can turn now, and besides them and yourself, I cannot say who would survive conflict with the so-called God of War, should it come to that."

Herakles snorted. "You've a great deal of confidence in me to think I would."

"I do, yes. But if possible, I'd not send you to face him alone. Rather, I think we can double our efforts to find him, then send word to the other and try to subdue him together."

Herakles sighed. He'd have to hire someone to do the planting this year, and he'd been so looking forward to the simple labour of it.

"I would not ask this of you if I saw another way for it."

"I know." He clapt a hand on her arm in reassurance. "I know it."

What was it about swords that they seemed to refuse to remain sheathed? As if the possession of such an instrument conspired with Ananke to present one with the necessity for its use. And now he needed to explain to Deianeira and Hyllus why he'd be gone, mayhap for months.

❧

"Fine," Deianeira huffed, arms crossed over her chest. "Then you'd best bring me a present to make it worth the wait for you."

"A present?"

"You brought Admete the girdle of Hippolyta, and she wasn't your wife. I'd expect no less than the sandals of Hera!"

Across the room Hyllus groaned as though he was even more put out than his father at the preposterous request. Had he thought Deianeira jested, Herakles would have laughed.

Instead he worked his jaw, trying to find the words. "Ares is in hiding and Hera dwells upon Olympus. It is not likely I'll find the two of them together or otherwise be in any position to steal the queen's sandals."

"Fine. Then grab one of her famed peacocks from her peacock garden."

Herakles stared at her. "If I should happen to see one, I'll consider it." Maybe being on the road a while would have its charms after all.

❧

THE THUNDER of hooves set the ground atremble, felt as much as heard, forewarning of a near stampede of cattle surging through the valley beyond Oikhalia. A billowing cloud of dust obscured Herakles's views of charging beasts but gave more than enough indication of their direction for him to know they headed right for him. A Potency-infused leap and he caught a tree branch, heaving himself up into the boughs of a cypress. Before he'd so much as settled, the herd came crashing by, dust stinging his eyes and setting him into coughing fits.

As he blinked tears away, he caught sight of a horse-borne man passing below, driving the wild animals before him. It had been years since last Herakles had beheld Autolykus, and, had the demigod not paused below, gazing up at him in his hacking fit, Herakles might not have recognised him at all. But the old man cast him a wry grin followed by a shrug, as if to remind of his reputation for thievery.

"Eurytos's cattle?" Herakles wheezed.

Hermes's bastard winked, his mischievous smile bringing Herakles back to their days on the Argo, as if naught had changed in all the years since. "You've little love remaining for your erstwhile teacher, or so tale tells it now."

"Can't say I'd shed a tear for his losses, no," Herakles admitted.

"And yet I'd have sworn I saw a glistening in your eyes."

Herakles grunted. Damn dust.

He'd come here in pursuit of rumours over Ares scouting for an invasion of Elládos, keen to begin the overthrow of Olympus at long last. The small kingdoms around Mount Pelion were the first lands one would come to, after passing through Thermopylae and into Elládos. Whilst Herakles had already sent word to Athene, they needed to know with a certitude whether the God of War haunted these hills and valleys before they came together, and that meant hunting for his half-brother.

"I take it, then, Eurytos's betrayal of his oath is a well-known thing," Herakles said, leaping down from the boughs and landing beside Autolykus's horse. The animal snorted in surprise, though surely it must have heard him from above.

Autolykus eased the distressed mount a few paces away. "Lying's a keen skill, I'll be the first to admit. Done well, I'd name it pleasing as a night in the warm arms of an eager lass, in fact. Oathbreaking, though—that I don't hold with." He huffed. "More like the difference between trickery and foul treachery, I'd name that. Mayhap you'd even call it justice then I relieve the man of the burden of caring for so many animals."

"I might indeed call it that," Herakles admitted. "Though I

imagine were you to name it thus, it would be one more lie, or at least in no way your motivation."

The other demigod smirked. "You give me little credit."

That drew a snort. "I credit you a self-proclaimed liar and a thief. Another day, in another land, I might take it amiss, seeing you steal from a man so brazenly." He shrugged. "And yet, I've pressing matters elsewhere."

"Well, if you've come for retribution for woes wrought those years back, best hurry, lest Ares beat you to it."

"Ares?"

"Indeed. Oikhalia lays besieged, along with the neighbouring lands. May have something to do with how a whole herd remained nigh unguarded. Did I fail to mention it?"

Herakles blanched. Much though he loathed their father, Herakles cared for Iphitos and most especially Iole. Given free reign, Ares would let slaughter and death flow across the valley like wine in a symposium, untrammelled and ever calling for more of itself. "I need your horse."

"Poor thief I'd be, allowing myself to be robbed of my mount in the middle of my—"

"Now!" Herakles bellowed. "Hand her over and I never saw you here!"

Grimacing, Autolykus chewed on it before swinging his leg over the mare's withers to hop down and hand Herakles the reins. A heartbeat more Herakles considered asking the demigod for his aid, but Autolykus would never surrender his prizes, much less deign to risk his neck fighting Titans.

So Herakles leapt astride the mare and kicked her into motion.

૪

COLUMNS OF SMOKE further darkened the twilit sky, rising from a city aflame. Even over the stench of burning flesh and homes, he could make out the reek of blood and bowel. Of death and pain smeared across this valley like butter over bread. Sporadic screams punctuated the awful moment. Only scattered sounds of the clatter of bronze on bronze, for the battle was over and lost, and Eurytos's warriors broken. Those who still held weapons now fought only to preserve their lives and the lives of those they held even more dear.

Adamantine blade in hand, Herakles leapt from Autolykus's mare —she was no beast of war—and raced through the streets. Not pausing in his stride, a swipe of his blade cut through the spine of a Gígas as it hefted a club to finish off a man sprawled in the dirt. Herakles wished he had the time to stop and check on the fallen victim, but Eurytos's manse, too, was ablaze.

Iole.

Potency and Alacrity leant speed to his legs, his passage streaking wind behind him. With a bound he cleared the manse's wall and landed in the yard amid a pair of Gigantes who had pinned a serving girl between them. Each of them was gnawing upon one of her hands whilst the girl wailed in her unspeakable agony. Snarling, Herakles swiped his blade, disembowelling one Gígas. A twist shifted his momentum and he rammed his xiphos up between the ribs of the other abomination. The brute looked down on him, eyes wide as if it could not believe a Man might dare to strike, much less slay a Titan.

The mauled servant fell, clutching her mangled hands against her abdomen.

"Me, I like the knees first," chortled another Gígas, the sound coming to him even over the sound of the girl's sobs.

Looking, he spied two more of the twisted giants assaulting a fallen guard.

"Naw," the other said. "Knees are all bony. Naught goes down sweet like a plump, chewy arse cheek slick with blood."

Herakles spared a glance to the fallen girl. "I'll be back for you, I swear." It was all he had time for before he launched himself at the Gigantes threatening to eat the wailing guard alive. One of the Gigantes turned in time to catch a blade through its throat. Herakles kicked it in the chest, freeing his xiphos and sending the soon-to-be corpse hurtling away.

It got the other's attention, who rose from the guard, brandishing a rusted cleaver and licking his lips. "Wonder how your arse cheeks taste?"

Herakles growled.

The beast lunged, a powerful but clumsy swipe of that blade. Herakles twisted aside and the knife wedged into the side of the house. Herakles's xiphos took off the Gígas's arm at the elbow. As the giant gaped at the wound, Herakles lopped off its disbelieving head.

The fallen guard stared at him, trembling, hand to his side, blood trickling betwixt his fingers.

Herakles knelt to check the wound, prying away fingers as though dealing with a frightened child. Not fatal. Not if stitched and cleaned. "Get up. Get the girl." He pointed at the mauled servant. "She's much worse off than you. Flee to the nearest village."

More screams resounded inside the manse.

Something rose in him, akin to a chorus of screams, not of terror like those coming from within the walls, but of fury. A bitter indignation at the iniquities so rampant here. Voices, summoning up chaos and death in *answer* to chaos and death, demanding he respond in kind, repay suffering and sweep clean the foulness.

His hand closed around the hilt of his sword. Some distant part of his mind knew the guard had risen, half running, half crawling toward the fallen girl. But the better part of his vision narrowed, closed in upon the blazing manse and the horrors unfolding within.

With a roar—something so primal it came not from him but from the army of voices rising in his soul—Herakles surged upward, heaving shoulder-first through the wall. Mudbricks, already cracking in the heat of the flames, collapsed inward, spraying over lower stone foundations. Smoke clogged the halls, a choking, obscuring fog of it. With the sun setting, even the courtyard beyond offered scant illumination, and Herakles found himself stumbling, half-blind, into roiling madness.

Waves of heat washed over his skin, flames tickling his unprotected flesh. "Iole!" His screams devolved into coughing fits, smoke clogging his lungs. Hand warding his face against the flames, he pressed into the courtyard where, at least, the fumes had somewhere to escape to.

"Little brother," a voice said.

Herakles turned. Beheld Ares there, one hand holding a blood-slicked xiphos, the other hefting the head of Eurytos. At his feet lay the body of Iphitos, a spear rammed through the base of his spine.

"Herakles!" Iole shrieked. He knew her voice; it had to be her, though he could not spy her through the clouds of smoke and the growing darkness.

"Swear allegiance to me, Brother," Ares cooed, "and join my army. Become mine, and I may yet forgive the insult of your murder of my son."

Herakles advanced. "Your son attacked me, unprovoked. As you have done to these people." Iole. Where was she? His soul longed to search her out, and yet he dared not tear his gaze from Ares for a heartbeat. Not half a heartbeat. "Your crimes end here."

Athene had warned him not to try to face Ares alone. They had agreed to do this together. But he had murdered Iphitos. Would no doubt do the same to Iole. Unless Herakles stopped him now, this night. Unless he put an end to his brother's insanity.

The thought of becoming a kinslayer no longer rankled with quite such bitterness as once it had. Now, the time had come to do what he must. "There was no call for the madness unleashed here."

Ares chortled, a fell sound, thick with glee. "Now you know what befalls those who fail to swear their loyalty. Last chance, little brother."

Herakles raised his xiphos. "Hades shall feast upon your soul, even as your monsters have gorged themselves upon these people's lives."

The answer, if aught, seemed to please Ares, a wicked grin spreading over his visage. In a blur of motion, he hurled Eurytos's head at Herakles like a missile. Herakles batted it aside, but even as he looked up, Ares had vanished into the darkness, inhumanly fast.

Without warning, the courtyard wall exploded, thrown inward by the ram-like charge of three Gigantes surging for him. Potency fuelled his leap, and Herakles bounded upward, caught the rim of a balcony, and heaved himself onto the upper level. The sudden snorting and slap of feet upon protesting planks warned him of danger, and he cast himself aside even as another Gígas rushed him. This one swiped at him with ursine claws and Herakles barely twisted away, those razors raking along his back in the process.

Even so, he rammed his xiphos into the brute's kidney as it passed. As the Gígas convulsed, Herakles kicked his attacker square in the back, ripping free his blade and sending the Gígas crashing through the wooden balustrade.

The floor beneath him burst apart, and he plummeted to the lower landing in a crouch before Ares. The shadowed form of his brother came at him in a blur and all Herakles could manage was Steadfastness to harden his skin against the incoming blow. Ares's kick took him full in the face. Though Pneuma blunted the impact, the force of it sent him flipping end over end, the World become a whirling haze of flame and smoke. He smashed through a table in the kitchen and lay amid the kindling, dazed.

Rough hands seized his hair and yanked him to his feet, another Gígas looming up before him. The beast reared back for a wild blow. Herakles braced. As the punch surged forward, he lunged, caught the Gígas's fist, and with his Potency, twisted until the bones in his foe's wrist cracked. His attacker collapsed, squealing, to its knees. Herakles's other fist to its throat silenced its cries.

He bent to retrieve his fallen xiphos, but only closed his grip around the hilt when Ares once more appeared as if from nowhere, slamming into him, sending him hurtling back out into the courtyard. The blade once more skittered free, lost in the consuming darkness that had swallowed this growing inferno.

"Iole!" Herakles rasped, struggling to gain his feet again.

A woman shrieked somewhere within the house.

Though he launched himself in that direction, two Gigantes moved to intercept him. Instinct rose in him, more primal than any edifice of Man, deeper than the most feral of animals. It was an atavistic movement of his soul, guiding muscles on courses that seemed woven into the fabric of time, as though he had always stood here. His foes lunged, seeming almost languid in their motions. Herakles ducked and dodged, twisting around them without thought, without consciousness. Without conscience.

His fist burst a spleen whilst his other arm enwrapt that of a Gígas. With a yank, he jerked that arm from its socket. His foot kicked out a knee, then he gripped the creature's head and jerked it so far around vertebrae burst out through its neck. The other foe was on its knees, gawping at violence—its same beloved violence in which it had bathed and thrived—wrought with such awful finality upon its kind. Scarce pausing in his momentum, Herakles slapped hands upon both the creature's temples, cracking its skull and leaving it sprawling across the burning yard.

"Hades's cavernous arse ..." Ares swore, stepping from the shadows, blade in hand, gaze flitting back and forth betwixt his fallen comrades and Herakles.

Skeins of Herakles's consciousness struggled to pull free from the corybantic haze that clouded his sight. A distant part of his soul called for Iole, and he mouthed her name but could not bring his desperate need to aid her to the surface enough to give voice to his plea for her. Concussive waves of warrior instinct washed over him, had him turning to face his brother, though Herakles was empty-handed and Ares bore a xiphos.

Wisdom bade him flee, find a weapon, and, if possible, return with allies at his back, for Ares surely had more of his forces. But Herakles was not himself. Or rather, he was more than himself, he was now certain. The chorus of voices lurked inside him, compounding their instincts with his, their voices no longer audible and yet thrumming inside his bones, nonetheless.

Ares lunged, point of his xiphos screaming toward Herakles's face.

Herakles slapped his hands together. Impossibly, the blade shattered between them, shards flying wide like missiles. A heartbeat, Ares gaped at his sundered weapon, disbelief writ across his visage.

For who—Herakles realised in the distant part of his mind that remained his—had ever heard of such an absurd manoeuvre?

But his stupor ended even before Ares's, and Herakles swung, fist careening toward his brother's head. Ares blocked it upon his forearm, dropping the hilt of the ruined blade as he did so. The two of them fell into a bout of exchanges, Ares blocking Herakles's furious blows. His brother had been faster, had possessed stronger Pneumatikoi. And yet, Herakles felt the speed of his blows increasing with each passing heartbeat. Moves he had never practiced, never heard of, they came to him, and Ares could no longer turn aside his relentless assault. Ares was forced back until the house wall gave him no further space in which to retreat.

The echo of gongs as his fists collided with Pneuma-reinforced skin, over and over, his attacks finding ribs and biceps and gut and face. A raw, bestial scream tore from Herakles as he pummelled his brother. The impacts drove the Titan through the wall, crashing to the floor even as flaming rafters sputtered and snapped, calling down a rain of debris.

Arm raised against the cloud of ash and dust, Herakles pursued his fallen brother.

Then another scream cut through the haze of Herakles's battle frenzy, a woman's cry, desperate and terrified, the sound like ice water cast over his inflamed flesh and burning mind. Sparing Ares not another glance, Herakles raced toward the sound. It had come from behind the burning curtain of an inner wall, and thus he raced at the wall without hesitating and flung himself from it, landing in a roll.

He came up to find Iole—his adamantine xiphos in her hand— and a Gígas she had been attempting to hold at bay, both watching him in shock. And why not, for his tunic lay in tatters, smouldering against his Pneuma-reinforced skin. Blood and ash caked him, head to toe, and grime no doubt turned his face into some ker-like demonic visage. Glowering at the Gígas, he moved to Iole's side, easing the xiphos from her trembling hand and into his own.

The giant, unarmed, glanced down at the blade and apparently decided it seemed more damning in his hand than it had in Iole's, for it fell back a step. An incensed piece of his soul demanded he pursue the creature and deprive Ares of one more murderous cannibal soldier. But he'd not let Iole out of his sight now, not for aught in the world. Instead, he took her hand, and together they fled the smouldering ruin of her home.

WRAPT IN A BLANKET AND TREMBLING—MORE with unshed tears and mounting rage than cold, he thought—Iole crouched by the tiny campfire Herakles had built in the wood. "The bastard took everything," she said, an ache deep as the Thalassa underlying such a simple statement.

"I know." He sat beside her, daring to glance at a face that had little changed in the passing of years. Such pain lurked behind her eyes now, and he'd have given aught he owned to ease even a hair of it. To see her smile, to laugh, he'd have faced any labour set before him. Too, how he had loved the strange swap of loving barbs that oft passed between her and Iphitos, even if the siblings' exchanges had left him flustered and speechless. "Mayhap ... it may help to speak to them. To say the things that ought not remain unspoken. The dead linger nigh to us, a time, and may yet bear witness to your final address." This he knew, for surely those years in which he had beheld his children by Megara meant it truth. They were gone now, but he had to believe they had walked beside him during his travails.

But Iole did not speak. She sang. It rose from her, slowly at first, a whisper, rising into a haunting threnody. Her song lamented the loss of brother and father stolen from her too soon, even as it bade them move on to their rest, in sunlit Elysian fields, where a gentle breeze would forever ruffle meadows of asphodels. Herakles did not know if such a place existed for the dead. Whatever he had beheld of the Underworld was all darkness and pain and loss, but perhaps, somewhere beyond the reach of Hades, some happy few souls found peace.

Mayhap, he dared hope, such was where now dwelt Kreontiades and Therimachus and Deikoon.

When at last her song trailed off, tears now streamed down Iole's face, and yet relief seemed to have eased her grimace, as though the sending of souls lifted her burdens as well. Her glistening eyes met his. Then she crawled closer until her breath warmed his face.

How long he had thought of that face, of those eyes, looking up at him. How oft he had cursed her father for his treachery in denying them the chance to wed, though they had both chosen one another. And now, here, with her looking at him thus ...

He cupped her chin in his hand, her skin so soft beneath his calloused grip.

Unbidden, Deianeira's haughty, childish glare flashed into his mind. Herakles had never betrayed his wife, leastwise not with his body, though he could not account for his heart.

Iole rose higher, her lips pressed against his, soft and sweet and desperate and pained.

Any thought of Deianeira burnt away in the fire of his passion for her. Herakles wrapt his arms about Iole and eased her down beneath himself.

"I FIND MYSELF IMAGING," Iole said, as they trudged along the beaten path toward Herakles's farm, "how astoundingly thrilled your wife shall be when you arrive at her home with your new mistress. My mouth salivates already in anticipation of the casserole she must surely serve as hostess. Admittedly, the recipe—which no doubt includes my eyes for filling—leaves somewhat to be desired, but alas, what can one do?"

Herakles kicked at a loose rock as he plodded, huffing. "Lots of men have concubines," he ventured with all the conviction of a self-righteous limpet.

"And me, I'm left wondering whether concubine qualifies as a step up or a step down from mistress."

He cast a wary glance her way. "I ..."

She quirked at brow at his discomfiture, enjoying it far too much for his liking. Not that she didn't have a point. Already, he could feel blood dripping from his ears at Deianeira's impending tirade. Mayhap he ought to have sent Iole ... somewhere else. But for the life of him, he could not think where she would find safety and refuge, and besides, the thought of parting from her again left his gut feeling like he'd swallowed a draught of drakon venom.

"Peace, warrior," Iole said. "Don't pull a muscle in your head striving for an answer when we both know you shan't find one. Regardless, the woman might not call for my eyes anyway. I imagine your stones might also fit well into her cooking."

"Deianeira is not much of a cook."

"Well, don't tell me she'll expect us to eat those things raw. Even skewered over a spit would be better than—"

Herakles winced at the mental image. "Please stop, I implore you."

Iole snickered. "Not even settled in, and already I've learnt the means to make my man beg. A mark of pride, if ever there was one, Hera be praised."

The mention of his father's wife only further intensified the sour roil of Herakles's gut. They made it little farther before he spied Hyllus, come running down the road to meet them. Maybe the boy had spotted them from atop a hill and come on his own? No, but there, in the distance well beyond, Deianeira stood, arms across her chest. So far off, Herakles could not make out her face, but her posture spoke volumes. Word had reached her that Herakles returned, and with another woman. Would her having had time to let her rage simmer make things worse, then?

Yes, he imagined it surely must, and for a heartbeat he considered seizing Iole's hand and pulling her to a stop. It was an idle fancy, this idea of running from this place and never looking back. But he could not break his oath to Meleager to look after his sister, and he could *never* abandon his son. This Herakles knew, even as he allowed himself a moment to indulge in the mental image of escape.

Instead, he strode forward to meet Hyllus, embracing the ten-year-old boy who rushed into his arms and squeezed hard. Then the boy pulled back, looked to Iole, and cast a quizzical glance at Herakles. So whatever Deianeira knew she had not quite made plain to their son.

"War captive?" Hyllus asked.

Herakles grimaced, for no doubt men across Elládos would think it. They would claim he'd taken the princess of Oikhalia to punish her father's treachery and warm his bed. Men ever thought the worst of one another, and oft enough proved right in doing so, though he preferred to tell himself the situation had shades of grey. "A friend I saved from war, rather. Battle spreads in the east."

Battle that would come here sooner rather than later, he imagined. Still, Ares had taken a beating and would need time to nurse both wounds and wounded pride. He, Herakles dared hope, would think twice before moving on mainland Elládos knowing it would mean facing Herakles again, to say naught of Athene, Hermes, and Zeus himself.

"Yes, we heard you were victorious over raiders," Hyllus said, shrugging a satchel off his shoulder. "Mother prepared a gift for you in celebration of your homecoming."

A gift? Honey instead of vinegar was a new tack for Deianeira, but Herakles would scarce complain. Opening the parcel, he found inside a fresh tunic, dyed so vibrant a cobalt he imagined it must have come from Phoenikia. Such garments cost more than most men could earn in a year, and certainly more than Herakles had thought their small farm could afford.

"Hera's sparkly tits," Iole swore. "I'd say your wife loves you."

Though he'd have preferred the princess not speak thus in front of Hyllus—neither the profanity nor the implication he'd doubted Deianeira's heart—Herakles found it hard to argue. And if he was to have peace in his home, he could scarce shun such a gift. He yanked free his tattered, grime-streaked tunic and slipped the new one over his head. The soft weave was luxury well beyond what he was accustomed to, and Herakles felt a mite *uncomfortable* from such *comfort*.

Also, despite the softness of it, it kind of itched.

"Let us see your mother, then," he said to his boy and started down the road, Iole and Hyllus in tow. Deianeira, too, had begun to stride toward him, though he thought perhaps he saw a tremble in her shoulders. Nerves?

Hades's crotch, his skin itched. Still, he dared not remove the tunic for fear of offending his wife. Maybe a good wash would solve the issue. A swim later?

"You come from the northern lands?" Hyllus asked Iole.

"North of here, anyway," she said. "Around Mount Pelion, ever in the shadow of its greater brethren."

Herakles's shoulder blades felt aflame now. A chill sweat streaked down his chest. His legs felt weak, his steps wobbling, feet no longer obeying.

"Herakles?" Iole asked.

"Papa?"

Herakles slipped to one knee, overcome by waves of enervation. His flesh did not merely itch, it felt as though he'd been doused in a vat of acid. Like ... like when Ladon's blood had washed over him in the Garden of the Hesperides.

By now, Deianeira had reached him, and she stood above him, glaring down, weeping and sniggering at once. "You thought I wouldn't know you bring a whore to my doorstep!" she shrieked.

"Mother!" Hyllus cried.

Beside Herakles, Iole stepped forward. "What have you done to him, bitch?"

Herakles's wife's lunge came fast. He tried to rise, tried to stop her, but all his strength had left him and his efforts cost him, sending him spilling sideways into the dirt. Deianeira collided with Iole, burying a knife in her gut.

"Worse than I do to you, cunt," Deianeira snapped. "You get off easy."

"No ..." Herakles moaned.

"Mother!" Hyllus wailed once more. "What have you done?"

"And you!" Deianeira whirled on Herakles. "I always knew you might one day betray me. Thus did I keep the blood of Nessus stowed, tainted as it was by your foul black arrow."

Nessus ... the centaur ...? Herakles's mind was not working. His skin felt as though he waded through a river of lava. The centaur he had poisoned with the blood of the hydra ... it was ... on the tunic? But whence had the priceless garment even come from ... Surely some enemy must have granted it to her. Ares? Another centaur?

His thoughts ran all ajumble.

He had to escape this burning torment.

Still on his side, Herakles wriggled, struggling to yank the hateful fabric from his body. As though melded to his skin, it clung. With a heave, with what little Pneuma he could muster, he tore it free, the flesh of his torso ripped away along with it. Cobalt had turned wine-dark, stained with his blood as he cast it aside, exposing raw, bleeding sinew. Veins of black putrescence streaked through his chest, like worms burrowing their way toward his heart.

Herakles wailed in agony, lacking the strength to do more than wallow in convulsions. From the corner of his eye, he saw Hyllus tackle his mother. He tried to roll toward them, to warn his son against kinslaying. All he managed was a wet, gurgling scream, coughing out bits of his liquifying innards.

Like this? The thought arose, almost indignant, that, after all the monsters he'd slain, he would die at the hands of his wife. *Like* this? A bitter irony crept in upon him, even over the unending torture wracking him.

Face, neck, and tunic awash in blood, Hyllus knelt before him, knife in hand. Herakles could not see if he'd slain Deianeira to get that knife.

"Papa ..." Tears streamed down the boy's face, washing rivets through the blood. "Papa?"

There was no surviving this. Mayhap, had he Ambrosia ... Or perhaps not even then. And it mattered little since he was no Titan to have a ready supply of their golden tonic. Once, his adoptive mother had saved him from draconic venom. Not this time.

"It's time ..." he managed, a wet wheeze.

"Papa ..." Hyllus repeated, hands trembling as he brought the knife toward Herakles's heart. The boy hesitated. Of course he did, for such an act must surely rip one's soul in twain.

But Herakles had not the strength to ask again.

And at last, in the child's eyes, Herakles could see his boy knew that.

INTERLUDE: ACHILLES

800 Bronze Age

A palisade warded the Myrmidons' camp on the Phrygian shore, its gate guarded by Achilles's fierce warriors. Along the perimeter of this wall he drifted, noting but little caring how the moon silvered the sea around his ships, though he knew his people felt the calling to sail from here. Home beckoned them, but Achilles would never leave this shore, of that he was now certain. Mother had warned him, long years back, and the invisible chains of Ananke had tugged his limbs where the Moirai willed.

Sleepless, he wandered, for what Man could welcome sleep when so beset? He could not hope for the reprieve of slumber when life itself had shifted into the liminal spaces betwixt waking and dreams. In grief, one walked in empty places, riven of light and colour, become like a shade. The dead, if one loved them dear enough, dragged pieces of the living down into the shadows alongside them. Sometimes, Men could climb their way back, gaze once more upon the sunlight, and praise the gods their time upon Gaia had not yet ended. But sometimes, he thought, grief became as weighty as the chains of Fate, and the path back toward light became an insurmountable slope.

All that remained to Achilles now was to amble, dolorous and broken, toward the inevitable end Fate had ordained for him. Each time his circuit brought him past Patroklus's pyre—burnt down to ash now, the last cinders stirred by the breeze—his forlorn state was reinforced once more. There was no way back for him; only the road that led deeper into the heart of those shadows clamouring for him now.

Thus did he come across the hunched figure approaching across a band of moonlight, cloaked and out of place before the Myrmidon camp. Should the man step before the gate, a pair of warriors would no doubt seize him, and from the furtive way the man glanced about, perhaps he knew that. An assassin, come to bring Achilles to his ignominious end? Part of him would welcome it, though he could not bring himself to present his throat without defending himself.

Well, Achilles could see why King Priam would send an assassin to avenge the slaughter and dishonour Achilles had visited upon his favoured son. But if that was the case, he ought to have sent more than one. More than ten, in truth. More than a hundred, though such a war band could never hope to rely upon stealth.

Brazen, almost daring to hope the man had the prowess to challenge him—though Achilles had already cut down Ilium's greatest champions—Achilles strode for the figure. The man stood taller at his approach and threw back his hood. Grey hair spilled about shoulders stooped by age and grief. Though Achilles had never seen him before, the diadem upon his brow made plain he looked upon King Priam himself. For the space of a heartbeat, Achilles imagined the king had come to avenge his son with his own two hands. Vain as such a gesture would prove, he could respect it.

Instead, on reaching Achilles, Priam dropped to the sand and threw his arms around Achilles's knees, planting shameful kisses upon them, upon Achilles's hands. Pensive, as broken as Achilles himself, Priam gazed up into his face, his sorrow landing like a blow on Achilles's heart. "You ... so blessed by the gods, Achilles." Priam's voice shook, the whole man seeming turned brittle ostraka ready to shatter at the slightest touch. "When you look upon me, upon my silver hairs, I beseech you to see the same silver as graces your father's head. Think of his venerable face, his trembling limbs, my equal in all save my anguish."

Peleus had grown aged, it was true, last Achilles had seen him, and that was more than ten years ago. Though he'd thought himself incapable of feeling any more pain than already he did, still it sat ill to think of his father reduced to such a state. But then, soon enough, Peleus would learn of his son's death, even as Priam had.

"I was there, more than seven decades back, when your father came here, alongside Herakles. When they slew my father, King Laomedon, and my brothers too. They spared me back then, only so I could come to such grief now. So I ask you to spare me as your father did. Spare, at least, the dignity to *bury* my son."

His words, soft and pained, struck like repeated slaps across Achilles's face. In his wrath, born of his grief, he had crossed all bounds of propriety and compassion. He had denied Hektor's kin their right to cleanse his body, to see his soul across the Styx. For such, Achilles not only welcomed his impending demise, but he also *deserved* it.

"Take him," Achilles rasped. "I will have one of my men grant you use of my chariot."

LIKE A HERALD OF DOOM, word had come with the tide of the abduction of Helen, famed daughter of Zeus and wife of Menelaus. He and Patroklus had returned from tutelage with the centaur Kheiron, but their homecoming brought him little peace. It was as if Achilles could feel the skein of his life pulled taut up hearing such news, and he found himself wandering bilious and distracted, though he could not explain to Patroklus his reasons. Whilst he had never demonstrated any propensity for the Sight like his mother, still, he could not help but feel a fearful portent, as of some looming intuition beyond the edge of his perception.

Without a word, his mother's visage confirmed it, when she came to him upon the seashore, bedraggled and dripping with seawater, eyes red, though the waves had washed away any tears she might have shed.

"What's happened?" Patroklus demanded of her, bold and brash in so addressing a Titan, a trait Achilles loved in him.

Thetis cast a scornful glance toward Achilles's friend before looking back to him. "There was an oath sworn on the marriage of Helen, that, should any move against her husband, the other suitors will come to his aid."

Patroklus groaned, as though some faded memory were suddenly varnished into blinding clarity. "I ... I was there, as a boy. I saw them, the mighty kings and aristoi of many poleis across Ellládos. But ... word was Helen was taken by the Ilian prince, Paris. It was hardly the intent of the oath to—"

"Agamemnon of Mykenai cares little for the *intent* of reckless oaths," Thetis snapped. "His brother's wife ran off with another man, and he names it abduction and thus it becomes a pretence for his wars. He thinks to conquer and loot Ilium and enrich his coffers, and perhaps in the process become king of half of Ellládos. He calls the men to fulfil their oaths, and they gather in a fleet unlike any raised afore now. Your father, he has told them of your prowess, thinking this the chance I foretold for your glory. And it is, though he forgets I also warned it would be your end, though your name would echo through eternity." Her voice caught upon those final words.

Mother had never been much for affection, and Achilles fought down the urge to go to her, to embrace her and still her fears.

"You were the only boon that ever came from my marriage to Peleus," she said. "I'll not see you dead on any account. Whatever we must do, we shall hide you from the eyes of warmongering aristoi until they have sailed off where they will."

Achilles folded his arms over his chest, noting that, even as his father had decided his future for him, so too did Mother make choices without consulting his desires. Parents, he supposed, cut and shaped their children out of pieces of their flesh and souls, and thus thought themselves as entitled to rule them as they were their limbs. Since no one had ever asked which choice he'd have made—a bitter, hard choice betwixt a short life of glory and a long life of insignificance—he'd never been forced to settle on the matter. Even now, he could not have said for certain on which side the coin would have landed, had he tossed it.

"I will take you to Skyros," Thetis said. "King Lykomedes has agreed to keep you in his care, concealed from the hungry eyes of those who see you dragged to the war."

Patroklus shook his head. "We cannot conceal the presence of a handsome prince among the court of Skyros." *Handsome, am I?* Such came as news to Achilles. "Word will spread of his presence, and his father has made certain half Elládos knows he's the fastest with a sword this land has seen in generations."

Achilles's mother sneered at his friend. "Yes, well, they won't take much note of a new *girl* serving as the princess's handmaid, will they? Men only notice women when they want something of them."

Now, Achilles cleared his throat. "You want me to avoid war by dressing as a woman?"

The stare his mother fitted him with brooked no argument, and yet, he could only imagine his father's face should he ever learn the truth.

MAYHAP, had Achilles never gotten Princess Deidamia with child, Odysseus would not have heard the rumours, tracked him down, and shamed him into joining the war. Both Thetis and Deidamia's father had thought little of the princess, if they believed she'd not discover her handmaid was, in fact, a boy, much though Achilles had amused himself trying to pitch his voice in feminine tones. Had King

Lykomedes thrown Achilles in with his daughter, rooming them in adjacent chambers even, out of naivety?

Rather, years later, Achilles now suspected it had been a ploy to mingle the king's bloodline with Achilles's demigod blood and thus fortify the royal claim on Skyros. Indeed, perhaps he'd also hoped to claim Achilles as a husband for his daughter—and might well have done so, had Odysseus not showed up to interrupt the engagement. Sometimes, Achilles wondered if the incident had given Agamemnon the idea of luring Iphigenia to Achilles with a false wedding, or if the king of Mykenai had done so to grind salt in Achilles's wound. He'd known, Achilles now realised, that Achilles could not protest overmuch without revealing his apparent cowardice.

On such musings, alone in his tent, Achilles lay awake. Once, he'd have confided in Patroklus. Now his friend's blanket lay as empty as Achilles's heart.

Had he spurned Deidamia's advances, maybe Patroklus would now live. Or perhaps, shamed by rejection, Deidamia would have seen him cast out, regardless. Sometimes, it felt as though Ananke conspired against him.

Or maybe that was but a means of abrogating his responsibility for all that had transpired. Had he heeded Odysseus's pleas to return to the war, Patroklus would not have gone in his stead.

Mother had foretold this war would prove Achilles's undoing. Avenged upon Hektor, he had but to await the fulfilment of that fate. She would have bid him leave these shores, now. But to what end? All life's joys had turned to ashes, tumbling between his fingers. There was no reason left to endure.

All he need find now was a foe strong enough to overcome him. And if no such foe existed amid Men, well, even the gods themselves had a hand in this wretched war.

❧

THEY COULD NOT BREACH the great cyclopean walls of Ilium, but they would force the Ilians to sally forth to meet them in battle. Or such was Agamemnon's strategy when his ships landed upon Trojan shores. They raided and conquered every polis and town under Ilium's domain. Achilles alone had captured eleven cities for the king of Mykenai.

From among the slaves taken, the Elládosi had awarded him the black-haired Briseis, widowed and orphaned by his hand. The girl was cousin to the slave taken by Agamemnon, though Khryseis had been abducted from Apollon's temple outside Ilium itself. Perhaps, the men thought in giving Achilles the kin of Agamemnon's slave, they honoured him. Or perhaps they thought to still the simmering resentment that had brewed betwixt them since those first days, when the king had murdered his daughter and used Achilles to do it.

As if it was that he had not received a wife that day which vexed Achilles.

Briseis sat upon the ground in Achilles's tent, arms about her knees, eyes lit with affronted pride and no little fear, though he had sworn to her that he would not force himself upon her. He had promised her, in fact, he would ensure no man laid an unwelcome hand upon her body. Achilles knew well what most of the warriors did with their captured female slaves. They expected them to cook and sew and tend their clothes, yes, and to warm their beds. Sometimes they traded slaves when bored of one, and it was not unheard of for men to expect to share in the charms of women thus taken. But it would not happen in the Myrmidon camp, of that Achille was resolved.

He could only imagine how much the thought of lying with him or any among the Myrmidons must appeal to Briseis, given Achilles and his men had slain everyone she had ever loved.

That odd combination of fear and defiance in her face spoke to the depths of him. It was not pity, he thought, stirring in him, and certainly not lust, but rather some other undefinable connection. Some threads were so thin that to even name them was to risk snapping them, and so he did not seek to define what he felt for the girl.

It had been days, and still she refused to speak. Not that he could blame her.

Patroklus ducked through the tent's flap, returning with steaming bowls of soup from the cook fire outside. The first he handed to Achilles, or tried, but Achilles motioned for his friend to give it to the girl.

"Eat," Achilles said. "I've sworn you safe here."

"Easy words," she spat, though she accepted the bowl from Patroklus.

Achilles's friend rocked back, shaken, perhaps, that she finally deigned to speak to them.

Achilles sighed. "I know it offers scant comfort, but I had no particular desire to slay your husband or your kin. In truth, I bear no ill will toward any Phrygians, save perhaps for Paris, who brought us all to this unhappy war." Or gave Agamemnon the excuse to wage it, at least.

"Really?" She set the bowl upon the ground and fixed him with her impassive gaze. "You know that offers no comfort, do you? That it, in fact, fails to balm my grief to hear you murdered everyone I cared for with all the emotion of a butcher slaughtering swine? That's good, then, that you know it. Otherwise I might think myself enslaved to an addlepated imbecile." Patroklus groaned, but Achilles quirked a smile at that. "Well and good. Glad to know it wasn't personal for you." Her feigned indifference melted like butter cast into a simmering cauldron, wrath now darkening her face. "It was some-what personal for *me*."

Achilles shut his eyes, trying not to flinch. What was he to say to that? That such was the way of war? That he'd not even wished to join this war? Such words would be as empty as the others.

"Today," Achilles began, "Agamemnon was forced to return your cousin to her father. He came some days back to ransom her, but the king refused him, priest of Apollon though he was. You've heard, no doubt, about the plague ravaging the other war bands? The augurs claim it Apollon's wrath, and so the king was left no choice save to return Khryseis to the temple." In truth, Achilles had been the one to force the issue, and he'd taken no little pleasure in spiting Agamemnon his prize. Besides, he'd hoped it would offer some measure of comfort to Briseis, knowing her cousin had escaped this life.

If it eased her mind, she gave little sign of it.

So Achilles left her alone to eat and, with Patroklus, took to inspecting his ships, fancying that he could still sail from these hateful shores. He liked to indulge in such thoughts, though he knew it impossible. It would rain shame upon him and the Myrmidons and, worst of all, upon his aged father, should he flee before the war was won. Even accounting for his mother's prophecy. Achilles had come to Ilium knowing it would mean his death.

He turned to Patroklus and sighed. "Should I fall ..." *When I fall, rather.* "Should I fall, see to it Briseis is safe. Wed her if she will have you but see her taken away from here at least. I made her a promise, and I'll see it kept, even ..."

"Even when your mother's foretelling comes to pass." Bitterness, thick as tar, dragged upon Patroklus's words. Achilles's friend had counselled them to leave, honour be damned. But Achilles *couldn't.* He could not do that to his father. Peleus wanted a son whose name would echo through the halls of history, and Achilles would give him that. He would not be remembered as the craven who fled the war. Patroklus heaved a great sigh, the wind blew all out of him. "I'll see to it."

Achilles knew the words must have pained him.

The day stretched on, and soon he spied Erastus scurrying toward the ships. The Myrmidon's face was streaked in sweat and, beneath it, dread. Achilles raced up the gangplank to meet him. "Battle again?"

"No, my prince." Erastus panted, making plain he'd run straight from the camp. "Agamemnon entered our gates in force. The king claimed, if he could not have his prize, you too would be denied yours."

Hollowness opened in Achilles's gut. "What?" But he already knew. Agamemnon had lost Khryseis, so he had stolen her cousin Briseis to replace her in his bed.

Growling, he leapt from the gangplank and charged toward the Mykenai camp. Agamemnon would pay for this affront, with his blood if need be. Not only did he shame Achilles in stealing a prize lawfully awarded to him, but his actions would mean Achilles had broken his oath of protection to Briseis. That, he would never abide.

Before he reached the Mykenian palisade, an iron grip seized his elbow and yanked him around. He was spun to face grey-eyed Athene, who shook her head in solemn denial of his plan.

"I cannot let this stand," he objected.

The Olympian's mouth creased in sympathy, but again she shook her head. "If you strike down the king of this alliance, the Elládosi will falter."

"I have not a single desiccated turd to offer for what happens to the Elládosi," he bellowed.

She seized him by the back of the head, fingers tangling in his hair as she pulled him up unto his toes, though he still could not meet her height. "There is more at stake here than your pride. Troy must fall, Achilles."

"He will force himself upon her." Such words damned all other arguments.

"No." Athene's face darkened. "I'll not allow that. Not that. I have a draught I can give her. Mixed in his wine, it will leave him flaccid and no doubt shamed, as well he deserves for this. But nor can I let the alliance break."

Achilles jerked free of her grasp. "I will no longer fight his war."

"Achilles ..."

"No! No Myrmidon spear shall be raised in defence of Elládos until Agamemnon comes to me on his *knees* and restores Briseis to me!"

Athene groaned. "Let his private shame be enough—"

"On his *knees!*"

Achilles stormed off. For there was naught more to say. The Elládosi would bleed and die for Agamemnon's affront. They would suffer and grieve until, in their rank desperation, the king's men forced him to come begging to Achilles. Only then, only *then*, would Achilles win this war for Agamemnon.

ILIUM's vaunted champion lay dead and buried, and still the city's cyclopean walls yet stood, inviolable. The Elládosi had granted the Trojans twelve days to mourn. Even now, once the allotted time had expired, they had made few sallies against the Elládosi, and Agamemnon had claimed their spirits broken. Odysseus had ordered construction of great ladders to scale the walls, and Achilles had begun to wonder if, now that he at last sought his death, Fate spurned him with the bitterest of ironies.

Then, before the ladders were ready, before the Elládosi had reached the walls, the Ilians had poured forth in a last, desperate charge. Achilles had ridden to meet them, driving his chariot now. To his shock, they had converged, not on the Elládosi army behind him, but on *him*. Hundreds of Trojans, all screaming for his blood.

He'd slain a half dozen with his javelins, but on they came, so thick a mass of bodies even his chariot could not pass. They snared his horses and dragged them to the ground, the animals shrieking as lances pierced their flesh. Achilles kicked off the rim of his chariot, flipped over his accosters and landed in their midst.

That was when that fearsome instinct had arisen in him, stronger than ever before. That was when death had become a dance, its steps well worn into the memories of his muscles. Twist and flow, pivot and sway, and men died around him. His sword severed tendons. It snaked around spear and shield to bite in the joints where even fine panoplies left exposed flesh. His shield crashed into the bridge of noses.

Blood flowed in raging torrents, and ever the dance to that music of voices in his head. Mounds of bodies arose, piled high, until he had to scale them, flitting about the battleground in leaps and bounds. Only the bare fringes of thought intruded upon his cory-bantic frenzy. Until, at last, he looked about himself and saw not men but fields of charnel strewn before the walls of Ilium like the last gasp of a dying behemoth.

Only then did he realise the Elládosi army had faltered, not joining him in the fray, gaping at the carnage he had wrought among the Ilians.

"Impossible ..."

He heard the word repeated, over and over, spreading through the throng, until it took on the ritual intonation of a prayer. As if his people, on seeing a Man—even a demigod—fell an army needed to invoke the gods in warding.

And as if summoned, one came, wading amid the gore as though passing through the soothing waters of a hot spring, his silver armour smeared crimson. Ares tossed aside his horsehair helm and grinned, exposing canine fangs, eyes seeming luminous. "Only once before have I ever beheld such glory in battle. Such unparalleled destruction begs *worship*." The God of War somehow infused the word with lascivious undertones that had Achilles's skin crawling.

This was what he had sought, was it not? A god to come and strike him down and release him from the mountain of grief that had settled upon his back, crushing the air from his lungs. But that primal instinct in him had not yet subsided, and now it rose afresh, one voice in the chorus drowning out the others until it poured from his throat. Until his limbs moved of their own accord, as though guided by a foreign power deep in his core.

"Then come, Brother," Achilles said. "Let us finish what we began in the palace of Oikhalia, so long ago. Even Gaia herself wearies from the oppressive tread of your sandals upon her back." Though Achilles could not understand his own words—did not know whence they came—he felt the primal truth of them as he advanced on Ares.

And the God of War, the fearsome Olympian, *quavered*, gawping at the demigod who thus addressed him. Achilles raced forward, kicking off a pile of bodies to fly at the god. Ares recovered in an instant, his sudden movement a blur of speed as he twisted aside and raised a shield to block Achilles's thrusting xiphos. The adamant blade clanged, gouging the bronze of the Titan's aspis. Ares yanked his shield to one aside, tearing the sword from Achilles's grip, even as he thrust with his blade, intent to skewer him.

Achilles turned, inside the Titan's reach, his elbow colliding with

Ares's jaw as he caught the god's wrist. He locked his ankle around Ares's and heaved, flipping the god over his shoulder and sending him sprawling. Ares lost his grip upon his xiphos and Achilles snatched it out of midair. Blade-first, he lunged to impale the prone god.

Shocked though he no doubt was, Ares still managed to fling himself aside with blinding speed, sweep up a fallen spear, and bring it to bear. Achilles avoided his thrust, caught the haft, and surged forward, relentless in his attacks. Ares was forced to abandon that spear and grab another, ever falling back.

Though a distant part of his mind wanted to spew taunts at the retreating Olympian, whatever dark portion of Achilles's soul had seized control of his body had no further desire to speak. Rather, it moved him with implacable fury and singular purpose, hacking through Ares's defences until fear began to limn the god's visage.

Ares had gained a new sword, though he'd lost his ruined shield. Blade out before him, the god parried Achilles's next thrust. Then he leapt, bounding upward as though weightless, primed to fly away. Achilles jumped too, swinging his aspis like a discus. The shield's rim caught Ares in the gut and sent him crashing back down to Gaia.

Before the god could rise once more, Achilles planted a sandal upon his armoured chest. Then he rammed his xiphos into Ares's throat, striking vertebrae and punching through.

That frightful aspect of his soul that had guided his limbs at last withdrew, and Achilles staggered, woozy and disbelieving of what he'd just done. An Olympian lay dead at his feet. An *army* lay dead before him.

Something struck him in the back, like being kicked by a horse. The impact had him stumbling forward. Then he looked down and saw the silver-tipped arrow protruding from his chest. All strength fled him and he collapsed to his knees. An Ilian chariot careened around, circling him.

Paris drove the chariot, but it was the silver-eyed goddess Artemis beside him who'd loosed that arrow. In those argent eyes, in that grim face, he saw a terrible wrath, a mirror of the fury that had overcome him upon the death of Patroklus.

Of course. Because rage begat rage. In that instant, he knew his apoplexy had served but to fuel her, though he would never know the details.

The World turned to grey, clouded.

Achilles pitched face-first into the blood-soaked dirt.

PART IV

Spellsongs seem to create some kind of harmonic resonance with the nature of reality, allowing the singer to somewhat reshape the World to his desires, although so doing ravages the singer's Pneuma. Theoretically, with sufficient knowledge of both the songs and of the World itself, the applications might prove almost limitless. And while we are certainly justified in delving into these mysteries, we might wish to ask ourselves whence came this tome that has begun to unlock the cosmos.

— Fifth Chronicle of the Circle of Goetic Mysteries

19

ENODIA

46 Bronze Age

*I*n bestial rage, Dionysus hurled from Thebes, an army of dryads arising from sylvan depths in answer to the livid cry he sent thrumming through the Ether. They came, his moss-drenched, bark-skinned followers, skittering over the woodland like lizards, vines and creepers bursting from the ground in herald of their arrival.

In the Mortal Realm, Sight attuned to the Penumbra, Enodia stood, awaiting their coming.

Given the choice, Enodia would not have met such an onslaught within the forest, and yet, her only alternative would have been to march on Thebes and launch mass slaughter among the possessed Maenads in the god's thrall. In such chaos, she could not predict what might follow. Better to strive here to delay and weaken the sylvan deity, even if it meant confronting him within his domain.

The dryads, like all eidolons, existed incorporeally, possessing mortal hosts whilst part of their essence remained tethered in the

Realms beyond the Mortal one. It was the one advantage she had when she sent her wraith legion streaming into the path of Dionysus's advance.

Shrouded, acrimonious ghosts rose up from wells of darkness, looming like towering shadows in the twilight. All at once, the dryad charge faltered, a chorus of indignant shrieks bursting from their throats as they piled into one another in attempt to scramble out of the way of two dozen soul-devouring, dead sorcerers.

Nephthys was the strongest among them, a brutal, frayed relic of her former elegance. The wraith caught the lead dryad—with a start, Enodia recognised Tithorea and grinned—digging skeletal claws into both sides of the spirit's neck. Fountains of blood burbled free the instant before Nephthys's hood closed in over the wailing dryad's face. Convulsions wracked the eidolon even as its Etheric form rippled before breaking apart. On the Mortal side of the Veil, an empty, auraless human corpse collapsed where a dryad had stood.

There was perverse satisfaction in seeing the destruction of her former servant, the one who had so betrayed Hekate when Dionysus brought her to the Gloomwood. Almost, Enodia wished she could have drawn out Tithorea's suffering longer.

Other dryads strove together to surround wraiths. Roots burst from Spectral ground to ensnare ghosts, pinning them even as dryads pounced. They ripped free tattered shrouds, then tore skeletal limbs off the seething darkness that comprised a wraith's core, before they, too, turned to feasting upon the abraded remnants of souls.

More oft, however, the dryads fell, torn down by the fathomless hatred of the damned. Some of her wraiths turned to spellsongs, their rasping, loathsome voices still sufficient to shred the Ether and break apart the fibre of roots and vines dryads relied upon as weapons. Others overpowered the Wood spirits with sheer, untrammelled malice, their hatred so thick it seeped off them in palpable waves.

When Dionysus strode amid the chaos, naked save for his mask of bone and antler, the god's irate gaze swept over the scene with contempt writ plain upon the set of his shoulders. Arms raised as if drunk upon his glory, Dionysus roared.

In answer, Gaia herself spasmed. Trees ruptured, spraying a hail of splinters that somehow reached even into the Spectral Realm, pelting Enodia's ghostly forces. The ground convulsed as though waves surged beneath the surface. The devastation that befell the Spectral Realm was even greater. Monoliths of vines shot from rents opened beneath the land. Pus oozed between writhing, fibrous tendrils that launched themselves outward in all directions.

Barbed strands of wood punched through wraith torsos and limbs. One poor wretch took such a lance through its hood before collapsing into a wrinkle and dissipating into shadow. Others were torn asunder from the inside out.

Ignoring the plight of the lesser eidolons on both sides, Enodia set to chanting. Dionysus, bloated with pride fit to dwarf the cosmos, had stridden into her circle blindly, the god not even imagining she'd have painted glyphs across such a wide area.

From the moment Hekate and Keuthos had fled, Enodia and her wraith sorcerers had begun preparing, sketching out a circumference nigh a half mile across. Wider, so far as she knew, than any ritual attempted since the days of Dark Faerie.

Other wraiths—those not pinned by vines or busy dispatching dryads—joined her cants. The circle leapt to life, pale, Etheric flame racing along the perimeter with the speed of a flashfire. In the Spectral Realm, furrows rent the air, partitioning off the interior as a prison fit to contain even a god, at least the piece of him residing within a mortal soul.

Dionysus's answering bellow sent a chain of detonations exploding through the Penumbra. Land and trees and vines blew apart in concussive waves that disintegrated the dryads and wraiths closest to the blasts and sent the rest sprawling.

Enodia released the Sight before the eruptions could claim her too, though her ears were left ringing, her footing unsteady. In the Mortal Realm, a profound sense of malaise settled in, plants desiccating while the ground collapsed into jagged pits of rock.

Expending so much Pneuma left Enodia wobbly, scarce able to stand as it was, and with the land's convulsions, she pitched down onto her knees. It might take days, or longer, to recover from such an expenditure of Pneuma.

She felt more than saw or heard the approach of Dionysus, the god now looming over her, quivering with divine wrath.

"I would claim your mind were you alive, ghost," the sylvan creature said, words more terrible as they dripped with honeyed sweetness. "Instead, I will content myself to consume your soul."

"Save your strength for escaping the barrier," she taunted, melting through the Veil even as she spoke.

Almost instantly, the god's form in the Penumbra began to take on substance as he embraced the Sight. It would allow him to seize her Spectral form. It would not, however, let him follow past the Echo and into the Roil. Enodia had chosen her battleground with intent.

Already the deepening shadows oozed into the swirling dark of this Realm, beckoned on by the spilling of more blood than any could count. Kronos's army besieging Thebes had been one of thousands to pollute these lands with death and suffering. The older a city, the more pain one could count upon.

Even as Dionysus reached for her, Enodia hurled herself into the rent, falling into the tenebrous grasp of a Realm darker still. Its suffusing chill seeped into her as the ultramarine shadows of the Penumbra gave way to the turbid, seething onyx fields of the Roil. Fingers of hungry Dark teased out of obsidian mounds, promising her blissful oblivion.

A lie, a lie.

There was no bliss.

Enodia collapsed, groaning and rasping, desperate to hold her form together and having not nigh enough Pneuma to do so. If another wraith found her thus, any other eidolon, they might feast upon her essence.

And all she could do now was drag herself deeper, hoping to find something even weaker than herself on which she might gorge and restore her strength. Given that Dionysus had kindly provided a plethora of dryads, surely one must have discorporated and found its way into the Roil.

Surely one.

❦

It took time—and great deal of feasting upon both souls and corpses—for Enodia to regain the strength she expended in delaying Dionysus. By the time she was able to follow Hekate and Keuthos into the forbidden north, the god had already set off in pursuit, Nephthys and the handful of wraiths still under Enodia's command following in her wake.

When she, at long last, reached the etiolated remnant of Vulgeth's former glory—the gate to the Underworld the barbarians termed Hel —she found Hekate and Dionysus gone, sucked into the future by the Box, leaving Keuthos stranded, beset by a swarm of revenants.

Her friend had fought his way free of the ruined library, but the hungry ghosts leapt at him from rooftops, from windows, from crumbling balconies. With rock-hard fists they pummelled Keuthos, punches cleaving through stonework when he ducked, or crunching rib if he failed to evade.

"Take them," Enodia hissed to Nephthys.

A trio of wraiths flowed within the shadows of the Penumbra, swirling up against hungry ghosts that sensed their peril too late. Skeletal claws lodged into necrotic flesh, rending muscle from bone even as wraiths leant in to slurp up ghostly souls.

Enodia herself leapt forward, seizing a revenant by the back of the neck. Hissing, she twisted until vertebrae crunched and the creature's sputtering, venomous maw turned to gape behind itself at her. Further, until tendons ripped. Until the whole head tore from its shoulders.

With his attackers distracted, Keuthos launched himself atop one of the hungry ghosts. The wraith inside the revenant must have come as a bitter, if brief shock, as it began to gnaw not on dead flesh, but upon the wretched soul housed within.

The remainder of the ghuls fled, scrambling into the dilapidated shells of once grand structures that must have sheltered them in daylight hours. Perhaps they would sink into hibernation, awaiting the coming of new blood foolish enough to walk these desecrated lands. Or, rather, they would have, had Enodia not had need to replenish her army before undertaking the task ahead.

"Find their nests," Enodia commanded Nephthys. "Find the deep places where they lurk, careful not to disturb ghosts greater than these." Frightful hints of other breeds of hungry ghost, of blood drinkers—these stories passed among the barbarians in Phlegra too oft to dismiss them out of hand. Enodia saw no reason to disturb such ancients at present.

When Keuthos had restored some of his strength, the revenant-wraith turned to her, fangs and jowls caked in gore. "What are you doing here? Where is Hekate?"

His ready-to-spring crouch and splayed fingers made plain he still had little trust for her, despite their alliance against Dionysus.

"The one you know has gone and still returned." A sudden anxiety had her fingers trembling as she reached for her hood. What if, despite his state, Keuthos rejected her now, repelled by her ruined beauty and accursed nature? What if he refused to accept that the threads of Ananke had woven her into something he would not recognise?

She already knew Dionysus would fail to catch Hekate. She could have remained in the Roil, began her plan already. She could have started the long, dark path into the unknown future. But she could *not* abide the thought of plodding such a road without Keuthos by her side.

So, despite the quivering in her hands, she lowered the hood, revealing her unglamoured, decaying visage. She watched as recognition battered Keuthos into mute submission, his fighting posture giving way to defeat.

When he spoke at last, it was but a whisper. "I do not ... understand ..."

He did not turn from her. And though Enodia needed no breath, she found herself blowing out a long, shuddering sigh of relief.

"I FOLLOWED you into the ghul-haunted desolation the savages call Hel," Keuthos said, when the two of them sat alone outside the ruins of Vulgeth, secluded in the Spectral Realm, at home amid the swirling shadows. Above, a play of virescent lights evoked the mercurial whims of the firmament in winter in the far north, though here it seemed more muted, sickly even. "Did you think, Hekate, there would be anywhere further I would not follow you? I would walk at your side to the gates of Tartarus."

She clasped his skeletal hand in her own. What a pair they made. "And would you challenge what lies beyond even those black walls?"

"I fear all capacity for love riven from me ..." Keuthos rasped. "Yet its echo remains imprinted unto my soul. For its mere vestige, I will stand against any you name foe."

How extraordinary. Hekate had not known any other wraith, ever, to give voice to such sentiments. What a man Keuthos had been, that, even corrupted and wracked by his damnation, some part of him *still* could care for another. Would it last? If the gods were not her bitterest of enemies, she might have prayed for such.

Instead, she was left only with the hope, however fragile, that Keuthos could still hold onto himself when all of this was done.

"First," she said, the bone of her thumb scraping over his knuckle, "we go to the Underworld and infiltrate the necropolis of Kek. We shall become the rot that eats away at Hades's empire until it is ours to claim. And when we have overthrown the King of the Dead, when you and I sit upon the dark thrones of his hall, then we shall turn our gazes to the neighbouring necropoleis."

"Their wars rage eternal."

Enodia shook her head, for she knew all too well of what he spoke. Oft enough, in the intervening years, she had skirted the Roil and learnt of its myriad dead cities and even more numerous horrors. She had walked the dark gates of Irkalla and gazed upon the arcing roofs of far Youdu. She had learnt of the unspeakable perils that lurked within the Roil's fathomless darkness. "The souls of Man have long served as recurring banquet for the Elder Gods. While we fight amongst ourselves, desperate for their leavings, obsessed with our illusions of free will, they laugh in corpulent ecstasy at our futile struggles. So, yes, beloved, I will do what no king or queen of any necropolis has done before. If it takes Age upon Age, I will unite us in greater purpose. Until, at last, we shall move against those fool gods who think us their prey."

Keuthos favoured her with a grim smile, exposing fangs dripping with acidic saliva. His gleaming red eyes gave her answer even before he spoke. "So shall the hunters become the hunted."

20

ARTEMIS

754 Bronze Age

For four years, Artemis and her siblings had lingered within Ilium, guests of King Priam. Though the king offered her a place in his court—Artemis declined. She did, however, arrange favourable trading rights between Ilium and Phoeba, and too Helion, for she found the king a kind and learned man. He had given her family a home, out of the sight of Zeus, where they could think on how next to accomplish their aims. It seemed only fitting that, if Priam proved a friend to her, she ought do likewise. Thus, she aided his city however she might and watched Ilium prosper.

Nearby towns and poleis came to rely on Ilium for protection, and in turn paid tribute, turning the greatest city in Phrygia into more of an empire than a simple city-state. Priam built a network of friendly monarchs stretching across his land and into Phlegra and Lydia.

When Artemis was not busy planning with Apollon, Phaethusa, and Kirke—who remained on Aiaíā for the nonce, despite Artemis's offer to bring her here—she spent time with Priam's wife Hekuba or their children. By now, Kassandra was approaching twenty years, and though her madness had not abated, there was truth layered beneath the surface, if one could parse it. Artemis left that to her brother, though he seemed to have begun to tire of interpreting the girl's ramblings and had taken up with other lovers within the palace walls.

For her part, Artemis, when she could, sought to draw Kassandra out of herself. She took her riding at least once a month. At first, the girl remained skittish, looking at a horse as though it was a lion. She would mutter nonsense under her breath, so incessant even trained steeds grew nervous around her. But Artemis found for her an ageing Anadolu, her coat white and pure, her nature so demure not even Kassandra's mumblings seemed to faze the animal. And after a while, as they raced across the plains beneath cerulean skies, Kassandra's grumbles would sometimes turn to laughter, fountaining up in beautiful streams. Artemis counted such moments among the greatest victories of her long life.

Still, Kassandra's progress was not all either Artemis or her brother hoped for, and so she wrote to Kirke in desperation. For surely, if anyone could help the girl, it would be another oneiromancer. Yet Kirke refused to break her banishment, unwilling to risk antagonising their father or Zeus until Artemis was ready to strike. Instead, Kirke offered to write for aid to someone else that might soothe a troubled mind.

Despite Kirke's letter and its promise of aid, Prometheus's arrival in Ilium came as a shock. It was difficult to look at the pyromancer now and not see the murder he had helped Artemis commit, long back. Because of him, she had been able to reach her grandfather Koios. Bringing down the Ouranid League had seemed so needful back then, and Prometheus had agreed to her plan, however much he had misliked it.

But Kirke's grandfather came, sadness and sympathy plain in his crystal blue eyes. "I do not know that I can help the girl," he said as he walked through the halls of Ilium palace with Artemis, "but I shall try. The reality is, the Sight is a burden, and, as with any glimpse of the Ontos, those whose minds apprehend such truths begin a spiral toward madness."

"Even you?"

She had meant it half in jest, but he'd offered her a weighty nod in return. "Immortals and Oracles both risk losing themselves beneath the relentless tides of history. Those who are both, then, face compounding waves beating against them from both sides, ever threatening to wash away both the vestiges of their humanity and the pieces of their minds others would recognise and thus call sanity. Even the most obdurate of stones erodes under ceaseless abrasion from the sea, and too, none of us remain unchanged."

Artemis snapped her mouth shut, almost choking on his bitter words. For they implied that the corruption on Olympus, and of the Ouranid League before them, had been inevitable. That the nature of Titans, become immortal through Ambrosia, was to lose pieces of themselves year after year. Would the Artemis of the Golden Age recognise the person she had become now? That she could not answer such a question left her shivering, even in the sweltering summer days of Ilium.

Or perhaps she had an answer, and it so vexed her soul that she refused to dwell upon it, and that thought only heightened the disquiet in her.

Prometheus spent months tutoring and counselling Kassandra, and some days, the young oneiromancer did seem better. Artemis did not know what the pyromancer said to her when they walked in the gardens or strolled the ramparts or sat staring at the stars. She could not guess what words he used to pierce the haze of dread that forever seemed to cloud Kassandra's eyes. But sometimes, if she saw the girl afterwards, Kassandra appeared lucid, able to dance, and drink wine, and laugh at jests.

By now, she had a little brother, Hektor, who was forever racing about the halls, pretending at being a warrior. Kassandra would chase the giggling boy, indulging all his fantasies as though she too could see the phantasmagoric landscapes conjured up by a childish mind. Perhaps she could. Artemis watched as brother and sister shifted one moment from naval battles against sea monsters to dancing between seams in the floor, fearing they flowed with lava the next. Neither seemed the least perturbed by the disparity of circumstances, and Kassandra maintained a child's capacity for whimsy that Artemis almost envied.

Once, she had come upon Hektor practicing with a tiny wooden sword, miming Phaethusa's stances and footwork as the Heliad worked through her forms. Artemis's sister pretended not to notice the boy training in her shadow, or so Artemis assumed, until the woman offered Hektor a gentle correction on a mis-angled parry.

It was after leaving them that day she found Prometheus again with Kassandra. The pair each had their legs folded beneath themselves, eyes closed as they sat in the garden. Artemis had heard of meditative techniques, though she followed no such practices herself. Was this how Prometheus had been helping Hektor's older sister? Kassandra, for once, was still, neither mumbling nor rocking, not casting about after voices only she could hear.

For time, leaning against a pine, Artemis watched the two. After a while, Prometheus opened his eyes and rose, whispering something to Kassandra. She too eased out of whatever trance she had rested in and lay back on the grasses. Prometheus left her there, making his way over to Artemis.

"I'm grateful you've helped her." When she and Apollon had failed.

"Your rides with her offered more balm to a weary soul than you realise." She'd told him of those? He hesitated. "I begin to suspect the weight upon her mind was fomented by one who wished to render her abilities moot and incomprehensible."

Artemis pushed off the pine. "Someone did this to her?"

"It's possible."

"Who? How?"

Prometheus shook his head. "I don't know. A curse from one

jealous of her abilities is possible. Another oneiromancer, perhaps, could have managed it. A sorcerer could have done it, if he or she set a spirit to prey upon the girl's mind. I've been trying to train her in the shielding of her mind from external influence, but such relies on her ability to protect herself."

"You cannot stop whoever is doing this to her?"

"I looked into the flames, but I could not find the source of her malady. I'm sorry, Artemis, but there are limits to what I can achieve for her."

Artemis sighed. Well, if she ever learnt who had done this, she would have some choice words for the bastard. Words, and worse. "You've already done much and more for her, and I'm grateful. Will you linger a while longer in Ilium?"

"A while."

❦

IN THE WANING SUMMER, on a cool, dry eve, rumours rampaged through the palace of the arrival of a goddess upon the ramparts. No one claimed to have seen her arrive by pegasus, and yet she was there, a golden-eyed, raven-haired Heliad, come asking after Artemis. Knowing of few who fit that description, Artemis raced up the stairs to the battlements, then skidded to a stop several feet away from Nike.

Though she hoped it not too apparent, she kept one hand by her side in easy reach of the dagger at her back, should the Goddess of Victory have come looking for a fight. "Did Zeus send you here for me?"

Nike was staring at her with such intensity, indeterminate emotion roiling over her face, that Artemis hesitated. Last Artemis had seen Nike had been after ... Orion. Where had the woman been in the intervening years? Nike seemed to try to answer her question, but instead some jumble of sob and laughter burbled from her mouth. The next Artemis knew, Nike was half-striding, half-stumbling forward, wrapping arms around her, holding her as though Artemis was all that kept her standing.

"Gods, Artemis," Nike mumbled into her shoulder. "I'm so sorry for everything ... what happened or will ... f-for the mistakes I've made. I want us only to be friends, always ..."

Artemis held the other woman back at arm's length to get a better look at her. Nike's eyes were red with tears, a dribble of snot dangling from her nose. "What are you on about?"

Nike laughed then, a sound more of anguish than mirth, and at last pulled away, wiping her eyes with the heel of her hand. "You know, I, uh, I missed you."

The words warmed her soul, almost too good to be true. "And I you." But she needed to know, even if she hated forcing the issue. "So you no longer serve Zeus."

Nike stared at her with those intense, red-rimmed, golden eyes. "I never served Zeus. I fought alongside him during the Titanomachy because Ananke wove it so."

"And the Gigantomachy."

The Heliad nodded. "A means to secure release for Prometheus, only. I had not the least desire to see Zeus's order endure a day longer than it must. And you? By your question and presence outside the sphere of Olympus, I take it you have broken with the Olympian Order?"

Artemis chewed her lip. If Nike spoke in earnest and despised Zeus as much as she seemed to, she might prove a powerful ally in the coming struggle. Besides which, Artemis had taught her, trained her, and so cherished her. She had lost almost everyone she had ever trained, either to death, or in Athene's case, to having chosen the wrong side. Could she keep Nike here, by her side? "A great war impends betwixt those who yet serve the corrupt kingdom of Olympus and those who would see Man freed of Zeus's yoke." A sadness crossed Nike's face, but Artemis pressed on. "Stand by me in this war, Nike, that we may rectify the mistakes of the past."

Already, the Heliad had begun shaking her head. "Would that I could. Maybe, one day ..." But now a fiercer shake of her head followed, and she shut her eyes. "I have other, more pressing ends I must attend to first, Artemis. Do you know aught of the Unseen Order?"

Now what? "No, I've never heard such a name."

"Well, it was worth asking."

Artemis shrugged. "You spoke of Prometheus. He is here, in fact." Pandora's face brightened with blossoming hope and the flush of the sort of love Artemis doubted she would ever again experience. Artemis beckoned the woman to follow. If she could not gain an ally, at least there was some relief in learning she would not need to have Nike as an enemy.

NIKE AND PROMETHEUS soon departed from Ilium, and Artemis knew not where they headed. The pair had ever the air of mystery about them, as if they waded deep into waters others did not know even existed. She would have liked either or both of them as her allies in her struggle, but as time passed, she pushed them from her mind.

Autumnal breezes turned the air crisp, and some nights, she noted a layer of frost had formed upon the stone ramparts above the palace. Most evenings, Artemis walked up here, basking in moonlight, soaking in its Pneuma, and pondering the course that would see the Thalassa world free of Zeus at long last. On some eves, Priam or Kassandra joined her in her strolls, though neither stayed out so late as Artemis, and in any case, she would not confide in them of her plans.

It was not the king or princess who sought her out this night, beneath Thoth's waning gaze, but her brother. The Heliad had inherited their father's gift for epic smugness, but this night, Apollon beamed, pleased with himself as a lion taking credit for a kill brought down by hyenas. As a Moon Titan, night was more Artemis's time than Apollon's—damn Sun Titans—and yet his aureate eyes seemed lambent and proud tonight.

"Well?" she asked, knowing if she failed to let him give voice to whatever he'd achieved, he'd mostlike begin wheezing from the building pressure of his pride. She could imagine his airs seeking escape from his orifices like so much flatulence, a thought that brought a disgusted smile to her face, as well.

"Uh ...?" Apollon faltered. "Do you already know?"

Artemis snickered. "I've no idea. Just an amusing thought. Do tell."

"After Prometheus's training, Kassandra's bouts of lucidity have grown. Or, at least, it has become somewhat easier to glean hints of meaning with the vast fields of her rambling."

There was something a little disquieting about the prosaic way he spoke of the princess and her tormented mind. Apollon had not wrought her madness—though Artemis had heard some in the palace whisper he had inflicted it upon her for spurning him, in the deepest of ironies—and he had, to some extent, even tried to help her through it. Still, his sympathies seemed limited. Too long upon Olympus? Or had he always been thus?

"There will come a great war that shall serve as the beginning of the end of the Olympian Order."

Artemis rolled her eyes. "Hardly news. We've long been making efforts to determine how to besiege Olympus."

He raised a finger. "Not a second Titanomachy, at least not yet. Rather, a war betwixt Elládos and Phrygia which will further sap the strength of Zeus and his followers."

Artemis blanched and looked about to make certain no guards patrolled within earshot. "You'd have me prompt Priam to invade Elládos?"

Frowning, her brother shook her head. "I don't think so. The king is a man of peace and would hesitate to do so. Even if he agreed, I mislike his odds of success for invasion. Kassandra kept mentioning something about Paris."

"Is that a name?"

"Not one I know. She also mentioned, once, the name Helen." At her questioning look, he winked. "Zeus, has a young demigod daughter by that name."

That could not be a coincidence. "So now we need to identify this Paris and what he has to do with Helen."

Apollon nodded. "The beginnings of a plan have begun to sprout." Small wonder he was so damned pleased with himself. Even Artemis allowed herself a slight smile.

PRIAM'S INFLUENCE continued to expand across Phrygia, at least in part, Artemis liked to imagine, thanks to her aid and counsel. Small wonder then, that foreign leaders began to take note of the rising star of the king of Ilium. With spring came two blessings.

First, Queen Hekuba gave birth to another prince, cause for celebration not only in the palace, but throughout the polis. Common folk festooned the agora with flower-braided ribbons, whilst wandering minstrels strummed lyres on street corners. Priam ordered his coffers opened and wine served to high and low alike. The palace was redolent with the smell of sweet breads, roasted pork, and savoury pies. Every which way she turned, Artemis found musicians plying their trade on harps or flutes or singing, until she thought the palace might fair burst from the abundance of food and song and cheer.

Thus, a smidge intoxicated—and having rather enjoyed herself with a handsome lyrist in a dark corner of a back room—Artemis found Phaethusa sitting upon the low stone wall rimming the garden. Her sister looked toward where a flutist piped a lively tune, though at Artemis's approach, she turned, a mischievous grin quirked. "You've heard what the king named his second son?"

Artemis thought. "If I did, I don't recall."

Phaethusa's smile widened, delight and something darker flashing in her golden eyes. "He named him Paris."

And Artemis too smiled, at least at first. Then the realisation of what it might cost settled upon her, a leaden weight upon her gut. Of a sudden all the wine and delicacies she'd enjoyed felt heavy inside her, sloshing about in her gut. If the Prince of Ilium was, along with

Zeus's daughter, the key to destroying Olympus, then already she could begin to see the shape of the plan. Too, she could imagine the ramifications of drawing the poleis of Elládos into war against Ilium and its allies. Years of slaughter turning the steppes and plains of Phrygia into fields of charnel, stained crimson.

But she had sworn to make an end of Zeus and his ilk, and such an end would always have come past rivers of blood. Seas of blood, mostlike, and she had known it already and would not turn from it now. No matter the cost, she would see Zeus destroyed.

She had not long to muse on the revelation, though, for a few days later, the verdant spring brought the second of its unexpected blessings in the form of an emissary sent from the nascent Babilimian Empire out of Kumari Kandam. Even across the Thalassa in distant Kumari Kandam, Emperor Kurus II had heard tale of Priam's glory and sought ties of friendship with him. This, Artemis could only take as a good thing, for it meant her efforts to build up Ilium had gone well indeed.

The man they sent was a Magus by the name of Mithra. According to Apollon, their kind were sorcerer-priests who supported the throne of Babilim. Though not numerous—sorcerers never were, perhaps because of the price they paid or perhaps because most Men could not attain the strange mental gyrations needful to pursue the Art—the Magi wielded enormous influence across Kumari Kandam. From what she learnt amid the courtiers, in the space of less than two decades, Kurus II had gone from a minor king in Kissatu to the ruler of half a continent, in no small part thanks to the wisdom and perhaps supernatural influence of his Magi. Fearing a threat from his grandson, Kurus's grandfather, the Emperor of Nineveh, had moved against him. And lost. Kurus had conquered Nineveh, then Babilim, and moved the capital of his empire there.

All of which had seemed so promising. Right up until the point she heard from Phaethusa that Priam had traded away his daughter as a bride for the emperor. Given that Kandamians oft took more than one wife, for all Artemis knew, poor, haunted Kassandra would become little better than a pallake, a thought that galled Artemis to no end. The girl had enough weighing upon her mind as it was, here at home in Ilium, without being dragged halfway across Gaia, wed to some man she'd never met, and left without the support of those who understood her situation.

"It is the role of princesses to serve as brokers of peace between kingdoms," her brother had said. "Indeed, we ought to see this as a boon granted to us. If Kurus II knows of her ... uh, condition ... and still deigns to marry the girl, it means he seeks alliance with Ilium with great dedication." Never mind that her brother had both dismissed Artemis's concerns and, in fact, tried to validate kings and priests trading girls like chattel.

"The *role* of princesses?" Artemis countered. "A person does not need to define herself by a role, at least not by the role alone."

Apollon scoffed. "You are not so naïve, Sister. Ananke forces all of us down paths not entirely of our choosing."

"I think your steps have proved far freer than Kassandra's ever have. Do you know what they say of what has passed betwixt you and her? Do you hear the rumours courtiers whisper about what you have done to the child's mind?"

A flash of anger bloomed in his eyes, fierce and seeming almost ablaze, all the more unnerving for her brother so rarely showed her his temper. "Enough, Artemis. We swore to bring down Zeus at any cost. He murdered our children in front of us ..." He rubbed his face. "What do you imagine *at any cost* means? That we shall have victory without anyone suffering for it? That we alone would pay the price for it? If it brings us a single step closer to our ends, then yes, I would have let the girl die for it. Compared to that, marriage to one of the most powerful emperors in the Thalassa does not seem so woeful a fate for her. She will be mother to a dynasty that may well rule an entire continent." He sneered at her. "So take your righteous indignation on Kassandra's behalf and shove it back up your arse, for it's worth no more than your shit."

He stormed off, and Artemis could not resist calling after him. "You put your shit back in after it comes out? Small wonder you've become cranky!" It had been a feeble retort, she had to admit, but it seemed better than letting him have the last word.

So, when Mithra was at last done with his interminable negotiations with Priam, Artemis manoeuvred the chance to speak with the Magus alone. She found the man, cowl half-concealing his shadowed face, lurking not in the voluminous great halls or verdant gardens but rather in silent chambers he had requested away from the bustle of palace life. His rooms were austere, the windows shuttered, the only light coming from an oil lamp whose fuel was nigh spent.

She wasn't even certain what she expected from the Magus—after all, the king of this city had already given his word—but somehow, Artemis felt she needed to see the man who had come to *buy* Kassandra. The Magus stood in the doorway, watching her. Standing close to him, she realised his height meant he might have Titan blood. With the light to his back, she could make out little of his features, save hints of a dark beard. After a pregnant moment, the man stepped aside and motioned her into his chambers. Artemis entered, and he shut the door behind him.

"Olympian."

"Not in years, as I have to assume Kurus's spies would have reported by now."

"Emperor Kurus II hears tales, indeed, most oft through our order, if we deem veracity lies within those rumours. Behind the whispers of ravens and sycophants one must take care when extracting nuggets of truth."

"And what need has the Kandamian emperor for a troubled bride from Phrygia? You know of her plight, I've little doubt."

Mithra gave no visible response, at least not at first. "Oracles are a rare breed. Oracles with royal blood, those through whom one might build worthy alliances of state, are rarer still. The Sight can manifest in some bloodlines. Imagine then the potential for a sovereign, himself descended of the Anunnaki, who could see the future and plot the course of his people using such insights."

Artemis could imagine it. "A god-king ..." As if the Titans had not already bent the backs of Man so far many cracked and broke beneath the weight. Or maybe Mithra's thought was the means by which Man could, indeed, one day stand on equal footing to Titans. She recalled that Nike had once asked after the Anunnaki, and now here she learnt Kurus II carried their blood. Thoth, perhaps so did Mithra himself.

"It vexes you, to think of losing your friend to distant lands," the Magus observed. Was Kassandra her friend? Artemis wasn't certain, but she did care about the girl. "If it would assuage the pain, perhaps you should come to call upon us in the court of Babilim, Titan. We have famed gardens that never fail to impress even those who have trod through the jungles of Nysa or Kush."

"Perhaps," Artemis answered, though she knew her time would be consumed in scheming against Zeus and Olympus. She had a war to plan, after all. "One day."

21

KIRKE

743 Bronze Age

*Y*ears dragged on, at once relentless and languorous, lacerating Kirke's soul with slow tortures. She had not yet seen the way free of Zeus's heel, but then, neither had he returned to grace her with his presence. So she continued perfecting the Nectar for him by testing it upon herself. What had she to lose? It was the question that danced through her mind with each tantalising dose she took, even knowing that she risked addiction and madness.

What had she to lose?

Such she had begun to ask herself, when a gentle rapping came upon the frame of her door, and Kirke quickly tucked her latest phial into the folds of her peplos. Then she almost choked upon seeing the two women who slipped into her house along with the honey light of the setting sun.

Artemis and Phaethusa, two of her half-sisters. By different mothers, of course. Father treated women like he did his clothes, aghast at the thought of being seen with the same one two days in a row.

Kirke lurched to her feet, wagged her open mouth like a cow chewing cud, and found not a damn thing she could summon to say. Last she had seen of Phaethusa was when the woman, after turning her in to their father for creating Nectar, had guided her to exile on this island, some five decades back. Artemis, well, *her* Kirke had not seen in much longer. Given the circumstances, all she managed was a moan of incomprehension. Still, she took pride in it being a rather articulate moan, for all that.

No doubt sensing her unease, Artemis leant against the interior doorframe, folding her arms over her chest. "You were right," the Phoebid said after a moment.

"Yeah ... well, I suppose that's usually a good way to start a conversation." Kirke shrugged. "And it's bound to happen, time to time. I mean, I aim for more often than not, but no one is perfect." She jerked her head toward Phaethusa. "Save for that woman, I suppose. You know with Father's light shining straight out of her arse and her farts smelling like summer dew and all."

Artemis and Phaethusa exchanged glances, and then the Heliad came forward until she stood before Kirke. Her aureate eyes glinted in the firelight, lambent and fierce, and yet, somehow diminished from when last Kirke had seen their blaze. "Forgive me, Kirke."

Kirke rocked on her heels. "Yeah. All right. So Artemis turns up saying I'm right ... about something or other. Then Phaethusa apologises to my face. I take it I've stumbled into a dream, and not the prophetic kind. Is this about to turn nightmarish, then? One of you will sprout a second head and start singing off-key whilst the other tries to gnaw upon my knees?"

Phaethusa blanched. "You dream such things?"

Kirke shrugged. With enough wine mingled with Nectar, she dreamt all sorts of interesting plays in her mind. Shows that would have put the great Atlantis Amphitheatre to shame, really. She motioned to the divan she'd had newly imported from Byblos. "If you've come here to be civil rather than to castigate wretched Kirke for some failing or other, then I suppose I can offer you up some wine. Phoenikian vintages, you know."

Old Khloe had died in her sleep last winter, and the woman's loss had stung Kirke more than she'd have suspected. Enough so she didn't visit *Dagon's Gullet* anymore, for fear of the emptiness that must lurk there without the kitchen mistress's presence to warm it. More than four thousand years of life, and still, she had never accustomed herself to losing mortals around her. Grief, each time it reared its head, was fresh and new, fierce. And ever in its shadow came then whispers of all those lost before, the lion's ever-growing pride.

Immortality necessitated one to block out the sea of faces haunting memory. Some found respite in forgetting, some in madness, some in cultivating narcissism and cosmic egos. Maybe that was how so many of the older Titans became as they were.

Artemis, rather than sit, drifted to her side, and when Kirke pointed out the amphora, she hefted it for her. Were Kirke in a cynical mood, she might have named Artemis's casual display of Potency a show of Titan vanity. But this night, Artemis seemed pensive and subdued, so Kirke chose to take it as her sister merely wanting to help. Thus, after Kirke grabbed some bowls, together they returned to find Phaethusa not upon the divan but on the wolfskin rug before the hearth, legs folded beneath herself.

By unspoken accord, Kirke and Artemis joined Phaethusa before the fire, though the skin was not large enough for all three, and Artemis sat on the no-doubt chilled marble floor. The cold seemed not to affect her, perhaps another demonstration of her Titan Pneuma, so much stronger than a Nymph's.

"You were right about Zeus," Artemis said before Kirke could dwell long on the differences between them. "You were right all along, and I ought never have convinced Father to back him in the Titanomachy. I ought to have slain him, despite Hekate's alliance with him. Maybe I could have managed leniency for her once that cur was dead. Maybe ..." Artemis let her head fall into her hands, raven locks spilling everywhere in the process.

"And I ought never to have turned you in to Father," Phaethusa added. "How did he ever have us so desperate to win his approval?"

Kirke huffed, having felt the same far too many times over the

Ages. What unforgivable things she had done in his name, even including creating the centaurs and unleashing them on Kolchis on her brother's behalf. "He only ever cared for his sons," Kirke said. As if that were an excuse for turning his daughters against each other. "The rest of us were tools to use or barter away as befitted his needs." And even now, after five decades his prisoner, after centuries dwelling upon such iniquities, speaking them aloud tasted sour as biting into a lemon peel. "Pasiphaë is dead, traded to Minos to win the favour of Zeus." She waved a hand at Phaethusa. "You and Lampetia are all but exiles on Thrinakia. I am banished here. And you," she looked to Artemis, "escaped such fates only because Zeus named you an Olympian and thus outside Father's authority. So, yes, Zeus is the greatest blight on the pox-riven face of Elládosi society, but he's hardly the only pustule."

"Such bitterness ill suits you," Phaethusa said.

Snorting, Kirke took the chance to pour wine into the bowls and pass them around. "Did the pair of you truly come here to the fringes of Father's domain to apologise to me?"

"That's the main of it," Artemis said. "That, and to join you."

Another snort escaped her. "Yeah, sure I've got rooms aplenty if you want somewhere to live a while in peace. I promise, few people come to bother us." Fewer still since word got out the Witch of Aiaíā turned intruders to pigs. "You can join me in my weaving," she indicated the shadowed looms barely visible in the firelight, "or we can braid each other's hair or whatever insipid activities normal sisters do when not at one another's throats." She took a sip of wine. "Perhaps gossip about men or other women or such."

Phaethusa shook her head and sighed. "Not to join you on this island, Kirke. We want to join you in the endeavour you began long back, to bring down Olympus."

Kirke stared from one sister to the next a long, drawn-out moment. Then she chortled with such bitter mirth she almost dropped her wine bowl. "Yeah, sure. Never minding that was a thousand years ago. Why not?" She set the bowl down. "Why not start again the vain pursuits that got me exiled in the first place? But before that, excuse me whilst I go bang my head upon the wall for the next fortnight or so."

"You're not alone, this time," Artemis said.

A vision of Kalypso flashed through Kirke's mind then. Having a partner had worked out so well the last time. It had gotten all seven of the Pleiades brutally murdered, innocent though they were, but who worried over such things? Surely not Artemis. "You two may be among the finest warriors in the Thalassa world. Rumour claims it, anyway. But still, the three of us cannot overcome the Olympian Order. You heard of those blighted witches, the Graeae, right? Sharing one eye betwixt the three of them? Hmm, yeah, that's us trying to live with one *brain* between us, and I can't imagine it enough."

Phaethusa glowered. "I did not come here for you to insult me."

"Eh. How do you know I wasn't insulting you before you got here?"

Artemis laid a hand upon her knee, a gesture almost shocking in its intimacy from a sister she'd barely ever had dealings with afore now. "Kirke. Please. We are offering you the chance to change this world for the better. I'm sorry we were not there for you long back, but we cannot change the past. We—"

"No one can change the past," Kirke cut in with a bitterness that surprised even her.

"The Olympians are not what they were," Artemis said, perhaps uncertain how to respond to Kirke's outburst. "Ares has left the order. My brother is with us, and I think I may yet win over Hestia, or at least ensure her neutrality. Poseidon finds himself embroiled with problems of his own, with his son Triton and granddaughter Triteia eroding his authority. A Telkhine civil war may well impend. Athene slew Demeter and Hephaistos long back."

Kirke raised a hand to silence her. "And besides Zeus himself, Athene remains your greatest threat. If you move against her father, she will defend him." Athene craved her father's approbation with even more desperation than Helios's daughters had sought for his.

"Of course, Hermes, too, is a danger. You never know when that arrogant cock is around." She sighed. "Can you recruit Ares?"

Artemis sneered. "He's a psychopath and a Gígas who feasts upon Man-flesh."

Kirke winced. Everyone knew about the former, but she had not heard he'd taken to cannibalism thus. "Hebe? Hera?"

"I don't know," Artemis admitted.

Kirke looked back and forth between the two women. "Why come to me, then? Why not one of them? They are Titans, and more powerful by far than me. Nyx, why not try to convince our father?"

"You're smarter than any of them," Phaethusa said. The brazen admission hung in the air between them.

Maybe it was the wine, but Kirke flushed. "Um ... thank you?"

"If the children of Helios all work together," Artemis said, "we can rectify the mistake we made in the Titanomachy."

"All? Aeëtes?"

Phaethusa frowned, making plain the answer. Her brother had lost himself to his Art, and there was no coming back from the Darkness in which he now dwelt.

"There's something else," Artemis said.

And Kirke nodded, for since Eos had spoken of it, she had oft considered it. "You are hunted by the reincarnated Dionysus."

Her sister nodded. "Before we can devote our full attention to Olympus, we must find the means to make a final end of that abomination."

Kirke looked from one to the other woman and back again. "You will ... not betray me again?"

"No, *never*," Phaethusa swore, and Artemis nodded, offering her arm.

Kirke took it. Swallowed hard. "Then I will dream for you an answer to this Dionysus. And once one monster is slain, we can attend to the next."

Sourceless lamplight guttered across shelves that stretched in winding, impossible paths along walls, floor, and ceiling. Each shelf housed hundreds of cubbies, jammed with crumbling scrolls that wriggled within their hollows, as if alive. But to follow the course of the strange library would have had Kirke walking unfathomable geometries that defied logic, even in dream, stirring a profound unease within her soul. Had her haunted mind conjured such insanity, or had she been pulled into the dreamscape of one cursed with madness greater even than Kirke's own?

The shelves, or perhaps the scrolls, they seemed to whisper in a thousand discordant voices, an incessant babble of nonsense that already began to fray upon Kirke's nerves. Was this the mind of Dionysus, one so alien as to thwart any semblance of understanding?

Though it set her stomach churning, Kirke followed the winding paths, her steps leading her from the floor and up onto the walls, then round onto the ceiling. Ever forward she trod until she came into some twisted antechamber, where shelves crossed and recrossed the room's periphery in ever more maddening angles.

Along another path, one perpendicular to the space where Kirke stood, an auburn-haired teenage girl burst into the chamber, casting furtive looks over her shoulder as she made a frenzied dash around the room. She took paths seemingly at random, treading stairs of books, and over, onto walls and ceiling, round and round, denied any means of egress.

"Kassandra ..." voices hissed at her from hidden recesses. "Kassandra ... Kassandra ... Kassandra ..."

The girl slapped her hands over her ears and, casting more glances about, dashed in pointless circles round the warped library, not seeming to notice Kirke's presence in the least. This was the girl's dream, and Kirke could scarce recall having witnessed such a perverse nightmare in the minds of any she had ever intruded upon, much less of one so young.

Inchoate faces began to take shape in the hollows between scrolls, mouths locked into moans. Each visage held for an instant before receding back into the gloom, and yet, Kirke felt a thousand of them now lurked upon the fringes, each desperate to utter laments they could not voice.

Kassandra stumbled, pitching onto hands and knees, and tumbled up a staircase to land upon the ceiling. The whispers burbling from the scrolls intensified, single voices rising to the surface, given evanescent expression.

"... Eteokles betrayed the ties of kinship ..."

"... the Sight is a burden, and, as with any glimpse of the Ontos, those whose minds apprehend such truths begin a spiral toward madness ..."

"... You fall prey to the Gnostic sin, it seems ..."

"... We're all these uncreated products of ourselves ..."

"... You are lost ... Wallowing in musings deep as the pits riving this place ..."

"... The Hidden God lies as far beyond them as they lie beyond those like you and me ..."

"... Tell me of the Unseen Order that tugs your strings even as you profess your actions as your own ..."

"... How can you, for centuries, live alongside a festering cancer and not smell the rot?"

Kirke's heart leapt to her throat. That one, that had been ... Artemis's voice?

"... Should Fate falter, should a single thread of the Moirai come unspooled, Khaos rises ..."

Hearing even these fragments drew further whimpers from Kassandra. On her knees, she rocked back and forth, arms wrapt around her head in a no doubt vain attempt to block the voices.

"... This is the only World we are given ..."

Kirke strode toward the girl, intent to pull her from such nightmares, but the library itself shifted and contorted, paths rising and falling in conspiracy to keep them apart. And Kassandra remained locked in her isolation, though it broke Kirke's heart to see the child thus.

KIRKE SAT on her portico with her sisters, Artemis and Phaethusa, breaking their fast, though Kirke found herself with scant appetite. Still, she forced herself to take some olives, for the dreaming had taken its toll. "She's an oneiromancer, and an unusual one. She hears voices in her dreams."

"You're already an oneiromancer," Phaethusa interjected. "What need have we for a Phrygian child when we have a Titan-blooded sister with the same gift?"

Kirke had little mood to entertain her sister at present. "Yeah, true. And have I ever mentioned how endearing I find it when people without the Sight advise me on how it works, though they couldn't tell the difference between psychic perceptions and an angry gut from sour wine? I haven't? Huh. I could have sworn I had. Perhaps I ought to have it carved above my door for future reference."

"I'm sure there must be a point buried in that mess of words," Artemis interrupted, "but I fail to see it."

Kirke snorted. "And they call you the greatest hunter on Gaia. Hmm." She sipped her apple juice. Sometimes, the fastest way through a conversation was to answer people's damn questions. "All right, fine, have a listen. The Sight is a term we use for psychic sensitivity and it can manifest all kinds of ways, yeah? So if someone is an oneiromancer, they use it through dreams, whilst pyromancers divine through fire, mediums see through the Veil, and necromancers hear the voices of the dead." She waved her hand, realising she was getting off topic. "Examples, only. The point is, even if you have two psychics cut from the same cloth, so to speak, they shan't be the same any more than the three of us are identical, though we share a common father. One psychic isn't interchangeable for another. I can dream whatever it is my mind can dream, and what I can't, I can't, so I won't, follow?"

"Yes," Artemis agreed, "despite your attempts at verbal acrobatics."

Kirke shrugged at that, amused despite her dour mood. "The tongue's a muscle, too, and needs exercise lest it atrophy." She waited until Artemis rolled her eyes. "So. I tried to learn of Dionysus and instead I dreamt of this girl, Kassandra, the princess of Ilium, hearing too much. Of course, there's always a chance she has as much to do with this as that hairy mole on Phaethusa's arse."

"I don't have a—" Phaethusa said.

"Anyway," Kirke cut her off, "there's also a chance Kassandra can dream up your answer, though I garner she can little control her talents."

"Sounds like *you* can scarce control yours," Phaethusa sniped.

Maybe there was a chance her sisters could help Kassandra escape the prison of her dreams. Either way, she had endured rather enough breakfast this morn. "Search out your answer in Ilium, and we can plan from there. If I can learn something else, I can have Eos send a message to you."

22

THESEUS

770 Bronze Age

The winter was past, Zeus be praised. Theseus had seen more than sixty winters now, and with each one, his joints hurt a bit more. Oh, courtiers and servants, they said he scarce looked a man of forty. Hints of Titan blood gave him longer life than most Men, true. But the weight of those years stooped his shoulders, nonetheless.

In the decades since Theseus had lost his beloved family he had oft caught himself glancing into the shadows, wondering when the spectre of Thanatos might at last come for him. With each nocturnal groan of the megaron, each unseen noise, he waited for death's black sword to relieve him of his post. But the winged god—if truly he served Hades—never came, and Theseus sat watching over Athenai to the ceaseless irritation of the rest of the aristoi.

Time to time, the Pallantides—fucking Menestheus now that his father was a doddering imbecile—stirred up trouble, and Theseus had not the energy to bother with them. Akamas had forestalled riots and mobs twice, in fact. Or, no, was it thrice now? Theseus wasn't certain any longer. Well, such hardly mattered to him.

Desolate, he preferred to be left alone to his morbid musings, and the servants had long since learnt to avoid him. Day after day, he sat upon his lonely throne, watching his empty hall, attended only by his cupbearer. With enough wine, Theseus could almost hear the voices of those he had loved best in his life.

So was it that, when Antigone's voice rang in the hall, at first he thought her conjured from the depths of his wounded soul, an echo of happier times. But no, time had touched her, despite her Titan blood. There were creases in her face now. As Theseus sat up to greet his foster daughter, he even noted a hint of grey streaking through one strand of her hair. Just a hint, but time chased her, too, and that thought only served to deepen the melancholy that suffused him.

"It feels an Age since last I saw you," he managed. She had come for Phaidra's funeral. A few times since then, she'd made the trek. Not recently. Not for a long, long time it seemed to him. Theseus, he could not bring himself to journey anywhere save to attend to the basic needs of the body, and only when he could no longer avoid those.

Antigone nodded, her mouth a grim line. "Things have grown increasingly ill in Thebes, and I could not, at first, find a way to leave. Now, though, I managed to get free, along with one of my brothers."

"Free?" Despite his protesting joints, Theseus rose and made his way before his foster daughter. Taking her elbow, he guided her to a more comfortable sitting room and ordered cups of wine for the both of them. "Tell me all that has happened."

"Oh, it is a long and bitter tale. The short of it comes to this: my brother Polynikes is deprived of his birthright, and I am left with no choice save to ask you to honour the oath you made to Oedipus long years back."

Theseus had not forgotten. He had sworn to the dying man to see to the interests of his children. But Kreon had abdicated and Polynikes and Eteokles had agreed to alternate years as king. Theseus had thought the children, the royal family of Thebes, well situated and in little need of his aid. Things, it seemed, had changed. He threw back a swig of Argosian red, then wiped his mouth with the back of his hand. "Best give me the whole story, then."

🙢

"It has sometimes seemed as though some dire curse lies upon my family. As if we, the children born of our father's unclean union with his mother, are ourselves damned for his mistakes. Such was it that my brothers remained forever querulous with one another, forever lacing their tongues with barbs. Every kind word carried beneath it an undercurrent of judgment. Every decision made by one became the subject of derision and mockery by the other.

"Perhaps then it was inevitable that the day would come when, asked to relinquish power when his year had ended, Eteokles would instead see Polynikes exiled. Our soldiers sided with Eteokles with a swiftness that tells me he had planned this long before it unfolded. Though I have no proof, I suspect he had cultivated a relationship with our general for years, with gifts and bribes, before making his move.

"Either way, Ismene and I, he intended to have confined until Polynikes was halfway to Korinth. Only, my betrothed caught wind of his schemes and helped me to slip away and thus join my brother in his exile."

"Your betrothed?" Theseus interrupted.

"Is that a jest? I sent word to you!" Antigone folded her arms over her chest, her affected pout evoking her teenage years so keenly Theseus had to fight from quirking a smile. "I am promised to Haimon, son of Kreon. And yes, I know well enough scandalmongers will say I'm too old to wed and ought to content myself as a spinster. 'Past childbearing years, she is,' I've heard more than once whispered when they think I am out of earshot. As if the only reason for the binding of lives together is procreation. Psht! Spare me."

"I said naught," Theseus protested.

Antigone unfolded her arms and heaved a sigh. "No. You said

naught when I wrote to you. How was I to take your silence save as judgment?"

Theseus rubbed his face, feeling bone weary all of a sudden. "Forgive me. I stopped reading the letters that came long ago. Akamas ought to have told me, but perhaps it slipped his mind." When had he last cared aught for the matters of state, much less those of personal import?

When ... when he had wept at the threnody sung for Phaidra. When he had buried the greater portion of his soul alongside his wife.

Antigone huffed, apparently deciding to let the matter lie. "I will say this for Eteokles: my brother saw Polynikes provisioned with enough drachmae to ensure we could live in comfort for a time, but not enough he need fear us raising any army to threaten Thebes. Knowing him, he must have calculated the amount down to the last obol. We did make for Korinth, of course, and en route we encountered Tydeus."

"Who?"

"A grandson of King Oeneus of Kalydon by his daughter Gorge. Tydeus slew a kinsman by accident—"

"Zeus's thundering arse! What *is* it with that family?" As if Theseus was one to talk, having executed his son. Still, between Meleager killing his uncle—and dying for it—and that loathsome bitch Deianeira murdering Herakles, Kalydon seemed forever entwined in its bloody curse.

"Yes, well." Antigone cleared her throat. "In any event, he bears a shield emblazoned with the boar in honour of the hunt his uncle led. Perhaps the irony is lost on him. Either way, he sought allies to help him reclaim his throne, and Polynikes swore to him that, should we take Thebes, he will help him claim Kalydon. But of course, we were only three, and I am no warrior. We had need of an army, and I had long back told Polynikes of the promise you made to our dying father. So he conceived a plan to come here, to beg you to help him oust our treacherous brother."

Theseus groaned. Though he might not look it, he felt old, and his fighting days were dead and buried. "You'd have me uphold an oath by Polynikes at the expense of my promise on behalf of Eteokles. I swore to see to the interests of all four of you, Antigone. How am I to then ignite a war betwixt two of my charges?"

"Eteokles betrayed the ties of kinship when he betrayed Polynikes!"

Theseus took another sip of wine. He had not even noticed the servants refilling it, but damn did he need a drink. "He thought enough of those bonds to not become a kinslayer."

"And that excuses all crimes?" She did not mention Hippolytus or what he had done. She did not say that Theseus had killed him for it. Not with words, though Theseus saw it in her eyes, nonetheless. The sight damned him and forced him to look away.

Long he sat, staring at the dregs of his wine, avoiding facing her and her request. Zeus, but he wished Phaidra were here! She would know what to do. She would know how to plot a course through the mire of this unhappy situation. Theseus had hung up his sword, but maybe, one last time, if he took it down, he could see Phaidra again. Maybe tell her he had done right by the daughter they had raised between them, even if she shared blood with neither of them. And there was his answer. Theseus had sworn to see to all of Oedipus's children, but his first loyalty lay with Antigone, whom he loved as his child.

At last, he lifted his heavy gaze to meet her own. "Thebes is well protected. We shall need allies to breach her walls. I will lead the army, but it will fall to Polynikes to deal with his brother as he sees fit. I shan't break my oath by striking a blow against any of Oedipus's blood myself."

THE ARGOSIAN ORACLE Amphiaraos had fought beside Theseus during the Kalydonian Boar Hunt, as an Argonaut, and later against the Pallantides. He had married Eriphyle, daughter of Talaus—a prince of Argos who had also aided Theseus back then. Talaus was gone now, as were his cousins Kastor and Pollux. Adrastus, son of Talaus, had taken the throne. His brother-in-law, Amphiaraos, the Oracle, he came, grim faced and stern, to counsel Theseus.

"If I go with you to Thebes, I shan't return," the Oracle warned in consult with Theseus and Akamas.

Theseus's son paced about his private chambers. He'd made plain his dislike for this entire endeavour. But then, Theseus had already sent out envoys calling for champions and could scarce back down now. Akamas could attend to the simpering Pallantides, and besides, Theseus was not certain he even wished to return.

"I'll not compel you to go then," Theseus offered the seer.

"Oh, but my wife already has. She is sister to King Adrastus, and he seeks the glory of the expedition. Indeed, he has wed his daughter to Polynikes and thus joined all our destinies with gossamer chains." The man groaned. "We think we can run from our fates but so oft instead find ourselves stumbling headlong into the Moirai's fearful embraces."

Theseus had known Polynikes went to Argos to seek aid from Adrastus. He had not known Oedipus's son had got himself a wife in the process and he wasn't certain he wished to know what the man had offered the Argosian king in return.

"Will we succeed?" Theseus asked Amphiaraos.

The Oracle shrugged glumly. "I cannot see past my death. I can tell you that you will lead seven champions against Thebes, each of them in command of his valiant war band. I can tell you, there will be battle, hard fought and full of the glory that fills the songs of bards."

That drew a huff. "I gave over chasing glory in war some time back when I found it comprised of dust and blood and little more."

"Then *why*?" Akamas protested. "Why do this?"

"I swore to Oedipus and I promised Antigone. And that, for me, is enough, Son."

So they came to him, champions under his banner. Amphiaraos and Adrastus, Tydeus and Polynikes. Then there was Adrastus's nephew, Kapaneus, a man so tall and broad-shouldered Theseus assumed he had Titan blood. There was Parthenopaios, a son Atalanta had born to Meleager, though his father had died before his birth and his mother shortly after. And last, Hippomedon of Lerna, cousin to Adrastus, and a man as eager for bloodshed as any Theseus had ever met. The Seven, they called themselves, to each Theseus and Adrastus gave command of a band of fierce warriors.

He might have thought it would be enough. He might have thought these gathered armies and their leaders equal to the challenge of breaching the mighty wall that encircled Thebes.

Theseus did not know what had prompted the old king, Kreon, to side with Eteokles over his brother Polynikes. Either way, when his host arrived at Thebes, the current king and the former stood side by side on the ramparts, rallying their archers. Though Theseus could not hear the words, he could imagine them, Eteokles stirring the fervour of his city in the name of famed Kadmus himself.

Then, from the seven gates of Thebes rode seven champions of the city, each come to meet a division of Theseus's army. Parthenopaios raced forward first of all, thirsting for glory, no doubt. And poor Amphiaraos, despite his dire prediction, did not hesitate to lead his men to their fates. Each of the seven champions who had marched against Thebes now churned the dust on their way to face a prince of that city.

And Theseus directed his chariot between them, guiding the army, preparing for the siege. As he raced across the battlefield, the arrows began to fall, sparking a terror in him he had all but forgotten. Sling bolts whizzed by, cracking against helm and shield, and laying low the unlucky. Hurled javelins felled some few among the phalanxes, but still, Argosian and Athenian men closed upon the walls.

With each of his men fallen, an ache in Theseus's chest deepened. Dread arose, not only for fear for his life but for his part in the carnage he could no longer stop. It had already taken on a life of its own, and he had agreed to become a party to it. He had led these men here to die.

As Parthenopaios had been the first to charge in, too, he was the first of the champions to perish, felled by mighty stones dropped upon his head from atop the walls. Kapaneus fell next, cast down from the walls by some opponent Theseus could not see. As he had predicted, Amphiaraos was struck down by a spear. Eteokles and Polynikes slew one another, even as Theseus watched.

He *tried*. He tried to defend his allies, but age and long years of drowning his melancholy and nursing his despair had slowed reflexes once viper fast. Still, even when he would have welcomed his death, Thanatos avoided casting his fell shadow over Theseus.

One by one, Theseus's gathered champions were slain, their blood the paint of a fresco of hubris. As if a city with unassailable cyclopean walls could be breached by brazen courage alone, without catastrophic loss of life.

In the end, only Adrastus was left of the Seven, the king wounded in body and pride, and helped from the miserable battlefield by a bone-weary and defeated Theseus.

With the death of his nephew Eteokles, Kreon once more ascended the throne of Thebes. In either spite or grief, he first refused Adrastus's pleas to allow the burial of Polynikes and the other Argosian fallen princes. Only after prolonged entreaties did the king of Thebes agree to take counsel with Theseus, the two of them meeting alone, between the two camped armies.

Whilst time's merciless ravages lay beneath the surface for Theseus, they had abraded ancient Kreon year after year. His flesh was sallow, his skin drooping. His hair and beard had turned the stark white of fresh mountain snow. Reflecting on the man's age, Theseus wondered if even Titan blood would sustain one so very long. He hoped not.

"Why would I consent to the honouring of a fratricide?" Kreon snapped when Theseus pressed for Polynikes's body to be interred in his family tomb.

Theseus sighed, shifting from one foot to another. Though he'd taken only light wounds in the battle, still, the bruises and cuts wore away what little strength he had. "He remains your nephew. He sought only the birthright that ought to have been his already."

The old man groaned. "Do you think I'd have supported Eteokles were he not the better king? This constant shifting of power betwixt two brothers forever at one another's throats weakened our city. Their schemes, their machinations, their rivalry, it had become a threat to the whole populace. Scarce a day went by without some poor fool getting knifed in an alley, caught up in power struggles. It became necessary to choose the wiser of the two and compel the lesser to step down."

"You had him exiled from his polis."

Now Kreon snorted. "Because if I let him live in the city, he'd have stirred up rebellion! Do not be naïve, Theseus. Rot left to fester grows only worse."

It made an unhappy kind of sense, he had to admit. There were pieces to this tale Antigone had left out or, perhaps, having the story only from Polynikes, not even known herself. "Polynikes is son-in-law to King Adrastus of Argos. If you do not bury him with honour, you will be planting your fresh rot in the form of resentment between your poleis. Enough have died here this day, Kreon."

The ancient king held his peace. Then he raised a single finger, in warning or concession. Or both. "Antigone must be returned to Thebes once more."

"For your son's sake?" Theseus imagined she would wish to return to her betrothed regardless, though things had turned out so ill here.

"For the sake of preserving the Kadmean bloodline. Only when she is returned to Haimon will Polynikes receive his state funeral."

Theseus nodded. "I'll send messengers ahead to Athenai. She'll be on the first ship here."

WHEN THESEUS LED his battered and broken army home to Athenai, they—or he, rather—found jeers in greeting. The people stared at their king with open disdain. They whispered behind their hands, they glowered, they made mockery of his effort to uphold his oath. All they saw was the king retuning home in shame, defeated. And how could Theseus blame them, for a great many husbands, fathers, sons, they would all need funereal rites in the coming days. So many shades must now gather along the banks of the Styx awaiting the shrouded ferryman.

By the third street they passed, Theseus could no longer meet the eyes of those he rode past, instead keeping his gaze unfocused, locked on empty space ahead of him. What explanation could he offer the grieving kin of the fallen? Did they care that he had sworn to aid a now-dead prince of a foreign city against his brother?

Even Antigone would be gone now, having sailed for Thebes before the army could return, and Theseus would find only Akamas here for him. He needed to see his son. Only his boy mattered now.

"I WARNED YOU." Wine slurred Akamas's words, the man's face cast in a dance of shadows by the dwindling light from the brazier. Midnight had come and gone, and still Akamas and Theseus sat drinking in the prince's private chambers. "I warned you ... not to go."

Theseus groaned into his empty goblet. Bestirring himself to reach the amphora for more seemed akin to climbing a mountain. Almost as hard as letting his throat go dry. Aching, he crawled the few feet to the wine vessel and snatched it with trembling hands. When he moved to pour, the damn thing slipped from his fingers. The vessel crashed onto the floor and shattered, spilling what little crimson treasure it had still held. A rubescent stain spread across the marble, slowly running out, like the course of Theseus's life. "Fuck."

Akamas rose—a hair steadier than Theseus felt—grabbed a towel from beside his divan and tossed it in the mess. "You had no business—"

Another crash sounded, outside the room but much louder than a shattering amphora. Shouts split the night's peace, and iron rang upon iron. Alarm cut through the wine-haze addling Theseus's brain. That was the sound of battle. Battle in his megaron!

He rose. He teetered. Looking about, he realised he had no weapons. Akamas though had already claimed his xiphos and moved to the door. "Stay behind me, Father."

"I ... I need my sword." Where was it? In his chambers, mostlike, though he scarce remembered what he'd done with his arms and panoply on arriving. For hours he'd sat here, with his son, drowning his sorrows. Or nursing his dolours, rather.

Grim faced, Akamas eased open the door and peeked outside. Assured at whatever he'd found, Theseus's son slipped from the room and beckoned his father to follow. Theseus did so, his boy leading him through the halls back toward his chambers. They passed a wide hall that opened into the courtyard, and there Theseus beheld the true horror of what unfolded. His people were embroiled in bloody rebellion, and from what he could tell, a good many of his warriors had joined the traitors. His loyal retainers struggled to hold back a massive throng, wild men and women bearing torches or carving knives as oft as real weapons. Looters pillaged the megaron while crowds bore down defenders, cracking skulls with whatever improvised tools came to hand. A score of dead littered the courtyard and rooms Theseus could see, and more seemed soon to follow.

He needed his damn sword!

Akamas looked back to him. "We must get you to ... Father!" His son shrieked in warning, and Theseus started to turn.

Something heavy crashed into the back of his head. Darkness surged up and engulfed him.

THE FIRST THING Theseus became aware of was pain. A mountain of pain vast enough to tower over Olympus itself, all pressing on his head. After a moment, he opened an eye. A mistake. Daggers of light lanced through his brain and Theseus groaned. Unless this was some fresh, vile chamber of Hades's Realm, he was sickeningly alive, if only barely.

"Father." Akamas's voice cut through the miasma of his agony.

Knowing he'd regret it, Theseus peeked once more at his surroundings. The light came seeping in through a crack in a shuttered window. Painful, though it turned out he lay in an otherwise dark room. "Where am I?"

"Elephenor's estate on Naxos."

"What?" Elephenor was a distant cousin on his father's side, and a loyal family friend. But why leave the island of Athenai?

Akamas's shadow fell over Theseus and his son settled down beside the divan they'd left Theseus to sleep on. "Menestheus and his ilk have taken the city, Father. The people rebelled and too few remained loyal to our family to hold Athenai against them."

Despite the pain, Theseus sat up at that. Fresh jolts of agony wracked him, and blood ran out of his head, leaving him ready to pitch over backward. He held himself up by force of will, though his gut churned at it. "We lost it?" He had lost the city his father had left to him?

The judgment he saw in his son's eyes cut like flensing knives, forcing Theseus to look away.

"Elephenor and his kin offer us sanctuary here. Menestheus is king of Athenai now, and we've no support to hope to change that." Akamas paused. "You squandered the pristine jewel granted to you." It was as if he had read the guilt from Theseus's mind.

"I ... You do not know what it is to lose those you love so well that their absence tears pieces of your soul away with each breath you take without them." First Pirithous, then Father. Beloved Phaidra and even Hippolytus. "I lost everything."

"You had *me*. Did you think I did not love my mother? My brother? Hmm. No, but you forgot you yet walked in the Mortal Realm, much less spared a thought for your other son. For nigh to thirty years I watched you wither away into a husk. Look at me! At least offer me that much grace, Father."

Theseus did so, though witnessing the wrath limning Akamas's visage was almost too much to bear.

"I warned you to leave off this thing with Thebes," Akamas said, rising. "Was it vanity that drove you down so fateful a path, Father?"

Oh, Theseus wished he had an answer for that, but he suspected none would ever come to him.

His son snorted. "Hmm. Well, you can live out your dotage in the sun of this estate. If I am fortunate, perhaps an opportunity to restore honour to our family may yet present itself. Time shall tell."

"Akamas ..." Theseus groaned.

But his son left him sitting there, alone in the darkness.

Theseus forever found himself alone in the darkness.

MAYHAP THESEUS OUGHT to have stayed upon Naxos, but knowing his son hated him had made even the wide estate feel as stifling as a tiny cell. As ... the hateful Labyrinth that forever haunted Theseus. So, when he was well enough to travel, Theseus had sailed for Thebes. Antigone was the last one he had left now, and if she could forgive him for his failure to save her brother, then perhaps his life still amounted to some good. In the end, he had to believe he had done right by at least one of his children.

The steps from the harbour leading up to Thebes seemed endless now. Cut from the cliffside, rising seven hundred feet in a circuitous route that carried one past a raging cataract, the path was beautiful to the young and fresh. All it left Theseus with was aching knees and burning lungs, and before he'd made it halfway, he had to stop, gasping for breath.

By the time he reached the summit, the sun had already dipped low on the horizon, seeming to light the city aflame. A man came from the gates to meet him, alone, relying upon a walking stick to carry him. With the sun behind the man, Theseus did not at first recognise Kreon.

"The king himself comes to greet me?" Theseus asked when

Kreon stood before him, looking almost as miserable as Theseus himself felt.

Kreon shuddered, looking so decrepit he might well collapse but for his stick. "I ... thought it justice, you know."

"What?"

"You have come for vengeance, no doubt, and now I welcome it, for I can no longer tolerate the shrieking erinyes of my guilt."

Theseus blanched. "I've no idea what you're on about now. I came to see Antigone." One last time. One last hope.

"You truly don't know?" Kreon grunted. "I ... I thought word had reached Athenai already." A heavy sigh escaped the ancient king. "My niece is dead. Of my sister's children, only Ismene remains, though she would never deign to speak with me again, I am certain. Huh. Who could blame her? I ..."

Though bone-weary, Theseus took a threatening step toward Kreon. "What wretchedness have you wrought, Kreon?"

"Antigone betrayed Mother Thebes. Thus, on her return, I commanded that if she so sought to join Polynikes, she must do so." Theseus's stomach dropped. He could not form words, and Kreon pressed on. "I had her sealed inside her brother's tomb. Granted a day's food, though it was cruelty to preserve her suffering, in truth. I was so ... enraged by her treachery, by Eteokles's death, I ..."

"Oh gods ..." Theseus moaned. "Antigone?"

"My son." Kreon choked on the word. "My son learnt of it and was taken enough with his betrothed to break into the tomb in a vain attempt to save her. But she was not one to await the slow terror of creeping death and took her life."

His words landed like blows, each raining upon Theseus until his knees gave out and he landed on all fours.

"I had not known how much my boy loved her until she was gone." Kreon's words spilled from him as if from a broken sluice gate. "Maybe he didn't either. But he came for me, tried to strike me down. My guards stopped him, damn them, and he fled. Cast himself from the cliffs in despair over what he'd lost." A pause. "I ... I ... Each night

I think to follow him yet remain too craven to take the long step down."

A shudder wracked through Theseus, tearing his insides asunder. Shredding the final vestiges of his soul. With that last breath, no human feeling was left to him. He was truly hollow. No longer panting, not certain if he yet breathed at all, Theseus looked up at Kreon. They were, both of them, shades now, damned to walk upon Gaia for one moment more. "So you come to me, that I may be the instrument of your release."

The old man nodded, once, shaking.

And Theseus rose, flowing toward the king's side as if he had become the shroud of Thanatos. "Then come." Theseus seized Kreon and dragged him toward the cliff's edge. Only at the end did Kreon begin to resist in the least, but the old man had no strength to break Theseus's grip.

Pirithous had taken his life. As had Ariadne. Phaidra. Antigone. The appalling weave of the Moirai had snared them each, dragging them all toward inevitable, bitter ends. Fitting now, that in the end, he and Kreon should join them, as shades in truth.

Still clinging to the king of Thebes, Theseus stepped from the cliff.

23

———

ARTEMIS

790 Bronze Age

In the end, when Paris was grown, Priam had almost—
inadvertently—thwarted the schemes of Artemis and her
siblings by arranging a marriage between the prince and the Nymph,
Oenone. It had taken a combination of Kirke's lust potions and her
influencing his dreams to get him to develop an obsession with the
demigoddess Helen. Once the idea had set within the prince's mind,
turned to a ceaseless itch by Kirke's oneiromantic ministrations, then
had come the practicalities.

Helen was, by then, like Paris, wed. In fact, she was wed to the
Mykenian prince, Menelaus, brother of prideful King Agamemnon.
All of which offered the perfect excuse for Artemis's war. Kassandra
had predicted it long ago, though Artemis did not think the princess
had known her brother would bring about such discord. Helen's step-
father, King Tyndareus of Sparta, had held a contest for his daughter's hand, and kings and princes from across Elládos had come. After
all, Helen was, according to tale, possessed of an Otherworldly

beauty fit to drive a man to madness with desire for her. Tyndareus extracted an oath from each of the suitors that, whosoever was chosen, the others would support him in times of strife.

Apollon told her that the idea for the oath had come from Odysseus of Ithaka as means to prevent war between the suitors after Tyndareus made his decision, probably in exchange for Tyndareus's support of Odysseus pursuing Helen's cousin Penelope. Artemis rather misliked the convoluted politics of it all, in truth, though it would not stop her from using it.

The marriage to Helen made Menelaus king of the young polis of Sparta after the abdication of Tyndareus, which, in turn, led the Mykenian brothers to control vast swathes of southern Elládos.

Artemis's brother well predicted how it would go. The Ilian prince, Paris, would abduct the Spartan queen and bring her to his city. Since neither Artemis nor Apollon could risk setting foot in Elládos, they sent Phaethusa to aid Paris.

Phaethusa, along with Paris and Helen, returned upon a swift ship, and the prince presented Helen as his new bride, having apparently gotten her willing acquiescence to his love. Priam, though aghast, could not turn aside his precious son. And Menelaus would look to his brother Agamemnon to avenge his affronted honour. Together, they would hold the suitors to their oaths, and the Elládosi would sail to Ilium, then break themselves upon impenetrable Trojan walls.

All the great kings of Zeus's land would spend their lives in vain war, depriving him of his assets and, sooner or later, forcing him to commit Olympians to the fray. When they did, when they came, Artemis would whittle away at Zeus's true power base until, at last, she could find a way to bring down the king himself.

Already, she had sent word to Ares, who had agreed to join Phlegra to the Phrygian cause. Already, the Elládosi ships darkened the horizon with their painted sails.

They said a thousand ships sailed to bring Helen home.

Most, Artemis suspected, would not return.

BUT THE WAR DRAGGED ON, neither side gaining much ground, though blood was spilled aplenty. Blood enough it became impossible to tell whether Elládosi or Phrygian had left the deeper stains upon the sands before Ilium. Months of siege turned to years. Priam's forces, at Artemis's urging, made sporadic sallies against the gathered Elládosi, but their enthusiasm for such waned as the war stretched on. Some believed they could outlast the foreign invaders who must already long for home and familiar faces. Ilium had stores enough already, and Agamemnon's fleet, though impressive, could not prevent supplies from coming in from the Axeinos Sea and Ilium's Phlegran allies.

So the Ilians sought to justify their reticence as strategy, though Artemis thought it had more to do with the spreading tales of the demigod Achilles, who, rumour claimed, had once carved his way through a hundred defenders almost single-handedly. Artemis would have dismissed such reports as soldier's gossip had she not, whilst walking the walls, once seen a man scythe through Ilian warriors like a threshing wind, more untouchable than even a Titan. That day, Apollon had launched an arrow at the golden-armoured Elládosi, but the melee had unfolded out of even her brother's impressive range.

"Should I seek him out?" she had asked.

"If we join the fray, we may play our hand too soon," Apollon warned.

So instead, Artemis had tracked the wilds on to Themiskyra to seek warriors brave enough to stand against indomitable Achilles. She found Penthesilea, the Amazonian queen who had succeeded Hippolyta. Like her half-sister Hippolyta, Penthesilea was a bastard daughter of Ares, well trained in the arts of war and a master huntress. And, too, she was one who blamed the Elládosi for the shame of what had befallen her sister, though Artemis knew Hippolyta had made her choices. She had died for Hippolytus to live, and the memory of him, of the boy Artemis had raised as apprentice, it sent fresh aches down to her bones. His face, as she imagined it in a rictus of agony when Zeus's lightning struck—that face stoked the fires of her wrath and steeled her resolve. Olympus must fall, even if the price would come dear for it.

From the ramparts, Artemis watched as Achilles cut down Penthesilea and the twelve of her finest Amazonian warriors. The demigod moved with speed and grace Artemis herself had to admire —flowing through battle like a siren threading the waves—much though she began to loathe the Phthian prince. One by one, he slew all comers. He destroyed the Phoenikian king, Memnon, who came to aid Priam when called upon. He conquered villages and towns across Phrygia, day by day depriving the Ilians of allies and resources.

"I must confront him," Artemis protested to her brother.

But still, Apollon shook his head. "Zeus and his allies lurk some-where in the midst of all this. If we show ourselves upon the field of battle before them, we face Olympus at a disadvantage. Besides, Sister, from what I've seen, I am not certain even you would survive clashing blades with Achilles. Never have I seen his like."

So they waited, ever upon the high walls of Ilium, ever scanning the mass of Elládosi for the familiar, hated faces of their former brethren upon Olympus. And for ten years, Men on both sides paid the price for her war against Zeus.

"Sooner or later, I must needs face the man," Hektor said, standing in the gloom of his unlit chamber, staring at his hands.

Artemis wondered if he said such hoping she would contradict his despairing proclamation. She stood leaning against the wall, beside his window's chambranle, half in shadow herself. Part of her wished she could tell him not to try. She had watched this boy, this beloved prince of Ilium, grow into a man. He was a champion, and some called him the finest sword behind these walls. She had hoped, in vain, that the Amazons would strike down Achilles. Even after, she had dared to believe Memnon could do so.

They had failed, though, and the people had begun to take note that Hektor, their peerless prince, never happened to be out in the same parts of the battlefield as Achilles. Somehow, by fortune—or perhaps the advice of Artemis's aeromancer brother—Hektor found himself always deployed on other fronts. He won glory, he slew Ellá-dosi heroes, and never did he clash blades with Achilles.

"Every Man and demigod who has ever stood against Achilles has fallen," Hektor's wife Andromache objected, wringing her hands as she paced about the room. The woman had seen their young son tended to by a handmaid when Hektor had begged counsel from Artemis. "No one can hold their ground and hope to survive that incarnation of destruction!" When the woman passed across the beam of morning sunlight streaming in through the latticed window, Artemis saw the flush in her cheeks and the redness in her eyes. "Achilles is more god than Man, and you tempt Ananke to even think of raising arms against him."

How Artemis wished she could offer him some reassurance, but a bitter truth did lurk behind Hektor's assertion he would have to fight the demigod. Someone did, and Apollon thus far had refused to allow Artemis to venture forth herself. Phaethusa, too, had volun-teered, but after what she had seen, Artemis was uncertain even her half-sister could match the man's speed and skill. The thought of losing the woman terrified her, even more than the thought of fighting Achilles herself.

"Is that what I am to tell our men?" Hektor shot back at his wife. "That no man can stand before Achilles's fury, and thus only a fool should try? After such a speech, we might find it difficult to get anyone to sally forth at all. Perhaps better if we open the gates and welcome the Elládosi into our midst, eh?"

A sudden fire seemed to seize Andromache, and she stormed over to Hektor and seized his shoulders as though intent to shake sense into him. "Gods *damn* your brother! By what stretch of monumental hubris did he think he could abduct the daughter of Zeus and not bring a tide of woe upon our heads?"

Artemis shut her eyes at the woman's words, trying not to wince. It would little help either the Ilians or the cause Artemis fought for to reveal that Paris was not wholly responsible for his actions. Oh, the truth might serve to somewhat redeem Paris's good name, yes, but Artemis rather doubted anyone would listen now, after years of suffering and so much death. Kassandra had claimed this war would spark the beginning of the end of Olympus. Surely that meant Artemis must stay the course and see this thing through. Surely, given time, opportunity must present itself for her to strike off the head of the serpent.

As Artemis opened her eyes, Hektor was already rising, shrugging free of his wife's furious grip. His face, which had been blanketed in despair and resignation, had turned dark with his anger. "The only people from which I shall tolerate ill spoken of my little brother are my parents, and they have thus far held their peace on the subject. I will not hear it from you, much though I love you."

"But you love him more."

Hektor sighed, his brief flare of strength seeping out of him as if from so many cracks in his foundation. "It is not a question of more. I would not allow him to besmirch you either, wife." Another sigh, and it seemed to pain him more than the first. "Goddess?"

How was Artemis to send this man, whom she had known his entire life, to his death? She could turn back now. She could, by force, take Helen from Paris—though the two now seemed much in love—and return her to Menelaus. Given a large enough tribute, Agamemnon might accede and make sail by the next morn. Even if the Mykenian king dreamt of conquest, he would be hard-pressed to convince his follower kings not to depart, with the woman returned and booty awarded, besides.

But then, what if Hektor's was the one more life necessary to bring Kassandra's prophecy to fruition? What if, in sparing this last man, she rendered the thousands dead before him moot? Not only their lives, but all those Zeus would destroy in the future, as his tyranny and madness stretched down through the ages ... If she turned back now, Artemis would forever wonder if every person crushed beneath Zeus's sandal henceforth had died because of her weakness.

Made weary by such thoughts, she turned to meet Hektor's gaze. She wished he had sent for Apollon rather than her. She wished she need not speak and thus, mostlike, decide the man's life or death within the next few heartbeats. She wished ... and wished ... she had never taken up arms on Zeus's behalf, long years back, in perhaps the greatest mistake of her life. "The day no one will engage Achilles is the first day of the fall of Ilium. If we declare him invincible, the spirit of your city will crack before the walls do."

Hektor nodded, grim faced. Andromache wept. And Artemis wanted to retch.

❧

WITH RAPT, disbelieving eyes, Artemis watched from the ramparts as Hektor slew Achilles. The Elládosi prince fought with valour but with none of the inhuman speed and fury which he had heretofore demonstrated. Part of her could not believe it had ended thus, as though someone had siphoned away the man's godlike power. Part of her almost wondered if somehow, across the sea, Kirke had worked sorcery to curse Achilles and slow his movements.

When Apollon by her side turned his gaze away from the rumbling, swirling clouds overhead, already the dire foreboding had crept upon her. Already, before her brother spoke, Artemis knew his words would herald doom.

"That was not Achilles," the aeromancer said. "Someone else wore his armour."

Artemis bent until she could press her head against the crenelation. Thoth's dark side take that demigod! She slapped the battlement. Despite the Titan Pneuma that infused her blows, her strikes remained as impotent to crack the wall as she was to fix all this.

❧

WHEN ACHILLES CAME ONCE MORE, when he carved his way through the Ilian army with frenzy more brutal than any he had demonstrated in the past decade, Artemis nocked an arrow to her bow. Almost, even when he called out Hektor in single combat, she loosed. He might have come close enough to the wall now, in the mindless fury of his grief. Artemis understood his pain too well, for she had suffered it, again and again, across the vast expanse of her life. So many she had loved had been torn from her.

Aidos and Aura, Orion, Atalanta, Ariadne, Hippolytus. A procession of loved ones ripped from her too soon. But her understanding of Achilles's grief did not mean his erupting wrath here, volcanic and sudden, held a candle next to the inferno she had long kindled within her.

With a gentle hand, Apollon eased the tip of her arrow down. "You cannot shoot a man who has challenged another to single combat, Artemis. We cannot win this by discarding the last vestiges of our honour."

So instead, she watched as Achilles slaughtered Hektor. She watched as the Phthian prince strapped the body of the boy she'd known behind his chariot, and dragged Hektor round the city, mauling and abasing his fallen foe. She scrubbed the tears from her eyes, and she waited.

MUCH THOUGH SHE might have wished to console Priam, she could offer the king no words for his grief over his son. She learnt, later, he had gone in secret to meet Achilles and beg for the body of his son. Achilles, in delayed recognition perhaps of the humanity shared between them, had allowed it, and Priam had held a grand funeral for his beloved child. Twelve days the Elládosi had granted, for Ilium to mourn and hold the needful rites. Twelve days of respite before someone would need to go and throw their lives down to slow Achilles's advance for another day.

Artemis had feared that, if they thought their prince craven, the spirit of the Ilian warriors would fracture. His death seemed to have had much the same effect. Their sallies became fewer, and the Elládosi pushed closer and closer to the walls of the ancient city. Now their foes brought vast ladders, intent to scale even the cyclopean fortifications and gain ingress.

From the ramparts, Artemis and Apollon shot as many of the Elládosi as she could. She rained arrows upon them until she ran out —even launching several at Achilles, though he deflected them upon his shield or one with his sword with Titan-like reflexes—then dashed off to gain more.

On her return, she learnt Ares had led a last, desperate sally.

"I warned him against this!" Apollon spat. "We cannot predict what response Olympus will have if he strikes down their champion."

So, it had come to it. Perhaps Zeus himself would soon show his wretched face. Maybe then Artemis could put an arrow through that face. She raced for the gates, trusting to Pneumatikoi to keep her safe as she leapt down a dozen stairs at a time, bounding to reach the Ilian forces before it was too late.

She arrived on the battlefield in time to see Achilles engaged with Ares. And, to all appearances, a Man had driven the God of War onto the defensive.

"Goddess!" Someone shouted.

She turned to see Paris, careening his chariot around toward her, and at once apprehended his intent. With Pneuma-infused legs, she leapt, caught the side of the chariot, and flung herself within, standing beside Paris. Apollon had convinced her before not to inter-fere with a duel, and her reticence had cost Hektor his life. She would not repeat that mistake.

As Paris banked the horses around to bring her in range, Artemis nocked an arrow to her bow.

By the time they drew close enough, Achilles had his foot upon Ares's chest, the God of War lying fallen in the dust. Artemis loosed. Achilles rammed his xiphos through Ares's throat an instant before Artemis's arrow punched through Achilles's back and out of his chest.

The great champion of Elládos fell to his knees, and, as Paris circled the chariot around and she could see the man's eyes, Artemis cast her fury at him. How many this man had slain. How many hundreds, perhaps thousands of lives had ended because of him?

Artemis leapt from the chariot, but not before Achilles pitched over into the dirt. The God of War, Ares, was dead, the final victim of the greatest of the Elládosi. Some sick part of her considered defacing his corpse as he had done to Hektor, but Artemis had better things to do than give in to petty whim.

"G-goddess!" Paris shrieked once more.

Artemis turned to where he pointed and froze. Even as Achilles had rammed his xiphos through Ares, so too did she witness the sword of Athene piercing Apollon's breast. That blade struck her brother, but it was Artemis who toppled to the dirt, somehow certain the impact had hit her as well. Staggering, rendered clumsy and numb, she gained her feet and took a wobbly step toward her brother.

A moment drawn into agonised eternities, Apollon hovered, impaled upon a blade, quivering as life left him. Athene eased him to the ground and freed her sword. Artemis tried to scream but managed only an aphonic rocking in place. The whole World swirled about her, heaving as though she stood in a storm-tossed ship, everything a blur, all order turned to chaos. To pain.

Her twin ... her brother ... He had said a cost ... a cost ... a cost ...

Artemis was only half aware of the hands that guided her back into the chariot and less than half conscious of the haze of the battlefield racing around her as she was ferried back within the illusory safety of the Ilian walls.

It had not gone this way.

It could not have gone thus.

It could not ... happen ...

24

ATHENE

800 Bronze Age

*P*atroklus, beloved friend of Achilles, was dead, reduced to ash on a pyre, and everything was changed once more.

In a paroxysm of rage, Achilles slew Hektor and desecrated the prince's body, despite the condemning stares with which his fellow Elládosi—and Athene—fitted him. Oh, she too well understood his grief, and the bleak mingle of despair and wrath it engendered. But Athene could not countenance the results of it, for she had walked those roads and knew well enough where they led.

It was chaos then, as had always been inevitable from the moment Titans had taken to the field. She saw it, as Ares closed in upon Achilles, their impending melee distant, too far for Athene to interfere. Still she ran, dashed around the fallen, dodging the surge of chariots, her sandals skidding in the mud created by rivers of spilled blood.

She had not made it far enough when she saw Apollon drawing a bead upon Achilles, prepared to shoot the man down should Ares fail to slay him. Reversing her grip on her spear, Athene broke into a run and hurled it at Apollon. The Heliad sensed it at the last moment, twisting aside, his arrow flying wide. Already, Athene was pulling her sword, racing at her former brethren upon Olympus.

Indecision warred across his face and the man considered breaking for the wall of Ilium. He had to know he could not best her in a contest of arms. But his gaze swept the field, and, decision made, he drew the xiphos hanging at his side. His golden eyes glowed lambent in the waning sunlight, his burnished panoply glittering as though Hyperion himself walked upon Gaia. The Heliad flashed his teeth, something between grin and grimace and no man there could have insulted his valour.

Panting, Athene slowed to a walk, circling the man, sword high, shield warding out ahead of her. Apollon spread the fingers of his empty hand to emphasise the disparity of their circumstances. Considering all that lay at stake, Athene could have denied him, held her shield, and demanded his surrender. In the Gigantomachy, she'd slain Demeter rather than allow Father to take the woman prisoner and vent his wrath upon her. She owed Apollon no less courtesy; besides, she doubted he'd be fool enough to allow himself to be taken alive.

Slowly, gaze locked on his face, she loosened the strap upon her aspis, then tossed it to the ground. "I wish it had not come to this." Yet she could see no way around it now. Father knew Artemis and Apollon—and Ares—had betrayed Olympus, and he would never stand for them to live now. Or worse, if he caught them alive, he would draw out their agony across the scope of Ages.

"Ah, then you'll not deign to join our cause, eh?" Apollon worked his shoulders, twirling his blade in the process. Unfortunately for him, his showmanship mostlike exceeded his swordsmanship. "Perhaps you ought to consider that we are the ones in the right here."

Athene glowered, pointing her xiphos at him and beginning to circle once more. "Because you protect the treacherous prince who absconds with another man's wife? Truly I wish more men were possessed of such a righteous sense of morality."

"The edifices of civilisation become cherished as a matter of course, tradition given weight by the voices of those who have gone before, until history becomes indistinguishable from *rightness* in the eyes of many. It is only the bravest who are willing to look beyond and consider their ancestors might have been wrong, might have been flawed. For us, immortals, who wrought this World ourselves, how much more courage does it take then to admit our creation suffers from our *failings*? If there is ever to be hope of better, we must tear down those etiolated edifices we erected."

"Apollon ..."

"History will judge those who fought alongside Zeus as tyrants."

Athene let the point of her blade dip and wanted to weep. "Only ... if you ... win." There was little more for it then. She lunged.

Twice and thrice he parried, each time falling backward. Until he stumbled over the severed limb of a hapless warrior, flailing his arms in a desperate attempt to keep his feet. Athene could have ended it then, but hesitation stayed her hand. She wanted to scream at the Moirai and demand they provide some third alternative to two paths she saw before her. But there was none.

Apollon steadied himself, hefting his sword once more, his eyes acknowledging she had spared him. Perhaps he thought it mercy rather than the weight of her indecision turning her arms sluggish. Either way, she had no further room left for indecisive action. Fate had decreed this all, perhaps, or else the Olympians had built this end all on their own.

The Heliad lunged. Athene beat aside his sword and rammed her xiphos into his chest. The sword plunged straight through, scarce slowed by panoply or any Pneumatikoi Apollon might have called upon. Stricken by what she'd done, Athene caught his arms and slowly eased Apollon to the ground.

"I'm sorry ..."

"Artemis ..." His breath was a wheeze. Ichor burbled from his wound, but already it had begun to slow. She had struck the heart, and not even Pneumatikoi would let him survive such a wound.

And then he was gone, and she withdrew her xiphos from his still form.

❧

*A*THENE SAW *the other Titan bounding between burning ships like some springing frog. The woman's preternatural agility meant she waded among Elládosi like a whirlwind of death. None of them could stand against her. No, but Athene would. When Artemis was tangled in the lines of a sinking ship, precariously balanced, Athene drew a javelin from her back. She had only one, but she would make it count.*

Taking aim, she flung it at Artemis, infusing it with Potency enough to pierce enough Pneuma-hardened flesh. But Artemis released her grip before the javelin struck. The woman slid down the ship's canted hull but caught herself in the rigging.

No, there would be no escape for Artemis. Whatever sisterhood had once blossomed betwixt her and Athene had now good and truly withered, and all that was left was the mouldering stench of decay clogging her nostrils. Athene needed this done, and now. She leapt from the pegasus's back and landed upon the angled mast. With a spear, she lunged for Artemis. The other woman twisted around, beneath the mast, and—impossibly— managed to flip around it and land beside Athene.

Athene whirled, swinging her spear like a scythe to cut down the Titan. Artemis toppled backward rather than take the blow. The Phoebid kicked her legs, and the two of them landed in a heap, then tumbled off the mast. Artemis might be faster, but Athene was fair certain she had greater Potency. They scrambled for pankration holds, even as they skidded down toward the sea, then Athene punched at Artemis's face. The woman twisted aside, and Athene's blow shattered the deck. Her fist snared the broken planks, jerking the both of them to a stop.

❧

S̀O MANY WERE DEAD NOW. Achilles gone, and Ares, and Apollon. Athene did not know what had become of Artemis, but since Apollon's last thoughts were of his sister, she had found it too painful to hunt for the woman. In truth, she knew, Artemis would mostlike come for her, given what she had done.

But the Ilians were nigh broken now, hiding behind the walls, and the Elládosi were desperate to make a final end of this. A decade of ceaseless, pointless war had drawn them out, some past their breaking points and others nigh to it.

And Odysseus had hatched a plan, a tribute that, with prescient certainty, she now knew would lead to the razing of Ilium. Her father had commanded the city be reduced to rubble, and soon, debris and ash would be all that remained of this place.

Those towering walls were so thick, so high, perhaps the Elládosi would never have breached them. No ladder could stretch so tall as to reach the top. The warriors could have landed blow after blow upon the gates without the doors cracking.

Hence the gift. A horse, the royal symbol of Ilium, standing nigh thirty feet high, wrought of wood salvaged from broken ships. And upon great wheels, they rolled it through gates thrown wide. Pride was ever the most human of failings.

Oh, not of Men, but of Titans, too. The greater power one held, the more jealously one guarded it and its accompanying pride. Where was Artemis? Had she already fled the city, or would she rain slaughter among those hiding within the horse?

Athene could have taken her place amid the invaders, watching over Odysseus herself, and ensuring his safety. She could have, but she had seen enough carnage upon these shores. So she would watch, and wait, that she could say in truth to her father she had seen the city fall. And if Artemis forced the issue, if she presented herself here and left Athene with no choice, then Athene would kill her, too.

Either way, the Ilian War would end this night. It would end as such things always ended. With surging fires and screaming and rivers of blood fed by the innocent and guilty alike. It would end with filth and pain. And in that ending, some would find new beginning, for a kindling of fresh wrath, and new furies, at ill-done deeds.

Flames that ever fed themselves.

25

PANDORA

382 Dark Age

*O*nce, in her studies upon Atlantis, Pandora had dreamt of far-off Nusantara, the eastern-most lands of the world known to Thalassan scholars. She had imagined ports clogged with exotic dhows, markets overflowing with silks, and a host of new foods to sample. Such had been the simple fancies of a hetaira hoping for more adventure in her life and a chance to see foreign horizons, even whilst knowing such would lie forever beyond her reach.

Now, for the second time, she walked the streets of Mugedang and found herself craving a life free of adventure. She and Prometheus had spoken of islands off the coast from here, places with scant people, where they could grow gardens and catch fish and raise a family. It seemed impossible. But then, no more so than her dreams as a hetaira had felt at that time. Would the Moirai permit her peace one day? Pandora remained resolved that, if they would not hand her the life she wanted, she would carve it out for herself, their wills be damned.

The sweeping saddle roofs greeted her and now she had a longer chance to ogle the elegant design than she'd managed on her first visit. She walked the breezeways, drinking in the aromas of roasting meat on sticks—though the fact she could not always discern what *sort* of meat gave some concern—or stopping to sip refreshing, sweet water housed inside fresh, green coconuts. Between the plazas, colonnaded breezeways created lanes where the traffic could flow in something—vaguely—resembling order. Thus, after enjoying the beverage, she slipped back into the flow of the crowd, following the larger groups in her stroll around the city. It would, she suspected, behoove her to have the lay of the place, and thus, she had begun creating a mental map of the districts.

The numerous, mountain-like temples rising around the city provided convenient landmarks should she ever need to orient herself. Her Nusantaran was poor, and she'd had little occasion to practice of late, save for her brief visit here before. Thus, she spent time eavesdropping on random conversations, helping her get a feel for the tongue, and truth be told, enjoying a voyeuristic thrill when she happened to overhear private titbits of gossip. The locals, she assumed, must think her incapable of understanding their speech. Thus, she struggled to keep a smile from her face when a woman—a harlot—questioned a potential customer's manhood after he haggled with a bit too much fervour for her liking. Too, she walked on without acknowledging an insult about the addled wits of fair-skinned foreigners, though, being Phoenikian, Pandora had never thought of herself as fair.

The next plaza over, she bought a dish of rice and egg that, though grilled right on the street before her, seemed about the finest food she'd ever tasted. It was served in a palm leaf and the locals shovelled great heaps of it into their mouths with their fingers. Pandora did likewise, licking her fingers in the end to make certain she'd enjoyed every bit of the savoury sauce. "What is this?" she asked in Nusantaran.

"Nasi goreng," the vendor said with a wink. "As for my secret ingredient, you'd not get that even out of my ghost, lady."

"It's rat!" the next vendor over shouted, earning himself what Pandora took to be a rude gesture from the man to whom she was talking.

"Well," Pandora said, drawing the first vendor's eye, "be it rat or otherwise, I'll have another leaf of that."

The man beamed whilst scooping out a ladleful into her waiting palm leaf. "My lady has fine taste."

"I like to think so."

When she had finished her second serving, Pandora strolled on. Last time she'd been here, that man, Nu'u, had referred to Prometheus as Maui. If she was to locate her beloved here, it stood to reason she would need to ask after him by that name. Thus, sated, she first booked a room at a guesthouse and then began to make some careful inquiries about Maui.

It did not, therefore, surprise her when he came upon her at the guesthouse that evening. Outside the house, a ways up from the sea but close enough to hear the sound of the lapping waves, the house had a dining area set aside for guests. They grilled satay over open flames, whilst the patrons sat beneath the shade of palm-leaf roofs, the thick smoke from torch poles keeping the mosquitoes at bay. Prometheus strode over to find her. He was shirtless, wearing a sarong similar to the one she'd seen him in before. Indeed, Pandora had bought herself one, and a local shirt to accompany it.

As he drew close, the amber glow of the torch pole illuminated his arms, already bearing some of the tattoos she had seen on him before. She raised a hand to indicate the new markings, and he quirked the bare hint of a smile. "Local custom." Indeed, she had seen other warriors with similar designs before the chaos began. He sat on the sand beside her, unbothered by how his sarong slipped off one leg. "The sorcerers here, long back they learnt strange arcana to infuse the tattoos with the power to enhance Pneuma. Not every tattooed person you see has such boons, of course, but some do, and it makes their warriors potent enough to challenge Titans, or so they hope. They've had few occasions to come into direct conflict with those who have turned their blood to ichor through centuries of Ambrosial addiction."

"And how much do those designs aid you?"

He blew out a slight breath. "When you have lost much, you strive harder to protect what is left."

It wasn't the answer to the question she had asked, but as she could see the tension spanning his shoulders, she decided not to press. He too knew the end of an Era loomed ever closer, and it weighed upon him. Prometheus did not want to allow the Eschaton; rather, he felt he must ensure it occurred, even as Pandora gave her all to try to avert it. "Why does love demand such strain from us?"

"You mean why do the Moirai not permit us more time together?"

"I mean, why must we find ourselves at odds." When he opened his mouth to object, she cut him off. "I know you have said our end goals are the same, yes. But I want us to be together now, to work together. I would, given choice, stand by your side in all things."

To that, he nodded, perhaps knowing no words could soothe such a hurt.

For a time, they ate satay in silence, Pandora tearing into hers with a fervour born as much from frustration as from hunger. When she had finished and tossed aside the stick, she levelled a heavy gaze on Prometheus. "Morpheus serves the Unseen Order and is, I think, perhaps one of the Anunnaki, as well."

"It would not surprise me. That one has ever kept his origins closed off."

"Unlike other men I know."

He raised a brow at her jibe and picked at the last remnants of his satay. "Tomorrow, I should introduce you to the Queens of Mu."

"So they have risen."

"Years back, yes. I find I am drawn to one of them, perhaps because of her affinity for flame."

"Mahuika." She recalled the name from her visit to the Soul Hollow, the queen she thought a reincarnation of Kelaino. He'd always had a special bond to her, extending it even somewhat to her daughter, Kalypso, Kirke's friend.

Prometheus's eyes widened, almost imperceptible. "I am not the only one who oft seems to know more than one should of things that ought not to be known."

Pandora laughed. "Well, see how it feels, then." She paused, hesitating. "Something occurs to me, love." He looked over at her, eyes searching, perhaps wondering what pain might tear them apart next. "We have travelled down through Ages together, hand in hand, oft as we may, and loved so much. Am I not, then, your wife in all but name?"

"Without the least doubt, you are. But would that last step please you?"

He had come from a time before such customs even existed. Perhaps to him, the promise of his heart was every bit as real as an oath spoken aloud before gods he did not believe to be gods. Perhaps far more real, in fact. But Pandora, though she no longer believed in gods, really, herself had grown up in another world, and it had left marks upon her soul that she could not erase. Perhaps, learning from childhood that a thing was how life ought to be, made the unlearning of it a momentous feat. In this case, it was not a battle she cared to wage, not when so many other struggles stood before her.

She swallowed. "Whatever foul twists the Moirai toss before us, whatever tribulations Ananke forces us to endure, I would know that we are bound with unbreakable bonds."

"Such bonds have held us together long before you were born, stretching back to the dawn of time. But if you would have us take another bond, I happen to know a few queens empowered to make the match."

She leant forward to kiss him. "It's been a good many lonely nights for us both, I think," she said when she at last pulled away. "Stay with me, tonight. Tomorrow we meet your queens."

"As you say, wife."

The word sent a tingle running along her spine. She could get used to the sound of it.

STRINGS OF FLOWERS hung lazily between poles dotted along the beach, demarcating a rough boundary for the wedding pavilion. Outside the periphery, to the beat of mighty drums, fire dancers twirled flaming batons, whooping and leaping in their wild, intricate performances. The whorls of fire spoke to the Phoenix quiescent within Pandora's soul, stirring a pleasant warmth in her breast, always drawing her gaze to the dancers, though other entertainments abounded.

Men and women tumbled and bounded in feats of acrobatics, whilst by the sea a poet sang an ancient song of love and longing, about a couple reunited by the sea, long after its vast expanse had separated them. Though she watched the flame dancers, Pandora found the song too tugged her attention, though more so because she had so oft been separated from her beloved by the sea of time. Had he chosen this song for its relevance, she wondered? Did he, too, forever wish for more time? Oh, but knowing the spans of time Prometheus waited, he must no doubt wish it with even more fervour than she did. Her beloved endured centuries, sometimes millennia of loneliness while the currents of time tossed Pandora hither and thither like swept-up driftwood.

Pandora was dressed in a crimson gown with the sleeves shaped into lace flowers that left plenty of skin exposed against the punishing heat. The intricate embroidery along the fringes of her dress must have taken seamstresses a fortnight or more to prepare. Pokoharau had even given her a bright golden crown they called a jamang, a piece with spokes that rose like the plumes of a peacock's tail, topped with trailing golden filaments. Too, Lilinoe had given her bangles of darker gold which clanked on her wrists, and Mahuika had placed on her finger a ring bursting with sea-urchin-like spurs. Never, in all her life, had she worn such fine garments nor born so much gold on her person. Indeed, she could not imagine most Ellá-dosi princesses dressed so fine for their weddings, and the thought had her flushing.

"As you begin your new life among us," Mahuika had said, when gifting the ring, "so too you should have a new name within our lands." And so, the queen had promised to make Pandora anew, come the wedding.

The scents of roasting pork and grilled fish filled the evening air, mingling with the smoke of torch poles and the brine, all of it somewhat intoxicating and surreal. Indeed, she could scarce believe such a vibrant celebration held in her honour. Did the Muians always pass through life with such vivacious joy, or did Prometheus—their Maui —enjoy such a special place in their hearts as to warrant this treatment of his wedding?

As the fire dancers finished their performance—to enthusiastic applause from the crowd, Pandora most of all—girls in grass skirts took their places. When the drummers took up a more relaxed rhythm, the new dancers swayed their hips like ocean waves, arms moving in gentle undulations, the whole motion almost hypnotic.

"The hula is a sacred tradition of our people," Mahuika said, startling Pandora from her musings. Because Mahuika was the closest of the queens to Prometheus, Pandora had spent the most time with her, though she'd had some interviews with each of them in turn. "Whilst we sorceresses use it to channel our Art, others use it as a form of worship, welcoming spirits of sun and sea and sky, praising the ancestors. In the end, I suppose the two applications come down to much the same thing."

Everything in Mu was fascinating in its differences from the life she'd known in Kêr-Ys, from their unique foods to their beautiful customs. Even their use of the Art, forever a source of terror across Gaia, held some perverse appeal to it. Pandora could not deny a certain fascination with their dances and songs and tattoos, though it was the fascination one saw when come face-to-face with a wolf. You could look into those alien, intelligent eyes and know the beast before it could, if whim struck it, savage you; yet you could not look away, for its majesty commanded respect. More than aught to do with the Art, though, Pandora found herself endeared to the Muians for their sheer love of life. Everything they did here, so far as she had seen, they did earnestly, true to themselves, and in open acknowledgment of their connection to Gaia.

"So you do these dances, as well?" she asked Mahuika.

The Queens of Mu had lived long, already, and Pandora had not arrived so early as she hoped. Already, they feared the growing might of the Babilimian Empire in Kumari Kandam. The queens were, all of them save one, born in the same year. The eldest, Pahulu, had called up the souls of her fellow Pleiades and had them reborn into the next generation, a feat of astounding sorcery that had Pandora shuddering at its implication. That a person should be able to reach out across the sidereal expanses and snatch up particular souls held a profound terror. It left her feeling impotent before the might of those who could hold intangible things in the palms of their hands and bend them to their wills. For all the might the Phoenix bestowed upon her, for all the strength of her limbs or the destructive abilities of her flames, Pandora could never achieve something akin to what Pahulu had wrought. Nor would she wish for such powers.

"Of course," Mahuika answered, and Pandora turned to her, to see her grinning. Each of the queens had their elemental affinity, with Mahuika drawing her strength from fire. It gave her a kinship to Pandora and Prometheus that might have drawn Pandora to the woman even if she had not already had a friendship with her betrothed. "The procession awaits you. You have but to give the word."

A jitter ran through her. Not that she didn't want this; she wanted it more than aught she could imagine. But still, life hinged upon moments of profound change. Such moments formed boundaries far firmer than lines of flowers across the beach. These moments would split a life, shuffling each memory into lumps of *before* or *after*. Naturally, it meant the birth of a new life, and thus, in a way, the death of the life she had heretofore known. So her mouth had gone dry, her palms were slick with sweat, and her heart fluttered. In answer, she offered Mahuika a nod, and the woman made some signal with her hand.

At once, a great conch horn sounded. The blaring call was taken up by another as the first one faded. Mahuika then escorted Pandora outside the flower barrier and, taking her by the hand, guided her along the wide periphery of the beach pavilion. Within, she spied others she knew. There, Lilinoe, the Queen of Snow, who had once teased Pandora by coating her sleeping form with a fresh dusting of powder, despite the tropical heat. Beyond her, Pokoharau, the Queen of the Sea, and perhaps the most powerful of the Queens of Mu. That Pokoharau was also the one who had demanded—would demand—they call up Tiamat, Pandora tried not to dwell on this day.

Beyond them stood Prometheus, wrapt in a royal blue, embroidered sarong. About his chest he wore an open white vest, trimmed with gold workings, that, whilst subtler than those of her garb, served him well, accentuating his masculine grace. The vest left his muscular, tattooed arms bare, save for a golden armband upon one bicep. The object seemed to catch the firelight, glinting at her, though not half so brightly as his sapphire eyes. He caught her looking at him then, and his smile, though reserved, seemed to sing with all the volume of a blaring conch horn.

After leading her along the full circuit of the pavilion, Mahuika lifted a strand of the flower line so Pandora could step beneath it without dislodging the jamang from her head. The queen next guided her toward a central bonfire. All the guests had made a wide ring around the great flame, and only Prometheus himself stood beside the blaze, its glow painting his skin golden. They had told her what to expect, so Pandora went to her husband-to-be, and he took her hand. For an instant, his calloused thumb brushed over her knuckles.

"The Wheel of Life spins us, again and again," Mahuika said. "And if we are bound strongly enough, we shall find each other, through successive births and deaths. Our souls yearn for one another and heed the cry of their other halves. For how many births wish you to be joined?"

"Seven," Lilinoe had instructed her to answer, that morning, for seven was the sacred number, though the promise could be renewed with each incarnation, thus maintaining the bond in perpetuity. "Seven," she was meant to say.

"*All* of them," she answered instead. Pandora had never much been one for propriety or doing as she was bid.

Mahuika gawped at the breach of the ceremony, and no few of the younger guests chuckled, and some of the elders drew in sharp breaths.

Prometheus, grinning, answered. "Perhaps seven circles will suffice, as I do not think our guests will await us making a thousand circuits of the flame."

"Seven seems prudent," Mahuika agreed. "And when it is done, you shall be not only Pandora but, among us, Hina, blessed by the moon."

Pandora's betrothed led her by the hand in circuits around the bonfire. During each pass, one of the seven queens stepped forward to speak a blessing and offer a prayer that their souls would find one another again in another lifetime. Given the prayers came from sorcerous queens of the highest echelons, Pandora wondered if they carried enough weight to ensure a favourable outcome.

When the seventh circuit was complete, Mahuika came forward and handed a garland of flowers to each of them. Prometheus placed the lei around Pandora's shoulders, then she did likewise for him. Afterward, she leant close to him. "Are we married now?" she whispered.

He chuckled at her question. "So it would seem, though in truth, I've not done this before, either."

She was grinning too. "Ten thousand years old, and I'm still your first wife." She liked the sound of that.

"Ah. Much, much older than that, my love." He pulled her close, hands upon her jaw, and kissed her, his lips brushing over hers with a desperate need that drew a moan from her. Dimly, she knew the crowd had begun whooping, but all Pandora cared for in that moment was the warmth and taste of him.

When at last they broke away, she stroked his smooth-shaven cheek. "You are mine and I am content."

For at least one stolen moment.

EPILOGUE

Asura Era, Bronze Age

Matarśivan's clothes lay in cinders, barely clinging to his form as he pushed his way out of the Spectral Realm and back into the Mortal Realm. The flames of Phlegethon had singed his flesh once more, and it seemed the Fates' blessing—or curse—only reversed time for him if he suffered catastrophic injuries. Not merely crushingly painful ones.

Stumbling, he pitched down onto the mountain slope.

His chest rumbled, the power inside lurching like an irate volcano primed to erupt and consume him from the inside out. Fervid power pulsed through him with each beat of his heart. Of their own accord, his hands burst into flames. His face felt so hot he thought it might ignite, might even melt his eyes once more.

A growl built inside him, like an animal caged inside his soul. Whatever it was lashed out at him, sending him tumbling down into the dirt. He pitched end over end, clutching at his chest as he fell, sure it was about to burst apart. He landed hard upon a plateau overlooking the expanse of Kumari Kandam and lay on his back gasping.

Graghah! The inarticulate roar had come from within him but was not *of* him. Not quite was it Agni, though it had a fraction of the ineffable timbre of Agni's voice.

The Flame Matarśivan had taken was alive.

Searing tendrils wormed their way through his chest and burrowed into his brain.

It was alive!

And it had some incipient intellect, though it seemed unable to form words as yet. But it tried to claim him, to seize his body.

Matarśivan bellowed in the agony and violation as this entity tightened around him. He beat his fist against the stone beneath him in vain attempts to cool the inferno raging inside him.

The ground trembled as if in response. As if his blow had somehow shaken the mountainside? He managed to push himself onto an elbow even as a distant peak shuddered. The rumbles intensified, then the peak exploded with the sound of a thousand thousand thunderclaps. An instant of ringing in his ears, then all sound was gone.

Raging incandescence scorched his eyes as a geyser of ash and magma spewed high into the sky.

He felt himself drawn inward, soul falling into the burning landscape around him. Swirling and breaking, even as the entity within his breast struggled to claim him. His mind lurched in Oracular vision.

"F*OREIGNER?*" *a woman asked.*

"Am I so foreign?" Matarśivan heard himself respond. "I have walked these lands often enough."

The woman's shoulders hunched, and she huffed. Slowly, she turned to face him. Her hair was blonde, her face different, but ... but ... Aditi? Matarśivan's mind roiled. He saw her soul. It was her.

Reborn, beauteous, Aditi.

She lowered her gaze. "Does walking in a land make you a native there?"

Matarśivan nodded slowly, realising he acted thus from having seen this before. He stood straighter, hands behind his back. "Given enough time, I believe most would argue it does."

Who was she? Who was this woman who housed Aditi's reborn soul? When could he see her in the flesh and know her and at last be reunited with his love?

"Are you with Jarl Odin?"

"Yes," Matarśivan said. "You can call me Loki. If you wish to see Odin, though, he is not with us."

THE VISION FLICKERED AWAY AS MORE of the landscape shuddered, torn apart by the raging conflict within him. Between his soul and that of the Flame ... Surtr. That name came unbidden to his mind, but it seemed to fit the consciousness of the Flame.

The First Flame of Phlegethon, brought now into the Mortal Realm.

With a steadying breath, he folded his legs beneath himself, placing the back of his hands upon his knees. Breathe. Prana was, in the end, much about breath, as was control.

The spirit inside heaved itself against his will. Its searing fumes scorched his sinuses, even as fresh trembles ran through the land. Matarśivan breathed it out. He had not claimed this power to let Agni rule him still through Surtr.

He had walked through flames for this. He had gone so far because he must spare Mankind from the Fate he had foreseen. And to do that, he must master this. His would be a long road.

The roars inside himself became warbling cries of a beast reluctantly submitting to its cage. Every time he called upon its power, he risked it gaining a foothold within himself.

But he could do this. He would bear the burden for Mankind. And for her. And he would see her again.

WITH THE ONTOS CONFIRMED, how was Matarśivan to serve the Archons that had so misled the Watchers? Now he had seen the Truth and it was worse than aught he had brought before the Dodecadic Circle. A more complete damnation than they ever imagined. Would they believe him now?

No, he thought as he plodded down the lower slopes of the mountains. The volcanic emissions had ravaged the landscape, with rivers of magma having flowed through valleys and lit whole forests aflame. The quakes had caused avalanches, though he dared to hope no Men lived so close to here.

He had trusted the Watchers before, and they had turned on him and cost him Aditi. He would never again commit such an error. He had sworn to serve the Fates and history and he would do so, but he would walk that road alone. For he alone had seen the scope of the Ontos and even if he could have shown others, their minds might break under the weight of such unfathomable burdens of knowledge.

None who knew such things might ever know true peace again.

So he would carry this torch and the pain of it alone and find a way to change what he had foreseen.

And certainly, he could not remain bound to the hateful Archons who had perpetuated the lies and abetted the consumption at the heart of the World. The orichalcum band upon his finger seemed to pulse with each beat of his heart. From the dawn of time, it had bound him to *them*.

Now, those bonds must be severed if Matarśivan was to make his way.

On a deserted slope, beneath the rising sun, he knelt and drew the hateful ring from his hand. Pinched between two fingers, he held it up. This thing had helped the Watchers maintain their immortality, ensuring they need no further apples of the Tree of Life to remain forever unchanged. But now the Fates had changed him and he could not have aged had he wished to. Could not have let go, nor strayed from this path.

Not quite sure whether in disgust or some perverse, lingering reverence, he laid the ring upon a stone. Forged orichalcum, it was all but indestructible. To destroy this, he needed to withdraw the power that sustained it. The piece of himself.

"I renounce my oath," he said in Supernal, the primal language of the Archons. "I cast aside the bonds that tied me to you. I reject all that was."

He hefted another rock, then sent it crashing down upon the orichalcum ring. The band crunched and split. A moment later, the shards melted into liquid, rosy gold.

Trembles of agony seized him abruptly, like a quake inside his core. His wings spasmed.

Then they exploded.

Blood and feathers and gore showered around him even as he screamed in pain and loss. It surged through him so violently that darkness rushed up to seize him.

AUTHOR'S NOTE:

"Andromache, dear one, why so desperate? Why so much grief
for me?
    No man will hurl me down to Death, against my fate.
    And fate? No one alive has ever escaped it,
    neither brave man nor coward, I tell you--
    it's born with us the day that we are born"
    —Homer, The Iliad, Book VI

Special thanks to my family and my team that helps bring these projects to life: Sarah, Regina, Felix, Shawn, and Francesca.

If you've enjoyed this book, I encourage you to join the Skalds' Tribe newsletter and get access to exclusive insider information and your FREE copy of Starter Library. **I generally send every week or every other; I promise not to mail more often than that.** No spam, no selling your email address to marauding warlords, none of that.

Join me here to grab a free novella and stay connected with me: https://www.mattlarkinbooks.com/skalds/

Thank you for reading,
Matt

PS Pandora's journey continues in *The Circle of Kirke* ...
https://books2read.com/circleofkirke

Join the Skalds' Tribe newsletter and get access to exclusive insider information and a selection of free books to kickstart your Matt Larkin library.

https://www.mattlarkinbooks.com/skalds/

ALSO BY MATT LARKIN

Gods of the Ragnarok Era

The Apples of Idunn

The Mists of Niflheim

The Shores of Vanaheim

The High Seat of Asgard

The Well of Mimir

The Radiance of Alfheim

The Shadows of Svartalfheim

The Gates of Hel

The Fires of Muspelheim

Tapestry of Fate

The Gifts of Pandora

The Valor of Perseus

The Inferno of Prometheus

The Madness of Herakles

The Threads of Theseus

The Face of Hekate

The Wrath of Artemis

The Circle of Kirke

Heirs of Mana

Tides of Mana

Flames of Mana

Queens of Mana

For my Juhi and Kiran.

Special thanks to my family and my team that helps bring these projects to life: Sarah, Regina, Felix, Shawn, and Francesca.